CRITICAL

HER ONLY SIN

"PURE PLEASURE."   —Joseph Heller

"Portrays Hollywood politics gone mad in the bigger-than-life way that only Hollywood could have invented."   —Los Angeles Herald-Examiner

"I LOVE THE WAY BEN STEIN WRITES ABOUT HOLLYWOOD."   —William Safire

"Jump right into the story and see if you can keep from caring as HER ONLY SIN confronts forces faced by a modern woman."   —Sacramento Bee

"[A] clear-eyed depiction of a Hollywood hierarchy whose ignorance and callousness are legendary."
—Washington Times

"Exciting! . . . The style is fast and full of real-life people."   —Library Journal

*R. Emmett Tyrrell, editor, The American Spectator

HER ONLY SIN

BENJAMIN STEIN

St. Martin's Press
New York

HER ONLY SIN

Copyright © 1985 by Benjamin Stein

Library of Congress catalog Card Number: 85–11771

ISBN: 0–312–90636–6   Can. ISBN: 0–312–90637–4

Printed in the United States of America

First St. Martin's Press mass market edition/January 1987

10 9 8 7 6 5 4 3 2 1

For My Goddess Wife

P·A·R·T

1

ORDEAL

May 15, 1979

Fire! Not the worst brushfire in the history of Los Angeles, but plenty bad enough. It started with three teenage boys riding an old ATC in Bell Canyon. The damned thing turned over. Gasoline poured out of its tank onto the dry grass. The driver lay on the ground, giggling from the effects of his marijuana joint. When he stretched out his arm the tip of the joint touched the gasoline. The parched brush and the gasoline and the joint went up like a bomb. The boys ran away, but in five minutes the fire had spread to a subdivision where every house was worth at least half a million dollars. The fire leveled nine houses, then raced to a shopping center nearby. Before it finished with a 7-Eleven, a Tastee Donut Shop, and Bangkok Taste, its sparks were already five miles away, borne in great clumps by the Santa Ana winds. The flames flew southeast, where they started fires in Hidden Hills, burning out the stables and the junior college. Then they spread northwest, rushing with a preternatural speed toward the new metropolis of Thousand Oaks, literally outracing the fire engines that ran alongside them on Route 101, the Ventura Freeway. By the time the fire engines reached the Thousand Oaks exit the fire had already leveled the timber substructure of the Princess Hotel, which was supposed to put Thousand Oaks on the map.

The worst wind was the westerly. It picked up immense bales of burning sagebrush, each one as big as a Buick, then hurled them over ten lanes of the Ventura Freeway as if they were matchsticks. The burning bales hit the bone-dry grass on the other side of the freeway and lit them into more messengers of flame. Like a runner picking himself up after a hurdle, the fire then sprinted down the steep banks of Las Virgennes Canyon toward Malibu. As the fire raced westward, it gorged itself on the creosote-filled mesquite, fueling itself for its final assault toward the ocean.

Ninety minutes after the boys had turned over on their all-terrain cycle, the fire had burned three thousand acres. Within two hours it had reached a line one-quarter of a mile from the Pacific Coast Highway in Malibu. There, like the defenders of a besieged city fleeing an overwhelming enemy, the firefighters turned and fought. Firemen from Malibu, from Santa Monica, from Trancas, from Santa Barbara, from Pacific Palisades, from Manhattan Beach, from Playa del Rey, convicts from Soledad, juveniles from the Pitchess Honor Ranch, deputies from the Agoura Sheriff's station made a stand with backhoes and bulldozers in a line from Cross Creek to Pepperdine College, directly in the path of the inferno. Like Marines on Tarawa Beach, they called in air strikes of watercopters and borate bombers. They tore down everything that could burn, including the Pepperdine infirmary. Then they put on their respirators and watched as the fire crouched and feinted in their direction.

Occasionally a torrent of sparks flew far over their heads past the Pacific Coast Highway, down toward the beach. The firemen chased after them with chemical foam and

4

water, but they were not winning their last stand. The entire beachfront of Malibu, the most prized real estate in western America, was built with wood. The wood was dry and weather-beaten from years of sun and wind. One spark could turn the whole waterfront into napalm. Those sparks were advancing with grim certainty.

As the fire marshaled its heat for its final push toward the Pacific, its thick black smoke rushed upward, sucked upon its own energy, and soared into a mushroom cloud that blocked the sun from the entire northwestern rim of Los Angeles. Two hours after the boys had fallen off their ATC cinders the size of pinecones fell in downtown Los Angeles. Sailors on Indonesian freighters eighty miles out to sea radioed that they saw the smoke and flames. Twenty-five miles away, on Rodeo Drive, shoppers put Hermès silk squares over their mouths because of the fine ash that fell in their paths.

In the fire area itself, for miles in every direction, the flames shed a red-orange tint all over the formerly light blue sky. The welcoming California light became menacing and bloody as the fire spread north and south, toying with the firemen defending Malibu. The weird red of the sky became so intense that it seared their retinas. The sky gave a crimson tinge to Mercedes convertibles parked in West Hollywood, forty miles away, as if the factory in Stuttgart had somehow embedded sparks into the finish. It was as if an atom bomb had been detonated in the sky in slow motion, shedding its light, its heat, and its winds, but leaving the final execution of sentence to be carried out later.

I watched it and felt afraid. I had been feeling afraid all day. By the kind of solipsistic interpretation of which only human beings are capable, the entire fire became, in my mind, a summary warning of the dangers of awakening huge, slumbering forces of nature. But then, I had been on edge for months, and the fire had only started on that day.

I took Susan-Marie's Jaguar out of the garage and drove a few miles along Malibu Road. Homeowners stood in front of each house or on the roof with shovels, pails of sand, and garden hoses. Playing a war game with toys, I thought, and yet perhaps in Malibu that was how war games were played. On the bluffs above the Road, though, fire trucks were lined up bumper-to-bumper with their water cannon pointing skyward, like forty-millimeter batteries in Hyde Park awaiting the Heinkels in 1940, and those trucks were not toys.

Terror had come to paradise. The entire mythos of Malibu life was that there was no such thing as fear, were no such concepts as danger and struggle. If a fire could come out of nowhere and threaten their homes and their lives, what was Malibu all about, anyway? In the cast of mind of those people who lived on Malibu Beach Road the process of denial had reached an apogee in which all previous fires, mudslides, earthquakes, storms, and tidal waves had simply not happened. All that ever happened in Malibu was relaxation and the enjoyment of an endless summer day. Therefore, each new catastrophe, especially a killer brushfire like this one, came literally as a bolt from the blue, a completely unexpected and, worse yet, unjustified intrusion into the life that God had promised them when they bought their homes. There was just something wrong with a situation where a fire could come out of nowhere and burn down their whole lives in thirty seconds. That is not the way it is supposed to be in a place where a front foot of land costs as much as most Americans earn in a good year.

But the people on Malibu Road could not argue with the fire. They could only stare at the red sky and choke on the flames and hope that this ghastly day would end with the next commercial.

A case in point: At the Malibu Colony Supermarket at the foot of Malibu Road, the manager decided to stay open during the fire. Not only that, he decided to have a sale on Brie and Dom Perignon. He had a salesgirl make a sign that explained that Dom Perignon and cheese would make an excellent gift for any firemen who happened to come by during the fire. All of the Brie was sold out within an hour.

Farther down the beach, at the Malibu Beach Colony

itself, there was a more realistic attitude. The men and women—and children—who lived within the Colony gates were largely without the illusions of their less affluent neighbors. To get to a worldly position where one can buy a two-bedroom house on a forty-foot lot for 2.5 million, before crucial renovations, one has to live without blinders.

The men and women in the fifty homes of the Colony were not burdened by the mistaken impression that catastrophes did not happen to them. Horrors did happen. The strong and the quick survived them. Those who lived by denying reality did not avoid them and perished. It was that simple. To be strong enough and quick enough you had to admit what was happening. You had to see that a brushfire which could travel across an entire county in part of a morning was something to be taken seriously, to be weighed and acted on, not made into a game. So, unburdened by the killing freight of self-delusion, the people in the Colony acted fast.

They took their Cartier jewelry, their Tiffany crystal, and their Revillon furs from their closets and safes. They loaded those valuables into the trunks of their Mercedes convertibles. Then they sent the cars off to a friend in Pacific Palisades or Hancock Park via Elena or Jesus, who were thrilled to be able to drive the car farther than to the Hughes Market. The patrons then loaded up the Jaguar with the F. Scott Fitzgerald first editions, the Jackson Pollock paintings, the Max Ernst lithographs, the leather-bound volumes of the first scripts for their TV series that had lasted for ten years, their life insurance policies, their original copies of their signed overall deals with Paramount. Then they got on the telephone with their lawyers—at home, because it was a Saturday, after all—and told the sons-of-bitches that their houses had better be covered by that brushfire supplement or there would be hell to pay.

Finally, they put themselves into their cars and wended their frightened but determined way out of the danger zone. They headed southwest on the Pacific Coast Highway, past Cross Creek, past Big Rock, past Topanga Canyon to safety.

They passed by the hippies fleeing their mountain redoubts above Topanga in rainbow-colored mini-vans, by the horse-women riding their Appaloosas out of the fire with the Pink's label on their jodhpurs turned out, by the Hare Krishnas in their saffron robes seated in the back of their Silver Clouds. They passed by the real estate agencies, the gas stations, the Nautilus weight-lifting rooms, the rare coin dealers, all of the flotsam of Malibu life. They passed by and they got out.

The princes and pashas of the Malibu Beach Colony were smart enough to know that living to fight another day was the only important thing. What did a house matter, anyway? If you're smart enough to get it in the first place, you're smart enough to get it again, unless you get incinerated first. By the way, even if Bernie or Michael can't get Aetna to pay for the destruction from a brushfire because there's a specific exclusion, you can load up the casualty loss on your income tax and come out just about even, especially if there's a little salvage in the property.

So the Colony emptied itself out rapidly and thoroughly, accompanied by the discordant throbbing of watercopters and the shrieking of ambulances and pumpers.

Meanwhile, the fire, which was uninformed about gross points, capital gains, and single-card billing, roared through the canyons and began to spread rapidly north toward Trancas and Camarillo and south toward Santa Monica. The fire knew no respect, only heat and hunger and speed.

The purposeful fear of the departing colonists, the willful delusion and terror of the homeowners on the Road, the tremors of the firemen whose lives were on the line, the confusion of the horses and riders on Topanga Canyon Road all rose up in a psychic swirl above Malibu, wound around each other, and formed into an almost tangible storm of emotion that mixed with the smoky haze relentlessly blanketing all of Los Angeles. The color of the emotional cloud was also red and orange, like the pall out over the ocean.

I watched all of this—because I am above all a tourist, even though I had lived in Los Angeles off and on for five years—and I felt the flight and the fear. Then I pulled Susan's XJ-6 into the garage at 77 Malibu Beach Colony. I pushed through the door and got ready to help Susan-Marie with her telephone call—if she needed any help.

Seventy-seven Malibu Beach Colony, which you may have seen in House Beautiful, *was the rambling brick-and-glass bungalow that Paul Belzberg and Susan-Marie Belzberg had made on three lots in the Colony. The small cottages that had been on those lots had been knocked down to allow Philip Stern to build a monument to the power and elegance of the people who lived there, a structure to house the dreams and realities of a man and a woman who lived by fantasy and power.*

When I walked inside the living room it was as if there were no fire nearer than Pittsburgh. The Bokhara carpets were still immaculate, thrown in front of the orange silk love seats and below the Poussin of a woman emerging from a bathtub. The crystal emblem of the Medal of Freedom still shone in its Lucite case below the Anuszkiewicz geometric. The air in the room was cool and dry and dim, as if it were air on Park Row in London, and not air half a mile from an onrushing twenty-thousand acre fire.

Psychically, Casa Contenta del Mare still emitted the deep blue glow of purpose and calm amid the magenta terror of the day. The air itself hummed softly with the effort of meeting the needs of Susan-Marie Warmack Belzberg. Those needs long predated the fire. They were formidable, and they were in the hands of a formidable woman. They would not be diverted by a fire, at least not right now.

I walked past Elena, who was, amazingly, dusting a Lucite coffee table. She looked at me with a cheerful but puzzled expression. "No caliente aquí, señor," she said to me.

"Sí, perfecto aquí," I answered and walked on into a maple-paneled den overlooking the red and orange ocean. It was adjacent to a "teahouse," a glassed-in structure right

9

on the sand, overlooking the beach and the swimming pool. I could see Susan sitting in the teahouse, flipping through a sheaf of printout pages. Susan, and the red-orange ocean behind her, were ignoring the fire.

I walked out through the den into the teahouse. To Susan's right, a thin young man in a Meledandri blue blazer and gray slacks sat at a Hitachi computer keyboard and pressed buttons. Instantly, rows of numbers appeared on a Televideo screen. The numbers flickered bravely among the other numbers, then disappeared forever into silicon eternity and were replaced by new numbers.

"How's the fire?" Susan-Marie asked.

"It's getting closer," I said. "I think it's time to leave."

"Not yet," Susan-Marie said. "It took a week to set up this phone call. And a lifetime to get to set it up."

"The fire doesn't care."

"I'll leave as soon as I make the call," Susan-Marie said.

The man at the computer spoke to her in a mixed English-Israeli accent. "I'm getting close to a total for Citibank," he said. "By subtraction, it looks like two-point-five mill, plus or minus two-fifty K."

The man was unlikely to make a mistake, since he had been drafted by Lazard Frères out of the Technion in Haifa, sent to study finance at Cambridge, become the youngest non-family partner in the history of Lazard, and had only two months before been solicited to help Susan-Marie take complete control of Republic Pictures. There were options on half a million shares in it for him if she won. I wasn't sure what was in it for me. Probably just the chance to see Susan-Marie have some peace.

"That makes them clearly the controlling block of shares," Susan-Marie said, "assuming the Justice Department blocks the Pension Fund in Sacramento from voting their shares."

"Exactly," the man said with a discreet cough of apology for his incomplete answer. So much for background.

"You can go now," she said. "No need to stay in this fire."

"Senator Coyne called this morning," the man said. "He said that Benjy's letter convinced him. No hearings."

"That's a big one I owe you." Susan-Marie smiled at me.

"My pleasure," I said.

"I never forget who does things for me."

The man stood up, shook hands with Susan, wished her luck, then turned to me. "You want to come along?"

"No," I said. "I'll stay with Susan and leave with the helicopter."

"As you wish," the man said, and then he left.

"Danny's a good boy," Susan-Marie said. "Nothing more for him to do. Might as well leave." She stopped for a minute and then added, "I'm glad you stayed."

"Where else in the whole world would I want to be?" I asked.

Susan-Marie looked at me and smiled. Her eyes were so dark and so blue that they seemed able to block out all of the heat and the redness of the morning. Her gracefully arching black eyebrows accentuated the soothing blue of the eyes, and the pale white skin set them off again. She wore a Perry Ellis dress blue enough to match her eyes. "This is the last call," she said.

"There are no last calls in this business," I said. "You know that."

Through the tinted window just enough light filtered in to bring out the facets of her one piece of jewelry: an emerald ring, square-cut, big enough to cover the entire third finger of her left hand from the first to the second knuckle. It had been a gift from the only man who had never wanted anything from Susan-Marie, but was now far too dead to help her. I think Sid gave it to her after the opening of Laser Tracks, but she didn't wear it until after Paul left her.

There was a chiming sound from the Call Director on Susan's Lucite desk. Without shifting her gaze, she reached out and hit the Speakerphone lever. "Yes?" she asked.

"You've had three calls from Mr. Belzberg," said the voice of Susan's secretary, calling from the office at the

*Republic Studios in Burbank. The Chinese accent in the ex-
ecutive suite never failed to surprise me, but why not? Why
shouldn't anyone work where everyone's fantasies lived?*

"*Thanks, Tai,*" Susan-Marie said and hung up.

She looked out at the ocean and seemed to sink back into
her chair. "*Now I know,*" she said. "*I wonder what's keeping that helicopter.*"

She stood up and went to the door, opening it for a
moment and scanning the reddening sky. "*If the smoke is
this thick, that fire is very, very close,*" she said. Sure
enough, just a moment's opening of the door allowed a
blue-gray mist into the air and made both of us cough.

"*Too close and too big,*" I said. But in about ten seconds
the Trane Eco-System III had completely changed the air
in the room, replacing the smoke with perfectly filtered,
highly uniform, negatively ionized, seventy-degree, sixty-
percent humidity breathing material. In the same time,
Susan-Marie cleared her mind of the fire and her ex-hus-
band's telephone calls and started to look through her
briefing papers about Walter Burns.

Susan-Marie had a lot of things, and she had fought for
every one of them. She was not about to let a fire distract
her from closing the biggest deal of all. "*I have most of the
institutional stock that Paul and Melvin Needle didn't nail
down right away,*" Susan-Marie said. "*I have all of the risk
arbitrageurs, because they know that only I can turn it
around and spin off the video division. The big question is
whether Melvin somehow got through to Citicorp. If he did,
the thing is cracked right open again, and I'm out on the
street.*"

"*That's a wonderful expression for a woman who could
be head of production at any studio in town,*" I said. "*For
a woman who could support half of Silver Spring with what
she makes.*"

"*If you lose, you're out on the street, no matter what
you're wearing or what kind of car you drive. If you win,
you're inside, even if you're richer going out than coming
in,*" Susan-Marie said. "*That's what it's about.*"

"Win or lose, you've come a long way from Montgomery Blair High School."

"Not far enough," she said. "Unless I win."

"You'll win," I told her. "I know Walter Burns. You've got everything you need going for you. He's careful and he doesn't like to back a loser. You're a winner. Paul's the loser, and everybody on Wall Street knows it."

"Do they?" she asked absently, and then she picked up a Cartier silver-framed portrait of her daughter from her desk. It showed Ava at two, in a blue dress with a yellow ribbon in her hair, on the beach in Montecito. Ava, with her black hair and her knowing smile and those eyes like Susan's, an island of light in Susan-Marie's cloudy, shadowy world. Even in the photograph, Ava seemed to have a nimbus of possibility and promise dancing above her head. Susan-Marie set the frame down and looked at me. "No point in thinking about her right now," she said.

She glanced at the watch on her wrist, the gold watch from Audemars-Piguet that was engraved, To Susan From Paul—Forever Young. She turned to show me the face of the dial. Burns's call was one minute late. She glanced at the photograph of Ava Elizabeth Belzberg and turned it to face the ocean.

I could see her point. Susan-Marie had a lot of experience. Most of it had come from wars, either financial or emotional. If you thought about the job at hand, you won those fights. If you started going off on emotional tangents, you wound up a victim, a loser in a room with soft walls. If you concentrated on the future, you got control of Republic Pictures Corporation nailed down tight.

"Susan," I said, "you've already won so much. Look where you started."

"That's not the point," she said. "The point is what happens tomorrow, not what happened yesterday."

"The point is that we're in the middle of a fire," I said. "The point is to live to fight another day."

"No," she said, "this is the point," as she saw a light

13

begin to flash on one of the lines she had connected permanently to her office at Republic.

At the same moment I heard the shuddering vibration of the Bell Long Ranger appearing over the roof and then we both saw it settling onto the sand in an immense cloud of dust and smoke.

Strictly speaking, helicopters were not supposed to land on the beach in the Malibu Beach Colony. But this was not a time for strict enforcement of the rules. A powerful woman was in the middle of a brushfire, staying behind to seal her control over a studio. She needed a helicopter to close the deal. It was a small thing, and it could easily be forgiven by the Malibu Sheriff's Office. They understood power.

The comm line button began to flash and a new, tinkling sound came from the Call Director. Susan-Marie reached into a silver cigarette case (inscription: From P.B. to S.M. —Forever Young) and took out a Viceroy. With one fluid movement, she snapped open her Du Pont lighter and lit her cigarette. She inhaled deeply, drawing the bluish smoke into her lungs, then replaced the cigarette lighter on her desk.

"I wish Sid could see this," she said.

"He knew you could do it," I said. "He thought you could do anything. So do I. I don't know if that's good or bad, but I know you can do it."

Susan looked at me with her special look for registering thoughts on a day when action counted. Just to be on the safe side, she took off her watch and slid it into a desk drawer. Then, Susan-Marie Warmack Belzberg, ex-girl without a father, ex-victim, ex-telephone company drone, ex-dreamer of a dream that could not possibly come true, ex-woman who played it safe, presently Chairman of the Board of Republic Pictures Corporation, Chairman of the American Film Institute, President of Women in Film, Trustee of the Getty Museum, Honorary Co-Chair of the United Jewish Appeal (only the second Gentile to be so honored), nominee to the United Nations Conference on the Status of Women, cover

14

of Time *and* Newsweek *in the same week, cover four times of* Savvy *magazine, creator of* Laser Tracks *and* Alpha Chi, *the first- and second-highest grossing pictures of all time, director of Reynolds Metals, director of Security-Pacific Bank, California Democratic Committee Co-Chair, mother of Ava Elizabeth Belzberg, former wife of Paul Belzberg, who had made* Estonia *before he was twenty-five and had two Oscars before he was thirty, a woman whom I had met in an obscure park in Silver Spring, Maryland, twenty years before, a well-prepared woman who knew what she wanted, put her hand on the receiver.*

She picked up the telephone and heard the familiar seashell sound of long distance. "Yes?" she said. Usually she waited for the other party to get on the telephone first. Not today. When you were fighting for control of a studio you didn't play games. You did what you had to do to win the fight. Today, Walter Burns was king of the telephone.

"One moment please for Mr. Burns," said a woman with a clipped New York accent.

There was a discreet click and then a surprisingly cheerful man's voice came over the line. "Susan," Walter Burns said, "you've got to stop becoming so famous, giving all those interviews to Barbara Walters about how women can do anything. You're making things very hot between me and Mopsy down here in Saddle River. She's threatening to come up to Manhattan to take the bank away from me."

Then Burns chuckled, to show that it was all in good bankers' fun and that whatever jokes he might make, as far as Walter Burns was concerned, Susan-Marie Belzberg was one of the boys. It was a forced chuckle, all the same.

"Walter, you just put Mopsy on the line and I'll tell her she should count her blessings and stay there in Saddle River riding to hounds. She's a lot better off than I am, having to knock people's heads together to make a picture on budget," Susan-Marie Belzberg said. Then she laughed, to show that she was not serious, that she loved knocking people's heads together.

15

"If I had any sense," Susan-Marie added, "I'd be working for you. It's hard work getting people out here to think about the bottom line. You can get that out of your employees naturally." She paused and then said, "I think I'll cash in my chips and buy your stock and get you to make me rich."

Burns said, "That's funny, Susan, because I was sort of counting on you making me rich."

"How could I do that, Walter?" Susan-Marie asked. "Oh, I know. Maybe, if you could see your way to doing it, I could get you some dividends on that Republic stock in your trust department. That might make somebody happy." Susan-Marie spoke in exactly the lighthearted way that bankers spoke when they were talking about money.

Walter Burns gasped in mock surprise. "We have Republic stock in our trust department? Are you sure?"

Both Susan-Marie and Burns laughed. Susan-Marie glanced through her window. She saw the sky growing even redder. Vividly burning sparks showered down upon the surf. Even with the air-conditioning, the smoke of the brushfire was beginning to mingle with Susan's cigarette smoke. Her voice did not change by one note. "Seriously, Walter," she said, "you know how I feel about Republic. I don't want it to be a playpen for directors anymore. I want to bring all of that top line down to the bottom line. If we had another year to get controls firmly in place, we could make three dollars a share next year. Maybe not."

A burning ball of sagebrush landed not twenty feet from the Bell Long Ranger. The pilot and co-pilot whipped out a small red fire extinguisher and stared at the burning bush warily through their reflector sunglasses. The fire was close. The wail of sirens was so intense that it penetrated the Thermo-Pane Ultra-Gard windows. The air-conditioning began to falter from the heat of the air. The room was growing distinctly warmer. I could taste the micro-ash on my throat. The fire was very close.

"I hear the same promises from Paul," Burns said. "You know I do. He says he'll put the whole company under the thumb of Goldman, Sachs. He'll put a CPA in bed with every director. He'll hang the first director who gives a star a Winnebago. That's what Paul says. He'll be Scrooge in Hollywood."

Susan-Marie let out a sigh. "I'm sure Paul means it when he says it, Walter. I'm not implying he intends to deceive you. But we both know Paul. He's got the attention span of a bumblebee. As soon as he gets back in the saddle it'll be business as usual, with Paul looking for the next deal and the people at the studio doing any old thing they feel like doing with your money. You know he's not going to change. He's got his talents, but he's not the slightest bit interested in your bottom line. He's interested in Paul Belzberg, and the studio can run itself and you know how that turns out."

"I know," Walter Burns said. "Red ink."

"Exactly," Susan-Marie said. "The way I see it, I'm doing everybody a favor keeping costs down, making sure there's a studio where they can work next year. If they think I'm too cheap, they can go to Warner. Look," Susan-Marie added, "I love movies. I love them as much as anyone in the world. But if there's no Republic Studios, there are no Republic movies, and that's clear. I have nothing against Paul. I was married to him for five years and he's an amazingly talented man. But Paul's looking for a studio he can play with. I'm looking for a studio to make pictures that win in Boise. I'm looking for pictures that'll give you a dividend, and those are the pictures that America loves, not the pictures that Paul loves. Not anymore."

"You're looking for the big story in Forbes," Walter Burns said with a laugh.

I could hear this through the receiver, even across the room. I got up and walked out of the teahouse, into the study, and then into the living room. When I got to the kitchen I was stunned. The smoke there was already thick. Elena was trying to fan it out of the open door with a towel. I ran out to the alley of the Malibu Beach Colony. At the far end, where Larry Hagman lived, there was already smoke pouring out

17

of three houses, and flames cavorted on their rooftops. Fire engines lined the street, bumper-to-bumper, pouring water on the houses, but beyond them, to the north, where the Malibu Road community had been, now there was only a solid wall of flame. There weren't even any cars coming out of the Road any longer.

I ran through the house and pulled Elena with me into the living room, and then into the study and then into the teahouse. I opened the door and shoved Elena out onto the smoky beach. A crewman from the helicopter ran across the smoky sand and pulled Elena into the copter. She looked terrified, an Inca suddenly carried into the bird that was the lineal descendant of Cortez.

Then I ran back into the beach house and wrote out a note on Susan's Francis-Orr stationery. "THE FIRE IS IN THE COLONY. WE HAVE TO LEAVE RIGHT NOW."

I handed it to Susan-Marie. She read it, nodded, then went on talking to Burns without missing a beat. "Walter, I need your help," she said. "If Paul takes over again, the studio is a goner, pure and simple. If I can stay in there, I'll make the stock pay dividends again next year."

"Susan," Walter Burns said, "you have our votes. You always had them. You know that." I could hear his confident laugh over the line. It rang eerily in the midst of the fire.

Now, even through the air-conditioning, I could hear the crack of falling timbers and the heavy crunch of vehicles on the melting gravel. I looked into the living room. Through the tinted windows I could see fire trucks and firemen pumping water into the house across the street.

"We have to leave," I said to Susan. "Right now."

Susan-Marie made a thumbs-up sign to me and said into the phone, "I won't forget this. If I can ever do anything for you, just say the word."

"Well, as a matter of fact, there is something you can do, and you have to say yes," Walter Burns said.

Now the smoke was starting to come through the Trane

vents into the teahouse. Susan-Marie took a silk handkerchief from her desk and held it over her mouth.

"Just name it," she said lazily, although I could see the fear on her face. She started to get up from her chair, as if she would escape if she were not tied to the telephone cord, and through that cord, to her destiny, which might mean staying in a burning house. I tried to frame it in my mind, to balance those perfectly, richly blue eyes and that confidence and that imagination on one side of the scale with a need so deep that it would keep her on the telephone in a house that was already burning.

I could only make the scale balance when I thought of the girl who was all arms and legs at a picnic table in Sligo Creek Park long ago, before anyone knew her name. There was no time to think of that now, though, because recognizable pieces of Susan-Marie's roof were now falling in flames on the beach all around the Bell Long Ranger.

"We have to go," I said in a loud voice.

Over the telephone, Walter Burns was saying, ". . . a trade panel . . . get a big-time Democrat like you on it . . . endorse free trade . . . big thing for the picture business . . . bring out a report this summer . . ."

Outside the window two immense redwood timbers, burning along their entire length, flew into the air and landed against Susan-Marie's window. Susan-Marie could hear the glass sizzle and crack, and so could I.

I leaned over next to Susan's ear. "We're going to die if you don't leave right now," I said.

Susan-Marie said into the telephone, "Consider me on that panel, Walter. Now I have to leave. My house is burning down, and I'm in it."

"Great God," Walter Burns said with an inexplicable laugh. "You're in that fire? Get out and run."

"Nice talking to you," Susan-Marie said and hung up the phone. She stood up and hugged me. She was warmer than the fire.

"We're over the top," she said. "Now we're going to make some movies."

"We're dead if we don't get out of here this second," I said and virtually threw Susan-Marie out the door onto the sand. She stumbled on glowing timber, and I reached over to pick her up.

"I couldn't believe that," I shouted. "Aren't you afraid of anything?"

We ducked and crept toward the copter through a shower of sparks. "I'll be afraid tomorrow." She winked. "Would that be all right? Benjy," she said above the sound of the helicopter's rotors, "now it's mine. I can make the movies I want without looking over my shoulder."

"If we live," I said.

Ahead of us the helicopter pilot opened the hatch door and gestured to us to get in. The force of the blades whipped stingingly hot air and ash against our faces. Susan instinctively put up her hands as if she were afraid of being struck. It was a reaction she knew well.

Suddenly she turned and ran back into the teahouse. Before I could stop her she opened the door, dashed to her desk, and grabbed the picture of Ava. In an instant, she took the photo out of the frame, tossed the frame onto the floor, then slipped the photograph into her briefcase. She started to open the drawer with the watch from Paul inside, looked at it for a split second, then slammed the drawer.

She and I ran closer to the whirling rotors, then were blasted backward for an instant by their pressure. Great joists from the Belzberg dream house sailed off the flaming roof and landed all around us. A shower of sizzling stud sheaths fell like burning raindrops.

There was a crash, and a ball of flame engulfed the teahouse where Susan-Marie had sealed control of Republic one minute before.

"I'm in charge now," she said to me. "I'll build another house." Then she laughed and added, "That was too damned close. You're the only one in the world who would've stayed with me."

"I'm the only one who knows you," I said.

But I don't think Susan heard that last part, because the

20

helicopter engines were revving up to takeoff speed, drowning out human communication with their power.

As Susan and I looked back one last time at the burning Malibu Beach Colony, at the flaming house that was planned to contain all of Susan-Marie and Paul Belzberg's dreams, and now would have to be rebuilt again by Susan's vitality, something caught my eye.

A man appeared abruptly from behind the helicopter. He was neat and well groomed in a cheap black suit with a cheap black tie and a white cotton shirt. Amazingly, even in this fire, he carried a black leather briefcase, which he pressed against his chest. He looked like a loan officer from a Dallas bank suddenly dropped into the inferno, a bill collector sent down to hell for a long overdue debt.

"Get in," I said loudly, pointing at the open hatch door.

"Where the hell did he come from?" Susan-Marie asked.

"I don't know," I said. "Let's get out of here."

The heat was so intense that I expected my skin to start melting like tallow and run down my face.

The man in the black suit shouted, "Miss Belzberg, I've been waiting for you." His face was pockmarked and weirdly enthusiastic.

Susan and I studied him for a moment and he seemed to glow in the heat of the fire. Then we turned back to the helicopter. All of this happened in less than five seconds, and we were moving when I saw the flash of the muzzle and felt Susan-Marie get blown backward and down by the force of two bullets. I stared at Susan. She looked amazed. I took one unthinking, violent lunge toward the gunman.

He flinched backward, directly into the arc of the Bell Long Ranger's blades. They cut him almost in half before he could get out a sound. I didn't waste any time looking at him. I had been inside a slaughterhouse and I knew what ground meat looked like.

Instead, I scooped up Susan-Marie and carried her into the helicopter. She shivered wildly, uncontrollably. Elena instantly laid two Norfolk wool blankets on the floor under her. Before her head touched the deck we were airborne. I lifted one leg to keep the blood flowing to her brain and looked at her wounds. One was in the shoulder and probably caused her severe pain. Another was in the abdomen. Abdominal wounds don't hurt as much, but they kill.

"Jesus," Susan-Marie said, "who was that guy?"

"Don't talk," I said. I cradled her head and put my hand over the wound to her abdomen. I could feel her blood flow out through my fingers.

In the cockpit the pilot spoke urgently into a microphone. "Santa Monica Tower, this is Bell Mystic Tango One-Four-Niner. I am carrying a gunshot wound, multiple wounds, including to the abdomen. Will clear UCLA Trauma in four minutes. Request trauma team and plasma, stat."

"This can't be happening," Susan-Marie said. "It hurts so much."

"Don't talk," I said, "we'll be at the hospital in a minute."

Susan-Marie somehow lifted her hand to grasp mine and looked at me with those blue eyes, still deep and alive, but now sinking into her head. "I wasn't looking for a fight," she said. "I never wanted anything like that."

"I know," I whispered, "don't talk," although by then it didn't matter because she was unconscious. I kept my hand on her abdomen and tried by some power of feeling to stop the flow of Susan-Marie's blood. Of course it didn't work. Man makes plans. God laughs.

The helicopter shuddered and raced southeast above Santa Monica Bay out into the green part of the city that was not in flames. The pilot and co-pilot threw the throttle forward and pushed the Long Ranger toward help. At the UCLA Trauma Center surgeons and nurses prepared for the arrival of a powerful and powerfully wounded woman. In the cabin Elena crossed herself and ran her fingers through her rosary while tears streamed down her Indian face. In my arms, in a world of her own, sailing above an orange-blue ocean, Susan-Marie dreamed.

2

STATIONS OF THE CROSS

■

Isn't it great? It's 1958, the year after Sputnik, and already Montgomery Hills Junior High School is doing its part. This little red-brick school right outside Washington, D.C., in the middle of a cow pasture ringed by tract houses, is actually offering a course in calculus. That's how America is going to catch up with the Russians. All the students have to take a test at the beginning of the school year, in September. The kids who do really, really well get to, *have to*, take a course in calculus, which is going to lead to a course in differential equations. The thirteen- and fourteen-year-old boys and girls who would have been barely past long division last year are way up in college-level math now.

Miss Morris, the squeaky-clean teacher right out of the University of Maryland stands in front of eighteen carefully selected boys and girls and writes equations on the board day after day. At first the kids hold back from the eager, buck-toothed woman with her talk of asymptotes and limits and sums. But little by little Neely Carpenter speaks up in class, although she always was a goody-two-shoes, as does Jeffrey Long, although he always was an ass-kisser, and pretty soon, the whole damned class is talking about summations and derivations as if they were little Russians.

The principal brings visitors from the Department of Defense and from the Department of Health, Education and Welfare. They stand in the back of the class in their uniforms and in their Robert Hall dark suits and short-sleeved white shirts. Miss Morris makes Jerry Akman and Jim Thompson derive equations on the greenboard right in front of the visitors. Then the visitors, General Sweezey or Deputy Undersecretary Kornberg or someone else, stand in front of the class. They clear their throats and say that these children are the hope of a nation. "Until I saw this with *my own eyes*," they say, "I had no idea at all that we really were going to win the life-and-death struggle for knowledge over the forces of totalitarian aggression." Then they hand out real, working slide rules with the logo of the Department of Defense, or real, steel—not plastic —globes from HEW.

Mr. Hall, the principal, is so proud he could burst. His little school, which had been a joke in the county system for seventeen years, is now goddamned likely to be in *Life* magazine. *Look* has already done a feature on them, and Mr. Hall has been on NBC radio twice.

Next semester, if all's well, a graduate student from the University of Maryland is going to come out and teach this same group of kids—maybe a few more besides—a regular, college level course in physics. By next year the whole school is going to be walking around with slide rules in their belts if Mr. Hall has anything to say about it. Not only that, but Mr. Hall is going to be getting offers—very major offers—to write a whole course of study for junior high schools all over the country about "gearing our schools for the challenges of the race for space . . . ." From assignments like that come jobs as supervisors of entire county systems. Entire state systems.

The only problem, and it's not really that much of a problem, is this girl, Susan Warmack. Susan-Marie Warmack. The only problem is that when these people come from the Department of Defense in their uniforms she starts to cry. Not only that, but sometimes she starts to cry and laugh at the same time. Once, when a colonel from the Office of Science and Technology started to talk about how if there were kids like this helping America then maybe Americans wouldn't have to ever fight any more wars, the girl actually got up from her seat and ran out of the room. It took a lot of explaining to the visitors about her father and Korea and everything, but it was still a close shave.

Things are going so absolutely great that there's just no reason at all to have any flies in the ointment. There are still plenty of teachers on the staff who can run to Senator John Marshall Butler, Joseph McCarthy's good, close friend, and tell him stories about students actually mocking visitors from the Army. Mr. Hall has had too many fire alarms about that whole subject in the last ten years, especially with all those completely untrue rumors about his wife. (The way people talked just because she had studied at City College in New York! You'd think she was a bomb-carrying anarchist instead of a statistician at the Treasury Department.) Mr. Hall has a smooth-running operation here, taking him to much bigger and better things. He doesn't need a little basket case in his calculus pilot program upsetting photographers and reporters.

What if one of them got the idea that Mr. Hall was driving his kids too hard? What if the articles started saying that he was a slave driver, an American who thought like a Russian, without any regard for the sensitivity of the American child? Why, the whole apple cart could turn over right on top of him any second.

Really, he should get her out of the class. That would

be the easiest thing. She wouldn't resist. She hardly ever says anything, except when she starts to cry and laugh at the same time. The problem is the mother, as it almost always is. The mother, who has blue eyes every bit as deep and piercing as Susan's, who has that same white skin that looks as if it might start to glow at any minute, made a huge fuss at the last PTA meeting about Susan's incredible test scores. The second-highest score in the whole school, when everyone had thought she was such an *average* child. If he tried to kick her out now, Mrs. Warmack would surely raise hell. No, not Warmack. That was Susan's father's name. What the dickens was the new step-father's name? Frazer. Something like that.

Mr. Hall sat in his office, which was the only room in the school with incandescent as opposed to fluorescent lights. He played with the plastic-encased letter of commendation from Governor McKeldin and thought about what to do.

Wait a minute! Wait just a minute! That new woman who worked in the afternoons in the nurse's office. Dr. Keiter. Guidance counselor. Some kind of psychologist. She could talk to Susan-Marie, give her some kind of tests, maybe even keep her out of class on the day when the photographers from *Life* were there. That was definitely an idea. As far as Mr. Hall was concerned, ideas were the fuel that would take America into the space age, and take him into the state supervisor of education's office, right there in Annapolis, three doors down from the governor, really not far at all.

■　　■　　■　　■

In her fourteenth year, while she was taking calculus and getting those really unbelievable grades on her tests, Susan-Marie had two dreams that came back to her night after night.

In the first dream she was taking a test in class. She stood in front of everyone in her leggings and the winter coat she had worn when she was five years old. Miss

Morris told her that she would have a test with ten questions. If she got all ten of them right, she would get a fabulous prize: she would get to see her father again and spend the day with him.

With all the other students giggling and making faces at her, Susan-Marie answered the first five questions about limits and sums and dummy variables. Then the next four were really hard, but she was able to answer them, too. She started to get really excited. She could actually start to see her father as he was when she was a tiny child, standing in front of the battalion headquarters in Ansbach, taking the salute of the battalion as they lowered their guidons and marched past in the freezing Bavarian wind. She stood in front of the class in the dream and could actually smell how he used to smell, of starch and pipe tobacco and the outdoors.

"Well," she asked. "What's the next question?"

Miss Morris looked at her in the dream and said, "There aren't any more questions. Go back to your seat," and the whole class burst out laughing.

When Susan-Marie had that dream she would awaken at the laughter. Then she would lie in bed with her eyes closed, playing possum against sleep, waiting for the sleep to come back so the dream could continue. She knew, lying in bed, that even if the dream came back she would only see her father in the dream. Even so, she would lie in bed for hours, hoping for the return of the dream. It never came and the tenth question never was asked or answered.

Susan-Marie was certain that if it ever were asked, she would know the answer. She had better know the answer, which is why she read the book so carefully, never missed a class, and got the best grades in calculus.

In the other dream, Susan-Marie had wandered across a desert and into a pyramid. At first it was dark and scary in the pyramid. There were spiderwebs hanging from moldy granite. There were even skeletons of men in armor.

Then Susan-Marie came upon a huge, brightly lit room

where servants in skirts but without blouses waited for her. They beckoned to her to come closer, speaking to her in a language she could not understand. In the dream the servants wore gleaming gold necklaces and headbands. They led Susan-Marie to a marble table. She lay on it and watched the ceiling, through which she could somehow see the desert sky and an expanse of stars.

Slowly, lovingly, the servants, all women, wrapped Susan-Marie in cotton cloth. It was warm and soft. They started at her feet and worked their way up her little legs to her waist, then to her chest, and finally, with a kiss, over her eyes. The servants wrapped and wrapped until Susan-Marie was completely covered in gauze so thick that she couldn't see or hear anything. Then Susan-Marie could somehow tell that she was alone in the room, unable to hear or see or feel any noise, any light, any pain. It felt wonderful.

In the dream, Susan-Marie's body grew light, then lighter, then weighed nothing at all. After a few moments, she could distinctly feel herself floating above that marble table, then through the ceiling of the room, away above the tip of the pyramid and far off into the desert sky.

There was still no sound, no sight, no touch—only movement. When Susan-Marie dreamed that dream she actually smiled in her sleep.

■　　■　　■　　■

MEMORANDUM　　　　　　　　　　November 20, 1958
From: Elizabeth Keiter, Ph.D.

To:　Richard C. Hall
　　　Principal
　　　Montgomery Hills Junior High School

Re: Susan-Marie Warmack

Per your instructions, I interviewed Susan-Marie Warmack on November 14, 15, and 16, 1958. I administered to her several standardized tests of personality, aptitude, and inter-

28

ests. I also questioned her at some length about her home life and history. My conclusions appear below.

Subject is an extremely intelligent thirteen-year-old girl about five feet four inches tall, weighing about 100 pounds. Subject has blue eyes and black hair and appears to be in excellent health. Her blood pressure, as measured by Hortense Krutch, R.N., is 110/80.

Subject was born in Stuttgart, Federal Republic of Germany, November 1, 1945. Father was a major in the United States Army, later promoted to colonel, killed in action in Chosin Reservoir action in Korea, January 5, 1951. Mother is Lydia Darnes Warmack, born approximately 1920, Prescott, Arkansas. Mother is trained as a school teacher per Oklahoma State University. In recent years she has achieved numerous promotions as an administrator of the federal program of educational aid to federally impacted areas. She served for a time as deputy assistant administrator of programs for Secretary of Health, Education and Welfare Oveta Culp Hobby.

Mother remarried in June 1955 to James W. Frazer, at the time a lawyer for the Railroad Retirement Board. Frazer was "furloughed" from that employer in 1956 or 1957 for reasons not known or stated by Susan-Marie. At present he is apparently working in Poolesville, Maryland, for a small construction company doing contracts.

(I probed about alcoholism and got no responsive answers except that subject did not categorically deny the existence of a problem.)

Subject has no brothers or sisters living at home at present.

I tested subject on the Minnesota Multiphasic Personality Inventory. Although the test bears further examination, I can preliminarily say that subject definitely shows abnormal paranoid responses. She also displays significantly overscale anxiety formation about the episodes of daily life generally.

Subject tests normally in terms of ability to distinguish social from anti-social behavior. Subject is definitely not violence-prone or dangerous at present. She is not over- or underscale in affective disorders as measured by the MMPI, but see my further comments below.

I tested subject on the Thematic Apperception Test. In the first case of this kind since I studied at the university, subject actually reached a significantly overlimit score on sexual content solely by reason of an impossibly high percentage of *denials* of sexual content. Put in layman's terms, subject refused so consistently to see any sexual nature to the drawings that this response is believed to be based upon a tightly repressed but well overscale sexual interest. The very strictness of the repression becomes, in this instance, evidence of subject's premature sexual interests. I attempted to learn whether subject had experienced sexual activity in her own life and was given negative or non-responsive answers. Given the extraordinarily high intelligence of this subject and the high educational background of her parents, I attribute this to her probable reading of sexually explicit literature.

(She said that her parents had a copy of *Peyton Place* at home and that she "might" have read it, although she "could not remember.")

By far the most meaningful results of my examination of Susan-Marie Warmack came in interviewing her. In almost two days of interviews I discovered what I must call an astonishing *flattening of affect*. By this, I mean that subject tested on paper as if she had a normal affect (i.e., live response to real situations, facial mobility, anger, concern, fear, laughter). But in conversation face to face subject had a distinct monotone, exhibited little change in facial appearance when discussing amusement parks or wars, and seemed indifferent to the need for food or rest.

Subject's flatness of affect increased markedly as a correlative of distance from the interviewer. That is, as I moved closer to her in the interview room, she became almost totally immobile. I must attribute this to her feelings of paranoia, very likely resulting from her father's violent death in Korea. Certainly, a woman of this age with such pronounced abbreviation of affect is distinctly unusual.

I sought to correlate this peculiar seeming absence of feeling with the subject's unusual behavior in calculus class and came up with a few tentative conclusions:

Subject is quite comfortable in situations in which a precise answer to a situation is required. This allows her to focus all of her considerable ability and energy on a narrow area. The area of focus involves no uncertainty and can easily be controlled.

When Susan-Marie is faced with a subject to which there is no precise answer, in which there are only vague and uncertain answers, she becomes highly agitated and anxious.

For example, when I discussed the MMPI with Susan-Marie, she wanted to know how it was scored, what levels of confidence were in different conclusions, and was generally talkative. When I discussed such seemingly innocuous subjects as the weather and her clothing, Susan-Marie became defensive, angry, and uncommunicative. She is able to cope with quite complex questions involving specific answers, but is almost completely paralyzed with anxiety about what I might call the more basic problems—and even pleasures—of life.

I suspect that subject's uncontrolled behavior in her advanced mathematics class does not result from her anxiety over seeing men in uniform in her class (especially since she has become extremely angry and frightened when journalists and photographers were in the class without any uniforms present). Her episodes probably are related to the intrusion of what she sees as a wild and uncontrolled outside world into the precise and carefully controlled world of mathematics.

I explained to her that any such visits would be temporary and harmless. I further explained that identification with your own path-breaking venture would probably enhance her chances of study in this field in the future. She was particularly taken with the idea that her picture would appear in a major national magazine, probably because it might help her get into an advanced program in mathematics at the high-school level.

Mr. Hall, I believe that Susan-Marie will be a docile and pleasant student in the calculus class from now on. I further believe that as a result of my testing, she knows that an exciting and secure future for her in a field like accounting or actuarial work lies ahead. She will never be a public or highly visible figure, to be sure. But kept in her own quiet niche, without other people around, and with numbers to keep her occupied, she will do well. She will be an excellent addition to any professor's staff as a researcher or statistician and will do us proud in a quiet, unobtrusive way in later life.

Keep this little mouse in her own den, Mr. Hall, and she will cause no one any harm, including herself.

I hope this is helpful.

Respectfully submitted,
Elizabeth Keiter

■   ■   ■   ■

As Susan-Marie's closest friends, Gale Helm and Gay Patlen, could have told Miss Keiter, Susan-Marie has another favorite activity beyond calculus.

Every Saturday and every Sunday afternoon Susan-Marie goes, by herself if necessary, to the Silver Theatre or the Flower or the Langley to see whatever she hasn't seen already. She sits way in front, where no one else wants to sit. She gets a big tub of popcorn and pours it out onto the floor in her excitement. Then she sits staring at the screen without moving for as long as the movie takes. She puts her long legs up under her, takes off her glasses, (oh, how she hates those glasses), and feels herself floating up onto the screen, much the way she floats above the pyramid in her dream. She is no longer in the theater, really. She is up there with the people on the screen, flat, two-dimensional, but forty feet high and sixty feet wide.

Susan-Marie will watch anything, from *Sands of Iwo Jima* to *Blackboard Jungle* to *Love Me Tender* to *Bridge on the River Kwai.* She is not partial to love stories, like her pals Gale and Gay. What she really gets lost in is anything, anything at all, that has a good, strong separation scene. If one person says good-bye to another person, Susan-Marie goes into a sort of trance. Her face becomes pale. Her eyes glaze over. Her hands flutter in her lap. Even in the stillness of the theater her friends *swear* that her hair starts to fly as if there were a breeze blowing through the auditorium, which of course there isn't.

The picture that has it all is *Estonia,* the fantasy epic by Paul Belzberg. It's the story of a part of Russia that was separated from the mainland by a giant earthquake and became a kingdom that, even in 1939, was still living by courtly, seventeenth-century folkways. The world around it has been torn apart by wars and machine guns and hatred, but life in Estonia is quiet and kind. Suddenly, just as World War II begins, there is another earthquake, and Estonia is rejoined to the mainland just in time for dive-bombing and poison gas. The flowered ladies and chivalric gentlemen are simply mowed down by the march of progress.

In the last reel, when the few survivors of that island gather in a hidden cove to flee by boat to the four corners of the world, Ricardo D'Amboise holds Amanda Bauman and says, "Let us dance one more dance before we leave. We can spare a minute surely if we are never to see each other again."

Then they dance a beautiful, intricate minuet while the Stukas come closer and closer, and at the last minute flee into separate fishing boats and watch each other disappear over the smoking horizon.

Susan-Marie has seen *Estonia* six times by the time it moves on. The last three times she sees it by herself. The final time she is one of only four people in the Silver Theatre. The tears pour down her face so profusely that her throat is parched by the time the lights come up. She watches *Estonia* in perfect concentration. When she watches Amanda Bauman as the Princess Alexandra she is not simply watching. Far beyond that, the line between fantasy and reality has disappeared. She *is* Princess Alexandra, of the Royal Court, saying good-bye to a gentler, finer way of feeling for all time.

When an usher tells her the show is over she slowly floats back down to the theater and glides out into the early winter Maryland dusk. She stands in front of the theater on Colesville Road and reads all the names, especially Paul Belzberg's, who wrote it, produced it, directed it, and, as far as Susan is concerned, *is Estonia,* wherever and whoever he might be.

She even writes him a fan letter at 20th Century-Fox,

but she tears it up. She had wanted to say that watching it made her feel as if she were floating over that pyramid in her dream, but how could she explain that to a big powerful man in Hollywood who has never even met her?

■ ■ ■ ■

Susan lies on her little knotty-pine bed, listening to Don Dillard, WDON, the rock 'n' roll voice of Wheaton, Maryland. It is nine o'clock at night on any one of three dozen nights, maybe more, from 1956 to 1959. Outside, it is cold and clear or rainy and warm. The leaves blow against the window or there is the patter of rain. Susan-Marie talks to her friends Gale or Gay on the telephone, reads *Seventeen,* drinks a grape Tru-Ade from a bottle. Sometimes she picks up her schoolbooks and reads them. Sometimes she hops up to her matching knotty-pine desk and starts to do her lessons in mathematics, her slide rule flying through her fingers.

She is alone in the house at first, because her mother is in New York or Cleveland or San Francisco or San Diego or San Antonio for a conference. Her stepfather has been "working late" at his "office." Susan-Marie has a few delicious hours of quiet and peace, almost as if she were bound up in gauze.

She lets her mind run free in her room with its dormer windows looking out onto Dale Drive. If she stares long enough out into the night, she can start to feel as if she were floating through the window, out onto the breeze, up into the night sky. Wrapped in gauze, sailing through the tree branches toward eternity, she can leave the final gear of calculus and race up to the fantasy sphere, where she is Princess Alexandra somehow finding Ricardo D'Amboise again after their painful, wandering separation. In her mind, she is on a rocky coast, watching as Paul Belzberg or Ricardo D'Amboise or Count Albert returns to a new, enchanted kingdom, telling tales of Germany or

Cuba or the Chosin Reservoir. Susan can feel herself moving, growing remote, powerful, and bright.

The front door opens and Susan cannot catch her breath. Just from his unfocused shuffling on the flagstone entryway, Susan can tell that her stepfather is drunk. Drawers and doors open and close erratically. Sinister noises of grunting and cursing climb up the stairs. Then there are the amplified, gutter sounds of her stepfather in the bathroom, the overpowering sound of the flushing toilet.

And then, oh God, there is that same sound of him opening the refrigerator and taking out the ice tray. The exclamations of pain as he supposedly cuts himself—always the same excuse—on the tray. Then his falsely cheerful singing of some football fight song from Georgia Tech or Notre Dame or somewhere. As if he were coming home to watch a football game on TV!

Susan-Marie's little room with its photos of Elvis Presley and Tab Hunter becomes suffocating with the high, keen scent of terror. Susan can hear the man stomping up the stairs uncertainly, still pretending that he has cut his fingers and is suffering terrible agony.

Susan-Marie leaps to the door and locks it. Of course, as always, the lock does not work. As often as she fixes it so it will lock, that is how often he "accidentally" breaks it so that it cannot possibly lock him out. She slams it anyway and turns off the light.

When he creeps into the room, still looking handsome, but sinister and dangerous beyond any movie monster, his hair slicked back and his after-shave reeking, Susan-Marie pretends to be asleep. It never works.

"Look here, Susan," he says. "I've cut my hand. Christ, it hurts."

Susan-Marie does not answer except to curl herself into a ball and pretend to be asleep. It never works.

"Christ, it's bleeding, Susan. Will you look at that?"

Susan does not look, does not even raise her head. It never works.

"If only your mother was here to look after me, but she's

35

a big, big wheel downtown. She doesn't really have any time for small fry like me," he says. "She doesn't remember it used to be me who called the shots. It was me who was general counsel for a whole department, Susan. She doesn't remember that." He actually lies down on the bed next to her and starts to stroke her back. "I guess there's nobody here to care about me but you, Susan," he says. "I guess we just have to care for ourselves now."

"Daddy," she says, "I'm sleeping."

"Daddy," she says, "I'm having my period."

"Daddy," she says, "I don't feel well."

"Daddy," she says, "I'm going to tell Mommy."

It never works.

"You can't tell Mommy," he says. "I'll tell her you're a little lying psychopath. She's not home to take care of you most of the time anyway, so they'll send you away to a home somewhere where nobody'll ever hear from you again."

"You can't tell Mommy," he says. "If the police ever come here, I'll kill her and then kill myself, and then where'll you be?"

"You can't tell Mommy," he says, " 'cause she's too busy making herself into a big wheel in that agency to even care. She won't want anybody making a stink."

Susan-Marie starts to feel herself going numb, as if she were retreating into one single solitary cell within her whole body, as if there were nothing of her feelings in that body that her stepfather is now stroking, now undressing, now kissing. In a rush, in a mad, headlong dash, all the feeling goes out of her body into this one, hidden cell that her stepfather cannot come anywhere near.

As if she were watching someone else, she can feel his whiskey breath. She can feel his sweat drip down onto her neck and chest. She can feel him getting excited, getting wild, getting frantic, then suddenly coughing and crying and becoming calm.

In that one little cell where Susan-Marie is hiding, she thinks, "I'll get even for this. I'll get back." But even that much feeling is too much, and the thought goes through her *mind over and over again: "This isn't happening at all. It's someone else. I don't feel a thing."*

Then the father, the stepfather, starts to cry, and says, "I'm sorry, precious. I'm sorry. It'll never happen again. Never again. I'm sorry. It's just that I need you, Susan. I need you so much."

He cries continually while he puts on his clothes. "I'm sorry," he says. "Won't you even talk to me?"

She does not answer. She has moved out through the back door of that one little cell, out through the window, up into the night sky, where she does not feel a thing except for the continuous motion of ascent.

"Oh God," he says under his breath. "Oh, God," and then he walks out and closes the door with astonishing gentleness.

Susan-Marie usually doesn't even know that her pillow is soaked with tears. She is in that part of the flight where she would not feel a waterfall. But far away, drifting away into the night sky, she thinks to herself that there must be a reason this is happening. If only she could understand exactly what made her stepfather do this, why he acted so brutally, so horribly, and then was so calm, and then so frightened. If only she could understand what this equation of torment was, if only she could somehow solve for the x in this infinitely complex equation, she could make sure that it never happened again.

That is what she thought when she went away through the back door of the one tiny cell off in space. When feeling returned, she felt fear and hate and terror and a consuming rage that this had happened to her when she was such a good girl.

■ ■ ■ ■

On December 3, 1958, the photographers and reporters from *Life* magazine appeared at Montgomery Hills Junior High School. They spent the morning taking photos of the students in Miss Morris's class standing before the newly installed high-contrast blackboard, covering it with complex equations. Susan-Marie did Miss Morris and Mr. Hall proud. She wore her best blue dress. She put her hair into long, shiny-clean pigtails so she would look like an especially young genius type. (See, pigtails and an equation twenty feet long! And they say the Russian kids are smart!) The photographers loved her deep blue eyes and pale skin so much they took color shots of her, all by herself, in front of an equation for figuring out how much water is in a kidney-shaped swimming pool. Susan didn't cry or become excited at all. She smiled and spoke cheerfully to all the visitors.

At the end of the morning, when the visitors from *Life* were leaving, Susan asked how many countries in the world got *Life* magazine.

"Practically every place there is, honey," the reporter said.

"Even communist places?" Susan-Marie asked.

"Oh, definitely," the reporter said. "It's a collector's item in Russia. I know that for a fact."

"What about North Korea?" Susan-Marie asked.

"Wow," said the reporter, adjusting his snap-brim hat and straightening out his Hart Schaffner & Marx jacket. "This kid isn't just a math whiz. She knows her geography, too."

"What about North Korea?" Susan-Marie asked again.

"Do they get *Life* in North Korea?" the reporter asked. "Is that the question?"

"Right," Susan-Marie said. "That's the question."

"Honey, I don't know," the reporter said. "I'm sure somebody there gets it, even if Henry Luce drops it out of a B-52. 'Bye, honey. Nice talking to you."

After school Susan-Marie looked up Henry Luce in *Who's Who* in the junior high school library. She saw that he was the publisher of *Life,* and an extremely important man. It was inconceivable to her that he could not get his magazine into North Korea.

Walking home along Dale Drive, the first snowstorm of

winter started to make the ground soggy and wet under Susan's penny loafers. She should have worn heavier shoes, but she wanted to make the image complete so that she would be sure to have a picture *by herself* in *Life*. She had just seen on TV that there were a lot of rumors that some U.S. soldiers were still in North Korea, in prison camps, thinking that nobody in America remembered them. She had also heard that at Chosin Reservoir some of the American bodies were horribly disfigured. You really couldn't tell who was who.

What if her dad hadn't been killed? What if he was a prisoner in North Korea, freezing, so cold he couldn't even remember what his family looked like? What if he thought he didn't have his little daughter anymore?

If he saw that issue of *Life* (maybe there was a library in the prison), he would recognize Susan-Marie right away. He would be able to see that she was alive and all right. Maybe it would cheer him up. Maybe it would help him stay alive. In a way, just thinking about his seeing it was the most, best communication Susan-Marie had had with him in a long, long time.

Susan-Marie didn't tell anyone about this notion. To her mother, it would seem just plain ridiculous. To her friends, who were kinder, it would seem silly. Even to Susan it was an incredible long shot. Susan-Marie considered the pigtails, the white socks, the penny loafers, the smile at the blackboard all worth while anyway, even if it was a long shot. In her life, the sure things were hell.

■　　■　　■　　■

I learned about these parts of Susan-Marie's childhood long after they happened. At a certain time in 1972 I decided to become a permanent investigator into her life, in the hope of possessing some part of her past, since her future seemed to be so clearly denied to me. From ancient records in Rockville, Maryland, I found out about Mr. Hall and the advanced mathematics class. I even tracked down Dr. Keiter and got a copy of her report on Susan-

Marie as a child. The rest I learned from Susan-Marie during lulls in her rise to Hollywood power, on drives in Talbot County, in her Burbank office long after even the janitors had left, on midnight walks on the sand in Malibu. In other words, I learned about the youth of the Hollywood legend when she was already in the executive commissary. But I first met her and knew her as a person who shared the cafeteria line and walked home with me from school and had skin that always seemed to be warmer than anyone else's skin long before that. I first met her as the star that would change my life before I even knew what life was, when Susan and I were children, in the summer between junior high school and high school, when I had just moved to Silver Spring and didn't know a soul my own age. That was a long time ago.

3

STAR JASMINE

My parents were both full on, totally happening high-domed brainos. They had met at the University of Chicago graduate school of economics in 1935 and come to Washington as idealistic young economists in 1937. They drifted through the usual assortment of Depression-era jobs for young geniuses—Railroad Retirement Board, War Production Board, Works Progress Administration, OPM—and gradually moved from Georgetown out to Silver Spring. They bought a split-level house of their own design about three-quarters of a mile from where Susan-Marie lived. It backed up to a magnificently green and endless park with the picturesque name of Sligo Creek. I had never heard of the original in Scotland, but I found this park a local miracle of escape and adventure. One day in 1959, when I was lying in the park on a June afternoon, reading *The Count of Monte Cristo,* which was advanced reading for a fourteen-year-old—but then, we were all expected to be advanced—I heard someone else walking nearby.

Through the high grass and the occasional oak trees, I caught a glimpse of black hair and fair skin and a girl of about my age. She was tall and thin, walking along wearing loose blue jeans and a red-checked cotton shirt. I think she was probably taller than I was. She gave the impression of being all limbs, with her legs and arms seeming to fly in many different directions at once, like a female Tom Sawyer in suburban Washington, D.C.

I knew Susan very slightly from the school bus, and so she came over through the grass to see what I was reading. She looked at the book and weighed it appraisingly. "It looks complicated," she said.

"It's a great adventure," I said. "It's unbelievably exciting."

"I bet it is," she said. "Listen, are you going to be going to Montgomery Blair in September?"

"Yes, I am," I said.

"Well," she said, "so am I. I'll tell you what," she said. "If you want, I'll show you where to catch the bus."

"I'm not going to take the bus," I said. "I hate the bus. People yell and scream and it's really slow. I'd rather walk home. My mom'll drive me there."

She looked at me with those magical blue eyes and said, "Well, I hate the bus, too. I'll walk home with you."

That was more than twenty years ago, but I can still remember taking my shy, bookworm's mind away from individual responsibility and feeling more than a twinge of excitement about this girl who stood nearby and offered to keep me company. Even in the way she stood, moving back and forth from one foot to another, focusing and refocusing her eyes, her black hair moving in a summer breeze, there was something excitingly repressed about her.

For the next three years we were in school together. We were never best friends, and certainly never boyfriend and girlfriend, but we were friends who saw each other almost daily, who swam in the same sea of suburban fifties and early sixties life. Obviously, her life had traumatic cliffs and abysses I knew nothing about at the time, but still I could see something of her.

When I go back through the catalog of photos of Susan that are stored in my frightened mind, I try to cull out those that tell something about the Susan that was to be. If the memories line up properly, if I can block out the clutter of the moment, I can sometimes see a pattern. Susan and I were both children of fear, mine the inherited fear of oblivion; hers far more immediate, and that bonded point of view sometimes admitted me to the meaning of certain snapshots that would otherwise be obscure nostalgia and nothing more.

For example, I can remember our cafeteria in tenth grade at Montgomery Blair High School. There we all were, a thousand of us eating at a shift, yelling and screaming, forming ourselves into little cliques. There were the tables of athletes, the tables of future scientists, the tables of hard guys with their leather jackets and their cigarettes rolled up in their T-shirt sleeves, the prisses with their cardigan sweaters and their blue ribbons and their straight hair.

I cannot remember what group Susan belonged to. I only remember one day seeing her sitting by herself at a Formica table, idly spooning Jell-O into her mouth, reading a completely unfamiliar magazine without any photographs on the cover. The magazine was called *The Paris Review*.

I stopped by with my tray of turkey croquettes and stared at the magazine. "What's that?" I asked. "Is that a travel magazine?"

"Oh, no," she said. "It's a magazine with all these wonderful writers. It has stories about places I've always wanted to go."

"Like where?" I asked. "Europe?"

"Oh, not places on the map," she said. "Places you

dream about. Places really far away from here," she added, pointing with her little chin at the cafeteria. "When I read these stories I don't know whether I'm asleep or awake."

I remember Susan-Marie and me working late on the school newspaper, *Silver Chips*. It was winter, maybe in our junior year, and I could see snow falling on the football field. It was past five and already dark. "We'd better go," I said. "Do you have a ride?"

"No," she said. "I still have a lot of work to do. I'll walk home when I'm done."

"It's snowing," I said. "It's cold. Let me drive you home."

Susan didn't say anything for a minute. She moved around little bits of columns and headlines and then she said, "Please don't make me leave. I like it here. If you stay here, I can stay here for another hour. If you leave, the janitor'll make me leave, too."

"It's all right with me," I told her, "but won't your mother be worried about you?"

"No, she won't be worried about me," Susan-Marie said. "It's pretty here, looking at the snow. Why would you want to leave? Why is it better at home than anywhere else where you can see the snow? What's so great about being at home anyway?"

"Well, I guess I could do a few more things myself," I said. I made myself busy reading an article about the Bi-County basketball league, and then I started to ask Susan for the scissors to cut it to fit the column. But when I looked over at her, she was standing in front of the window, silhouetted by the streetlights and the falling snow, with tears streaming down her face.

"I don't know why everybody makes such a big deal about home," she said. "What's so great about it?"

I remember the day General Curtis LeMay, the commanding general of the Strategic Air Command, came to speak to our whole school. The general was a portly, white-haired cold warrior. He stood in back of a wooden lectern with the school motto on it ("Crescens Scientia") and told us that the retaliatory might of the Strategic Air Command was "the strong shield protecting you children and guarding the American way of life."

The general was dressed in mufti on this occasion, specifically, in a gray suit with a white shirt and a blue tie with little eagles on it. "I can tell you that the only purpose of all of our hydrogen bombs and B-52s and Atlas missiles is that they shall never have to be used. If they ever do have to be used, our mission and our purpose will have failed. It will be the saddest day of my life," General Curtis LeMay intoned solemnly while we sat on wooden bleachers and listened in awe.

Next to me, Susan-Marie nudged my forearm. "What a joke," she said. "He'll be the unhappiest guy on earth if he *doesn't* get to use 'em. That's why he's got the job."

I looked at Susan in shock. "That's an incredible thing to say. Do you think he wants to blow up the world?"

"I think he wants to show how big and strong he is," she whispered, "and he doesn't really get too concerned about anything else. If it takes blowing up a few continents, he'd do that, too."

We walked back to class across the great rolling grassy hill that separated the boys' gym from the classroom buildings. "I'm really surprised at you," I said to her as we trudged up the slope. "What you said about General LeMay."

"Benjy, don't be mad at me. It's just that it's all about power games, and people who work with atom bombs are not doing it because they hate loud noises. That's what power's all about. Really. Some day, well, some day we'll have a long talk about it."

I was insulted and hurt that she thought she would be able to explain about power games to me, since I had just won the *Time* magazine contest for knowledge of world affairs (a hundred multiple-choice questions, such as the location of Quemoy and Matsu). For about a week we didn't speak, but then one day I stood next to her in line at the cafeteria, she handed me her hot apple crumble, and all was forgiven.

I remember Susan-Marie talking to me about girls one night after a Thanksgiving hop in the same boys' gym. This was a "stag" affair. As usual, I was madly, frantically trying to pick up one of a few different "hard girls." These were the girls who wore straight skirts, fuzzy angora sweaters, bobby socks, and little silver crosses hanging from their necks.

For all of my young life I had been obsessed with bad girls. In our high school of bureaucrats' children there were probably no really bad girls, such as I have since met in places like Hollywood and Van Nuys, but there were most definitely some girls who were "badder" than others. Like Humbert Humbert with his rule about nymphets and how to spot them ("I know them when I see them"), I also had a knack for finding the girls who would swoon for a date with a guy with a missing tooth and motorcycle grease under his nails. As any fool could tell you, these also tended to be the girls who would rather be caught dead than spend a minute of their time with a notorious braino type like me who didn't even have a lowered car and, worst of all, got really good grades.

So, at the Thanksgiving hop, I spent two hours in my brown Lord & Taylor suit, carefully hand-picked by my older sister, struggling to pick up girls in their Maybelline eyeliner and J. C. Penney sweaters. As always, they preferred the Pep Boys kind of guy.

Standing nearby in a corner was Susan-Marie. The band played "Rip It Up" and Susan said, "Let me explain something to you. This is really simple. Never try to date a girl who doesn't appreciate what's best about you. Those girls don't have the slightest idea of what's inside you. Cast not pearls before swine," she said with a wink. "There're lots of girls who'll like you for the real you, not for your imitation of Ricky Nelson."

In retrospect, her ideas ring even truer than they rang at the time. But Susan's advice would have been best directed at Susan. It makes perfect sense to choose a lover who appreciates you for who you are, who values what's inside you. But then, how do you explain Susan's choice of Paul Belzberg? How do you explain her putting up with him for so long after they were married?

For that matter, how do you explain the 1962 affair of Susan's three-year-long crush on Bobbie Bagley? Bobbie was the son of our vice-principal. He was a good-looking, sandy-haired boy, and he was president of our class for three years running. But he was mostly interested in refinishing cabinets even then. He was nothing but a pretty face and a connection to a high school vice-principal. But Susan-Marie had that worst kind of crush on him, a *well-known* crush, from tenth grade to the middle of senior year. It was that crush that led to another snapshot of Susan-Marie from those years.

It was Valentine's Day, 1962, in our senior year of high school. As usual, I had sent out fifty Valentines to practically every bad girl in class, only this time hoping that possibly I might have found the girls that Susan had been talking about, those who would love the inner me. But, alas, I had only received the usual polite but noncommittal ones from the same girls I had known since elementary school.

As I was walking home along Dale Drive in a bleak fog of disappointment, I passed by Susan-Marie's little colonial house. Incredibly, on that bitterly cold day, I could hear loud music pouring out of Susan's open dormer window. I stopped to stare and listen ("Come Go With Me" by the Dell-Vikings). Susan's face suddenly appeared in the window. She saw me, waved, and called out for me to wait there for her.

As I stood on the sidewalk, Susan erupted from the house in jeans and a winter jacket and actually did a series of handsprings that flipped her high into the air and landed her right in front of me.

"Don't tell anyone," she said. "You promise?"

"I promise," I said.

"Bobbie Bagley sent me a Valentine's card," she said. "A really, really sensitive one," she added in subdued tones.

"Great," I said moodily. Nobody had sent *me* a really sensitive Valentine's card.

"I think this means something," she said. "The big question now is whether he'll invite me to the Valentine's Dance this Saturday."

"I hope he does," I said. For my own part, I was going to the dance with Susan Jacoby, a girl who now owns a Nautilus fitness center for women in Berkeley, which tells you all you need to know about her.

"Well," she said, "I'll see you there." She had a big smile, bigger than I had ever seen before, and she was actually holding up crossed fingers on both hands before she did a cartwheel into the house.

Bobbie Bagley didn't invite Susan-Marie to the Valentine's Dance. He hadn't even sent the card. It was sent by a prankster named Arne who later told me he had done it just to keep the pot boiling in our class.

Susan never let on. She never embarrassed herself. But Bobbie Bagley never gave her the time of day, either. I often think of her doing that cartwheel on the frozen grass in February, happier than I had ever seen her before. When I think of that I'm glad Arne sent her the bogus Valentine's card. For a few days she lived in a fool's paradise, but then, what other kind of paradise is there? And from then on, if Bobbie Bagley cut her dead, she could at least imagine that he was doing it, snubbing her in front of the wood shop, because he simply had an uncontrollable crush on her and didn't trust himself to speak. Susan always had a great imagination. Now she had something to feed it, at least from February to May.

The final photograph in the exhibition of Susan-Marie in high school is a big, lush Kodachrome glossy from our Senior Prom. Susan and I went to it together. The background was that I had been planning to go with a tall, willowy girl named Judy Bloome. She was a friendly, carrot-topped girl who had been with me in Advanced English for two years. I considered her *almost* a hard girl because she wore a little cross and angora sweaters, even though she was going to Duke the next year.

The problem was that I had taken her to the movies twice and to dinner once, and then her parents told her, pure and simple, that they thought this low-level dating was fine, but they certainly did not want her going to the Senior Prom with a Jewish boy.

She tearfully passed this news on to me, then made plans for the prom with "Deuce" Walker, my close friend. So much for guilt. But I was so thunderstruck, so absolutely overwhelmed at this blow, that I was unable to collect myself to ask someone else. As the calendar of high-school days slid relentlessly into history, I planned to stay home and brood while the rest of the class sang the school anthem one last time. ("By old Sligo's clear blue waters, gentle hills of green," to the tune of the Cornell anthem, for a change.)

Two days before the event my mother told me that I would regret it for the rest of my life if I didn't go to the prom. Wasn't there any girl who also lacked a date who might want to go with me just so she, too, would not miss the life experience of the prom? She went into a long, sincere song and dance about how neither she nor my father had been able to go to their proms because of the Depression, passing on real insight in front of the Formica counters.

I called Susan and told her stammeringly of my plight. I will always remember what she said, and some day I will write it down and put it on her wall as a masterpiece of tact and generosity.

"Benjy," she said, "we've known each other all these years and we've never been out on a date. The Senior Prom would be the absolutely most perfect way to have our first date and celebrate all the time we've known each other. I'd love to."

The prom was at the Shoreham Hotel, in Washington,

D.C., itself. The dance was in a large room overlooking Rock Creek Park. In appearance, it was a *natural* prom. The high-school oligarchs got their final chance to lord it over everyone else. The football players, who would be insurance salesmen, and the cheerleaders, who would be Amway reps, had their final moments of pride. The last gasps of a police state as severe as Oceania in *1984* were gasped, the last exactments of teenage thought control were exacted, and the bonds of life before adulthood dissolved tangibly along with the ice replica of the school seal.

Susan-Marie wore a light blue prom dress made of imitation silk. She also wore high-heeled shoes exactly the same color as the dress. Her dress was daringly low cut. The idea that she, whom I had met in the park while reading *The Count of Monte Cristo* all those years ago, had beautiful breasts was an exciting revelation. To think of Susan, the whiz at differential equations, the parser of Keats's poetry, with white, firm breasts that pressed against the carnation in my lapel, that actually pressed against my chest, was dizzying.

We both ducked out to the veranda overlooking the park and took nips from a bottle of vodka I had brought. By midnight we were in a much more candid frame of mind than when we began. In the peculiar grasp of vodka and leave-taking, we began to feel both excited and saddened.

Around us swirled the faces of boys and girls with whom we had learned and laughed and who had judged us and whom we had judged. In their rented tuxedos and homemade prom dresses the boys and girls to whom we swore we would be closer than we were to our families kissed and danced and made a thousand small speeches beginning with "This is the last time . . ."

Susan and I paid our court to the class presidents and service club debutantes and then made our way seamlessly to midnight. We stood in a corner of the room. I had my arm around Susan's shoulder in the way that high-school students do, and I kissed her on the neck in the way that high-school students think is cool. The band played "In the Still of the Night." I thought, "This is a moment to remember." Aloud, I said, "This is sad. I'll probably never have friends like this again. I'm really feeling sad about this."

"Why?" Susan-Marie asked. "What's so great about high school? What's so great about having these people in charge of your life?"

"It's not that," I said. "I know it's not that great having to worry about whether Neely Carpenter thinks we're worth talking to, but I'm scared of whatever's coming. I'm going away to a big city where I don't know anyone, and I'm scared about that. I felt safe here."

Suddenly Susan-Marie looked me in the face with eyes so blue they looked like sapphire light bulbs. She grabbed my hand off her shoulder and took it in hers. Then she led me out the door back to the balcony and found for us a secluded spot next to a flower box filled with small white and green blossoms that gave off an intoxicating, woodsy smell in the midst of the city.

"You are so lucky," she said hoarsely. "You don't even know how lucky you are."

Then, without another moment of explanation, she kissed me. I had been kissed before, and I had even known long, heavy-breathing kisses in the car while the winds of teenage passion had swelled and ebbed. But this was a different embrace. So much heat came from Susan that I actually felt frightened for a moment. I felt as if Susan-Marie were giving me a transfusion of heat itself on that chilly balcony next to the heady smell of the flowers. The sensation was like an unexpected exposure to a warm, open window while walking down a cold, empty street. The draft of warmth was startling and vertiginous.

Then she stopped kissing me and said, "You are so lucky. You're leaving someplace where you feel safe." She was leaning next to me and I could hear her words and feel her breath on my ear. "Your life has been the way it's supposed to be."

"Not really," I said. "You don't know everything about my life."

"I know," Susan said, "but I know enough. I know that if you're afraid to leave it, it must have been all right. It must have been pretty good. I know that."

"Well, your life is just like mine basically." That was what I knew at the time. It says something about making judgments.

"You don't know," she said. "You've been a friend for a long time, but you don't know at all. It's all supposed to have been one way, with football games and bonfires and coming home out of the snow and feeling like you belong somewhere. It's never been like that for me. Not ever. There's never been a day in my whole life when I felt like I belonged where I was. None of it's ever been the way it's supposed to be."

Then she kissed me again, and this time I felt a definite promise. She pulled her head away and looked at me.

"This is it for me," Susan-Marie said. "Now my life is my life. It's not under anybody else's thumb. From now on I'm in charge, and it's going to be exactly the way it's supposed to be. Now I'm making the rules for me and I'm going to make my life so it's the way I want it to be."

Susan-Marie pointed with her nose at the prom in progress, cocked an ear to listen to the band playing "Story Untold." "I'm never going to be the belle of that ball in there," she said. "That's not going to happen. I mean, this is the last one, and I'm not ever going to be wearing the Homecoming crown."

"Susan, you're much better than that. This isn't for you and you know it. You're on a different level. You know that."

"No, I'm not," she said. "I'm just like everybody who wants things and doesn't get them." Her face looked open, vulnerable, on that balcony. When she spoke, her voice was barely above a whisper.

"You don't know what I want," Susan said. "Maybe I wanted more than anything to be in the Blair O'Debs and be a cheerleader. You don't know. *I* don't even know. I just know that I never got whatever it was I was supposed to get, and that's why I'm dying to get out of here."

"Well, then you're getting what you want now."

"Yes," she whispered. "Now I'm going to go to Duke and I'm going to spend the summers in France and I'm going to work in New York and in Paris and do all the things I wanted to do. That's what I'm going to do. I'm going to make the kind of life where I belong, *where I'm not a stranger in my own life.*"

I didn't know what to say to that, so I said, "The prom is ending. Let's go inside."

I held her hand and we walked indoors. On the way to our table I brushed by Betty Jones, who said, "There's a big party at my house afterward for breakfast. If you want to come, I'd love to see you there."

"I have to be home by two," Susan-Marie said. (Imagine the woman who said "yes" or "no" to Goldie Hawn saying she has to be in by two! Only seventeen years ago, the batting of an eyelash, and this is where she was.)

"Well," I said. "I don't know."

"You go ahead without me," Susan-Marie said. "You don't have to be home by any particular time."

"No," I said to Susan. "I'll take you home and then I'll just go home myself." I turned to Betty Jones, who had worn the Homecoming crown, and said, "Maybe not, but thanks."

She smiled and walked away. Susan-Marie squeezed my hand and said, "I don't want to hold you back."

"This is the best date I've ever had," I said. "I feel like killing myself that it took me so long to ask you out."

Then Dana Beers, the prom chairman, took the microphone. The lights in the Cherry Blossom Room were dimmed and the band began to play our school song. The prom-goers joined hands and sang the song as if they were making the only plea they would ever be allowed for eternal life. We were that sincere. Even Susan got into the spirit and sang, tears pouring down her cheeks.

When we got to the final stanza, which ended with "Alma Mater Queen," the entire cheerleader squad suddenly materialized out of thin air behind the stage and, in their red-and-white uniforms, held their arms above their heads, turned in a slow circle, then gradually lowered their arms to their sides, while still turning, fighting off their own hysteria at the thought of no longer being cheerleaders in high school and knowing that everything else would be a downhill slide.

In hushed, reverential tones, Dana Beers took the microphone and said, "Now, it's time to say good-bye/To all the friends and all the years/We'll keep their memory always alive/Warmed by smiles, watered by tears."

The band began to play "Good Night My Love," and then Dana Beers whispered into the microphone, "Now, while we dance our last time, while we're all together *for the last time,* let's all make a wish together, and I know that mine is going to be that we all stay close for the rest of our lives and look upon these years as the best times of our lives and always know that Montgomery Blair is the home we can come back to. Now, let's all make our wishes."

I obediently closed my eyes and made my wish, which was indeed that I might keep some of the friends I had made in high school for the rest of my life. Friends were crucial to me then and now. In the event, I have lost touch with all of them, except for Susan-Marie, but then, wishes rarely come true.

After I made my wish I put my arms around Susan-Marie and kissed her while we danced. "Good—night, my —love, pleasant dreams and sleep tight, my—love . . ." I felt as if a flower bud of life's possibilities had just opened for me in the person of this wonderful, this dazzling Susan-Marie, who had the warmest kiss on earth.

While we danced, Susan-Marie put her head on my shoulder and stroked the back of my head. Her hand, like her lips, was unusually warm, as if it, too, had a natural heat of 108.6 instead of 98.6.

"You know what I wished?" Susan-Marie said, holding the back of my head. "I wished that I would have just one day some time in my life, just one day when I felt like I belonged somewhere and I was there where I belonged."

The band played, "May tomorrow be sunny and bright, and bring me closer to you . . ." I felt as if I were sailing through an unknown universe of vodka and infatuation, loss and revelation, and mostly I felt as if I were in love with Susan-Marie, the brilliant, frightened, overwarm girl in the light blue dress who danced and cried in my arms. I knew exactly where she belonged.

■ ■ ■ ■

That is the last photograph in my scrapbook of Susan-Marie in high school, of Susan-Marie and me as children growing up together. The Kodachrome is fading now, and the corners are turned up, but when I examine that photograph in my mind it still has that lush, gorgeous richness of color that can make me stop in the middle of a day of a hundred telephone calls and feel dizzy that time has passed and that we are grown, make me beg for a dream that would take me back.

I drove Susan-Marie to Luigi's on Nineteenth Street for pizza. We ran into Jim Thompson and Marvin Bernstein with their dates, Patti Magidson and Linda Keller. We ate pizza and drank wine, then headed for home, down Sixteenth Street, past the red-brick embassy mansions, the Carter Barron Amphitheater, the endless churches, out into suburbia.

I parked in front of Susan-Marie's house and we kissed. I touched her and pulled her to me.

She pushed me away very politely and sweetly. "I feel like I could get very close to you tonight. Maybe really close. You were very good to me," she said softly.

Susan-Marie traced the outline of my mouth in the

dark, in my parents' 1957 Ford, and said, "I mean to take me home and not go to Betty Jones's party."

"Well," I said, "it would be a good way to end high school."

"But I'm not going to," Susan-Marie said after thirty seconds of silence. "I'm not going to, because I'm starting anew. And if I got involved with you, it would be getting involved with the past. Do you understand?"

"Yes," I said. "I understand," and I did, even though I felt as if a velvet door had been slammed in my face.

"I think after what I told you tonight, we're almost too close to get involved anyway."

"I don't want to force you into anything," I said, although I felt dismayed. This evening was obviously good-bye and not hello.

"I won't forget this evening," Susan said. "I'll never forget it. Never. I told you things and you heard me. I'll never forget that. That doesn't mean anything to you now, but some day it will." She looked at me and I nodded.

We kissed once more and then I walked her to her door. It was a normal wooden door with six panels and a brass knocker in the shape of a horse.

"Good night," she said. "Stay like you are and you'll do all right. And stay close."

Then she gave me a big, 1962 good-night-sized kiss with tail fins, opened the door, and went inside.

The next day I drove to the Shoreham Hotel and found the balcony and the flowers next to where we had kissed. Their smell was gone, as Susan-Marie was. I tracked down the hotel gardener, a wizened Japanese, and asked him what the flower was called.

"That flower very delicate," he said, "is called Star Jasmine."

4

POWER GLIDE

■

The most haunting of life's mysteries is simply that time, which seems indelible at the moment, passes and is gone.

The days and months and years after graduation from high school seemed as permanent as concrete when they happened. Now they are a moment's remembering of days in summer jobs adding columns of numbers, terror at final examinations, dates with girls who couldn't stand me, speaking out in class, being locked in a closet for fraternity initiation, finding a girl who would love me, thinking love would go on forever, sinking back into hopelessness, taking standardized tests, drinking, getting sick, buying a suit at Brooks Brothers, getting yelled at in a law-school classroom in New Haven, seeing a beautiful girl at a summer dance at the State Department, marrying her on a scorching day in Arlington while her father wore Army dress whites, yelling back at the professors at Yale, singing songs and carrying signs, working in a cubicle I shared with another loser so deep within the bowels of the bureaucracy that Satan couldn't find us with a microscope, arguing, getting divorced and signing ghastly papers that said I didn't love my wife, and then starting to date girls who couldn't stand me.

These things seemed as permanent as granite and as vivid as a blowtorch when they were happening, but then they were gone, only remembered when I got stuck in a traffic jam on Virginia Avenue or was waiting for a doctor's appointment to have my colitis monitored.

In 1970 the only thing that mattered was that I was living in a one-room apartment in a renovated but still murderous section of southwest Washington, D.C., and that I spent my days carefully studying the claims of dog food manufacturers as to whether their products really were (a) "meaty," (b) "moist," (c) "nutritionally balanced," and (d) were "what your dog would choose for himself if he could."

I worked in a paperboard-walled cubicle without windows. Across from me was a woman who sat in a similar cubicle studying diet soft drink claims and crying softly all morning. My boss was a man with flaming red sideburns who often refused to discuss legal matters with his staff and instead ostentatiously studied the writings of Mao Tse-tung in a plastic-jacketed little red book. He was known to reply, when unavoidably confronted with a legal problem, with such aphorisms as "When enemy attacks, we retreat. When enemy retreats, we attack."

Day by day, I walked the humid, smoke-filled streets of Washington, D.C., wondering where I had gone wrong. Somehow, I had fallen off the track of success and achievement I thought I had been on. I brooded about it constantly, but something was about to change in an unexpected way, from an unexpected quarter.

■　　■　　■　　■

First, at a party at Jim Thompson's house during the Christmas vacation of our first year of college, across a room of boys and girls boasting and laughing about college ("Well, Oberlin had the most Rhodes scholars last year," "Yes, but Reed has the most out of the class admitted to medical school . . .") I saw Susan by herself drinking slightly alcoholic punch out of a plastic punchbowl. Amid the welter of yelling and greeting, we talked about her life at Duke and mine at Columbia.

"It's wonderful," she said. "I can stay out as late as I want on most nights and I can stay up in my room reading all night if I want to. And the kids are so nice . . ."

She said that, and yet her eyes had an even darker tint than usual, and her hands actually shook. "I'm so happy," she said. "I'm going to take advanced statistics next semester and I'll have a tutorial on topology and I'm already working outside of class with one of my professors."

Still, she looked frightened. She told me she was not staying at home during her vacation, but with her friend Lois Rosen, because her parents were "out of town . . ."

I didn't see Susan-Marie again for eight years, although I didn't completely lose touch. I heard, for example, that she had consummated a furtive affair with the head of the mathematics department at Duke, and that he had briefly left his wife for her. When I heard that I thought of the heat on the balcony and I envied that professor.

I also heard that her mother had been killed in an airplane crash in Nebraska while investigating a grant from the Department of Health, Education and Welfare. The funeral was in her mother's home town of Idabel, Oklahoma, or else I would have gone.

By the time Susan was in graduate school in mathematics at the University of Maryland her stepfather had sold the house on Dale Drive. I would never walk by there again and hear loud music and see Susan-Marie come running out the door and do cartwheels in front of my eyes, tumbling gleefully on the frozen ground.

(This is what I mean when I talk about the mystery of

time and its concreteness and evanescence. I can still drive by that house sometimes in the winter and look at Susan-Marie's dormer windows. I expect to hear the Dell-Vikings and see Susan in shadow at the window. That expectation is as real to me as whatever I will do that day, as real as arguing a case or hiring a writer or meeting the Cabinet. But it is based on something that is as gone as the pharaohs.)

By 1968 I heard that Susan-Marie was married to a fellow graduate student of mathematics at the University of Maryland. Then I heard that she was divorced. In *The Washington Post* I read that Susan had won an award for developing a formula that would allow a machine called a "computer" to generate random numbers more rapidly than previously possible. For this achievement, she had been given a large fellowship by the Chesapeake and Potomac Telephone Company.

In 1971 I ran into Susan at Garfinckel's. I was shopping there for a necktie to add to my pitiful collection. I bought one with little paisley figures, paid for it with a credit card, then waited for the elevator.

When I got into that ancient paneled elevator there was only one other passenger. Her eyes were like two blue diamonds, but, fleetingly, they looked frightened and defensive.

When Susan saw that it was me, though, she became almost wildly excited. She hugged me, threw down her packages and kissed my cheek, flushed as if she might start to cry. She wore a smart, tailored linen outfit of a brownish beige, and once she stopped looking frightened, she looked authentically "together"—a buttoned-down, completely well-organized Washington career woman.

"Let's talk," she said. "Let's have lunch."

"Fine," I said. "What about next Monday?"

"No," she said. "Right now."

So we walked over to the Hot Shoppes on G Street and ate.

Susan told me that things were going pretty well. "I'm

at the telephone company," she said. "I work on optimizing number theory for them, which means getting the most that you can possibly get out of the existing number of phone lines. It's really difficult."

"I'm working on a lawsuit about dog food commercials," I said.

"I was married," she said. "He was in my class in grad school. He was all right. It was just that when he got stuck in a problem he drank a lot. He really drank a lot. In fact, he got so drunk he would throw me around the apartment. The first time he did it I told him if he did it again, I was gone. The second time he did it I left. I didn't work like a dog all the way through school to get beat up. Nobody's ever going to beat me up. Not ever," she said. It was surprising to hear such frank, outspoken words coming from a woman in a tailored suit at the Hot Shoppes. It was especially strange to hear a tone of such fear, such vulnerability, in the middle of an afternoon at a restaurant filled with well-to-do women carrying alligator bags.

"I had a hard time there for a while at Duke," Susan-Marie said. "You might have heard about it. It was just such a change from home that it was hard to adjust."

I nodded and said I knew what she meant.

"When I lived at home it was pretty tough," she said warily. "I don't know if you knew anything about that."

"No," I said. "I didn't know about that."

"Well," she said. "It was just that my stepfather drank a lot, and things were pretty bad. So I was always on my guard, if you know what I mean. I mean, I was always prepared and watching out. When I got to college I didn't have to be so buttoned-down, you know, inside, and I sort of went haywire in the other direction," she added with a cheerful let's-get-on-with-it smile.

We ordered sandwiches, but I was too excited to enjoy them as much as I usually did. In her own, buttoned-down, number-theoretician way, Susan also was still running on the burst of excitement she had allowed to be unbuttoned in Garfinckel's elevator.

"I've been to France three times," she said. "It was wonderful. I saw Provence and Mougins and I ate in two three-star restaurants. It was really great. Now I'm trying to organize the research division at the phone company to go on a charter to Europe this summer. I've already arranged for us to have a little part of the cafeteria where we can get French food that we bring in ourselves and pâté and things, and even wine."

The conversation went on for an hour, with my usual whining about my work on dog food commercials. "I thought I was destined to have something big," I said. "I guess I'm not."

Susan's personality suddenly changed drastically. It was as if my remark had thrown her entire psyche into a new, deeper, lower gear, a more truthful gear.

"You think so?" she said. "Benjy, let me tell you something. You get to work with advertising, with something dramatic that's seen by millions of people every week."

"It's dog food advertising," I said.

"I don't care," Susan-Marie said. "It's still drama. It's incredible high-tension adventure compared with working out telephone circuits for the phone company."

"So," I asked, "what're we doing? This is our only life. What went wrong?"

"Nothing went wrong," Susan-Marie said. "We just know better than we did. Life's much more scary than we thought it was. We went for a safe way out. Nobody can blame us for that. There are a lot of dangerous people out there. A lot of dangerous ways to live. We're keeping our heads down and staying out of trouble at the Federal Trade Commission and the phone company. We don't get the big prizes, but we don't get into big trouble, either."

"Yes," I said, "but it hurts to keep your head down all the time. It makes me feel like a schmuck and a loser when I'm keeping my head down and everybody else is getting ahead."

"You don't know about their lives," Susan-Marie said. "You don't know anything about their lives. Compared with almost anyone's in the world, our lives are pretty good."

"I feel like a loser every day I work at the FTC," I said. "Look at Goldie Hawn. She was a year behind us in high school, and everybody used to feel sorry for her then, and look where she is and where we are. Look at Connie Chung, who was a little mouse, and now she's on national TV. She used to sit behind me in chemistry and I never even noticed she was there."

"Yes," Susan-Marie said, "and when I was a little kid I used to think I'd be up there on the screen with Charlton Heston and Jean Simmons, and I'd be getting an Academy Award from Paul Belzberg. But that's not the way life is. We're not them. What happens to people like Goldie Hawn or Paul Belzberg is a million-to-one shot. It didn't happen to me and I'm just as happy. I'm not in the line of fire, and that's just fine with me."

"Yes, but what about self-esteem?" I said. "Every day I feel devastating blows to my self-esteem."

"I'm not worried about self-esteem. I'm out of trouble, and that's what counts. Period. I keep my fantasies that someday I'll be like those people, like Goldie Hawn, but I know what's real and what's not."

"Goldie Hawn is real," I said.

"So is winning the lottery. It's nice if it happens, but only a crazy person spends the money before he buys a ticket."

"A personality is not a ticket," I said. "A personality is a live, moving thing, and you've got a lot more of it than Goldie Hawn ever did. And Goldie Hawn wasn't that good in math," I said, trying to return the conversation to a friendlier tone.

"Benjy," Susan-Marie said, "I have my dreams, and if they come true, great. If they don't, I'm staying out of trouble."

Susan became edgy after that. We finished our sandwiches and I kissed her good-bye on her cheek. Even for that moment, the smell of White Shoulders was stunning.

Then Susan-Marie hailed a cab back to her office at the telephone company. I strolled back to the Federal Trade Commission along Pennsylvania Avenue, watching the winos leaning against the granite blocks of the Post Office Department.

From what I saw of her energy to do and to be big, and from what I saw of how she was marshaling all of her own strength to fight against that great, frightening event, to keep herself perpetually locked away, I could see a dizzying future for Susan: if she should ever stop fighting against her own daring and let that daring, that heat on the balcony, that somersault on the frozen lawn, that seething need mixed with that creativity—if she should ever let that tiger out of the cage, there would be plenty of noise in the jungle.

Frankly, I was not sure it would ever happen, just as I was not sure that I would ever be released myself to do the great things I wanted to do outside fiberboard walls. "Full many a flower is born to blush unseen, and waste its sweetness on the desert air . . ." was the unwritten motto of Washington life, after all.

But Susan was within days of being released. More amazing than that, her savior was to be Richard Milhous Nixon.

5

VICTIMS

∎

Richard Nixon. Let's start with my connection with him.

In 1952, when I was seven years old, I read an official campaign biography of Ike and Dick passed out in school by the Montgomery County Republican Committee. Only one fact from that document lingers in my mind: When Richard Nixon was a young man he met and fell madly in love with Patricia Ryan. Alas, Pat Ryan was already going with someone else. But Richard Nixon would not take no for an answer. He insisted on sitting on Pat Ryan's porch each night to wait for her to come home from work, to plead with her to change her mind. Eventually she did.

In essence, that fact summarized Richard Nixon for me then and now.

Here he was, a poor boy from Yorba Linda, which ain't much, believe me. He had no money, no especially great looks, no family background, a father who was barely there, a mother who had to work raising other people's children, and a personality barely covering up a bottomless well of hypersensitivity to everything that happened to him.

So here he was, this nothing from nowhere, and look where he had gotten by sheer persistence and willpower. Kennedy had all that charisma and all that money. Lyndon Johnson had great big steel balls that clanked when he walked across the room. Eisenhower was made of leather inside and out. But Nixon was, to me, always the outsider trying desperately to cover up his fear and his loneliness and act as if he were one of the boys.

Even as a child I could see that Nixon, alone among politicians, actually bled when he was attacked. Look at him talking about Checkers. Look at him on the night he lost to Kennedy. Listen to him telling the press in Los Angeles in 1962 that they wouldn't have Richard Nixon to kick around anymore. This was not a Ronald Reagan, tough from the inside out, and not a Jimmy Carter, wrapped in a trance of religiosity. This was a man who bled, a real live human being with feelings.

In fact, to compound my felonies, I have always believed that the main reason the press and many, many other Americans hated Richard Nixon had nothing to do with his politics. (William Buckley is far more conservative than Nixon, and he is invited to the best dinner parties in Manhattan.) No, the reason the press liked to go after Richard Nixon, why it became a national sport to go after Richard Nixon, was the same as the reason children in a schoolyard pick certain children to taunt and certain ones to ignore: human beings like to go after other human beings who will show their hurt.

I do not pretend that mine is an original theory. Far from it. The part that's *my* feeling about Richard Nixon is that he was always, all his life, that child taunted in the schoolyard. He tried, oh, how he tried, to pretend that he had a rhinoceros skin. He tried to pretend that he was tough and that "the hotter it gets, the cooler I get . . ." It didn't fool me. I could see in any press conference, in any give-and-take with reporters, that Richard Nixon was bleeding profusely, that his opponents could smell it, and that they wanted more.

I have to say that after sixty years of this kind of struggle, Richard Nixon had probably even fooled himself about who he was. He might even have believed that he was the big, tough, conservative gunfighter that all the liberals were after. But to me, the siege of Richard Nixon in the Watergate years had nothing to do with conservatives and liberals. It had everything to do with bullies and schoolyards and victims. I had been the playground victim enough to know which side I was on.

In 1971, when I was working at the Federal Trade Commission behind fiberboard walls, I stopped reading the replies of the dog food companies about their advertising and strolled across Pennsylvania Avenue to the National Archives and walked into its cool, marble reception room, with the brass engravings of the Founders and their words. The thought suddenly struck me that movies and TV shows were a sort of national archive as well. They told of how the nation felt at any given moment and what the nation was willing to believe.

In a day I wrote an article about how the movies of 1971 predicted with perfect clarity that despite all the qualms about Richard Nixon's policies, the public wanted a Machiavellian, cunning, *seemingly* dominant type as president, almost a Godfather figure. That meant R.N. By a small miracle the article appeared almost instantly in *The Wall Street Journal.*

Within one day after the appearance of the article, about two weeks after my lunch with Susan at the Hot Shoppes, my immensely fat secretary, an Okie who actually brought her children to work and let them play in the corridor outside my office, buzzed me to say that there was a "Mister Hollerman" on the line.

I picked up the phone and heard a pleasant woman's

voice say, "Mr. Haldeman will be with you in one moment."

Click-click, and then a voice like a buzz saw in low gear said, "Ben, let's get together and talk about your article."

That day at lunch, instead of eating in the FTC cafeteria (whose special that day was fried turbot, $1.15, with green beans, tea, and a roll), I ate at the White House with Robert Haldeman. In a basement room called the "White House Mess," I sat across from "Bob" at a small table.

Bob told me that he had been impressed with my article. He had also been able to show it to "The President," and "The President" agreed there was something there. Bob looked at me with his steel-gray eyes, his crew-cut, which gave him the air of a religious fanatic, and his high forehead reminding me of a bank vault. "Ben," he said in a perfectly sincere way, "how would you like to come over here to work at the White House?"

"Doing what?" I asked.

"Writing a comprehensive study of how the mass media reflects our political and social views or doesn't reflect them," Bob said. "That would help us shape our own TV commercials for the 1972 campaign."

"You mean the president has decided to seek a second term?" I asked. Bob Haldeman laughed, and I laughed, too, and I took the job. It would be fun working with a jolly steel buzz saw, far from the winos and the cardboard walls, right there in the White House, helping the child in the schoolyard who was now president. It would be a big, big step above working on dog food commercials with a secretary who brought her children to work.

It had nothing to do with politics. It was about a chance to get out of a pit, to work on something big, somewhere important, for someone whose personality had always touched me.

A clean-cut fellow named Craig who had left off business school at USC to work on assigning offices at the White House showed me to my new digs. They were in the Executive Office Building, a massive Victorian wedding cake of a building immediately adjacent to the White House. My office was off a large, wide hall with fluted gray columns and a checkerboard pattern of black-and-white marble tiles. The suite had a reception room with secretary, a small file room, and then two offices, each with a conference table, a couch, and a huge antique maple desk. Each office also had floor-to-ceiling French doors and satin drapes that matched the upholstery on the couch and the desk chair. To compare it with my office at the FTC would be like comparing a Midas Muffler shop with Versailles.

"Who's got the other office?" I asked.

"That's for your assistant, your numbers person to help you with the study. Mr. Haldeman says you've got one slot for an assistant up to twenty thousand, exempt from Civil Service," Craig said, reading from a sheet of paper on a clipboard.

"Does that telephone work?" I asked, pointing at a beige Call Director on my new desk.

"Absolutely," said Craig.

I picked up the receiver and dialed Susan-Marie's number at the telephone company. When Susan got on the line I said, "How would you like to come to work at the White House?"

P·A·R·T

II

6

ASCENT

■

People are drastically influenced by their surroundings. Psychiatrists say it, and it's true. Take a man and put him in a gun show, surrounded by Mausers and Lugers and Uzis, and he thinks of killing. Put a child in an airplane hangar and he thinks of flight. Put a woman in the boardroom of Revlon and she thinks of cosmetics and money. Put any human being on the marble of the Acropolis and he or she thinks of idealism and history. Put small children in a yellow room. They act aggressive and excited. Put them in a pink room and they act dazed and quiet. Put them in a green room. They are subdued but playful. This is not an article in a magazine. This is true.

By the same token, take a smart young woman who is already deeply locked in against the dangers of the intimate world. Put her in a windowless room in a telephone company regional headquarters next to a Burger King.

You get a resentful drone. Put the same woman in a corporate headquarters next to a garage and you get a bureaucratic cipher. Take the same woman. Put her in the White House, seat of supreme power for half the earth. Have her enter the building past Marine sentries. Give her a large, airy office with a line to the Oval Office, with a cherry-wood conference table, satin drapes and matching slipcovers, a telephone that chimes rather than rings, a Chrysler and a driver to pick her up and take her home in the rain or snow, and you have an awakened woman with a vision.

Susan-Marie's first day at work was a scorcher, a miserable summer day in Washington, and even with the air-conditioning our offices in the EOB were sticky and enervating. Our very White House appointment certificates in their black frames and non-glare glass dripped condensation.

At nine-thirty in the morning Cheryl, my blond, primly attractive secretary, rang my buzzer—which made a tiny noise like a discreet cough. "Miss Warmack is here," said Cheryl.

When I walked out into the reception room there was a woman standing about two inches taller than I thought Susan-Marie stood. Her hair, yes, her hair, neatly arranged in waves to her earlobes, looked more alive, more vivid, as if each strand had a story to tell. After a moment I recognized her tan suit from our meeting at Garfinckel's, but it looked like a newer, more up-to-the-moment version, perhaps made with silk threads. Her shoes were definitely new, with that tight, dense look of leather that only shoes from Delman or Gucci or some other expensive store might have. But most startling of all, Susan's skin and eyes looked as if they had received a transfusion of energy, a jolt from a psychic Grand Coulee Dam that lit up her whole face.

She hugged me, and I could smell her perfume. It smelled great. I made an exaggerated sniffing sound and Susan said, "White Shoulders." But I already knew.

I let her go and smiled at her. "Honey," she said, in a nasal, 1950s TV voice, with a touch of a Cuban accent, "I'm home."

From then on Susan-Marie was off and running. Working at the White House, even as despised as it was by much of the ruling class of America, transformed her. First, and not just on her first day of work, was her appearance. She not only looked cool and elegant on her first day, like a cover of *W* served on ice: she looked smart. She looked like she was there to get the job done.

It was not a question of money. She didn't have money to spend on new clothes, except in dribs and drabs. Salaries at the White House, then and now, were nothing to tell the people at Salomon Brothers about. Susan's new ingredient was a sureness about herself that gave her a style, a look of accomplishment and poise that apparently had always lain dormant within the girl from the Senior Prom and the telephone company mouse.

From that first day, she walked down the wide, black-and-white-checked hallways with pride, in a hurry to get things done. When she ran into Julie Eisenhower or Ron Ziegler or Len Garment she greeted them deferentially, but definitely as if she were one of the boys. From those hallways, those "corridors of power," Susan derived the strength to renew herself and emerged as if she had always belonged at the Executive Office Building of the President of the United States.

One day about two weeks after she began work Susan and I were walking down the hall toward the Executive Office screening room when we ran smack into Henry Kissinger muttering to Brent Scowcroft. He looked over at Susan the way a professor at Harvard might look at an attractive graduate student in the hallway of Widener Library.

"Good morning, young lady," said the National Security adviser.

"Good morning, Dr. Kissinger," Susan said with perfect equanimity.

"Are we having a White House fashion show?" Dr. Kissinger asked, with the deft humor that had made him a Society favorite.

"No," Susan-Marie said with a smile. "A screening of *Cisco Pike*. Would you like to see it with us?"

"I would if you could bring the Shah of Iran into it with us," Dr. Kissinger said. "I have to talk to him."

Without a moment's hesitation, Susan-Marie took two steps toward Dr. Kissinger, put out her hand in a perfectly engaging way, and said, "I'm Susan-Marie Warmack and this is my boss, Ben—"

Dr. Kissinger cut her off with a wave of his hand. "I know him," he said, as if to say "Who cares about him?" "What do you do here?" he asked Susan-Marie.

"I analyze popular culture," Susan-Marie said. "I'll be happy to send you a copy of our report."

"And I would be happy to send you Madame Binh," said Kissinger. Then he smiled and walked on, with one long, over-the-shoulder glance at Susan.

"Do you know him?" I asked Susan.

"Not until now," she said with a disarmingly girlish giggle.

While we watched Karen Black and Kris Kristofferson struggle and die in the world of heroin trafficking, I looked at Susan's profile in the dark. I was pleased with myself, proud that I had faith that Susan, the woman who had told me only days before that the way to live is "to keep your head down and stay out of trouble," was now completely at home striking up a conversation with Henry Kissinger. Susan was almost instantly able to talk to Julie Eisenhower thoughtfully about needlepoint and to John Ehrlichman knowingly about urban mass transit. She was able to almost, but not quite, flirt with Fred W., a notorious lady-killer, and to appear perfectly buttoned-down to Frances George, the seventy-year-old woman who controlled the computers at the White House. I felt as if Susan-Marie had landed in New Guinea, hiked into the depths of the tropical rain forest, and, without any warning, known how to speak the native dialect of fifty naked savages with bones in their noses.

When I cast my mind back and remember her briefing the jolly steel buzz saw himself, I can still feel the dizzy grasp of surprise as she responded to Haldeman's most demanding questions evenly, calmly, as if she were a deferential but completely tenured faculty member briefing the head of a department: no disrespect, plenty of courtesy, but no fear.

"How do we know this isn't just out-and-out pie in the sky?" Haldeman asked one day when Susan was adding a few words to my explanation of why a renaissance of cowboy shows on TV was a good sign for the commander-in-chief.

"Well, you asked us to do this in the first place," I said, somewhat exasperated. "Apparently you felt we had some judgment."

"What have you done to make us think we were right?" Haldeman asked, as if he were talking to a galley slave.

I took a deep breath and started to compose a reply about the vague nature of all cultural analysis, the iffy nature of social content study, and other scholarly camouflage.

Susan, on the other hand, standing in front of a chart, looking like the owner of the building, sparkling in a red silk blouse, pearls, and a white linen skirt, white patterned stockings, and rainbow leather shoes, understood the question.

"Let me ask you this," she said with an equable smile. "Do *you* think we're on the right track? Do you have any ideas about where we might be going wrong?"

"No," he said instantly. "It sounds right to me. It's the kind of thing I've always believed, and I think we're pretty much parallel on this one. But I do want to be sure we talk every few weeks."

"That's what we want, too," Susan said. "Ben was just saying that he wished we could talk to you more often as we worked on this."

"Well," the jolly buzz saw said, "I wish I had time, but I'll certainly be glad to consult with you whenever you need my input." He gave us a smile, claps of encouragement and praise, and showed us out with his blessings.

Susan had understood what Bob Haldeman wanted: to feel involved, to feel as if we were proceeding under his direction, to reassert his control. With the kind of instinct that I could only wish for, she had divined what a man like Haldeman would be interested in: not statistics, not academic speeches, but a chance to express his power.

Susan's intuitive knowledge of that need in powerful men was only glimpsed slightly by me as we walked back across West Executive Avenue from the White House. Now, from the vantage point of twelve years, I can see that was the first hint that Susan had the key that would unlock the doors to all the dreams and terrors of her life.

But I am getting ahead of myself. Another fact I noticed when Susan and I were coming back from the meeting with Bob Haldeman was that there is a price for everything. After about twenty steps inside the gray darkness of the EOB Susan looked sickly pale, as if she had been poisoned. Without a word, she ducked into the women's room of the first floor. She emerged about ten minutes later looking no longer pale, but now a medium green, with her hair disheveled.

"It don't come easy," Susan said, with a smile.

"It never does," I said.

"This is our secret," Susan said. "When people start to smell fear they don't think you're a contender any more. And I always could have been a contender," she added with a heavy New York waterfront accent.

(For some reason I am always reminded of that episode by a producer in Hollywood whom I have come to know recently. This man is the shyest, most fearful man I have ever known. Nevertheless, he goes to five meetings a day, yells and screams with the best of them, and drives a $48,000 Porsche 928 painted a lustrous, magical wine red. Once when he drove me to the airport he stopped short and five empty bottles of paregoric, all dated within the last month, slid out from under my seat. "You didn't think all of this was free, did you?" he asked me matter-of-factly.)

Days and weeks went by. All of this was pre-Watergate, so the main concern was inflation and student demonstrations, at least at the White House mess. But Susan and I were not involved in Cambodia or Selective Service. Each day, morning and afternoon, we sat in upholstered orange wing chairs in the White House movie theater or the EOB screening room. An ancient projectionist named Elmer who had once shown *It Happened One Night* to FDR and Eleanor showed us the pop culture effluvia of Hollywood day after day. While battles of price control and Operation Menu raged above us, we watched *Shaft* and *Charleston Blue* on the big screen, and videotapes of "All in the Family" and "The Mary Tyler Moore Show" on the small screen.

We concentrated and thought and perceived and wrote summaries. There was a major difference between the way we watched the movies, though. I watched as an academic, sometimes interested, sometimes appreciative, sometimes angry at the betrayal of the medium. But Susan-Marie watched as if her life depended on it. She stared at the screen the way a dog stares at a slice of roast beef on your plate. She watched as if eternal life might come through the acetate and cotton and enter her soul through her eyes.

One day I brought her a bag of popcorn and while she was eating it, preparing for *Welcome Back, Shaft*, she let out a long sigh. As the titles and action shots of Richard Roundtree moved across the screen, Susan grasped my forearm. "The people here at the White House think they have power," she said. "That's wrong. They have laws and taxes, but they don't have power. The people who make these," she said, taking away her hand and gesturing at the screen, "they have power."

"They can't arrest you," I said.

"They can get inside your head," Susan-Marie said. "They can tell you whether you're alive or not. They can completely take control of everything you see and do, change the way you feel, everything that happens to you, and that's power. They can change your dreams. They can make your life bearable."

"Well," I said. "That's power."

One day, around the middle of January of 1972, Susan and I flew to Las Vegas to attend a meeting of the National Organization of Theater Owners. We were to attend a session on "Character and Caricature in the Media Marketplace." I still don't know what it was supposed to be about. We sat on a panel with a number of professional academic worriers who used words like "psychic disintermediation" and "intergroup value transmission." Susan and I mostly laughed and passed notes to each other. At night we slept separately in small rooms at the Tropicana. One night, about two in the morning, while I was wondering what it would be like to be Sammy Davis, Jr., Susan called on the house phone. She asked if I felt like a walk through the casino.

I got dressed and met her at the two-dollar blackjack tables. I wore a blue blazer and a pink Brooks Brothers shirt. Susan wore a white silk suit with blue pinstripes. She also wore a string of pearls. As I walked with her through the casino by night, I was struck—and she was struck—by the faces we saw. There in Las Vegas, in the gambling center of the gambling West, the men and women had hardened looks beyond what either of us had ever seen in the East. The women's eyes seemed to have several layers less of retina and iris. The men's faces were tighter, pulled shut against other hard faces. The teeth and the lips were perpetually pulled apart, like the mouths of coyotes.

There was in the air the snap of electrical circuitry from the slot machines. There was the sizzle and pop of the numbers coming up in keno or roulette. Through the sea of two A.M. faces there were flashes of money being laid down on the tables in endless profusion, then being watched, followed, searched by the hardened eyes of the hardened people, as if they were Indian scouts perpetually on the lookout for edible game.

Somehow, by growing up in Washington, the only place in America where small amounts of money are not important, the only place where socialism works, we had been spared the fixation on money that screamed off the walls of the Tropicana casino at two A.M. Walking hand in hand with Susan-Marie through the pits and the ranks of black-jack tables, I felt as if we were Hansel and Gretel walking in the dangerous forest. Somehow, we had wandered into a place where we did not know who we were.

As I say, this was a two A.M. feeling in a strange town, and yet I think Susan felt it as well, because, after a few minutes she said, "Thank God we don't live in a place where people only care about how much money they can take away from each other."

"The war of all against all," I said, and Susan nodded.

"This is the first place I've seen that makes the phone company look good," Susan-Marie said.

We wanted to get an omelette and then go back to our rooms. But we got lost among the rows of tables, as if we were on an uncharted sea of unreasoning greed, far out beyond the shoreline. We turned down one row and then down another, and suddenly we were at the high-stakes baccarat table. By then it was almost two-thirty in the morning and there were only four players at the table, as well as two beautiful black shills. Two of the players were Japanese men in polo shirts. The third was a heavy-set Italian man smoking a cigar and rolling quarters over his knuckles as he played.

The fourth was a tall, thin man with sunken eyes and an out-of-place look. His face was sensitive, interested, feeling. His lips were thin and alert. There was an air of mournful vitality about him, like the air I imagine to be around artists who have just pawned their brushes. The man wore a brown suit and a striped necktie against a blue shirt. He looked almost like a college professor.

In fact, the man was gambling against the bank for a thousand dollars a card, and from his look, and the look of the Japanese who was the bank, the man was losing.

Susan grasped my arm at the elbow as if she were about to impart a tremendous truth, and she did exactly that. "I heard he was in bad shape," she said. "I heard he's been having trouble."

"Who?" I asked.

"That's Paul Belzberg," she said.

We watched the play for about ten minutes. Paul Belzberg won a few cards, but mostly his cards and his hunches went against him. After ten minutes he slid off his seat, tossed a blue chip to the pit boss, and walked away from the table, brushing right past Susan-Marie. She stiffened, as if she had just been given a shot.

As Belzberg walked away, Susan looked after him for a moment, and then I asked her if she still wanted to find the hotel coffee shop for an omelette.

"I don't think so," she said. "I think I'd like to lie down."

The next morning, I stood in line at the cashier to pay my bill and Susan's with our government travel orders. As I waited, Susan appeared, dressed in a dark blue silk suit and a red scarf. While we studied our hotel bills, Paul Belzberg appeared again. He was dressed in the same college-professor mode, but this time with a plaid jacket with leather elbow patches. He looked much more pulled together than he had at the baccarat table six hours before. He was accompanied by a bellman pulling a cart of elegant blue canvas luggage.

He was also accompanied by a razor-thin woman in a tan pantsuit. Her hair was short and straight. She had light blue eyes that darted around the room like the eyes of a Secret Service agent. She had a number of heavy silver bracelets on her left wrist. On her right hand she wore a silver watch with a circle of diamonds around its face. Her nose was short and pointed, like the nose of a toy poodle. Her teeth were also like a poodle's—even, small, but very sharp.

"That's Deirdre Needle," I said to Susan-Marie. "I went to college with her. We used to call her Madame deFarge in a Villager dress."

"I think that's the woman he lives with," Susan-Marie said. She watched them closely while I signed the triplicate forms at the cashier's window.

Outside, in the baking sun, Susan and I waited for a taxi. Only a few feet away, Paul Belzberg stood looking at an air-mail edition of the London *Times*. Next to him, Deirdre Needle stood and reamed out the doorman. "What do you mean, the car and driver aren't here? Just get on the phone and get them. If we miss this plane, we'll never stay here again. This is supposed to be a place that shows Republic Pictures very special treatment, and this is the head of motion pictures. You think Sid Bauman's gonna like this?"

"He'll be back in just a minute," the doorman said.

Deirdre was far too agitated to notice me. "If you don't get us our car in two minutes," she said, "it's your job. I can promise you that."

The doorman was an ancient man who looked as if he were going to either hit Deirdre or pass out from sheer humiliation. But, in the event, he did neither, because the Cadillac limousine suddenly appeared with Paul Belzberg's driver.

"Lucky for you," Deirdre said in a low hiss.

She got into the car and as she did, Paul Belzberg glanced up from his paper. He looked in our direction, either at me or Susan, maybe at both of us. He shrugged and turned his palms upward as if to say "What can a fella do?" Then he very distinctly winked at Susan and got into the limousine.

Once Susan and I were airborne on our way back to Washington, D.C., I ordered my usual Dewar's and waited for Susan to recover from the excitement. I had cadged first-class tickets out of the White House travel office, and we had the section almost all to ourselves. There are few high rollers in Washington, D.C.

"In college," I said to Susan, "Deirdre used to go out with one of my best friends. Guy named Larry. I think he's in the Marines now."

Susan didn't answer for a while. She looked out the window at the desert and drank a white vermouth.

"She's the granddaughter of Yitzhak Pincus," I said. "The investment banker. Her Dad is Melvin Needle, who's very tied in with the right kind of people, if you know what I mean. People in the linen supply business. Parking lot operators. Jewish funeral homes. Went on from there to be a very big investment banker in the picture business at a time when the white shoe firms wouldn't touch Hollywood because it was too Jewish."

"She looks like a smart cookie," Susan-Marie said without turning her face, but with a faint catch in her voice. "Very sure of herself."

"You bet," I said. "We used to say that when God was on vacation he put Deirdre permanently in charge. On the other six days she was only second in command. Once, when Larry said he was going to break up with her, she said he wasn't allowed to, and that was that. She said that if anyone was going to break up with anyone, she would do the breaking up. I swear to you, Larry went off to fight the Viet Cong rather than stay with her while she was in grad school."

Susan-Marie shook her head slowly and stared out the window at Utah.

"I used to sit next to her in economics," I said. "She was amazing. She once told Steve Saulnier, the teacher, right to his face, that economists had no idea of how the economy operated. 'You know who understands the economy?' she said. 'Not professors. Peddlers like my grandfather.' It was an incredible slap in the face for Saulnier, because the *Post* had just run a story about how Yitzhak Pincus made three million dollars that year, I

84

think it was 1965, and Saulnier, who had been chief economic adviser to Eisenhower, had made thirty-two thousand."

Susan-Marie turned around and looked at me defiantly. "Paul Belzberg makes great pictures," she said.

"I agree," I said, "although I think he's had some problems and he's a studio executive now."

"I know he is," Susan-Marie said. "And that Deirdre person helps him run Republic, and maybe she's good at it."

"Maybe she is," I said.

"There has to be some reason he's with her," Susan-Marie said. "These things don't just happen. Paul Belzberg must see something in her you didn't see."

"I was wrong," I said. "We didn't call her Madame deFarge. We used to call her the Dragon Lady in a Villager dress."

"I don't care," Susan-Marie said. "I know his last few pictures haven't made money, but what an eye that man has. Really. What a feeling for what it means to be an American."

"She was always very well organized," I said. "That must mean a lot in business."

"He's not in *business,*" Susan-Marie said. "He's an artist. He has unbelievable insight. Look at that scene in *Mother,* which didn't make a dime. The kids are all grown up and they're all trying to get the mother to sell her house so it can be knocked down for a freeway, and the mother tries every trick in the book to keep the house, to stay in it with her memories, and finally she realizes that she'd rather have the money than the house, exactly because the kids don't give a damn about the memories. They only want her to get the money so they won't have to support her. But you know, just from the look on Katharine Hepburn's face, that her insides have been crushed because her kids are so greedy."

"It was a fantastic scene," I said.

"Look at what he did in that final scene with the bulldozers coming up on the house, and she's telling a neighbor that it'll be just as good living in an apartment house, and you see her belongings and her photos all on the back of a rented trailer. It's an incredible, amazing scene," Susan-Marie said.

"What's the point?" I asked.

"The point is that I don't like you running down that woman he lives with because it sounds like we're making fun of him, and he's put some wonderful fantasies on the screen," Susan-Marie said. "He's the best of Hollywood."

I drove Susan-Marie home from Dulles Airport in my little blue Subaru. In the cold Washington night I could feel her heat coming through her gray cloth coat across the gearshift console and then into my life. My feelings about Susan-Marie were changing, as much as I wanted to fight them.

I dropped Susan-Marie off in front of her condominium on Forty-fourth Street near Battery-Kemble Park. She didn't invite me in, but then why should she have?

We went back to our pop culture-watching at the White House and I tried to keep my mind on artifacts of national happiness or dissatisfaction with perceived leadership strengths and weaknesses. But night after night I returned to my newly rented house on Thirty-fifth Place in Georgetown, fed Mary, my glorious Weimaraner, and then threw a stick for her in the darkness of Glover-Archbold Park. In front of the flickering Sony in my lonely bedroom, I could smell White Shoulders, see Susan's magnificently deep blue eyes, trace the delicate black eyebrows, hear her voice. I could also see her silhouette in her tailored clothes and imagine what she would feel like lying next to me. I imagined that it would feel as if I were going to live forever. I used to dream that Susan would press her face into my neck when we were finished and tell me that we would always be together, and then she would say something that would make me laugh and cry because it would explain everything that I had felt I had lost in my life. I never knew what her words would be, but they would explain what I missed, and they would float over me like the blanket my mother would cover me with when I was sick and had the chills, warming and soothing. Her words, whispered into my skin, would heal all the wounds of my young life.

7

TRIAL

■

One night in February, after a hard afternoon watching love scenes in rural Mississippi from *In the Heat of the Night*, I decided to make a stab at hearing those words.

As we rode down in a maple-paneled elevator toward the ground floor of the Executive Office Building, I complimented Susan on her observations about the underlying regard that Hollywood paid to the white redneck cracker, and then, as if it were an afterthought, I said, "How would you like to come over to my house and I'll get us a pizza and we can get totally into Rod Steiger movies?"

It was a lame opening, but Susan had no trouble figuring out what it meant. "Not tonight," she said in perfectly cheerful tones. "I have to go over some of my notes. I want to start thinking about an introduction to our report."

"We can do that together," I said.

"No," she said. "Not tonight. We can work on it together tomorrow morning."

"Susan," I said. "I didn't really mean we should just work tonight."

She stepped out of the elevator as it opened on the ground floor. "I know," she said. "When this is over, when everything's done, we'll get together in a different way. For now, let's just get this work done and make sure we're staying out of trouble."

"I don't want to stay out of trouble," I said.

"That's because you've never been in trouble," Susan-Marie said, and then she walked out into the night to her car.

I drove home, took the dog to the park, threw a stick for her, mused on how a dog could see to catch a stick in the dark, mused on how I could not see what was going on with Susan in broad fluorescent light, and then went back home to watch television.

At about ten I turned off "Starsky and Hutch" and began instead to empty the small straw wastebaskets throughout the house. Although it was an obsession with me to keep current about prime-time television, I hated to watch it by myself. When I took the wastebaskets out to the trash can, I saw to my shock that snow was falling hard. Already there was an inch of densely packed stuff on the ancient brick sidewalk in front of my house, giving that somber place an almost festive air.

In fact, I could hear young people laughing out on Thirty-fifth Place, yelling and screaming, falling heavily onto the pavement, whipping themselves up into a frenzy of snow hysteria. My dog began to bark with her own eagerness to be out in the snow, burying her long nose in the white stuff, running and sliding across the park nearby, catching new, large snowflakes in her mouth. All of this, combined with the crisp, businesslike rejection of my clumsy advances by Susan-Marie, made me urgently want company.

I put the dog into my pitiful Subaru and headed up

Wisconsin Avenue to a bar where I sometimes went on similar mental self-help missions. The Barkentine was just below Calvert Street in a small shopping center, next to a fish store and a laundry. It was a popular hangout for the people who lived in the déclassé north end of Georgetown. Nurses from Sibley Hospital, interns from Georgetown Hospital, single men and women who were not quite on the first rung of Washington success but still wore plaid pants in the summer and L. L. Bean corduroys in the winter drank Lowenbrau instead of Miller's at The Barkentine and told themselves that they would soon be legislative assistant to Proxmire or deputy assistant secretary to Shultz or would own not only a home in Wesley Heights but also a waterfront farm near Easton, Maryland.

I skidded along Wisconsin Avenue, then turned into the parking lot. I left Mary in the car with the engine running and the heater turned on. The Barkentine was packed with its usual clientele, some of whom were wearing madras trousers in the snowstorm. I ordered my Dewar's from a grinning Irish bartender, then turned to scan the room for a friendly face.

I did not find one. Instead, to my left, next to the pong game, Susan-Marie stood with her back to me. She looked wonderful, even from behind. Her legs were wrapped in tight light blue jeans. She wore a dark blue sweater. Her feet were lifted off the floor by backless high-heeled pumps. Her hair was curled and alive.

I started to walk over to Susan when I realized she was deep in affectionate conversation with a man of about thirty-five with a wide Georgetown University jaw, a cable-knit red sweater, wire-rimmed glasses, tan wide-wale corduroy trousers, and, God help me, Sperry Topsiders on his feet. I did not like him.

After a few sips of my Dewar's I decided to rescue Susan from this obvious mistake. Before I had even started my mission across the room, however, Susan set down her drink on a table, slipped her arm through Topsiders', and walked out of the bar with him, into the snow, carrying her coat in her other hand. In a trance, I watched them get into his elderly Saab and drive away.

If a man had come at me in the bar with a straight razor, I could not have been more upset, terrified, and bewildered.

I drove home with Mary and brooded through the night while the snow covered gray Washington with its light magic. At first I felt cheated and furious. Why had Susan turned me down, lied to me, broken my heart, to pick up a stranger in Topsiders at a bar? Affects do not lie, and Susan had clearly never seen that man before.

As the first distressing hints of pink came through the window, my feelings changed. Now I felt as if I were in a strange country. Obviously, Susan went for human comfort to bars, to take home strangers. That was not the Susan I knew, or had ever known. What if I were completely wrong about the kind of woman Susan was? More to the point, what if Susan-Marie were a far more desperate, unreachable type than I thought she was, and yet I still loved that stranger?

By the time I left for work my feelings about her were thoroughly mixed up into a lumpy, vile-tasting sauce of anger, betrayal, curiosity, and love. The human heart has its ways, however, and the simplest of those emotions—anger—was on top by the time I parked my car on the Ellipse.

Susan-Marie looked fresh and clean, in contradiction of my expectations. Somehow I had expected her to wear a mark, perhaps a scarlet letter, that told the world she had gone home from a bar with a man with wire-rimmed glasses and Topsiders. The more compassionate part of me expected her to wear some kind of mark of confusion about self, of despair, perhaps an audible mark, such as a deep sigh. But Susan wore nothing unusual and, in fact, looked exactly as she did every morning—attractive, businesslike, intelligent, and just alluring enough not to lower her status within the White House team.

I avoided talking to her throughout the morning, then went to lunch with my father at the White House mess. In the afternoon I walked over to the National Archives and examined a movie about the British Eighth Army in the Sahara, then came back to the EOB just as the secretaries were leaving.

I hoped and expected that Susan-Marie would have gone as well. Perhaps she needed to rest. Perhaps she needed to prepare for that night's adventure. But she was there, sitting in my office. She had turned on the incandescent lights with the Chinese ceramic bases and had even turned off the overhead fluorescent lamp to give the office an almost homey look of light and warmth on a cold, snowy evening.

Susan looked like a particularly intelligent, flashing, dark stewardess welcoming a passenger onto a night flight, and I greeted her in the most detached voice I could muster.

She stared at me, her eyes blazing with curiosity. "What's the matter?" she asked. "You look as if you'd just as soon kill me as look at me."

"Nothing," I said. "Nothing."

"No," she said. "Something's really wrong. What is it? What did I do wrong?"

"Nothing," I said. "I only thought I might have seen someone like you in a crummy place called The Barkentine last night, only that couldn't possibly have been you, because you were too busy to come over for a drink. And it couldn't possibly have been you because that girl was getting picked up by some guy with a complete phony Georgetown outfit and you were at home making notes for a report and couldn't even spend one minute for me."

Susan looked down at the floor, at our blue White House carpet, then looked up at me, and I swear her eyes were two shades darker, almost black, but with lights flashing out of them, like quartz halogen shining upon onyx. "That's none of your business," she said evenly. "I'm really surprised at you," she added.

"You're surprised at me?" I almost screamed. "I've been your friend for twelve years, and I just wanted to spend time with you and you go out and get picked up by a stranger, and you wonder about me? You're surprised at me? Are you crazy?" I took a breath for air and said, "After all I've been to you, after all I've done, after I had faith in you when no one did, when you were hiding at the phone company . . ."

Susan raised her voice and said, her eyes suddenly on fire with smoldering feeling, "You don't own me. I pull my weight here. You know I do damned well. You think because you gave me a job you own me?"

"Right," I said. "I don't own you and I guess I really don't know you, either, and to tell you the truth, I guess I made a mistake when I started this whole project." By then I was completely wound up into my own rage.

Now Susan-Marie looked at me with yet another kind of expression in her eyes, this time almost pleading, as if those blue irises were telling me I was doing something cruel to an innocent animal that deserved no harm.

"Look," she said, "it's a lot more complicated than you think. There's a lot about me you don't know. I *have* known you for a long time. That makes it harder. Can you believe that? Can you understand that the fact that I didn't know that guy was exactly why it happened?"

She got up from a yellow upholstered chair and gripped my desk. She looked at me and said through clenched teeth, "And I wouldn't care if he lived or died, and that's the whole thing, and that's what it's all about."

"I don't know," I said quietly. "I don't know. Maybe it would be better to just wind up this whole project and call it quits. That might be the way to resolve this whole matter. I just don't feel good about it anymore. I'll tell Haldeman we don't want to go any farther with it tomorrow morning."

I got up and looked out the window at the Ellipse, pink and white from the snow and the high-crime lights hitting the snow. Behind me I heard a long sigh, and then Susan-

Marie's footsteps going to the door. I heard the door close. But Susan-Marie was still in the room. I could hear her walking to the couch, then to a lamp. I could hear her switch off the lamp so that the office was now only lit by the pinkish light coming in the window.

When I wheeled around to Susan her face had changed expressions yet again. It was softer, younger, more resigned, like the face of a child. It was a more seductive face, the face of a courtesan. But her eyes were remote, almost unconscious even in that dim light.

She had removed the top of her suit and was on the last button of her silk blouse. She undid that button, then stood before me in her skirt and her bra. Her skin was white and alive in that office. Her breasts moved up and down inside her bra as she breathed almost like a sleepwalker.

She walked to where I stood and ran her hand behind my head, stroking my hair. She turned her face sideways and pressed it against my chest. Her skin was warmer than any other skin I had ever felt, and I remembered the night on the balcony next to the Star Jasmine. She ran her hand down the back of my shirt and started to pull out the tail from my trousers.

"You're right," she whispered to me. "I've been bad. I've been selfish. You were so good to me, and you needed me, and I was bad." Her voice was almost that of a child. "I'll make it up to you," she said. "I want to make you feel better."

"Stop it," I said. "I get it. You don't need to go any further."

"You've done so much for me," she said. "We should be really close. I've been bad not to see it."

She pressed her legs against me and started to wrap one leg around mine. She began to pull me toward the couch. "Come here," she said. "I want to hold you."

"Susan," I said, "stop it. You're making me feel terrible. I'm sorry. I acted like a fool and a bully and I'm sorry. Just forget it."

"No," she said. "Come here to me."

She stepped back from me, then unhooked her bra. She let it slide down her arms to the floor.

"This is right," she said. "This is right for both of us. I know it is."

She put her arms on my chest and I pushed them down. Then I bent over and handed her her brassiere.

"I'm sorry," I said. "I acted badly. I'm very, very sorry and I won't do it again. Go home, Susan, and we'll come back tomorrow and forget this ever happened, if you can forgive me."

Susan looked at me with eyes like those of a somnambulist coming awake. Her eyes came into focus as she put her clothes back on and I slumped at my desk.

When she was dressed she ran a hand through her hair and shook her head, as if shaking herself awake.

"That man at the bar wouldn't have stopped me," she said. "That's the difference. And now I guess I'll go home."

She walked out of my office. I could hear her going into her office, then hear the lights switch off, then hear her walking down the hall. After she got onto the elevator and I couldn't hear her any longer the office grew cold and oppressive and dark, so I put on my coat and went out into the snow.

8

PLANS

■

After the incident in my office Susan hit the ground running. She came to work the next morning looking only slightly tired, dressed as neatly as ever in a green wool suit that was clearly not expensive but was just as clearly made high fashion by the intelligent elegance of the wearer. She wore slightly more makeup than usual, but that didn't surprise me because I always thought that for women makeup was not only for attraction, but for armor.

(I recently became close friends with a woman who had to enter a hospital in Thousand Oaks for a complete hysterectomy. All of her anxieties about the operation boiled down to one outward wish: that she be allowed to wear full makeup into the operating room. The appeal went from the surgeon to the head of the hospital. When it was granted the patient entered the operating room with nearly total equanimity.)

Susan-Marie walked into my office and sat down on the same couch she had tried to pull me onto the night before. She gave it a meaningful look and smiled a co-conspirator's smile. "Now for something *really* interesting," she said, and we both laughed. She cleared her throat and said, "I assume you will agree that the way our report gets treated, that is, whether anybody pays attention to it at all, depends largely on whether the people at the White House take it seriously?"

"Absolutely," I said.

"And whether they take it seriously or not depends about ten percent on how good the report is and about ninety percent on whether the powers here like us and think we're good guys, right?" Susan asked.

I had to think about that for about five seconds. It was a sad conclusion, but nonetheless obvious. "All right," I said. "I agree with that one, too."

"So, we have to put out the best report we can," Susan-Marie said, absentmindedly patting the couch, "and we also have to make sure that the powers that be like us."

"I think I get it," I said with a smile.

"Well, here's how we can make some friends," Susan-Marie said. She then outlined to me a simple idea, which drew upon the basic fact of American life that everyone has two businesses—his own and show business. Susan would start telling the more important people at the White House which movies we would be screening and invite them to come along to offer their impressions. Not only that, she would offer to change the schedules for really important people like Haldeman or Ehrlichman or Garment. We would offer the battle-weary White House troopers another perk: the chance to get some respite from price control, Days of Rage, textile quotas, and budget deficits in a darkened room with Karen Black and Angie Dickinson and Joey Heatherton.

Within a very few weeks we had regular attendance by the White House illuminati at our small screenings. We not only regaled them with motion picture lore and our erudite impressions of how these films—and their box-office grosses—foretold the electoral future of the nation, but we gave them peace and quiet in the center of several thunderstorms.

Clarence Bakshian, the president's chief speechwriter, was a particular fan of the films we showed. He persuaded us to show him *Eye of the Condor, Fists In Pockets, Tell Them Willie Boy Is Here,* and *Gimme Shelter* twice each within the first six weeks of the project. Bakshian, a tall, gangly Armenian from Muttontown, Long Island, was close to everyone who counted at the White House, from R.N. down. I suppose his gratitude to us, and those good connections, were what led to a visit from him in early April 1972 while we were laughing at "All in the Family" on videotape.

"Benjy and Susan," he said, "this is your lucky day." It was our lucky day because Clarence had arranged for us to be invited to a luncheon the next week in the White House solarium, with Richard Nixon himself as host. "The idea is that we're going to impress this big wheel from Hollywood named Taft Schreiber and send him back there to impress other people."

"The Taft Schreiber from MCA?" Susan-Marie asked.

"Exactly," Bakshian said. "He's a loyal Republican out there among those Godless atheists in the picture business. He's given his twenty-five thousand. He says he can raise two million out there. For two million you get lunch with the president."

"Sounds fair to me," I said.

"I told Dwight Chapin that you two knew all there was to know about Hollywood. R.N. likes to have someone there to keep the conversation going, if you know what I mean," Bakshian said.

"I love it," I said.

"I can't believe it," Susan-Marie said. "I've seen pictures of the solarium, but I thought it was only for the family."

"Only for the family and people who raise two million

and their best friends," Bakshian said. "It's great. It's all furnished in white cotton and wicker. It's on the fourth floor, and it looks out over Virginia, and you're a heavy hitter if you go there."

"What can we do to thank you?" I asked.

"How about a screening of *The Honeymoon Killers?*" he asked.

"It's done," I said.

"Bone up on your movies," Bakshian said. "Taft's bringing a very high-powered artiste with him. A Jewish guy from Alabama. Young genius turned middle-aged. He made that fabulous picture *Estonia*. You ever see it?"

"Fifteen times," Susan-Marie said dryly.

"He's an amazing guy," Bakshian said, clearly warming to his subject. "The only Jew in Albion, which is probably worse than being the only Armenian in Muttontown. He leaves there to wait on tables when he gets out of the Army, and five years later he's this great killer in Hollywood, married to the former Miss Netherlands."

"Is he a big giver to CREEP?" Susan-Marie asked. "He doesn't seem like the type."

"Anyone can be a big giver to CREEP if he thinks America needs President Nixon for four more years. If he can study and learn just how this president has given direction to the American spirit, if he can hear the driving beat of an unashamed drummer, he can give with a full heart," Bakshian said.

"I get it," Susan-Marie said.

"Plus, his boss is coming," Bakshian said. "This guy Sid Bauman, who owns a big chunk of Republic. He's coming just to see the fabrics in the solarium."

Susan-Marie nodded her head slowly. "Talk about heavy hitters," she said.

"Not only owns a big chunk of Republic, not only chairman of the board, but also used to be married to Amanda Barton," Bakshian said.

"Anyone else?" I asked.

Bakshian shook his head, then suddenly changed his

mind. "Mind you," he said, "I won't be there. But I think that a woman named Deirdre Needle will. Very amazingly cagey little monkey. I met her at a conference in Santa Barbara. She made the Biltmore change the menu for the whole weekend because there wasn't enough fresh fruit on it. Thinks very highly of herself."

The morning of the luncheon Susan and I quizzed one another about our project. We made up twenty-second capsule answers to any possible questions, no matter how off the wall. We each also made mental summaries of answers to questions like "Why should Hollywood support Richard Nixon?" ("Because a strong, confident America is an America that loves movies and can afford to go to the movies." This was not a doctoral dissertation defense.) Frankly, I wondered if anyone at the lunch would need more than a few words about political trends being endorsed by the audience or not. But Susan had extremely detailed data about exactly how much different genres of picture cost on the average, how much they grossed, what pictures were financial exceptions to the rules, and what pictures might show that argosies of profit lay off in an as yet uncharted direction.

In my innocence I thought this showed Susan's extreme devotion to showing that we were earning our keep at the EOB. In fact, of course, her facts and figures were meant to get her out and not to keep her in. Yet on the morning of the luncheon I marveled at what an ally I had in Susan-Marie. There she sat in my office, a *Vogue* magazine cover girl of intelligence and preparation, with the eagerness to please of a 1959 applicant to Wellesley College. She wore a tailored suit made of green silk, black-and-blue Rayne shoes, and flashing red lipstick like the television anchor-women were wearing that year. Most amazing of all to me, her loyal colleague, Susan-Marie's nails were painted for the first time I could remember, a vivid dazzling Cadillac red.

9

PLAYERS I

■

As we walked across West Executive Avenue to the residence in unnaturally warm April sunshine, Susan took my arm and held it with her right hand. Again, I could feel that peculiar heat through my jacket sleeve.

"I can't imagine why Paul Belzberg is bothering to come here," she said. "What does he have to do with any of this Washington stuff?"

"You mean you can't imagine why he would want to have lunch with the president of the United States?" I asked.

"That's right," Susan-Marie said firmly. "He's an artist. He's not a cookie-pusher."

"You don't think R.N. is a piece of art?" I asked.

"You have a point," Susan-Marie said. We walked into the bright spring Washington sunshine and I saw the Executive Protective Service guards staring at Susan. There

101

were a number of beautiful women at the White House, particularly Shelley Buchanan. But Susan-Marie was not just elegant that day. She was resplendent. Maybe, I thought, she will be so carried away with how great this lunch is that she will decide she loves me with eyes open, not in any kind of trance. After all, I had done a lot for her, and she might find me worthy of her love. I would magnanimously forget the incident at The Barkentine and we would make our lives together as the perfect Washington couple.

On a fatefully different track, Susan-Marie said, "I don't meet many people from Hollywood. I don't think I've ever met any before."

"We never meet any artists of any kind," I said.

"We will today," she said. We stepped off the elevators onto the third floor of the residence and walked past two Secret Service men whose jackets bulged.

We walked across the hall and up a half flight of carpeted stairs into the solarium. Mr. Nixon's guests were already there. Leonard Clothier, the president's counsel, a short, gray-haired, gray-eyed man without a smile, greeted us tonelessly at the door. He then introduced us to Sid Bauman, a man of medium height with a bald spot and graying hair combed carelessly across it, wearing the best-tailored suit I had ever seen—a suit that practically screamed "handmade"—carrying a short glass of Scotch in particularly delicate fingers, looking jauntily around the room as if he were overjoyed to be there, and equally determined to be the most relaxed and suave man in the room. Something about his blue eyes made me suspect that this man, the son of a handbag designer in Brooklyn, was saying "Tennis, anyone?" to himself over and over again in the solarium.

"How are you, doctor?" he asked me. He was the kind of man who habitually called everyone "doctor," perhaps as a way of saying that he didn't really give a goddamn about titles. He would simply award the most prestigious one his mother had told him to everyone and be done with it and see how much you left on the table.

Next to Sid Bauman stood a shorter, plumper man with jowly cheeks, a mottled red complexion, and an irritated air about him. He was Taft Schreiber, a high muckety-muck at Universal. Apparently, he had been arguing about something with Sid Bauman, who was not simply a high muckety-muck at Republic, but personally owned more than twenty percent, making him effectively The Owner. Taft Schreiber seemed to be too aggravated by whatever he and Bauman had been arguing about to give Susan and me more than a cursory nod. Then he and Bauman returned to their argument, which carefully avoided any raising of voices or mentioning of clues as to what the subject in dispute might have been.

Clothier then walked us across the small room to where a surprisingly tall man stood holding the elbow of a shockingly thin woman. The man turned at the mention of his name. He wore a simple blue pin-striped suit, which looked definitely off the rack. He also wore a look of cheerful, rather boyish enthusiasm, which ran from his brown eyes down his long, Lincolnesque face to his fingertips, which shook my hand as if he had not seen me for fifteen years, but, boy, had we been pals before. It was hard to dislike Paul Belzberg.

"How are you, Ben?" he asked, in that marvelous way that some truly effective people have of seeming to really mean it. His greeting to me was the greeting of a man who knows communication.

But his greeting to Susan-Marie was like the application of a finger to a high-tension wire. Paul Belzberg looked at Susan-Marie as if time had just started, as if the world had just begun at that moment. There was a palpable static in the air when he took her hand, not shook it, but *took* it as if he were going to do something unique and unheard of with it. There was a dancing lightness in his eyes and a timbre of vivacity in his voice about double what he had employed when he met me. He bore no resemblance to the

103

beaten baccarat player Susan and I had seen months before at the Tropicana.

Susan's response was at least as intense. Her eyes shone and I could feel her elevated temperature even standing two feet away.

Susan said, "I've always been an admirer of your work. *Estonia* is the best movie there has ever been."

Belzberg reeled backward and pretended to be dodging a blow. "Don't talk that way. It makes me crazy. That was more than fifteen years ago. It makes me feel old. What have I done lately that you liked?" Then he laughed to show that it was all in good movie mogul's fun. "Thank you very much," he said. "What kind of work do you do?"

"Before I tell you," Susan-Marie said, "I'll tell you what I liked lately. I liked the way you showed in one scene how money scrapes away the glue that's supposed to hold families together."

"The scene with the bulldozers in *Mother?*" Paul Belzberg asked.

"Exactly," Susan-Marie said.

"You see, Deirdre," Paul Belzberg said to Deirdre Needle, the thin woman standing next to him. "There are people who appreciate that movie."

"I'm glad to hear it," Deirdre Needle said. "It didn't make two bucks. It didn't make enough to buy a lamp shade."

"The picture business is not the jukebox business," Belzberg said. "Sometimes things are beautiful but don't make any money."

"You ought to know," Deirdre said, and then she turned to me. "Ben and I were in college together at Columbia," she said pointedly to the man who had not finished high school, Paul Belzberg.

"Susan and I love movies together," Paul Belzberg said, then he took one look at me and winked.

Deirdre grasped me by the elbow and said, as predictably as if she were a clockwork personality, "How is Larry? Do you ever hear from him?"

"Last I heard, he was in a mental hospital in Tupelo," I said. By then Deirdre had walked us into another corner of the room, where she pumped me for every detail of Larry's life.

From a distance of about fifteen feet I could see that our leave-taking was the only thing necessary to put an almost tangible curtain up around Susan-Marie and Paul Belzberg. The Leonard Clothier–Sid Bauman–Taft Schreiber axis rotated around them, but they were off in a world of their own talking about movies.

From the looks, the postures, the smiles, the laughter, the microscopic pauses and starts, the aura of separateness that Paul Belzberg and Susan-Marie gave off, it was clear that a connection had been made at a deep level. When Paul touched Susan's elbow she winced with pleasure. When she leaned forward to compliment him he quivered with joy. This was not a conversation between a Hollywood executive and a White House staffer. This was Romeo and Juliet in the White House solarium.

Susan gave him a smile wider, more radiant, than any smile I had ever seen. Belzberg gave her a low, confidential tone that was meant to include her in his feelings—and no one else.

I have enormous difficulty understanding my own feelings about anyone else. But I can read the feelings of others with precision, and I could tell that Susan-Marie and Paul Belzberg were off in a world of their own that had nothing to do with raising funds for the Committee to Re-Elect the President.

Above Deirdre's questions, I could hear an occasional snippet of their conversation. ". . . Amazing . . . an intellectual type like you at this White House . . . with all the things you have to think about . . . you remember that? . . . it's all two things . . . all of making a picture, just two things . . . seeing the picture in your mind and then getting a whole big bureaucracy to at least see little pieces of that same vision . . ." Then, from Susan, ". . . But your thoughts get to be everybody's thoughts

. . . that's power . . . inside people's heads . . . no elections, just ideas . . . my idea of heaven is to be where you can put your own ideas up there . . . share your dreams with the nation . . ."

After about ten minutes even Deirdre was catching on. The sense of mutuality between two strangers was a blowtorch of human feeling in that cool, white White House solarium of self-promotion. "My work at the studio isn't that exciting," Deirdre said, as if she could pull the focus of the entire room to her by talking to me. "I mainly help Paul with what he's doing. He's a hell of an artist, but he doesn't have much idea how to administer a big operation like Republic. I do all the little jobs, like deciding who gets to go on vacation and deciding who gets what office. I go through the deal memos with the people from legal and business affairs. I just generally clean up a lot of the garbage that's involved with running a studio," she said with a self-sacrificing sigh. "My dad wonders why I didn't stay in New York, working with autistic children like my cousin, and like your cousin, who used to go to Chapin with me."

"I've been wondering about that too," I said.

"Ben," she said, "everyone in Hollywood wants the glamour jobs. Writing. Directing. Acting. Producing. That's *kinderspiel*. Those people need someone to clean up after them, to take charge of them, to make sure that everything's neat and orderly. A studio can't be run like a playground. It's a business. Someone has got to make sure that it runs and makes money.

"When I started out at Republic I told Dad that it would be easy for me to try acting or directing, but it would be wrong. No, what I needed to do was stay out of the limelight myself and just make sure the studio ran efficiently for the people who need to be in the spotlight. The guys who need to have the applause have one foot in the grave anyway. That's not for me."

Then, seamlessly, she said, "Who's Miss Georgetowner over there with Paul?"

"She's my dear friend," I said. "She's the smartest woman I've ever met. I've known her since high school."

"Smart doesn't mean a goddamned thing in Hollywood," Deirdre said grimly. "Out there, it's balls and connections. The smart ones are waiting tables in Santa Monica."

But Deirdre was talking to herself. In her affect of jerky head movements, her constant running of her hand though her hair, her repetitive, meaningless questions about long-gone classmates was a symphony of crisis. Her man was fifteen feet away talking to a young, beautiful woman with black hair and a perfectly relaxed, confident posture. Her relaxed, eager self contrasted with Deirdre's frantic, angry self, and proclaimed volumes about what was to come.

I dimly heard the prophecy, and it started a slow, soft rustle of music inside me. Obviously, this moment with Paul Belzberg was what Susan had been waiting for. Whatever she had been doing with me at the White House was no more than the dress rehearsal for meeting Paul Belzberg. The music inside me was a concerto of impending loss.

These thoughts, and this soft, murmuring concerto, were interrupted by the entrance into the room of President Richard M. Nixon. As he always did, he came in wearing a Nixon mask. (There is more to this remark than there seems to be. If I am right about Nixon, he was *always* wearing his Nixon mask, the mask that was meant to tell the schoolyard bullies that he was not afraid of them. "The hotter it gets, the cooler I get. . . ." The mask never fooled his enemies, only his friends.)

The president greeted us with his resonant Irish voice, then moved from guest to guest, shaking hands. When he got to Susan he said to Bob Haldeman, who was at his side, in a stage whisper, "How long have we had anyone this beautiful working at the White House?"

Susan blushed and said, "I'll bet you say that to all the girls."

"Only to the beautiful ones."

When he got to Deirdre he said, "How is Melvin? I haven't seen him since I worked at Mudge Rose."

The difference in what the president said was not lost on Deirdre, nor on Susan-Marie. Their eyes met, deep blue against flint, and, like fighters at a weigh-in, they acted calm, while desperately seeking to size up each other's strengths and weaknesses.

The rest of the lunch was a blur of conversation played out above that sad, ineluctable concerto of adieu, almost as intrusive as audience-talking during a performance. There was a miserably homeopathic chicken broth, a salmon mold of some kind, and one memorable piece of conversation. In the Nixon White House, against all of that tragedy and betrayal, even the saddest moments were accompanied by a sliver of the absurd, and this sad day for me was no exception.

When I had taken two bites of my salmon the president said to me, "Ben, do you know that I would cheerfully switch places with you at any time?"

"No," I said. "I didn't know that."

"Would you like to know why?" he asked, looking at me as if he might stick me with a hat pin.

"I certainly would," I said.

"Because I have always wanted to be a sportswriter," he said. "I was never good enough to be a professional player. But I could be a writer and I think the writers have the best part of the deal, anyway."

I started to speak, but Haldeman shot me a glance that would have melted granite.

"There are a lot of times right now," the president said, "when I pick up your paper, the *Star*—we don't get the *Post,* although I understand they use it in the kitchen for wrapping fish—and I read the stuff you boys write, and I wish I could just take off in the middle of the night and go write about the baseball games every day."

"That's really a surprise, Mr. President," I said. "I would have thought you were perfect for this job."

Again, Haldeman shot me a warning look.

"Oh, this is a good job," he said, "and somebody's got to do it," he added with his patented look of modesty, arms outstretched but crooked at the elbow, palms facing upward, as if trying to see if it were raining, head and neck in a protective, ducking gesture, as if he might suddenly find himself the victim of tomatoes thrown at the stage by irate burlesque theatergoers. "It's just, it's just, well, I don't like to complain, because that isn't in my nature. I take them the way they come. But I imagine you out there covering the ball games, not even the big ones, the ones that decide the pennant, and I think of you in Wrigley Field or Three Rivers stadium, and you really don't have a care in the world."

"That's not quite true, Mr. President," I said. This time Haldeman quite audibly brought his fork handle down against the table and looked at me, shaking his head slightly in further warning to keep quiet.

"Oh, I don't mind the work I have to do here. It's a great job. But the twenty-hour days, the endless crises, the bickering over who gets this and who gets that, the empire building, the political infighting, it wears me down so I can't spend as much time as I'd like thinking about the big picture, about peace and diplomacy and arms control.

"I'm not complaining," he said. "That's not the way I am. It's just that I have to do everything myself. It's almost as if I had to look at every little detail all by myself. I don't mind, because someone's got to do it, but I just have to tell you that I don't always have *time*. I might want to do it all myself but I just can't. There's too much. That's when I wish I were a sports columnist like you."

"It is a fine life," I said, and then an aide came in with a note for Mr. Nixon. "This is just what I was talking about," he said with mock desperation as he stood up. "Word from the talks in Paris. Just go on eating as if I was still here, and come see me in the Oval Office on the way out." That clearly did not include White House staffers, and I knew that Haldeman knew who I really was even if the president did not. (Of course, it turned out that the president knew. His was an extended joke, although only he and I got it. He had a unique sense of humor.)

So I sat and made small talk with Deirdre, who was seated next to me, until she came to the real question she had wanted to ask since I walked into the room. Gesturing in a tiny way with her chin, she pointed toward Susan and Belzberg at the other end of the table. In barely more than a whisper, she asked, "What's her story?"

That is a hell of a question, I thought. I was tempted to answer, "She is a Woman. Look out." But instead, I said, "I already told you, Dee. She's a very smart woman I went to high school with who works with me now at the White House."

"But I mean, what's she interested in? What does she want out of life? Politics? Academics? Is she from a big Republican family?"

"You know," I said to Deirdre, "she never talks about her family. Obviously, there's something there, or else why would she be at the White House?"

"Obviously," Deirdre said, rising to the bait.

"I don't know how interested she is in politics," I said. "I suppose she'll stay until after the 1972 elections and then she'll go on."

"Where?" Deirdre asked.

"I think she's interested in pictures," I said. "Holly-wood would be my guess."

Deirdre let out a low chuckle. "Good luck," she said contemptuously. "Hollywood's a small town. It's tough on strangers."

I gestured deftly toward Susan-Marie and Paul Belz-berg and said, "I'm not sure she's a stranger."

Deirdre said, "Oh, that's nothing. Paul is very gregarious. He's terribly overworked. I have to stay until ten every night helping him get everything straightened out. He's an artist, sort of, but he's a sloppy administrator."

"Why do they have him doing it if he's not a good administrator?"

"Sid Bauman brought him in because he thought Paul's connections with the major people would be helpful. The Zanucks, the Friedkins, the Schaffners, the Huycks, those kind of people. They respect Paul. They would be more likely to see Republic as a possible home if they saw a fellow auteur at the helm. It's worked pretty well. We got Schaffner's latest, *Ice Maiden,* and it got ten million in rentals in eight weeks," Deirdre said. "I think we've got a good shot at the next Clint Eastwood, and it may be from a script by Jay Allen, so I'd say it's working out very, very well. The only problem is that he can't keep track of everything that comes across his desk, and he isn't even interested in most of the different deals that need his attention. He won't even meet the people from business affairs or legal. I have to do all that."

"But you're not complaining, are you?" I asked.

"Not at all," Deirdre said quite unself-consciously. "Someone has to do it."

I had never liked Deirdre, so I said, "I think that's the kind of work that Susan-Marie could do really well."

Just as I could feel the heat coming off Susan-Marie, I could feel a chill distinctly peeling from Deirdre. "If she thinks she can do it in Hollywood, she's got her work cut out for her. It's hard to pull people together. When I started working for Paul he had just made four pictures in a row that didn't make money, including *American Traveler,* which was an incredible stiff. He was spending his time in Vegas, gambling, letting himself run down, brooding all the time about what it was like when he was a kid in Alabama and he was the only Jew in the county. I pulled him back together. Got him into shape so that he'd start going to the office like a normal *mensch* instead of feeling sorry for himself all day. In Hollywood we don't need people who feel sorry for themselves. I made Paul look like a winner again."

"But he hardly has any time to make his movies anymore. *Mother* was his first in a few years."

"Benjy," Deirdre said, "he's making a lot of money for

Republic, and some of that money sticks to his ribs. He's doing great, and he doesn't need any help from your pal. Maybe she could come out and go on the Universal tour and then she could get it out of her system."

"Maybe," I said. "I wouldn't bet on it."

After the lunch Deirdre and Sid Bauman were taken by Dwight Chapin on a tour of the East Wing and the White House Garden. Paul Belzberg walked back to the EOB with Susan and me.

He kept up a steady patter about how hard it is to judge the public's mood, about how every gamble costs five million dollars, about how it's all like playing roulette, only with a blindfold on. "Nevertheless," he said cheerfully, "we keep shoveling money onto the table."

"Yes," Susan-Marie said, "but you can't win if you're not at the table."

Paul Belzberg paid her the respect of looking at her quite levelly and saying, "You can't win if you're not at the table and you can't lose if you're not at the table."

"You've already lost if you're not at the table," Susan-Marie said.

Susan, Paul, and I talked for another half hour about art and money. ("They used to say there was no art without money. Now I think maybe there's no art with money," Belzberg said.) We talked about how to get things done. ("Benjy and I have a rule. If you want to get something done, you do it yourself, preferably without telling anyone about it. If you don't want it done, ask someone else to do it," Susan-Marie said.) We talked about how rare smart people are. ("If Susan were to leave, I think I'd just pack my bags and live in the desert," I said.)

While we talked, I marveled at Susan's not having said ten words to the president of the United States, and having mesmerized the head of motion pictures at Republic. But then, to be fair, what could the president have done for her? Was he going to put her in a position where she could put her own fables and fantasies up on a sixty-foot screen?

Was he going to allow her to alter the world so that it could share in her imagination? No, even then it was clear that Susan had made the sensible conquest.

With the passage of time, I have come to realize two more truths about that afternoon at the White House solarium. First, Richard Nixon was pulling my leg. The rigmarole about my being a sportswriter was a gentle form of teasing. God knows, he was entitled to give some of it back.

Second, and closer to the bone, Susan was not paying attention to Paul solely out of calculation. I often mistakenly thought of Susan-Marie too much as a calculator and too little as a woman. The fact of the matter was that Susan-Marie had just met a man who had been her idol at a time when she was lonely and desperate. In a setting of almost tangible achievement, she had met the man who held out light and hope in a dark, forlorn time. She had met a Great Man, to put it briefly, and that great man had been far more than polite. The Great Man had lit up with joy at her face and her words. He had drawn a circle and included only Susan-Marie within it. Everyone else was outside, including the woman he lived with, the owner of the studio, and the president of the United States.

If Susan-Marie were overwhelmed—and she was—it was not by calculation, but by the real weight of amazement and gratitude that the Great Man saw her as great as well.

But at the time, I saw only effects and not causes. So I watched while Paul Belzberg lit Susan-Marie's Viceroy—one of her rare cigarettes—and then heard him say, "Ben, you and Susan-Marie are doing some very important work here. It's the kind of work we need at Republic to get us back in touch with our audiences, to see what they think about the directions we're taking before we go broke taking chances."

"That's kind of you," I said. "Who knows if we're on to anything at all?"

"I can tell you are," he said. "And I can tell that I'd be

113

able to make a place for you two in our studio. I know that Sid Bauman would go for it in a big way."

As if on cue, Sid Bauman himself bounced into view. He looked slightly ill at ease without a drink in his hand, but I could still see him trading his Meledandri tie for an ascot, changing into white flannel, saying, "Tennis, anyone?" and then laughing at himself and everyone else. "Did I hear my name?" he asked in real life. "What've I done wrong?"

"Sid," Belzberg said, as if he were Edison struggling to tell his railroad employer about the invention of electricity, "Sid, I think we could use these two at Republic."

For the first time I could see that Sid Bauman also had an unusually acute look directed at Susan-Marie. He tried to look as if he were making a joke, but he did not fool me. "I know we could use the girl," he said, "but what would we do with Ben?"

"Oh, you'd find something," Paul said, jumping in the merrymaking. Then, sober and serious again, "Really, Sid. I think we have a shot at making some real connections between what audiences want and what we make."

"Artists make what they want to make," Sid Bauman said nonchalantly, and then he added, "You know that better than anyone. But you're head of production, Paul. You do what you want to do."

"How about it?" Belzberg said. He acted as if he were talking to me. "Could we lure you out to Los Angeles?"

"Not me," I said. "I love working at the White House. But maybe Susan would like to think about it."

In a voice of absolutely perfect composure, Susan-Marie said, "I'll think about it."

■　　■　　■　　■

Susan-Marie stayed another two weeks. She told me she was going the day after Paul Belzberg made the offer.

"You know it's what I wanted," she said. "I'm not just a movie fan. I don't just want to watch them. I want to be part of it. Part of the fantasy."

"I'm not sure Hollywood has much to do with fantasy," I said. "It's a business. Businesses are very different from poems."

"It's the fantasy business," she said. "That makes it all worthwhile. Different kinds of people. There are very different kinds of people involved in making movies compared with people making plumbing supplies or mining coal."

"I'm not sure," I said. "I had a great-uncle who was a vice-president of Columbia. He died in a mental hospital in Agoura, somewhere outside Los Angeles."

"That was a long time ago. Anyway, I want to go. In a way, it's your fault for putting me where I'd meet people who could take me out there."

I was too sad to say anything at that moment.

"This town means very bad memories for me," she said. "It's not just the Capitol and the Pan-American Union. Some terrible things happened here. I want to try a new place."

"I understand," I said in a monotone. Even though Susan was leaving on a hot day in June, the offices already seemed cold, clammy, and lifeless without her. The suite that had looked so elegant now had a good thick coating of dust on the cornices. The doors were splintered. The satin drapes were faded.

But there was nothing for it. The Susan who was still there with her bags packed was only a cardboard cutout of Susan. The real Susan was long gone, flown west out of her caterpillar past, spreading her yellow-and-black butterfly wings over California in her mind.

One morning at the end of June I picked up Susan in my Subaru. I packed her bags in the trunk and drove her out that long, mournful road to Dulles Airport. The usually green, rolling Virginia hills were ugly and mocking, and the blue sky promised to turn to rain as soon as I dropped her off.

"Hollywood is so far away," I said, "and so dangerous. Please, please come back if it's bad."

"I will," she said. She sounded confident, but her hands were trembling visibly.

When she stood at the gate, she kissed me on the cheek. Then she hugged me, looked at me carefully as if she were trying to memorize my face, and said, "You've been a lot to me. I never forget. You were my only friend."

"Now you have new friends," I said.

Susan thought about that and then she kissed me on the lips, for the first time since our high-school Senior Prom. Again, I felt the warmth of Susan through her white silk suit, the extraordinary warmth of a woman with a mission.

The announcer called the final-departure summons for Susan's flight. She hugged me again and said, "Do you have my address? Do you know where to reach me?"

"Yes," I said. "I know where to reach you," although by then I was fighting back tears and couldn't see Susan well.

"Where?" Susan asked carefully. "Where will you reach me? Where will you know how to get in touch with me?"

"In my dreams," I said. Then she was gone.

10

EYESIGHT

■

Exactly one month after Susan-Marie left Washington I received a postcard from her addressed to me as "The Honorable" and sent to the White House. The postcard showed four scenes of Los Angeles life, all surrounding a small circle of the way Los Angeles must have looked in 1930, before smog. The city was small, sparkling clean, and in the distance there were snow-covered mountains, as microscopically visible as if they had been on Wilshire Boulevard. One of the small squares showed a Rolls-Royce on Rodeo Drive. Another showed the entrance to Paramount Pictures, that familiar inverted U-shaped gate with its wrought-iron tracery and "Paramount Pictures Corporation" spelled out in grammar-school perfect script. The third picture showed a wave crashing off Malibu. The fourth picture showed Barbra Streisand on a sound stage for *Hello, Dolly* over at the old Fox lot.

On the other side, Susan had written: *Flash, Cash, and Trash. This place is unbelievable. I don't understand how anyone can live anywhere else. It's like a giant insane asylum where no one has the key any longer so no one can be put back inside. I love it. Letter to follow. Best, Susan.*

One week after I received Susan's card, Cheryl, my blond secretary who was clearly glad that Susan was gone, buzzed my office with that famous White House Communications Agency buzz that sounded like a discreet footman at the Reform Club in Pall Mall announcing a visiting bishop. It was Susan, calling from Los Angeles.

"Listen," she said. "I miss you. I miss you a lot. All anybody wants to talk about here is money."

"Well," I said, "I guess you can adjust."

"I guess I can," she said, but she wouldn't be put off by my tone of voice. "How are you? How the hell are you?"

"I miss you," I said. "Everybody in town has gone off to fucking Northeast Harbor, Maine, wherever that is. It's lonely here. We're supposed to get the report back from the White House printers next week."

"So I hear," Susan said. I didn't press her about how she had heard. Obviously, she had friends in high places. "Can I get about a hundred copies? On that real thick White House stationery?"

"Of course," I said. "Where shall I send them?"

"Oh," she said, "just send them to me at Republic Studios." Then, to show she was the same old Susan, she actually giggled. I laughed, too, and then Susan added a realistic note. "Is my name still on the cover?" she asked. "I wouldn't blame you if you took it off."

"Yes," I said. "You pulled your weight. I wouldn't have thought of taking it off."

Susan sighed with relief. "That means a lot to me," she said. "There are a lot of people out here who pretend to be things they aren't. A lot of people who really believe the lies they made up about themselves. This report sort of helps to locate me for people out here."

"I understand," I said. I was answering shortly to keep

the conversation from lapsing into the personal, which would have meant an inevitable deposit of loss at my end when the conversation ended, as all personal telephone conversations do. For at least a few minutes on the phone I could pretend that Susan was a former colleague, not a woman whose office I had kept sealed since she left. I swear to you that I could still smell White Shoulders on the couch where she used to take her afternoon rests, reading statistics while lying on White House satin.

"I hope you're coming to see me soon," she said.

"I will," I said. "And I'll send you the reports. And Susan, the president's been asking about you."

"I'll call him." Susan-Marie laughed. "From now on, tell him he's welcome in Hollywood any time. A guaranteed three-pic pact."

Susan had to go into a meeting so we said good-bye.

The next week I got ten huge cartons of the report, *The View From The Writers' Guild—How Hollywood Sees America and Vice-Versa.*

I read it and liked it, if I may say so. I had to agree again that Susan-Marie had at the very least pulled her own weight. Every analysis bore the stamp of her imagination and care, and I surely could not have had what I had without her—a report with my name as co-author that was already being discussed on the editorial page of *The Washington Post,* and which would serve as a focus for discussion for many years to come. (I never made a dime from it, but Susan made enough for two, or two thousand, but, again, I am getting ahead of the story.)

I sent Susan one hundred by REA-Air, and I enclosed a letter. *What I want to know, in exchange for all this freight, is just how and when did the little person who told me to "stay down and keep out of trouble" turn effortlessly into a completely self-assured blockade runner, a privateer of ambition and easy determination? I think about this— and you—night and day.*

I received Susan-Marie's response almost immediately. It came on heavy vellum stationery with the familiar Republic logo of a globe with a megaphone and a strip of film in front of it. The note was typed, letter perfect, a sign that Susan-Marie had typed it herself. In the upper right-hand corner was a note saying DIRECTOR OF RESEARCH—MOTION PICTURES.

After a preliminary thanks for the reports, Susan-Marie wrote: *When I got your letter I thought maybe it had been misdirected to me. "A privateer of ambition and easy determination"? Are you kidding? I am just the same as everyone else: a lot of parts of a human being that don't really fit together, a sum total of a human being who feels as if she will never belong anywhere. The only two differences are that I had a friend who got me a job in the White House, so that I saw that anyone can do anything, and that I love movies as much as I love life.*

Please come out here as soon as you can. I have a wonderful red Mercedes convertible. Let me take you for a ride along the beach at sunset and show you what it's like to wrap all of Los Angeles around your shoulders.

P·A·R·T

III

11

FREEWAY

Susan-Marie was met at the airport the first day in Hollywood by a studio limousine. The driver was very sorry, but Mr. Belzberg, who had wanted to meet her himself, was in Zihuatenejo on location, watching some shots from Republic's latest, *Sleepwalk*. But Miss Needle had laid on the car, and she had arranged for offices at Republic that she hoped Susan-Marie would find adequate.

The driver was apparently an out-of-work actor, a USC dropout with an authentic bushy-bushy bon hairdo, just as if he had stopped waxing his board long enough to drive the Caddie to LAX to pick up Susan-Marie. He talked continuously as the car threaded its way through town to the Republic Studios in Burbank.

"It's been hot here. Ninety-five some days. You wouldn't know about that, coming from Washington, I guess. I hear it rains there every day. Not here, I can tell you," he said.

"I'm from Washington, D.C.," Susan said. "Not Washington State. It's an entirely different climate."

In a good-natured way, the driver asked, "What's the difference?"

"One is a large state in the northwest, and one is a small city in the mid-Atlantic area and it's the capital of the United States."

"You're kidding," the driver said with perfect sincerity. "That's why I like this job. Because I learn so much. Which is which?"

Susan watched the cityscape slide by. It was far lower, far flatter, far more on a human scale than she had realized. This awareness thrilled her. She related the size of the buildings to her own size everywhere she went. For that reason she had always felt helpless and overwhelmed in New York City. The buildings were huge and endless, and she was a flea by comparison. In a city like New York, she could get no purchase, no vantage point from which she was not small. But in Washington there was more of a human scale. And in L.A. the scale was perfect. Few of the buildings were more than two stories tall. What buildings were more than bungalow size were bunched together, as if they were seeking refuge from the more normal scale of things. Susan passed by Century City, saw its tall buildings, skirted downtown Los Angeles, saw the ARCO Towers and the Bonaventure Hotel, but also saw that they were rarities.

In this city, even from a slight rise on the Santa Monica Freeway, Susan could oversee everything. Her vision was not met with concrete, blocking out the sky. Instead, she saw bodegas and car washes and appliance stores and burger stands and donut shops and film laboratories and even hospitals, rarely more than two stories. Next to these easily manageable structures were empty sidewalks. This was a welcome sight as well. The absent pressure of strangers allowed her to feel as if she could think long thoughts.

"I guess you're not used to having so many cars on the streets," the driver said. "Out where you come from, I guess it's mainly evergreen forests and stuff."

"Exactly right," Susan-Marie said.

Presently, the car drove through the Cahuenga Pass on the Hollywood Freeway. Susan was astonished at the amount of traffic. Twelve lanes, all fully packed at two in the afternoon, all moving at seventy, with the relentlessness of machine-gun fire. What if a car should become disabled on the freeway. Where would its driver go?

Susan asked the driver. He just shook his head and laughed. "Man, this whole city's a freeway," he said. "If your car breaks down, you're in big, big trouble anywhere in L.A."

For a few minutes, while the limousine turned off the freeway onto Barham and then down onto Pass Avenue, Susan reflected upon the possibility of her own personal vehicle breaking down on the freeway. For those few minutes she felt chills and wondered what the hell she was doing so far away from home, or, since she never really felt the notion of "home," what she was doing so far away from places that were familiar to her. In Washington there were no freeways. If your car broke down, you pulled off to the side of a leafy street, walked down to an embassy or a drug store and then waited calmly for help from the Auto Club to arrive, perhaps reading a book while you listened to WGMS.

But here, on this freeway, if your car stopped in lane three, you would simply die as other cars crashed into yours. At that speed, who could possibly stop? Not only that, but if you were crazed enough to try to walk across the six lanes on either side of the freeway, they wouldn't even find enough of you to bury.

Stop it, Susan said to herself. The driver was wrong. The whole city was not a freeway. She had just seen parts of it that were perfectly small and peaceful. Not only that, but she was going to have a vehicle that never broke. The vehicle she brought out with her, the vehicle of nerve and imagination and flexibility and hard work and the knack of making friends; that vehicle wouldn't break down on the freeway or anywhere else.

Besides, she would see to it, as soon as she could, that she was never riding in that vehicle alone—at least not on any particularly hazardous part of the freeway.

The driver pulled the limousine off Pass Avenue onto the single-lane Warner Boulevard entrance to the Burbank Studios and suddenly the freeway seemed far behind. Even though the entrance was across from a Taco Bell and a gas station, it marked the beginning of an entirely new and different world. To the right was a Spanish-style two-story building, as harmless and cheerful-looking as a chipmunk. Across the entryway was a large, perfectly manicured Kentucky bluegrass lawn with several perfectly trimmed oak trees standing in it at attractively spaced intervals. In front of the building, off the entryway, ran a semicircular driveway. Every car parked in the drive had a whimsical, cheerful look about it—Volkswagen convertibles, Mercedes coupes, three Porsches, a BMW. The kinds of cars bureaucrats would kill for. But here they were fripperie, just tokens for happy, grown-up children who were astride the mechanism of mass culture. They were exactly what Susan had in mind for herself—just so long as they would not break down on the freeway.

The building at the top of the semicircle was simply the most beautiful private structure Susan-Marie had ever seen. It was a long, low, uncluttered Spanish-style building like a Bauhaus version of the most magnificent hacienda in Mexico. Along the ground floor ran French doors leading to small, tiled patios rimmed with mulberry bushes. In the center of the first floor were four Spanish Art-Deco doors with chromium trim. Above that, in 1940s moderne script were the words *Republic Pictures*.

On the second floor, above the French windows, was a row of balconies, each one with four French doors leading onto it. Susan lowered her window and stared at the offices on the second floor. She could see that some of them were paneled, from floor to ceiling, with wood that gleamed from oiling and polishing, even through the windows.

She thought, but only thought, that she might have seen Sid Bauman bouncing jauntily along in front of the windows, peering out onto the street, then turning back into his office, holding a telephone receiver in his hand.

Then something struck her. The air! The air was not humid. It was dry and balmy and crisp to the touch, even to the breath. It was the air of welcome and health, not like the clammy, fetid summer air of Washington, D.C. Susan saw no sign at all of the smog that Johnny Carson had so often mocked. Why, this was air not only to breathe, not only to live from, but air through which a woman who knew what she wanted could *fly*.

The limousine drove right past the headquarters building of Republic Pictures. It paused briefly at the guard gate, where the driver, whose name was Robbie, told the guard, a pencil-thin man with alert blue eyes, that he had a passenger from Washington, and she didn't mind the heat at all.

"That Washington State or D.C.?" the guard asked with a distinct Scottish accent.

"What's the difference?" Robbie asked insouciantly. Then he waved his arm at Scottie, like the waggle of a bored seagull off Catalina, and drove onto the lot.

Once inside the lot gates, the buildings were decidedly less opulent, but far from grim—at first. The buildings were still Spanish style, but they lacked the elegant touches of the headquarters building. They were made of stucco and had wrought-iron, mullioned windows, but there were no carefully manicured mulberry trees, no small balconies, and no brushed and polished chromium borders on the French doors. Still, the afternoon sun of Los Angeles reflected dazzlingly off the pale salmon stucco of the buildings. By any reasonable standard, Susan thought, they were vastly superior to any building she had ever worked in before, except possibly the White House, and that was a building she could only have on the short-est possible lease.

These buildings, this whole studio set in the clear, beck-oning California air, was exactly what Susan had in mind for a much longer stay. They were on a human scale; they stood out in sharp, approachable relief in the sunshine; they were obviously designed to serve as launching pads, not prisons, for the human imagination. They shimmered with the possibilities of human existence.

Robbie drove the limousine down several streets and alleyways. Off to one side, along a deserted way, Susan saw a glimpse of a back lot of a Western town street. She saw the saloon and the "Tonsorial Parlor" and several rails for tying up horses. It looked just as it had in *High Noon*. Then the limousine wound around a sweeping curve and entered an industrial portion of the lot. Now the buildings were far more modern, functional, and featureless than the splendid Spanish buildings of the front portion of Repub-lic. There was no grass, and certainly no trees. In fact, most of these small buildings directly abutted scarred blacktop asphalt parking lots. On these lots there were no status tokens, no tokens of the media's ruling class. In-stead, there were broken-down trucks and vans and com-missary buses.

The limousine came to a slow stop in front of one of the buildings on which was written, in a recent stencil, TV DEVELOPMENT AND RESEARCH. In front of the building was an ancient Oldsmobile on which three men with long sideburns were working. The building was as ugly and stark in the sun as a drying pool of motor oil.

"This is it," Robbie said cheerfully, as if to him there were no difference between this building and any other building. "Miss Needle wanted you to see your office be-fore you unpacked."

Susan felt as if an ice pack had been put on the bottom of her spine. She looked out the window but didn't touch the door. Through the open window she could see a row of low foothills off to the south. They were dotted with gravestones. Then she saw that the hills were Forest Lawn Cemetery. Of course, she thought. Deirdre wanted her to see the office while there was still time for Susan to actually make it back to the airport and leave town this very day. That thought, and Susan's anger, made her step out of the door Robbie was holding open for her, smiling an oblivious smile.

"Let's see now," said Robbie. "You're supposed to report to Room 101A, and you're supposed to have the office right next to that."

Susan grimly walked into the building, which was instantly reminiscent of the corridors of a public junior high school. There was the same smell of desperation and futility, of utility-grade floors and walls and ceilings worked over too many times with wax and then finally ignored. There was the same industrial strength despair that came in an aerosol can and could be sprayed into the hallways to dispel hope and light.

Susan could not hear a single sound in the hallway except for a tinny radio playing Aretha Franklin at the other end of the hall.

"All right," Susan said to herself. "All right. If this is where I start, this is where I'll be for a few weeks or a month. No more than that." She had been around long enough to know that if you acted like a prima donna the first day of work, the reputation stuck for five years. If this was the pit she was destined to start in, she would work her way out of it. God knows she had done it before.

Robbie led her down the hallway. He ostentatiously read off the numbers as if he were proving to her that he could count. In the middle of the hall, where a four-bulb fluorescent light hung from the ceiling, Robbie proudly read, "Room One-o-one-A."

There was a small, hand-lettered sign next to the door saying RON SILVERMAN. The door was ajar and Robbie pushed it open. He peeked in and saw a secretary reading *The Hollywood Reporter*. The secretary looked as if she was one millimeter from sleep.

"Excuse me," Robbie said in his same carefree tone. "This is Susan-Marie Warmack. She's supposed to have an office somewhere near here. That ring a bell?"

The secretary turned a thin, pockmarked face toward Robbie, taking him in without any interest whatsoever. She laid down her newspaper and said, "I think I got a note from Miss Needle's office about her. Just a minute."

After a moment she picked up a slip of paper and read it. She stood up with a distinct look of disgust and walked out to the hallway, as if she had been asked to shoulder an enormous boulder. She pointed at a gray metal desk covered with dust and an upturned, greasy, gray metal typist's chair, surrounded by two months' worth of casually tossed trash.

"This here's your desk," said the secretary, with a distinct Okie accent only hinted at before.

Susan looked at it and felt red flashes of rage going through her entire nervous system. She ran a finger along the desk. The fingertip came up covered with black dust and grime. She looked at it for a second under the fluorescent light.

"Where does the desk go?" she asked, unsuccessfully trying to keep the edge out of her voice.

"Right here in this wide place in the hall," the secretary said. "Miss Needle said to tell you there's no offices right now, but one may come up in this building in a few weeks."

Susan kept her wits about her long enough to ask, "Is this a joke?"

With the malice that only an Okie can direct toward a college girl from the East, the secretary said, "No, ma'am. We're crowded here now. This place is right busy."

Panic swept over Susan, an occlusion of fury and terror and abandonment. She felt light-headed, suddenly swimming far away from this grinning surfer and this bitch secretary.

Nearby, someone had come out of an office, and Susan could see him, portly, with a beard, just out of reach of awareness. For her part, she was no longer in that hallway at all. In her lapsed consciousness, she was a small child and her stepfather was teaching her to play cards. Every time she tried to shuffle, the cards came flying out onto the floor, and every time they did, her stepfather slapped her across the face. Her mother sat in a corner reading *The Washington Post.* Blood came out of her nose and her lip was split and bleeding, but she was floating out the window, out into the night sky, where she did not feel a thing. Now, at Building H of Republic Studios, Susan had left through the window at the far end of the hall and sailed off into the blue sky over Burbank, where she didn't feel a thing.

She was actually flying, actually holding out her wings and soaring over Southern California, high above the freeway, where her car could not possibly have broken. She was flying higher and faster, and then a pilot's voice came out of nowhere. The voice said, "Are you all right? You can't lie here on the floor all day. What will all the other people who've been fucked over by Deirdre Needle use?"

Susan-Marie opened her eyes to the here and now and saw a middle-aged man with a kindly face, flushed red cheeks, brown, sad eyes, and a little beard bending over her. She was half sitting, half lying on the floor, against her new desk. How did she get down from those clouds to here so fast? She saw that the man had his black hair combed into a veritable bird's nest over his bald spot, and that made Susan-Marie smile.

The man was sitting on the floor next to Susan and he had spread out a tweed jacket under her suit. Susan looked at it, and then at him. "Jet lag," she said calmly. "Thanks for letting me use your jacket."

In a minute they were walking outside, down the streets of Dodge City. The sun was warm and bright, but Susan felt distinctly cold. Ron Silverman, the man with the bird's-nest hair, was talking to Susan about the studio, and Susan was trying to pull herself into the moment.

"Listen," she said, "I have never been a good traveler.

I should've gone to the hotel and rested for a while before I came over here."

"Bullshit," Ron Silverman said, not at all unkindly. "I've seen what Deirdre Needle can do, and that's a lot worse than jet lag."

"Plus," Susan said demurely, trying to find the right role for herself after her vertiginous departure and return, "it's the first day of work and that always makes me a little nervous."

"Bullshit," said Ron, laughing merrily. "It's coming here, thinking you're going to be treated like a human being, and then getting treated like shit. That's the problem."

"You've got something there," Susan said. "Who else is in that building?"

"People Deirdre doesn't like. People like me, who wrote the first thirty episodes of 'Valentine's Day' and now I can't get a pilot on the air, but they keep me around anyway in case some day someone at the network invites me to his son's bar mitzvah and I get a pilot deal."

"I'm not even supposed to be in television," Susan-Marie said. "I'm supposed to be in features."

Ron Silverman laughed happily again. "That's what they all say. Listen, at least you should know you're in good company. If you're on Dee's shit list, you have to be a fine human being."

"I feel as if somebody's made a mistake," Susan-Marie said. "Maybe I should call up Deirdre."

"Not bloody likely," Ron Silverman said. "She didn't do this by mistake. Just let me take a guess. You were hired by Belzberg, right?"

"Right."

"Look, I envy you the pampered life you must have led before you came here if you *didn't* think Deirdre would do this to you. Why should she let you hang around here to compete with her? This is the NFL, kid. People play for big stakes. If she can blow you out with this little trick, she's got to go for the shot."

"This is great," Susan-Marie said. "I'm out here in the middle of a swamp."

"You got it," Ron Silverman said cheerfully. "But the little alligators are afraid of the bigger alligators. Who do you know? When Belzberg hired you did you meet Sid, too?"

"I did," Susan-Marie said. "I'm not sure he remembers me."

"Where did he meet you, if it can be told?" Ron Silverman asked with the same twinkle in his eye.

"I was working as a special assistant at the White House," Susan-Marie said.

"He'll remember you," Ron said. "Count on it. He doesn't know a thing about this."

"Can I use your phone?" Susan-Marie asked.

In a moment she was in Ron Silverman's whimsically decorated office, with its pinball machine, its gum machine, and its Boys' Town poster of one boy holding another on his back. Above it, Silverman had written, *He ain't heavy. He's the producer.*

When Susan asked the studio operator for Sid Bauman's office the phone rang twice, and then a woman's English-accented voice said, "Mr. Bauman's office."

12

ACROBATICS

■

"Hello," Susan-Marie said, as if she had just brought the controlling interest in Exxon out to California with her. "This is Susan-Marie Warmack. From the White House."

The other voice became noticeably warmer. "Oh, yes," it said. "Of course. Mr. Bauman will be right on."

"Just a minute," Susan-Marie said cheerfully. "I've just gotten onto the lot. I'm at the Hollywood Way gate," she added, nodding at Ron Silverman, who held up his forefinger and thumb joined together to form a circle. "I haven't even been to my office yet. I thought maybe since it's a nice day, and since Sid told me he loved to go on walks, I'd come over there and Sid and I would walk over to my new office together."

"That's a very fine idea," the secretary said confidentially. "Mr. Bauman is always talking about exercise, but he never gets any. I'll make sure he does, and we'll be expecting you." Then she hung up the phone.

"I was right, wasn't I?" Ron Silverman said.

"If he knew about it, his secretary should get an Oscar," Susan-Marie said.

"Oh, Bauman didn't know a thing about it," Ron said. "He doesn't worry his little head about where people like you and me have offices. He worries about who's running the Federal Reserve."

"We'll see," Susan-Marie said. She looked around at the office of the comedy writer, took note of his three Emmys mounted on a plywood board hanging from a fiberboard wall by obviously do-it-yourself brackets. "Listen, let's keep this between us, okay? I don't want people thinking I'm Butterfly McQueen, fainting whenever something goes wrong."

"It's between us," he said. "When you get to be head of Republic maybe you could get me a better secretary."

"When I get to be head of Republic," Susan-Marie said, "you'll be a very big wheel."

■   ■   ■   ■

Sid Bauman's office was a song of power and success. It was forty-five feet long by thirty feet wide. Along the interior wall there was solid oak paneling, with a black marble fireplace inlaid in the center. Above the fireplace was a portrait of a beautiful, middle-aged blond woman wearing a black cocktail dress and smiling as if she knew a secret about you, but it was a good secret, the kind that would make you happy if you shared it. Susan-Marie assumed the woman was Amanda Barton, Sid Bauman's late wife, a legendary California beauty and sometime actress.

On the facing wall there was a row of eight French windows looking out onto the green lawn Susan had seen before. One of the walls had low bookshelves. The other had photographs of Sid Bauman with Gerald Ford, John F. Kennedy, Lyndon Johnson, John McCormack, Ronald

Reagan, and even a few movie stars. Behind the photographs was enough oak paneling to build an ark. Miss Pilkerton, Bauman's English secretary, cast a steely glance at Bauman as she brought in Susan. "Now you must walk for a half hour, mind you," she told him, then left, as if she had been lecturing a wayward schoolboy.

Sid Bauman, looking at Susan warmly, lit his pipe, brushed ash from his blue blazer, adjusted his ascot, and said, "Welcome to Republic, countess. I feel like a complete idiot not meeting you at your office your first day here. You probably think we're all complete slobs." He rose from the desk and walked toward Susan on a thick gray carpet. "And you're not wrong," he added.

"You're a busy man," Susan-Marie said. "I don't expect you to drop everything. It's just that your secretary said you liked to walk, and I thought maybe we should walk over together, since Paul isn't here."

"Paul isn't here?" Sid Bauman asked with genuine surprise. "That's rude. We're acting terribly. Now you're going to tell everyone back in Washington that we're pigs."

"Not at all," Susan-Marie said. "I shouldn't take much of your time. The driver said I was in Building H. Do you know where that is?"

"Frankly, I don't," Bauman said. "But we'll find it. I'm sure it's very nice, because we don't take people out of the White House and put them in offices overlooking parking lots. Did you have a good flight?"

"I only need a place that's quiet and peaceful, where I can concentrate and try to help you," Susan said. "It doesn't have to be like this." She gestured at the sweep of Bauman's office.

Neither Miss Pilkerton nor Miss Neese, the other secretary to Sid Bauman, had any clear idea of Building H's location, but Sid Bauman wanted to be outside, so he and Susan headed in a vague way toward the back of the lot, where Miss Pilkerton said she "thought" Building H was hidden.

"I probably should have picked out your office myself," Bauman said. "I didn't know we still had offices in the back of the lot. I know that Columbia was building some very fancy offices back there for Ray Stark, and I bet you have one of those. They're not my taste, with all that glass and skylights. I prefer the more traditional look, but maybe you'll like them. That must be where you are. I don't want Ray Stark stealing you away from me. You won't let that happen, will you?"

"Of course not," Susan-Marie said, and anyone who saw her, heard her voice, saw her appealing, confident posture would swear that this was the same Susan who had been at the luncheon in the White House solarium, who had attracted more approval and admiration than the president himself. Surely the Susan-Marie who went pale and dizzy when she saw her office—her pit of gray steel, grease, and trash—was someone else, an imposter, not Susan-Marie Warmack at all.

Susan-Marie and Bauman walked down a narrow alleyway that passed the costuming department. The windows were crammed with shepherds' dresses, suits of armor, outer-space headgear, army uniforms, deep-sea diving suits, and a few ordinary basketball uniforms. Once again, Susan had the delicious rush she had felt when she first walked onto the lot, the feeling that she was on a launching platform, about to fly into the most fertile parts of her own imagination.

Then Susan-Marie and Bauman passed a great, rambling stage filled with backdrops—Pacific Oceans, Sahara deserts, New York City skylines, Oklahoma wheatfields, Texas oilfields, Everglades swamplands. As Susan and Bauman passed, workmen in front-loaders, extras in milkmaids' aprons, freelance producers in leather jackets and pressed jeans passed by. No one said hello to Sid Bauman first. Any one of them who was greeted by name by Sid Bauman beamed.

"You're like royalty," Susan-Marie said. "The blessing

of the king is now being bestowed on the Republic back lot."

"Better than royalty, countess," Bauman said. "The king doesn't own twenty percent anymore anywhere except Saudi Arabia. I have twenty percent and options on two million more shares at five bucks each and the market is at twenty-two."

"It must be nice to know you did it from nothing," Susan-Marie said.

"From nothing!" Sid Bauman said indignantly. He shook his head furiously. "From less than nothing. From a family in Brownsville, Brooklyn, who thought we were Rockefellers if we had chicken once a week. From a father who didn't even know what a twenty-dollar bill looked like, who didn't see a decent job until he worked at the Navy Yard starting in 1940. But I always knew what I wanted. I was in the Young Communist League, but I always knew I wanted to be one of those Communists who rides in a limousine. I always knew I wanted to be one of the ones who gets a house taken from the capitalists on Park Avenue."

"Young Communist League, Sid? You?" Susan-Marie asked incredulously, or seemingly incredulously, because although it was in no biography of Sid Bauman, if it could have been found out by perfect diligence, Susan-Marie would have found it out.

"Oh, totally," Sid Bauman said. "Totally," putting the entire force of the word on the first three letters, like a wolf of totality blowing down the house of parts and percentages. "Everyone in my neighborhood was in the YCL. You know why they expelled me?"

"Because you wanted to make the clubhouse into a cosmetics factory?" Susan-Marie asked cheerfully. They were now heading past a stage set where a sign in red letters said HOT SET—NO TALKING. Through the prop backs, Susan could see a woman getting into and out of a Dodge station wagon while immense lights flooded out the day.

138

"Not at all," Sid Bauman said, puffing happily on his pipe. "Not in the slightest. No, you're too young to remember the fury about the second front, I suppose."

An assistant director in a thin leather jacket peered angrily from behind a prop tree at the noise. He started to make a shushing gesture, but when he saw that the noise came from Sid Bauman, he simply smiled and disappeared into the polystyrene foliage. Sid Bauman gave him an absentminded wave and he popped his head back out again and whispered a hello, now positively beaming with joy.

"Of course I know about the second front," Susan-Marie said. "Stalin complaining endlessly about Churchill allowing Hitler to bleed Russia white."

Sid Bauman stopped in his tracks and grabbed Susan by her silk-and-linen elbow. "You are amazing," he said. "How did you know that? You're the only person on the lot who knows that, I'm sure of it. And how old are you?"

"Twenty-seven," Susan-Marie said modestly. "But everyone knows about the second front."

"No," Sid Bauman said. "You and I are the only ones. Now I know I can't have you over here on this side of the lot, away near Ray Stark, so when he sees how smart you are he steals you away. I'll bet you have a little Park Avenue penthouse over here, but I don't care. We'll just see how they've got you fixed up, and then we'll see."

"I just want someplace bright and quiet where I can work," Susan-Marie said.

"Yeah, but what do I want? I want someone near me who can talk about something other than yesterday's grosses that he just got out of the *Reporter*. I know you'll have something really nice here, but I just want to see if it beats what I might find for you near me."

"Well," Susan-Marie said, "it's just great to be where I'm appreciated. It's a long way from the phone company."

"Yes, I was opposed to opening a second front," Sid Bauman said. "All along. The whole time. I was opposed to sending any Americans to go fight. I hate war. When it's over all the good people are dead and the bad people just got richer. So they called a meeting where everybody criticized me and then they threw me out. And I was so angry that they had done this *tot*ally unjustified thing that I went out and got a job decorating windows at Tiffany, which was the archenemy of what any good YCL kid would think of. And there it was. That was what I had always been meant to do: make things pretty. Make things pretty so that people would buy them instead of somebody else's things, so their lives would be pretty, at least for a minute."

"You've done it well," Susan-Marie said. "Just look how beautiful you've made this studio."

"Yeah, well it could be better, but lemme tell you, princess, when I was still a young guy, when my father was working at the Navy Yard and complaining, but also telling me every day how lucky he was to even have a job, I already had ten guys working for me doing what I told them at Arnold Constable. I was in charge of the whole thing, right down on Fifth and Fortieth, and I was taking home five hundred a week, and giving half of it to my mother without my dad knowing a thing about it. 'Cause he wouldn't have wanted to take the money because of his pride, and he wouldn't have believed I could make it from doing windows, which he always thought was sissy work anyway."

"Fantastic," Susan-Marie said. "Five hundred dollars a week in those days."

"Exactly," Bauman said. "That would have been around 1942, 1943, and I was living like a king. Better than a king. Living like a Rockefeller. But I still remembered that people have feelings, and I treated the ten guys who worked for me better than they'd ever been treated and I swore that when people worked for me they'd be people that I'd make life prettier for, just the same as I made those windows. That's why I've kept up these buildings here just like they were in the glory days, back in the twenties and thirties here. I treat the people at Republic right, and Deirdre knows that's my first priority. To treat people as if they had feelings."

While Sid Bauman had been talking, he and Susan had turned a corner, and they now stood in front of Building H. Susan made a coughing sound and said, "I want to hear every word of this, Sid, but this is my building, I think."

"Oh, no," Sid Bauman said. "No," he repeated, shaking his head. "If this is even one of my buildings I'll be very surprised."

But Sid Bauman looked worried, and his face, which had been glowing with proud remembrance of youth and promise, now suddenly looked red and fearful. "I'll just walk in here and check," Susan-Marie said. "I'm sure it's great inside."

Sid Bauman walked in with Susan. Again, Susan felt as if a sprayed mixture of gloom and failure had been evenly and repetitively applied to the linoleum and the peeling paint every day for a century. Sid Bauman's springy step became slow and heavy. "I recognize some of these names," Bauman said. "But this isn't even features. This is just people out to pasture because they've done something a long time ago, and I didn't even know we kept them in a place like this." He stopped, looked around solemnly, and said, "This building will not be here next week."

Ron Silverman came out of his office and showed him Susan's greasy metal desk at a wide place in the hall. Here Bauman's reaction was even more emphatic. He looked, Susan-Marie said later, "as if his blood had started flowing the wrong way."

"This has to be a mistake," Sid Bauman said. "Or a joke."

"Sid," Ron Silverman said. "This is the way Deirdre treats people. Wake up, Sid. Deirdre is a little dictator here."

"Ron, from right now, you're in the main executive building. Just because I'm so embarrassed. Susan, you're getting Schmooey Lipsher's office. It's right next to mine. *Emes,* Ron, I had no idea this building was even here. I'm going to talk to Deirdre. You don't humiliate someone at his studio. That's not the way it works here. There are going to be some changes, and you can bet every dime on that."

●   ■   ■   ■

In less than an hour the office one down from Sid Bauman's was Susan-Marie's. That was the one almost as big as Sid's, with cherry-wood paneling and two skylights and three custom-made Bokharas over a hand-inlaid tile floor, with a marble fireplace from Duncan Phyfe, bought in Banbury, Oxfordshire, with a teak desk specially made for Schmooey in Manila, and a thirty-five-foot bookcase facing the four sets of French doors, with the late afternoon sunlight streaming in through the silk curtains.

Schmooey had been head of marketing. He had been fired, locked out the day before when the auditors told Sid Bauman conclusively that he had been taking bribes and kickbacks from research and advertising contractors he had hired.

"A fifteen-year man here," Sid Bauman said as he showed Susan-Marie the office. "The guy's always looking so *febissineh,* and I'm feeling sorry for him, and now he's got two million in a Swiss bank account, and I look like dog meat to the Board of Directors. I put in these carpets myself. Red against the red tile. My idea. Everybody said it wouldn't be pretty, but I knew it would be."

"It's fantastic, Sid," Susan-Marie said. "The president doesn't have an office like this."

"The president doesn't work for Sid Bauman," he said. He walked over to the bookcase and scanned the leather spines. "Listen, this is your office. If Deirdre raises any problem, tell her to talk to me. Never mind. I'll be talking to her myself right away. If you don't have any plans for dinner, I'll work something out."

"That would be perfect."

"I don't even want to think where Deirdre has put you in an apartment," Sid Bauman said. "I'll have Joyce Pilkerton find you something decent at the Beverly Hills Hotel."

"That would be even more perfect," Susan-Marie said. "I hardly know how to thank you."

"We workers have to stand together." Bauman raised his fist in a clench. *"Non pasaran."*

"Right on," Susan-Marie said, raising her own fist and smiling.

Sid Bauman left, closing the door behind him. As soon as he did, Susan-Marie looked at the rich carpets, the sun on the tile, the look of perfect, eternal comfort, and twirled her way across the room to the Herman Miller couch. She collapsed onto the fabric like a ballerina and threw her arms out in a gesture of total acceptance.

13

SILENT NIGHT

∎

On that first day in Hollywood there were none of the usual problems of jet lag for Susan-Marie. Sid Bauman arranged for Bungalow 12 at the Beverly Hills Hotel. It was two hundred bucks a night in 1972, when a dollar was a dollar. But Sid Bauman wouldn't hear of "the next generation of power" at Republic staying anywhere else.

Waiting on the teak enamel coffee table was a basket with a jar of Beluga caviar, a fifth of Stolichnaya, and a basket of fresh fruit including two pineapples already sliced. The bungalow had its own porch overlooking a large lawn sloping down to Crescent Avenue. It had a king-size bed and the whitest linen Susan-Marie had ever seen. The maids had just finished cleaning it up after Barbra when Susan-Marie checked in.

At eight, after Susan-Marie had time for a nap, a studio limousine (mercifully without Robbie at the wheel) picked up Susan-Marie. Sid escorted her to the car. He was filled with apologies, but Susan and he would not be dining alone. Jules and Doris Stein had called and were in such a good mood that Bauman just had to invite them along.

"When I go with them they only talk about antiques," he said. "I'm hoping that with you there they'll talk about something more interesting."

"This is the Jules Stein who is chairman of Universal?" Susan-Marie asked, half serious, half unsure if she were dreaming.

"I know," Sid Bauman said sorrowfully. "It should be someone younger, more interesting for you. I'm sorry."

"Don't be sorry," Susan-Marie said. "This is nothing to be sorry for."

In fact, Jules and Doris were sick of antiques that night, and they mostly wanted to hear what was going on in Washington, especially if Taft Schreiber made a good impression on R.N. "I should worry," Jules Stein said with a laugh, "I'm the one who's paying him."

"You think too much about money, Jules," Doris Stein said to him, tweaking him playfully on the elbow.

"If I thought about Susan-Marie, you'd lock me out of the house," Jules Stein said in mock terror. Sid Bauman raised his eyebrows in a theatrical gesture of agreement and amazement.

"She's not just beautiful," Sid Bauman said. "She's not just a gorgeous *talena*. She's one of those smart girls from the East."

"Like Doris," Jules Stein said, in what seemed like a never-ending effort to please his wife, who looked perfectly pleased already. "What did you do at the White House, Susan?" Jules Stein asked, fixing her with a startlingly intelligent stare.

So you see how it went. Not only were Jules and Doris Stein and Sid Bauman with her at La Scala, at the best table, the red leather rolled and tucked banquette right inside the door to the right, but they were hanging on her every word. Jon Peters and Peter Guber could walk by and nod, but no one looked. Jackie Gleason passed by, hoping for a nod from the A table, but nobody nodded. Angie Dickinson got a wink from Doris Stein, and Bob Evans got a slightly raised hand from Jules Stein, but basically, the A table was listening to Susan-Marie.

"The mood of this country is changing," she said. "You think it isn't, or somebody thinks it isn't, because there are still demonstrations about the war and kids still lie down in front of the Justice Department. But out on the prairies, out in the neighborhoods where the real America is, things are changing.

"People in this country looked at the faces of those people at the Democratic Convention, then they looked at the faces of the cops, and they got scared. They looked at their children, and at their brothers and sisters getting clubbed, getting ripped on acid, dropping out and letting their lives run down the drain, and they got really worried. The pendulum is going to swing back.

"The country is sick of change. There are still small groups in important places, network people, newspaper people, who want to keep the pot boiling. But, basically, the country is hunkered down waiting for things to return to normal," Susan-Marie said. "This isn't something I made up. This isn't something from exit polls at a shopping center in San Jose. This is from hundreds of thousands of Americans right now, today, in interviews and focus groups by people who know what to ask."

"I wish we had them in research at Universal," Jules Stein said.

"You just try to imagine a person who's been up all night drinking and taking drugs and then he wakes up with a terrible headache to find that he's overdrawn at his bank. That's what's going on now," Susan said. "The inflation on top of the hippie era, and people just want things to settle down."

Sid Bauman puffed on his pipe and nodded in emphatic approval.

"There could still be a big blow-off somewhere," Susan-Marie said. "A finale bigger than anything that's come before. But," Susan-Marie went on, "whatever happens, you may have this one more giant post-sixties blowout, but then you're going to see amazing changes. People are going to want a much quieter America. The colleges will have fraternities and goldfish-swallowing again. The kids and their parents won't want to hear about the ghettos or social responsibility. They'll want to escape."

"You have data on this?" Jules Stein asked hopefully.

"She does," Sid Bauman cut in, "and Republic is paying her for it. Maybe in a few years we'll let you see it."

Jules Stein looked dignified and offended for a moment. Then he slouched into his seat, turned up his collar, and in the best Yiddish accent of a peddler, he said, "Sidney, you can't blame a guy for trying."

"Escape," Susan-Marie said. "That's the ticket. Think of what made people forget in 1935 or 1936, update it, jazz it up visually to appeal to a country that's known LSD, and you've got what this country's going to want for the next ten years, maybe more, at every theater around the country."

The waiter brought another round of drinks. Susan-Marie sipped from her white wine, Puligny-Montrachet, which Sid Bauman always ordered, which Tony at La Scala brought him without his even having to ask for it. Jules and Doris and Sid waited expectantly for more from her. For a split second, before she plunged onward, Susan-Marie relished a thought: She was not in a cafeteria on 17th Street NW, Washington, D.C., pretending to be with studio executives, talking to Benjy and wondering what it would be like to try her ideas on moguls. No, she was there, in real time, doing in real life what she had imagined and pretended she was doing so many times. Only better, more fluid, more lucid, and the moguls were listening to her far better than the bureaucrats ever had. Small wonder. They had money riding on it.

"The same formats that were really big in the Depression are going to be big again," Susan-Marie said. "Pictures with monsters. Science fiction. Serials about people from other planets. Plain, straightforward love stories, all the forms that people have been laughing about for ten years are going to come back with a big bang, and all those exotic European pictures with people dressing up like Death are going to just be a joke."

"We have this monster picture about a big shark in development right now," Jules Stein said. "It's a TV movie. Nothing more than that. Good for one night and that's about it."

"We'll see," Susan-Marie said.

"Think about it," Sid Bauman said to Jules. "This girl is new. She's not jaded from being at your story meetings. She's real and she comes from somewhere out there in America. She knows what's going on, and you ought to pay attention. She doesn't work for you, Jules, so she can tell you the truth."

"It's a point," Jules Stein said.

"Read the script," Doris Stein said. "Maybe it's better for theatrical."

"But science fiction," Sid Bauman said. "That never works. Every few years somebody tries it, and the only one that ever made a dime was *2001,* and that was so slow it could put a shark to sleep."

"Yes," Susan-Marie said with a deferential smile. "But that was science fiction that wasn't about escape at all. In fact, it was about really deep subjects like evolution and the unconscious mind. It made the viewer feel stupid that he didn't understand it, not happy that he wasn't worrying about inflation."

She paused for a moment and ate a forkful of angel's-hair pasta while Jules Stein and Sid Bauman exchanged looks.

"If you imagine all the escape potential of the colors and

148

special effects of *2001,* but with a straight escape plot like Buck Rogers, you've got what Americans will be interested in later on in the seventies," she said. Then she added, "Of course, this is all theory, and it might not mean a thing to you when you've had experience actually building a studio, and you've probably thought about it all before."

Jules Stein folded his napkin into fourths as carefully as if he were setting up instruments for a corneal transplant. "This is a smart girl," he said to Sid Bauman. "A very, very smart girl. Only don't apologize when you're making so much sense. Apologize when you're wrong."

"If you're going to try to steal her away right in front of me," Sid Bauman said, "I'll have to leave."

"I'm not trying to steal anyone," Jules Stein said. "I just happen to want Susan to know what you and I already know, which is that there are several different studios in town, not just one. That's all. So sue me."

After dinner the limousine took Susan-Marie and Sid Bauman up Coldwater Canyon Drive to Mulholland, the road that runs along the ridge of mountains that divide Los Angeles in half.

From a vantage point near Outpost Drive, Susan saw the lights near the gigantic international airport where she had been a bewildered immigrant only hours before. Moonlight fell on a sliver of beach next to the airport, then became the prelude to a torrent of lights that swept up from Redondo Beach and Playa del Rey, through Venice, across to Inglewood, into Hawthorne and Culver City, then through Beverly Hills, growing brightest in West Hollywood and Carthay, and running up the Hollywood Hills to where the limousine sat silent in the moonlight.

On the Valley side, which Susan-Marie saw from just east of Coldwater Canyon, the lights were fewer and more orderly. They ran in neat lines out Lankershim Boulevard and Laurel Canyon, past Studio City, through North Hollywood, sweeping by Van Nuys, then out through Burbank and Sunland, until they petered out in the utterly dark Santa Susanna Mountains. Occasionally Susan could make out the lights of a 727 circling for a landing at Burbank Airport.

"It belongs to you, kid," Sid Bauman said. "But it's like everything else that belongs to you in Hollywood. You have to be ready to kill to keep it."

The limousine brought Susan-Marie and Sid Bauman back to the gracefully curved, sweeping driveway of the Beverly Hills Hotel, then dropped them off on the red-carpeted steps.

"I feel wound up from that dinner," Susan-Marie said.

"From Deirdre Needle's games," Sid Bauman said. "Do you want a nightcap in the Polo Lounge?"

"No," Susan said. "How about getting one at the bungalow?"

In the living room of the bungalow Sid Bauman drank a Bombay martini while Susan sipped a Courvoisier on the rocks.

"Deirdre said she didn't know a thing about it, of course. She said she just told the buildings man to find you someplace nice and then she forgot about it. She's a liar," Sid Bauman said. "I told her I was humiliated and that I would keep a very close eye on her. I'd fire her except that nobody would get a check for a month if she left."

"Let's not think about it," Susan-Marie said. "Maybe she really didn't know."

"Are you kidding?" Sid Bauman said. "She plays hard-ball, Susan. Always. That's the only game she knows. That's the only game anyone here knows."

Susan-Marie got up from her chair and sat on the arm of Sid's couch. "This has been the kind of day I never thought I would have in my whole life," she said.

"No, you're just tired," Sid Bauman said. "And you had a rotten trick played on you."

"I'm not tired," Susan-Marie said, "because you saved me."

She said it to Sid Bauman in such a matter-of-fact, yet

girlish way that it was as if she were reading part of a fairy tale about princesses and enchanted towers. It was momentarily difficult for Sid Bauman to reconcile the girlish tone with the careful analyst of culture he had seen at La Scala.

"I'm a designer, Susan," he said. "I see what looks right. I could see you looked very right for Republic the first moment I saw you at the White House. I could see you were wrong for Building H and right for the Main Exec building just as fast. One thing fit and the other didn't. Now I think I'd better go."

"No," Susan-Marie said. "You being here with me tonight fits."

"I don't know if it does," Sid Bauman said. "I'm really not sure of this part. I'm not sure it's pretty."

"I am," Susan-Marie said, leaning toward him with her lips half parted.

Sid Bauman stayed until about three in the morning. The limousine driver had left and Sid simply walked the few blocks to his home behind the hotel. As he walked along the empty streets, he looked up at the coconut palms arrayed against the moonlit sky. All of the cares and fears of middle-aged life melted away from him. He felt as if he were young again, with the frictionless walk of youth, the serene calm of forty years before. To Sid, even after he arrived home and got into his own bed, his skin was still glowing from the warmth of Susan-Marie's skin. Sid Bauman didn't even pick up the day's *Wall Street Journal* that lay carefully folded on a silver tray next to his bed. Why should he look to see what the other seekers of the world were doing that day? For now, Sid Bauman was the only man in the world and the world had just begun that morning. What news could there be?

Back in Bungalow 12, Susan-Marie looked through the Levelors and the white mullions to the moonlight on the green grass. The moonlight was blue and palpable on the grass. There wasn't a sound except the swish of an occasional automobile and the constant din of crickets. Once, before she fell asleep, Susan-Marie heard an owl distinctly hooting off toward the park. She did not regret her night with Sid. He had made her feel safe, wanted. He had told her she belonged. Now Sid knew her, and knew she belonged. She felt *connected,* and that was a good feeling in a new city.

14

BREADCRUMBS

■

There are no visitors' parking places at any major studio in Hollywood. There never have been. There are no orientation programs for new employees, no assigned spaces for young executives on their way up to park their new red 280 SLs. There never have been. If you want a space, you take somebody else's space or you park off the lot. That's how Hollywood works.

On her first full day at Republic Susan cruised through the Warner Boulevard gate and told her name to Scottie. He smiled at her and gave her a broad wave onto the lot, as if to say, "There it is. Take it."

Susan didn't even look for new employees' parking or visitors' parking. She saw a space near the Main Exec building that bore the white-stenciled name of Paul Newman. She figured there was probably one of those spaces at every studio in town. He wouldn't be needing this one today.

In her office, sitting lazily on a stenographer's chair, was Susan's new secretary, Sheila Wallen. Sheila was a lively Filipino-American with round, full cheeks like the cheeks of a chipmunk in September. She wore her thick black hair in a ponytail and swished it through the air when Susan-Marie entered, as if she were brushing away flies in a stable.

Sheila Wallen also distinguished herself by wearing an Asian *ao dai* instead of a dress. It was black silk and slit up to the top of her thigh. "It was Sid Bauman's idea," Sheila Wallen said languorously. "He had a couple of Chinese secretaries and he used to design women's clothes, so he got all of us black silk *ao dais*," she said. "Everyone on this floor had to wear them once a week in the old days. Schmooey used to crack up about it. I still wear mine once in a while. What the hell. It didn't cost anything. I don't know. I guess Schmooey's more worried about the grand jury now."

Sheila Wallen, Schmooey's ex-secretary, knew every single person and almost every deal on the lot. Her first official act as secretary was to note which kinds of diet sodas Susan wanted. "Most people on the lot take Perrier and grapefruit juice. A few prefer Tab. Then there are a very few who take V-8 juice. If you want to fit right in, I'd go for the Perrier and a few others just as spares," Sheila Wallen said.

"Nobody drinks regular soda?" Susan-Marie asked her sparkling, engaging, guilelessly talkative secretary.

"Oh, a few *writers*," Sheila Wallen said. "They're the only ones. They don't care what they look like. They're so far down at the bottom of the heap they don't even bother to be thin."

Susan-Marie's first official assignment was to sit in on a meeting of the marketing committee. "It's a rump session," Sheila said. "Sid Bauman left town real early this morning for a NATO meeting in Chicago. That's National

Association of Theatre Owners. Paul Belzberg's in Mexico on location. Deirdre Needle's out of town. So it's just Marco Castro and Bryan Fitzpatrick, the two guys who used to be just under Schmooey, and then Robin Wright from advertising and Ann Jastrow from research. And you. I guess you're there to tell them what life is like in the big wide world outside."

"I guess so," Susan-Marie said.

"While you're at the meeting, I'll make sure you get plenty of raw carrots. You don't want any salted peanuts, do you?"

At the meeting Marco Castro was first to speak. Castro's real name was Caldwell. He was the eldest son of a major stockbroker and grandson of the president of Yale. Rumor had it that he had changed his name to Castro to get into a training program for minorities at the American Film Institute after he graduated from Wesleyan. He was a heavy-set man of about thirty with thick glasses and a charming desire to please.

"Campbell and Ewald have submitted a proposal on the *Trade-Off* campaign," he told Susan. "Now this is a movie about a man who leaves his family to become a used-car salesman in a small town in Wyoming and gets involved with an Indian girl there and decides to try to become an Indian."

"The way we see it," Bryan Fitzpatrick said in a cheerful, eager, boyish voice that belied his bald head and graying eyebrows, "we're selling the idea of sex with an Indian woman. We're selling a fantasy of an Indian woman who'll love to ball and won't ask for alimony and won't start carrying around a placard if he leaves her with a little papoose."

"I hate it when you do that," Ann Jastrow said. She stared at him through wire-rimmed glasses. Her light blue eyes darted at him from different angles, like bees attacking a guinea pig. "You can't belittle everything."

"Why not?" Bryan Fitzpatrick asked. "We know we won't get anybody to buy a ticket if we show him on a poster standing in a teepee with his shirt off and a woman with granny glasses reading *The New Republic* in the background."

Ann Jastrow sputtered, took off her glasses, and cleaned them with the sleeve of her silk dress. "Really," she said.

"The poster we plan has the hero, Masterson, standing at the window of a ranch house. He's wearing tight jeans and no shoes and his chest is bare. Out the window we can see a corral with a horse. In the background, in the room, is the girlfriend in the bed, with the sheets just up to the top of her breasts, and she's looking like she really would love to ball this guy until he drops dead," Robin Wright said in a matter-of-fact, earthy tone. She was the oldest person in the room, perhaps fifty, wearing a sloppy cotton dress covered with ashes from her never-ending puffs on Camel cigarettes. Sometimes she had more than one lit at a time.

Ann Jastrow groaned.

"What the hell's wrong with it?" Bryan Fitzpatrick asked. "It has everything."

"It's just like a hundred others," Ann Jastrow said. "That's what's wrong with it."

No one had an answer for that, so Marco Castro fingered his paisley necktie and said, "Susan, what does the White House have to say about this?"

So they find out that fast, Susan thought. She took a deep breath and said, "Well, what does your research tell you about it?"

Ann Jastrow shrugged her shoulders. "Horse is a powerful symbol. Window is a good one. Girl in bed is a good one. If the guy's chest is good, that's one too. I'm not saying it has any glaring flaws," she said. "It's just ordinary."

"Well," Susan said, deferentially, "I'm new to the business, but if no one'll hate me, I'll offer a few ideas that are probably totally wrong."

"Listen," Bryan Fitzpatrick said, "if they're totally

wrong, we'll love you. If they're right, we'll hate you. You know how that works."

"I know exactly how that works," Susan said.

Robin Wright grunted. "So what's on your mind?"

"Well, I haven't read the script or seen the rough cut," Susan-Marie said.

"Nobody has except the director and Belzberg," Bryan Fitzpatrick said. "Go on."

"When the Committee to Re-Elect was testing places to have the president stand to get himself into the right psychological spot with the viewers, we basically got a rank order of places that evoke good feelings in the viewers of TV commercials." She spoke very calmly, as if she were talking to Haldeman. "This is what we got," she said. "First, the ocean, preferably the beach. Second, the top of a luxury apartment building overlooking a city with a lot of lights. Third, a forest, but only if we could get a really good, leafy green off the leaves. Fourth, an airplane really high up in the clouds. Fifth, a school classroom with young children. That's what gave us our best readings for adding authority and charisma."

Everyone in the room looked interested. Ann Jastrow said to Castro, "See what we could do if we laid out a few dollars on research instead of spending it all on Winnebagos?"

"Why should we do that?" Castro asked. "We have Susan now and she can just call her pals in Washington and get whatever we need." He turned to Susan and said, with a broad smile, as if it were a boast, "We're takers here."

"The people at the Nixon White House are very shy," she responded. "That's what we got for authority," she said. "But to close the loop, we picked up answers for locations for sexiness and excitement too. Of all locations for sex, highways got the highest reading. Highways beat out bedrooms, bars, cars, anything. An open highway is where it's at if you want viewers to start thinking about sex."

"Oh, for Christ's sake," Bryan Fitzpatrick said to Robin Wright. "Put a fucking highway there instead of the horse."

There was a moment's pause and then Robin Wright said, "Of course we'll hate you forever for this, but we'll dummy one up and test it." She took such a deep drag on a Camel that in one breath she turned a third of it to ash. "We don't hate you, honey," she said. "It might work and it might not, but it shows that somebody's doing something unusual here: thinking about what's going on and not just working off the seat of his pants."

"We've got a saying here, Susan," Ann Jastrow added. "It's called 'every woman for herself,' but that only applies when the woman did something wrong. When she does something right we all hang on for the credit."

"We're takers here," Castro repeated. "It's that simple."

After the meeting, as Susan walked down the hall to her office, Bryan Fitzpatrick caught up with her and squeezed her arm above the elbow. "You did good," he said. "Come have lunch with me and I'll tell you how to have fun here."

In the Burbank Studios commissary, in the blue-painted room where only executives could eat, Bryan Fitzpatrick methodically drank his soup and laid out his role for Susan.

"What Deirdre tried to do to you is all over the studio. Ron Silverman's secretary made sure of that. How you turned it around is all over the studio, maybe all over town. It's already on its way to being one of those Hollywood classics."

"Just trying to get into the ball game," Susan said. "Just trying to protect myself."

"And you did it right." Fitzpatrick smiled, showing a mouthful of white, even teeth. "I started out my life in a military academy, planning to be a general, and I guarantee you that everyone there would have approved of what you did. It was organized and it was definitely smart. Why not go directly to Sid if you're coming from the White House?"

"I don't want to seem like a crybaby," Susan-Marie said.

"You don't want to be losered out on your first day either," Fitzpatrick said. "You handled it just right. Now, now comes the big test. You're here. You're Bauman's pal. You're from the White House. You're in a dress and not in jeans, and everybody's wondering what you're like. And Deirdre Needle's got plenty of pals here just praying for you to fall right on your face."

"Is it really that desperate?" Susan-Marie asked. She looked at a plate of ravioli, poked it with a fork, but decided not to risk it. She ate raspberry Jell-O instead.

"Not at all," Fitzpatrick said. "She's been here a few years. She's made enemies. Don't think you're alone. Plus, you have Sid."

"I don't have Sid," Susan-Marie said tartly. "We're friends. I met him twice and he took me to dinner. I'm not counting on him to hold my hand every day."

"And a good thing too. That's one of the major lessons of life on the lot."

"What's that?" Susan asked.

"If you need someone to help you, he won't be there. If you don't need him, if you can stand alone, he'll be right by your side."

"That's a lesson everywhere," Susan-Marie said as she scanned the toughened faces at the nearby tables.

"Absolutely. It's just as true at the academy in Scranton as it is on the Republic lot. Only losers need anyone and winners don't need anyone. And I'll tell you another thing. That goes not just for connections but for the job itself." Fitzpatrick scowled as he ate his chicken salad. (Susan made a note to find other places to eat in a hurry.) "If people think you need the job here, they'll put you through hell. If they think you don't need the money, they know they can't hurt you as much, so they don't even try."

"That's worth remembering."

"Yeah, it sure is," Fitzpatrick said. "I don't know what kind of family you come from, but you've got a leg up, because if you come from the White House with a Republican in there, everybody here's going to just automatically assume you're rich."

"Well . . ." Susan-Marie said with the beginnings of a smile.

"Don't even tell me." Fitzpatrick held up a hand. "If you're not from a rich family, I don't want to hear about it."

"And I wasn't going to tell you," Susan-Marie said. "My family's money is a private matter."

Fitzpatrick made a high sign with his right thumb and smiled. "You got it, kid."

"Not only that," Susan-Marie said, "but no matter how much money my family has, I wouldn't want to sponge off them."

"You got it, you got it, you got it," Fitzpatrick said.

"So now we understand a little bit about each other. How come you're telling me all this?"

Fitzpatrick lowered his fork and ducked his head in a protective gesture. "I've been here for six years," he said. "The first time I met Deirdre in the hall I called her 'Dee' instead of Deirdre. I guess I just heard her name wrong. After that she wouldn't give me a chair for my desk for a year. I had to buy it myself. So you get the picture."

"I get it," Susan-Marie said.

"You have a sensitive look on your face. You showed you were smart at the meeting. That's a problem, not a plus."

"Great."

"Let me just tell you one story. I used to work with a guy who reminded me a lot of you. He was a new producer who had great ideas all day long. He had gone to Harvard and won the Wells Prize in poetry. Really smart guy. Really felt things. You can't believe the way people here would cut him up just to watch him bleed. No other reason. He took it for a long time.

"Then one day he was talking to Deirdre about how Wordsworth had written 'Tintern Abbey' after one afternoon at a ruined abbey. He started quoting from 'Tintern Abbey' about 'sportive rows of trees,' and Deirdre interrupted him. 'Out here, we make more money with our ass than with our head,' she told him. I thought the guy was going to fall through the floor. You get it?"

"I get it," Susan said. "It's sad."

"From that day on the producer never told anyone about going to Harvard or winning the Wells Prize or Tintern Abbey. He moved over to MGM, and when people asked him how he got into the picture business he said he used to work in the slaughterhouse business and he inherited some theaters in Georgia. Now people don't bother him as much. You get it?"

"I get it," Susan-Marie said. "Sounds like a wonderful business."

"Best place to work in the whole world," Fitzpatrick said. "I wouldn't trade places with anyone. Listen, if you ever need anyone to talk to, a shoulder to cry on, just call me. I love hearing confession."

"I have nothing to confess," Susan-Marie said.

■   ■   ■   ■

Back in her office Susan-Marie looked at a sheaf of yellow message notes from Sheila Wallen. Sheila handed them to Susan-Marie as if they weighed a thousand pounds and she had been carrying them for a week. "My, but you're popular," she said. "Was that Bryan Fitzpatrick you were eating with?"

"Yes, it was," Susan said. She leafed through her messages while she stood in front of Sheila Wallen. There was one from Robin Wright inviting her to come to a meeting of Women in Film, which had lunch every Wednesday at the Polo Lounge. "Take it," Sheila Wallen said knowingly. "A very heavy-hitting group of women. Hadassah couldn't offer you such connections already."

"Tell her I'll be there," Susan-Marie said.

The next message was from Beverly Hills Mercedes. It told Susan to call the service department about the "recommended engineering maintenance intervals" for the 280 SL. Susan handed that to Sheila and said, "You take care of it."

The next message was from the Gulfstream II on which Sid Bauman was flying from Chicago to Toronto for more meetings with theater owners. "Sorry to have missed you this morning," Sid Bauman said. "I'll be back on Friday and I'd love to hear your impressions of your first week at work."

Susan folded that one and put it in her skirt pocket.

The next one was from the payroll department. Stapled to the message was a long chart of what Susan's paychecks were going to be, allowing for all the usual deductions. "I usually just ask a friend in accounting to go over that for me," Sheila Wallen said in her drawn-out way. "It's too complicated to understand."

But Susan's eyes were already flicking down the chart like an optical reader. "Well, I can see that payroll is deducting as if I had been earning this salary all year," Susan said. "In fact, this is already July. So they're over-withholding by about four thousand dollars."

"My Gawd," Sheila Wallen said. "You just did that *in your head?*"

"Well, where else would I do it? I could teach it to you in ten minutes."

"Wuhhh?" Sheila Wallen said with exaggerated dumbness. "I know that the people in accounting can do it. I just never saw anyone in a designer dress who could do it. Can you do that with all kinds of numbers?"

"Sheila," Susan said with a smile, sitting down on an orange cotton-covered love seat, "don't let this little thing impress you. I used to work with really hard problems of generating random numbers. I used to work with people who could keep logarithms in their head and simplify quadratic equations in the shower. This is nothing special."

Sheila Wallen looked positively ecstatic and shook her head in the peculiar way that people do when they mean to say "yes" with extreme emphasis. "Madame Boss," she said, "if you can carry these things off at meetings, you've got a long way to go. We have a saying here. 'Whoever controls the numbers controls the meeting. Whoever controls the meeting controls the deal. Whoever controls the deal controls the picture.' You follow me?"

"I follow you," Susan said, "but what happens to the woman who controls the picture?"

"It hasn't happened yet," Sheila said.

A few minutes later Susan-Marie went through her next three messages. One from Herb Melnikoff, who was studio coordinator for the United Jewish Welfare Fund. Apparently, he had come through the hall earlier and seen that Susan had Schmooey's office. He had learned from Sheila that Susan was a Gentile, and he was eager to get her involved with the UJWF. "They love to get the occasional Christian to sit at their dinners and watch slides of irrigating the Negev desert," Sheila told her. "Go to a few of them. You'll die of boredom if you go to any more."

The next message was more interesting. It was from Brooke Halpern in the Secretariat of Administration. The message had apparently been very carefully dictated to Sheila. It said that there had been a "deplorable error" about Susan's office in Building H. Without apologizing, the message then said that there was now an office available for her in Building G, which was across from Building H, and which Susan should go and check to see if it was satisfactory.

Susan-Marie crumpled that one and threw it into the wicker wastebasket.

Then she noticed the blinking button on her telephone. Sheila pressed it and picked up the receiver. "Paul Belzberg calling from Mexico," she said with thinly disguised interest.

"I'll take it in my office," Susan-Marie said. She walked

to her desk, picked up the receiver, and looked out the window. There was a series of seashell noises and then Paul Belzberg was on the line.

"Listen," Paul said, "we're just between takes, but I hear you're all set up there in the Main Executive Building. Don't you love it?"

"I love it."

"I couldn't be there when you arrived," Paul Belzberg said. "I had to see this week's shooting."

"Thanks for letting me know in advance."

"It just came up at the last minute," Paul Belzberg said. "Don't be mad at me. It's just business."

"I'm not mad at you," Susan-Marie said. "I was surprised, but Sid Bauman took care of everything."

There was a pause and then Paul Belzberg said, "Listen, there's a big conference at the Santa Barbara Biltmore next weekend. Maybe you could go there with me. Give us a chance to learn more about each other."

"I'd love to, but Sid has asked me to go over some marketing plans that Schmooey Lipsher left behind," Susan-Marie said. "I hope you won't take it personally. It's just business."

"You're a fast learner," Belzberg said. "Listen, I really mean it. I really did have to come down here suddenly just to make sure everything was going all right. They were way over budget, and that's the truth."

"I'm sure," Susan-Marie said. "When you get back you can let me know and we can talk about my job. I want to be helpful right away. That's business too."

"I'll be back in a few days," Belzberg said. "Maybe we can straighten this out."

"There's nothing to straighten out. It's just business."

15

GLORY

■

At exactly eleven P.M. Susan-Marie put aside a stack of papers on her teak desk. She laid the marketing reports in one pile. Then she placed the marketing plans for the future in chronological order according to the release date of the film. She divided her telephone messages into two piles—those to be returned, like the Women in Film invitation, and ones requiring no return, like a second message from Brooke Halpern inviting her to investigate an office in Building G in the back of the lot.

Then she took out a lace handkerchief from Lord & Taylor and brushed off her desk. She studied her office in the perfect silence of late evening in an office building. It looked like a spaceship of power and status that would take her to any planet of creativity she wished to visit.

Next, she flipped off the desk lamps, the floor lamps, and the indirect lamps hidden behind the bookcases.

There was no overhead fluorescent light. She closed her door and went out into Sheila's office.

She walked out past Sheila's still-humming typewriter, reached under it, and turned it off.

Far down at the end of the blue-carpeted hallway she could hear the whir of the maids at work cleaning for the night. Charwomen, they were called in the East, but how could anyone working in the clean, sparkling, sootless halls of Republic ever have that name?

Susan-Marie passed by the life-size blowups of movie stills from Republic's past—Joel McCrea and Ronald Reagan as cavalry officers. Joan Fontaine and James Cagney as star-crossed lovers. Humphrey Bogart and Audrey Hepburn as master and servant. She walked by Sid Bauman's immense oak door, with its whimsical sign announcing only S. BAUMAN, as if he were an actuary.

She walked down the stairs one flight to the ground floor. There she waved at the guard, a skinny, cheerful young man with a bobbing Adam's apple, listening intently to a baseball game. The announcer's voice barely escaped from his earpiece. She waited while he silently opened the door, then saluted her as she walked out into the Los Angeles night.

Susan headed across the lawn to her/Paul Newman's parking space. Aside from a few fugitive sounds, the night in Burbank was as quiet as the night in Idabel, Oklahoma. The buzz of crickets sounded faintly, almost like background noise on a tape, serving only to sharpen anticipation of more distinct sounds.

As Susan rounded a corner and located her Mercedes, she could see a thick shaft of bright blue light coming from the back lot. It stood out clearly from the surrounding darkness, as if it were an Athenian pillar in the Acropolis night. No, it was far larger than a pillar. It was a temple of light arising on the dark hillside of the Capitoline.

From the direction of the light came the faint sound of music and laughter. Susan stopped thinking about her luncheon with Bryan Fitzpatrick and got into her car. She started it, backed out, and headed down alleyways and tiny avenues toward the light. She passed no other cars, no pedestrians for at least five minutes.

As Susan came upon a sign on the Republic back lot telling her she was nearing a "hot set," she realized she had found the spot.

She parked her car behind a mobile makeup wagon and stepped out into the night air. It was a precisely comfortable temperature, cool and dry and bracing. All around her there was activity. Children were dressed as altar boys in flowing white smocks. At least ten severe-looking men in priestly black paraded by en route to a sprawling, artificial, bombed-out cathedral. Twenty-five nurses in World War II nurse uniforms walked by in a row. Hundreds of peasants in wooden shoes and floppy trousers and dresses strolled toward the ruined cathedral.

Surrounding all of the players was a circling, buzzing orbit of cameramen, boom men, gaffers, sound men, handlers of lighting meters, electricians, and set dressers, all moving with a delightfully relaxed purposefulness. Behind them was still another circle of men and women, who lounged about the set doing nothing but waiting for their few minutes of work—makeup women, costumers, wardrobe mistresses, teamsters, security guards.

From a trailer to the right of the set came a group of men and women who were noticeably thinner and more well-dressed than the others. The director walked over to the stars, a priest played by Richard Partridge and a wounded soldier played by Lee Marvin. He talked to them for a few minutes while Susan stared.

A young woman carrying a tray of doughnuts and coffee approached Susan and offered her food. "It's gonna be a long night," the serving woman said. "You in makeup?"

"No," Susan-Marie said, "marketing."

"We don't see too many of you people actually coming onto the set," the woman said. She had a friendly, open face. She wore jeans and a T-shirt and no makeup. In her wholesome look, she was a million miles away from the faces Susan had seen around her at the executive dining room of the commissary at lunch. "Mostly you people are out at some fancy restaurant or else home reading scripts," the woman said.

"I'm new," Susan said. "This is my first day."

"Well, enjoy it, because if your pals in the Taj Mahal see you here, they'll never let you out here again." The woman had a smile on her face and in her brown eyes.

"I can't believe it," Susan-Marie said. "This is the best thing at the studio. Is there something like this every night?"

"Not every night on the lot. But somewhere in town, just about every night, either for movies or TV, we've got something going."

"This is like a party," Susan said, as red lights like ambulance warnings began to circle and flash. "It's like a party where everybody's invited."

"Except that you have to be in the union to even get a ticket."

"I'm in the union," said Susan-Marie.

"If you're in the union," the woman said, "and if you're over in the Main Exec building, you're in the shark union."

An amplified voice said, "Quiet on the set," and there was utter quiet. Then the same voice said, "Give me speed." An answering voice said, "Speed."

Then in front of the altar of the set, a stagehand clicked a clapboard and said, "*Wilderness,* take three. Quiet on the set."

In front of the altar the wounded soldier carried a small, bandaged boy in his arms. A spotlight struck a brass cross in the night sky, casting highlights into the darkness. Behind the soldier came a priest, also carrying a wounded child. Then, slowly, somberly, an entire parade of nurses and priests approached the cross with wounded children in tow. Behind them, the villagers were stretched out by the light of huge bonfires that suddenly flared out of the

168

night. The camera panned across the line of the wounded and their helpers, and then across the somber, dirtied faces of the peasants.

"Father, how could this have happened? How could God let these little children . . ." the wounded soldier started to ask the priest in a faltering but angry voice.

The priest handed the wounded child to a nurse and then stroked the face of the child in the soldier's arms. "Your quarrel is not with God, my son," the priest said. "Your quarrel is with man."

That scene was reshot six more times between eleven o'clock and one-thirty A.M. Susan stood riveted, watching, for the entire time. Twice, a rugged, bearded gaffer approached Susan and offered her a beer. He was a handsome, confident man, but Susan-Marie shined it on. Let Deirdre do her worst and let Fitzpatrick tell her scare stories. Nothing would move her now that she had found her home.

P·A·R·T

IV

16

NECROMANCY

When I look back from the vantage point of seven years, Susan's triumph at Republic comes into far clearer focus. At the time, hearing about it from Susan-Marie, reading occasional tidbits in the newspapers, then viewing it from the scene (yes, I too moved to Hollywood), the whole sequence was confusion. There were random bursts of light and shadow, seemingly unconnected with each other, simply the gropings of four people to establish their lives. But in retrospect, knowing what I have heard in late-night conversations with Susan-Marie, sickbed confessions from Sid Bauman, and relayed confidences through new friends about Paul Belzberg and Deirdre Needle, the blur takes on meaning and order.

Now I see the whole sequence as a ballet. The steps are a perfect blend of energy and control and imagination. The players are attached to their movements inevitably.

Even death is camouflaged in swaying grace until the very end. The arguments, shouting, persiflage, and heartbreak appear as glissades, tour jetés, pas de quatres.

As in a ballet, the action is choreographed and every step charged with meaning. But unlike a ballet, the movement of Susan-Marie Warmack in Hollywood was not plotted by Perrot or Diaghilev, in salons or theaters in St. Petersberg or Paris or Vienna. The choreography of Susan-Marie's ascent was made in the human heart, and crafted out of a long-buried need. Finally, as in a ballet, the motivations and action are explained partly by character, partly by what has happened before, but in Hollywood, as in *Giselle,* much of what becomes of a woman is the result of witchcraft, spells, and destiny.

* * * *

The day after Paul and Deirdre returned from Zihuatenejo, Susan-Marie had to discuss printwork for *Trade-Off* with Marco Castro. As she walked along a white gravel path with him, Sid Bauman came around a stucco corner. Castro stopped talking to Susan and grinned at Sid Bauman.

"Don't let me stop you," Sid Bauman said. "I hear Susan has become a meteor."

"No meteor," Susan-Marie said. "Just a working stiff."

"Ahh, the working masses," Sid Bauman said. "The revolutionary proletariat."

"She's hot, Sid," Marco Castro said. "She hasn't been here long enough to get spoiled. She still knows about the country outside."

"East of Burbank?" Sid Bauman asked in mock surprise. "My good doctor, you mean to tell me there's life east of here?"

"Ticket-buying life," Susan-Marie said with a laugh. "In other words, intelligent life."

At just that moment Paul Belzberg stepped out through the French doors of the Main Exec building, talking animatedly to Deirdre. Paul wore a tweed sport jacket with leather elbow patches. He looked like a harried professor escaping from a particularly tenacious assistant dean of administration. He said, "Look, I can either make the picture or make the deal for the next picture."

Deirdre said, "You have to do both."

But neither of them said another word, because then they saw Susan-Marie, Sid Bauman, and Marco Castro talking cheerfully in the sunshine. Paul Belzberg's jaw dropped minutely, then he set himself into conversational position and walked over to Susan-Marie. He started to kiss her on the cheek, but she held out her hand at too great a distance for him to do that. Behind Paul, Deirdre sidled along, looking as if she were about to be introduced to the groundskeeper.

"Susan," Paul Belzberg said, "I hear you're burning the place down. I'm sorry I wasn't here when you arrived."

"It was okay, Paul," Sid said. "We had a problem with the office accommodations. Someone on Deirdre's staff screwed up."

"You're kidding," Deirdre said, deadpan. "Can I help?"

"It's all taken care of, thank you," Susan-Marie said. "How was shooting in Mexico?"

"Is this for your plan of advertising the movie?" Deirdre asked. "I hear you've just about taken over."

"Not in front of Marco," Sid Bauman said.

"Were you able to make the sandstorm come off all right?" Susan-Marie asked.

"Think you might be able to make a campaign around that sandstorm?" Deirdre asked. "Planning ahead?"

"The sandstorm was great." Paul smiled. "Dickie Daumit did a great job."

"Do we have marketing people in the rushes now?" Deirdre asked. "Is Susan-Marie working on that now, too?"

Sid Bauman scowled. "Deirdre, have you had any rest since you got back from Mexico? Aren't you feeling well?"

"I feel terrific," Deirdre said. She was so angry that she

couldn't close her lips. Her teeth were bared and gritted between her thin lips.

"Well, why don't you just listen for a minute instead of making jokes?" Sid Bauman said. "Susan-Marie had a few ideas about *Trade-Off* that were pretty strong."

"I'd love to hear her ideas," Deirdre said. "It's so much fun to hear how everybody thinks she knows Hollywood better than the pros."

"I think in this case maybe it's true," Sid Bauman said. "I love her ideas."

"My housekeeper has incredible ideas for reaching the Mexican-American market," Deirdre said.

"That's enough," Paul Belzberg said. "That's plenty, Deirdre."

"Just trying to help. My housekeeper's already here. We wouldn't have to fly her out or anything."

"We have to go," Paul Belzberg said.

"I'm going to tell Schiller over in comedy development about you." Bauman winked at Deirdre.

"We have to go," Belzberg repeated. "I'm going to come over to talk to you this afternoon, maybe around four. See what you've been up to."

"No, you have dailies at four," Deirdre said acidly.

"We'll change the fucking dailies," Belzberg snapped.

"It's too late," Deirdre said evenly.

"I agree," Susan-Marie said.

■　　■　　■　　■

A few days later Sheila Wallen wore black pajamas to the office. She also wore a straw conical hat from a Pearl Buck novel. She walked into Susan-Marie's office and plunked down a memorandum addressed to Sid Bauman. From Deirdre Needle. Copying Paul Belzberg and Susan-Marie Warmack.

"In the interests of administrative review, I would like to be certain that all occupants of the Main Executive Building need to be there. This particularly applies to persons in the marketing area. I am planning to centralize all marketing functions in Building G to cut down communication time and optimize creative interaction. May I please have your comments on this as soon as possible?"

"What about it, Madame Boss?"

Susan-Marie took from her pocketbook a package of Viceroys. Next to them was a gold cigarette lighter. Well, really, it was imitation gold. It had a plastic laminated photograph of Dick Nixon on one side and Patricia R. Nixon on the other side. On the top was a lid in the shape of an elephant. Susan rolled Deirdre's memo into a cylinder, held it over a yellow marble ashtray, then lit it. The flames and smoke were drawn away through the powerful air-conditioning ducts in the ceiling. "This lighter's from the man I used to work with in Washington," Susan said.

"I see."

"Physics," Susan-Marie said. "Matter can be neither created nor destroyed. Unless it's a memo from Deirdre Needle."

■   ■   ■   ■

That night Susan worked until after eleven o'clock. She then packed her papers into a Mark Cross briefcase. It had been a gift from the Hollywood Central Printers to Schmooey Lipsher. It had arrived after his departure. "Take it," Sid Bauman said. "I guarantee you Republic's paid for it."

Susan walked over to the back of the lot. The set of *Stained Glass* was still "hot." It still emitted a bluish glow into the Burbank night. Susan had been coming to watch every night for a week. She usually stood by the makeup trailer until her friend Jodie appeared. Jodie was the woman who had offered her coffee, doughnuts, and a warning her first night on the set. Usually the routine was just that Jodie introduced Susan to a few of the gaffers and the lighting assistants and the teamsters. They ate fragments of doughnuts. Then Susan left—alone. Susan felt closest to her reasons for being in Hollywood when she was on the set. It was difficult for her to drag herself away even after midnight.

Tonight a blazing tank was being made to careen toward a group of huddled, frightened children crouching next to the cathedral wall. After the second try Susan said to Jodie, "It's so real it makes me frightened. I keep trying to think what those children have had to go through and then they have to worry about this tank. It's a fantastic effect."

"You could almost believe you were there," said Jodie.

"The looks on the kid's faces though," Susan-Marie said. "They don't look beaten enough. They look like they're scared of losing a game. Not like they're scared of losing their lives."

"They just don't look tired enough," Jodie agreed. After a minute of silence Jodie spoke again, in a different tone of voice, without looking at Susan. "My father was taken away from his home at bayonet point by the SS in Lodz in 1939. He and his mother and father and brother were put in a cattle car. My grandfather was dead of starvation by the time they got to Auschwitz.

"When they got off the train the kapos just threw my grandfather's body into a pile of other bodies. My father pinched his cheeks and his little brother's cheeks to make them look healthy, like they could work. The guards, Poles, put my grandmother in one line and my father and his brother into another line. My father's little brother started to cry, so a guard asked him if he wanted to go over and stand with his mother. He looked up at my father and my father said, 'Sure. Fine. After the showers we'll meet outside.'

"My father went into a building and got deloused. Then he waited for a minute by the door of the building his mother and brother had gone into. A guard says, 'What are you doing, Jewboy?' My father says he's waiting for his mother and his brother. The guard knocks my father down and points at the smoke coming out of the building. 'They're up there, Jewboy,' he says."

Jodie Sugar said this in a surprisingly animated tone. Susan-Marie was too stunned to speak. "From what my father told me, I know those refugee kids don't look tired enough or hollow enough. But I did their makeup, and I didn't want people to see that kind of look," Jodie Sugar said. "Maybe I was wrong."

Susan-Marie held her arms against her sides and said, "No, you're not wrong. Movies aren't life."

"That's what I thought. Movies are something bigger. When my father got out of Europe in 1945 and got to Canada, the first thing he did after he got through immigration was to go to the movies in Ottawa. A rerun of *Gone With the Wind*. He said when he got into the theater and the picture went up on the screen that was the first time he knew the war was over."

■　　■　　■　　■

After about three weeks on the lot Susan-Marie was called to a meeting with Bron Gless, the producer of *Lips*, a movie about a woman with supernatural kissing powers. It was to star Elvis Presley, and it was still in early development. The King was holed up at Graceland, and there was some doubt about whether he would bother to tell MGM that he wanted out of the deal there.

Susan was shown into a cottage on the lot. In the cottage a middle-aged man with a sharply pointed beard and a pale, emaciated face talked animatedly into a telephone. Behind him were two posters advertising two of his movies, *Snowslide* and *Deep End*. Neither one had been a success. The man was apparently talking about how he wanted his swimming pool finished. "No," he said. "Not Palos Verdes stone. Gray flagstone. Dark. I can always hose it down."

Susan sat on a white couch and waited for ten minutes to discuss any marketing ideas he and she might cook up. In that time he took two more calls, made one, and got up to feed his parrot birdseed. After fifteen minutes Susan pointed at her watch.

Bron Gless held his hand over the receiver and said to Susan, "Talk to the parrot until I get through with this call. Please."

Susan looked at Gless for ten seconds, then picked up her notepad and walked out of the office.

When she got back to her office, Bron Gless was on the phone for her. "Tell him whatever it is, tell it to the parrot," Susan-Marie said. "If the parrot has any good ideas, I'd like to hear them. I'll be free in about a month."

The next day Bron Gless called Marco Castro to complain about Susan-Marie's attitude. After Marco heard the story he told her, "If it happens again, shoot the bird first, then Bron."

■   ■   ■   ■

On the Friday of his first week back in town Paul Belzberg came to see Susan-Marie. Sheila showed him in. On this day she wore blue denim coveralls and a stevedore's hat. Paul Belzberg wore a well-fitting blue suit and a striped shirt with a blue necktie. He sat on the yellow couch across from Susan's desk and said, "I'm sorry, Susan. What more can I say?"

"What are you sorry for?"

"For a lot of things. For being in Zihuatenejo when you got here. For not talking to you from Mexico. For Deirdre acting the way she did."

"I'm getting along all right," Susan-Marie's voice was pleasant. "It was a mystery, but I'm getting along fine now, thanks. A lot of people here have been very kind to me."

"So you think you're just about getting the hang of it?" Paul Belzberg asked.

"Just about." Susan-Marie had not moved from her desk. Her hands were starting to shake. "I think I'm learning a lot of things I didn't know about the business."

"Like what?"

"I'm discovering some real surprises." She got up from behind her desk and walked over to a French door. The sun coming in off Pass Avenue backlit her black hair and caught a deep spark from her dark blue eyes. "I'm learning that you can meet a man at the White House and that man can look at you as if it meant something, as if it meant a lot, and then the man can come down to your office and promise you the moon and change your whole life around. I'm learning that that guy can take you out of the town you grew up in and move you across the country and get you jacked out of your mind so that you think something big is really going to happen, and then that man can go out of town when you get here and not call for ten days. And when he does get in touch he can make you a proposition over the phone and then when he sees you for the first time, he can have his mistress dump all over you. He can let his mistress dump all over a woman who's just trying to get along as if that woman were a beggar in the street." Susan's voice had become angry and deep. "I'm learning that the man who showed the whole world so much about human feelings in a few movies must have gotten the ideas from someone else, because he sure doesn't have too many himself."

She took a deep breath and walked to the yellow love seat across from the couch where Paul Belzberg sat. "So that's what I'm learning," she said. "You think I've missed much?"

"Not much."

"I'm sorry. I'm a numbers person. I'm not a diplomat. Remember, you met me at the White House. Not at the State Department."

"I remember where I met you." He hesitated before he spoke again. "It's complicated."

"It always is."

Susan-Marie was determined not to light a cigarette. She was determined not to shout. She picked up a copy of the Annual Report of the Republic Corporation and flipped through the pages, pausing to look at a bar chart of Republic earnings. They were up.

"The way I looked when I saw you in the White House," Paul Belzberg said. "That was real."

"So you say," said Susan-Marie, looking at a graph of motion picture revenues. They were down.

"My life has been in a confused way for a long time. I've done pretty well here. Damned well," he said.

"Very interesting," Susan-Marie said icily.

"Don't be sarcastic."

"Don't tell me how to talk. You're the head of the motion picture division. You're not the head of the Gestapo. You can't tell me how you want to talk. If you don't like the way I talk, fire me. Get your little pal Deirdre to fire me. Or be a man and do it yourself."

"I'm not going to fire you. You're under Sid's protection now, anyway."

"I won't go running to Sid if you fire me. If I'm not needed here by you, I'll just leave. It's one thing to fight to get a decent office when a jealous woman screws me over. It's another to stay when the man who brought you out here fired you."

"That was terrible, what Deirdre did."

"You didn't lift a finger to help."

"I didn't know about it," Belzberg said. "If I had known, I wouldn't have allowed it. It's complicated."

"You didn't have a clue? How well do you know Deirdre? Who do you think you're talking to? Maybe you should just get into her corner and stop trying to play both sides."

"Look, I said it was complicated. I thought she'd try something. I didn't know what it would be. I'm telling you, it's complicated. I owe a lot of what I've been able to do to Deirdre. She pulled me together when I'd had a lot of bad breaks. That's even been in the magazines."

"A capable woman. You were lucky to find her."

"I also owe a lot of not knowing where the hell I am to her. I owe her a lot of confusion about what's going on. You saw the characters in *Mother* and *Estonia*. You know the people in my work. You know they're me. You know when I get confused I really take a lot of wrong turns."

"Very unusual for a head of motion pictures," Susan-Marie said, tossing the annual report on the glass-topped table in a gesture of dismissal.

Belzberg picked up the report, glanced at it for a moment, then neatly tore it in two before Susan's eyes. "I'm a very unusual guy," he said. For the first time Susan laughed.

"Don't be so hard on me," Belzberg said. "You don't have to be so cold—"

But Susan-Marie cut him off. "Look, don't you dare tell me to not be hard on you. I'm out here three thousand miles from home and anybody who cares whether I live or die. You brought me here with your looks and your insights and your genius ideas. I had a good job at the White House. I didn't have a big office and I didn't go out to dinner with Jules Stein, but I worked with a guy who cared about me. I got brought out here and if Sid hadn't taken me in, I'd be back in Washington as a bad joke. That's because of you, Paul. So don't tell me not to be cold. You have your problems with Deirdre, fine. You work them out. You want to tell the people who work here how they should feel when they've been treated like dirt? Fine. Fire me. Get a bunch of Koreans. Get a bunch of robots. Don't get me, Paul, because I've got feelings."

Paul pressed his hands to his temples and then wiped his eyes. He started to get up and walk to the door. He actually took two steps toward the door. Then he turned around and walked over to Susan. He stood in front of her and looked down at her. "Could you just stand up for a minute?" he asked. "Please?"

"Why?"

"Please."

Susan-Marie stood up. With her Rayne heels, she was able to look directly into Belzberg's endless brown eyes. Very gently, Paul Belzberg touched Susan's arms and held them as if he were holding a fragile, irreplaceable icon.

"When I think of the hope that it took for you to come out here," he said. "When I think of the faith in me you had just from seeing me in my movies. When I think of the love and the hate you must feel right now I feel like being here with you in this room is the only place in the world that I ever want to be."

Then he deliberately moved his head forward and kissed her. He kissed her for a long time and then pulled her toward himself and held her. When he released her his eyes were damp. "I've been terrible," he said.

"I know it." Susan-Marie stood next to him and laid her head on his shoulder.

"That person who made *Estonia*," Susan-Marie said. "Is that you, Paul, or is that someone else? I have to know."

"I hope it's me," Paul Belzberg said. "God, I hope it's me."

"I'm not going to be the fifth wheel with you and Deirdre. Even if you are head of the motion picture division."

"I'm not going to take Sid Bauman's leftovers," Paul Belzberg said.

Susan-Marie slapped him across the face with her right hand. She slapped him so hard he reeled backward against a French door.

"Where the hell do you have the right to even ask me about Sid Bauman? Get out of my office. Right now."

Paul Belzberg grasped her wrists and pulled her close to him. "I have the right because Sid Bauman likes you and takes care of you, but I need you. Because Sid Bauman will never feel the way about you I feel. Not ever."

"Sid Bauman will never treat me like dirt, either," Susan-Marie hissed. "And let the hell go of my hands."

"Because Sid Bauman didn't fall in love with you the minute he saw you," Paul Belzberg said, "and I did. That's what gives me the right."

Susan-Marie shook her hands loose. As she did, Paul Belzberg kissed her again and pulled her toward him. She fought herself free and said, "Get out of my office."

"Because Sid Bauman likes you, but his life won't change because of you. And from now on, you're everything that's ever going to matter in my life, *and you know it, and that's what gives me the right!*"

"I'm not going to be the fifth wheel," Susan repeated. "I didn't come here to do that. I came here to work on pictures with you, to share something with you, not to be your mistress."

"I promise you, you'll have more than you ever dreamed you would have or I'll die trying. That's from the man on the screen. The one who feels things and says things and means them."

"I don't know, Paul. I don't know if words mean anything to people here."

"You'll see," Paul Belzberg said. "And you've already seen, and maybe words don't mean anything, but you could see how I felt the minute I saw you. You know that. You know how you feel."

For a moment they stared at each other again, then Belzberg pulled her toward him. They kissed again, in front of the French windows.

"It's getting less complicated," he said after a minute.

"You'd better be real," Susan-Marie said. "We're playing with something important. Something that could hurt if you're not real. So you'd better be real, and I'd better think about it. You could hurt me, Paul. I'm telling you, you could hurt me a lot."

"I never will," he said. "Never again. I don't expect you to believe me, but I never will again. Don't trust me. See what I do."

"If you're lying to me, Paul," she said, "if you're lying to me . . ."

But she didn't finish because she didn't know what she would do if Paul were lying to her.

■   ■   ■   ■

One month after Susan-Marie drew up a comprehensive plan for marketing *Trade-Off*, she got a memo. Susan's

185

plan suggested concept testing of the four possible trailers, a series of focus groups around the country, general market trend studies for middle-age change-of-life pictures, early market outlook studies aimed at preview audiences, performer familiarity and appeal tests calculating which actor in *Trade-Off* would draw the largest response, recruited previews with word-of-mouth opinion leaders on selected college campuses and in metropolitan areas, key ingredient focus group testing of specific images in the advertisements, and release time alerts directed at specific opinion leaders in the northeast and west.

The document was a hundred and ten pages long. Susan-Marie had drawn upon the expertise of Professor Philip Borosage, the head of marketing at Northwestern University, and Emil D'Antonio, head of statistical sampling at Cornell. She had also spent two Saturdays hiring college students in Westwood to sample other college students about print advertising concepts. Finally, she had called upon Carl Ally to get his response to the trailer she found most provocative.

The memo in response came from Bryan Fitzpatrick. It read, *Here at Republic we can't really get our heads around such complex concepts. As you know, out here we make more money with our ass than with our head. But thanks for the effort.*

Sheila Wallen sat with Susan when she read it. She wore a coal-miner's hat and a painter's smock.

"He's just been given a whole new suite in Building B," Sheila Wallen said. "And two assistants. Courtesy of Deirdre Needle in administrative review."

Susan-Marie looked at the documents and moved her long fingers over them.

"More money with his ass than with his head," Sheila Wallen said.

"He's lucky it works out that way," Susan-Marie said. "He'd have trouble any other way."

■ ■ ■ ■

A few weeks later, Susan-Marie was shifting restlessly around her new apartment on Horn Street, just above Tower Records. The day had been terrible. Angry fights with Marco Castro about the campaign for the negative pickup of *Latigo Bay*, a story from Petrovich about children marooned on an island turning to cannibalism. It was a frank rip-off of *Lord of the Flies*, only with far better production values and both boys and girls on the island. Then there had been the visit from Bryan Fitzpatrick absolutely forbidding her to summarize her proposed ad campaign for *Trade-Off* and put it in the *Harvard Business Review*. Finally, her furniture had still not arrived, so that she ate off the top of a carton and slept on a bed from Abbey Rents.

At about ten o'clock she drove down to Beverly Hills. She wore her jeans and her high-heeled pumps. Her hair was pulled back from her head. She wore bright red lipstick. She went to The Red Onion bar, sat down, and ordered a Tequila Sunrise. The bar was crowded with men with shirts open to the navel, girls in baggy trousers, tight trousers, clown suits, leather jackets with studs.

A man walked over to Susan. He was handsome in a sharklike way. He bared his teeth and wobbled slightly as he approached her.

"Hey, pretty lady," he said, "want some toot?"

"No," Susan-Marie said. "Thank you."

"You new here?" the man said. "You're a foxy lady."

"I'm new here," Susan-Marie said.

"Where you from?" the man said. "I'm from Sacramento."

"I'm from Washington, D.C.," Susan-Marie said.

"You're kidding," the man said. "I used to sell rack overstock on the road up there. It rains all the time there, right? Big forests?"

Susan-Marie spent the night alone.

At five in the morning, when she thought that Arlington Florists would be open, she called them. "From today on," she said, "I want you to put hollyhocks, jonquils, and plain old honeysuckle on my father's stone every Sunday morning. There's no need for a card. I'm the only one they could possibly be from."

After she put down the phone she went to a box she had kept sealed for over five years. She dusted it off, untied a ribbon, and took out a sheaf of her father's letters to her mother.

She worked her way through the ancient envelopes until she found the one she dimly recalled. It was a flimsy blue V-mail envelope, postmarked April 3, 1945. She took the letter out of its envelope and read.

Dear Lady-Bug,

Well, it's been three days of pure you-know-what. We got into Aachen without too much trouble. But on the way out, we ran into a brigade from the Tenth SS Mountain Division who were well dug in on two sides of a small valley. I won't bore you with the details, but we were fighting just to get out of there alive, and forget clearing the valley of the Krauts. The artillery finally got them out, but it was a close-run thing.

I swear that when I get back to Arkansas I'm going to just sit on the porch of Big Daddy's house and rock back and forth for a year. The only time I'm ever going to leave is to go to the picture show to see Clark Gable. Maybe Claudette Colbert, too. Did I ever tell you that you look like her? Only a lot younger and prettier.

A boy from West Point, just one class behind me, got hit by shrapnel from a Kraut 88 when we first got past Aachen. We gave him morphine and he didn't even know he was dying. I swear to you, he was dreaming and he thought he was a kid in the movies. I think he was watching Flash Gordon until he died.

Well, I know you're all alone there in Prescott, but I swear to you that when this war is over, we'll be holding all the aces. I miss you every minute.

Love,
Dale

Susan read the letter four times and held it in her hands while she slept in her rented bed.

■   ■   ■   ■

The next afternoon, while Sheila Wallen was on her break, Susan-Marie looked up from a survey on the fears of American young people. The data were fascinating. They showed—according to the American Enterprise Institute —that young Americans feared not having a job and not having a good standard of living far more than they feared war or big government.

The telephone rang, Susan picked it up herself. The nasal, insistent voice of Deirdre sounded throughout the office. "Listen," she said without preamble, "listen. I'm going to do you a really big favor. Bigger than you know."

"What's that?" Susan asked coolly.

"Our Rome office. We just lost the head of marketing for Italy. It's a plum job. I think I can put you in there. The money's good. The perks are fantastic. It's a good chance for you to learn about the overseas part of the business. I'm sure you'll be a credit to Republic there."

"I'm flattered that you thought of me," Susan said. She lit a Viceroy with her Nixon lighter and took in a puff of smoke. "I'll have to give it serious consideration."

"You better give it goddamn serious consideration. It's a lot better than what you'll get from me next." Then she hung up.

Susan took another puff of her Viceroy, then went to Sheila Wallen's Selectric II and typed.

Dear Deirdre,
    I have decided to try to serve Republic best by continuing to work on marketing here in Los Angeles. But thank you for your vote of confidence.

She copied Sid Bauman and Paul Belzberg and put the letter in Sheila's Out box.

"Can we go to lunch?" Paul Belzberg asked as he lounged on Susan's yellow couch. "To talk about the business?"

They drove out to Venice Beach. It was a Thursday in the fall, and the beach was deserted. They bought corn dogs from a woman with a catering truck, and walked along the cement boardwalk. They walked in silence for a few minutes and then Susan-Marie said, "It's an amazing business. Every business you ever hear about, people say, 'Oh, this is a crazy business,' and then it turns out to be just like any other business. But this picture business really is crazy. You make a picture without any consultation with the people who are going to sell it to the exhibitors, without any talking to the people who are going to sell it to the customers."

"People don't consult anyone before they decide what they're going to dream. I used to think the business was tacky. Money crazy, too Jewish, too lowest-common-denominatored out. So right after I made *Estonia,* I took a job at San Francisco State. Just for a month. Talking about film theory. The CBS station there asked me to come on for two five-minute segments of their morning show to talk about film in American life. 'Boy, this is great,' I thought. Just great. Journalism, TV, reaching *film* lovers, not movie lovers, *film* lovers. So I went to the station and there were two women there with a chimpanzee that could count. The studio audience loved that chimpanzee so much they held him over for a segment out of my two segments. I left for L.A. right from the studio. I didn't stick around for my five minutes. I figured the monkey could have that, too." Paul Belzberg squinted out toward the ocean. "It's all Barnum time everywhere. Washington, Wall Street. Everywhere. The only time it isn't is when you're fighting for your life in a war."

Susan-Marie said nothing.

"I know about your father," Paul Belzberg said. "I know he was a war hero in Germany and in Korea."

"How do you know that?"

"Because your pal from the White House told me. He told me you had hero's blood in your veins. He called me up and told me that before you started here, so I'd know to treat you right."

"You're a slow learner," Susan-Marie said.

"But then I don't forget."

"We'll see."

"When I was a teenager I used to go to sock hops at the National Guard Armory," Belzberg said. "It wasn't much of a place, but I could smell the jasmine coming in the windows. There'd always be some guys from the barber shop waiting around outside in their trucks, hoping for a fight. Inside, the girls would dance in their jeans and their fluffy skirts, with their scarves around their necks and bobby pins in their hair, and a ponytail tied with a ribbon. I'd just look at them. Once in a while I'd dance, but not very often. I'd look at a girl and I'd dream that if I could just take her out in a pickup on a county road and neck with her and smell her perfume, her cheap perfume from Woolworth's, I'd be the happiest boy on earth. No sex. Just her kissing me and making me feel like I belonged as much as Buck or Bill or Tim or any of the other boys, that I wasn't an outsider."

"Did you ever do it?" Susan-Marie asked.

"No, I never did until I met you. I don't mean you're those girls. There's no cheap perfume around you. Nothing but White Shoulders. Nothing but the best. But you're part of the inside. You belong. Just being with you makes me feel like I'm not on the outside anymore. That's the blood in you. You're the girl in my dream, on some torn-up seat of a Chevy truck, out in the moonlight next to a lake somewhere."

"I don't know," Susan-Marie said. "I never felt like I belonged anywhere myself."

"I told you it was a dream. That's where you belong. It doesn't matter whatever you felt before in Silver Spring or at Republic or anywhere. You belong in that dream where I've been keeping a place for you all my life."

"You're a poet," Susan-Marie said. "And what are you in my dreams?"

"I'm the man who takes you out of the cotton swathing in the pyramids and brings you out into the desert sky. Is that good enough?"

Susan-Marie turned white and stared at him. "How could you possibly have known about that?"

"I told you I've been holding that place for you in my dreams all these years. I learned a little bit about you in all that time," he said. "I've been studying you in my dreams."

"Jesus." Susan took his hand. "You'd better not be playing with me, Paul. People who know my dreams can't do that and get away with it."

"Out into the desert sky," he said.

▪ ▪ ▪ ▪

Paul Belzberg opened the door of his Jaguar and stood back to let Susan in. As she sat on the red leather she turned her dark blue eyes up at him. They were so dark, so charged with feeling, that they seemed to eclipse all the light of a California afternoon at the beach.

"Would you like to see where I live?" she asked.

17

INSIDE

■

A sunny afternoon in a light blue room in a rented apartment in West Hollywood. A rented bed next to a sliding glass door facing a lanai. Bamboo shades filter the sunlight into thin shadows across a bedspread of brown and white cotton in the pattern of cocoa leaves. On the lanai, palm fronds blow in the breeze, scraping softly against the glass of the sliding doors. The sun moves lower in the sky and the shadows of eucalyptus leaves grow broader on Susan-Marie's pale, slender legs. The straight lines of bamboo shades cover Paul Belzberg's dark, muscular back.

At three o'clock, the wind comes up from Santa Monica, moves across Century City, through Beverly Hills, into West Hollywood and into Susan-Marie's bedroom. It blows Susan-Marie's hair down from her forehead and across Paul Belzberg's eyes.

Susan-Marie lies in her own dampness and Paul Belzberg's sweat. The air itself in her room is charged with a dry, sweet reassurance. She turns over on the bed so that her back curves into Paul Belzberg's chest. He covers her neck with a thin sheet and then pulls her against him.

Susan falls into a light, dreamless sleep. In her sleep she turns toward him and he embraces her again. Later, she turns so that he can hold her. She stares out the window, through the bamboo shades at the waving palm fronds.

"Are you asleep or awake?" Paul Belzberg asks.

"I don't know anymore," Susan-Marie says.

■　　■　　■　　■

The next day, when Susan wakes up, a messenger is at her door. He has for her a package in a small blue box. Susan opens it in her nightgown. Inside the box there is a gold Audemars-Piguet watch with a ring of diamonds around the face. On its back, in a surprisingly large and elegant script, is the legend, *To Susan from Paul: Forever Young*.

■　　■　　■　　■

At the meeting of Women in Film two days later, the topic is marketing. Darcy Beaupre, Ann Jastrow, Arlene Zeller, and Susan-Marie Warmack are on the panel.

There is talk for forty minutes about large breaks versus small breaks. There is comparison of regional spot TV buys with network household rating point package buys. Then there is a subpanel on "The Essence of Advertising —How or How Many." Darcy Beaupre talks about reaching campus opinion leaders. Arlene Zeller talks about making the media an arm of the studio.

When it is Susan-Marie's turn to speak she says, "I have only three propositions. Movies are dreams made visible. Advertising is part of the movie. Good advertising is the beginning of the dream."

The audience sits dumbfounded for thirty seconds. Then Arlene Zeller, the most powerful woman in Hollywood, the only woman who raises her own money, stands, walks four steps to Susan, and hugs her in front of a crowd that breaks into tumultuous applause. When the clapping finally stops Arlene Zeller says, "Friends and colleagues, bet the whole farm on this woman. She will show us all the way."

■   ■   ■   ■

One week later, on a hot, dry afternoon, when Susan lies asleep, Paul gets out of bed. He walks to Susan's kitchen and takes a glass of ice water. As he walks back to Susan's bedroom, he sees a sheaf of papers spread out on her breakfast table. They are her plan for a marketing strategy for *Trade-Off*.

Paul reads for an hour straight without stopping. Then he gathers them up and takes them in to Susan-Marie.

"Why didn't we use this?" he asks Susan. "This picture is dying."

"Out here we make more money with our ass than with our heads," Susan-Marie says.

The next morning Paul calls in the marketing executives. In a calm voice he tells them the essence of Susan-Marie's plan, then shows them her documentation.

"Why didn't we use this?" he asks. "Is there any reason besides office politics?"

No one has another reason.

"It goes into effect right now," Paul Belzberg says. "Whatever can be used post-premiere is operational right this minute. Susan is in charge of getting it going this morning."

Within the day, time has been bought for Susan's first-choice television spots. They show a man in a lane of commuter traffic on a highway. Suddenly, the man presses a button on his radio. Whirring, rushing music floods his car. The man and his car are suddenly in a futuristic tunnel at fantastic speed. When the man and his car stop, they are on a deserted highway outside a small town, with mountains in the distance. There is a beautiful teenage girl in a torn flimsy cotton dress and bare feet by the side of the road. The man steps out of his car and a voice (Orson Welles's voice) says, "Needing. Wanting. Daring. Danger."

Then a gigantic truck rushes by at deafening speed with its horn blasting and is frozen just before it reaches the man. Lettering flashes on the screen saying *Trade-Off*, and, under that, "Pray that it's not too late."

In the first weekend after the start of the new campaign, box office per screen was up forty percent. After the first week it was up fifty-five percent.

The next issue of *Variety,* one week after the meeting in Paul Belzberg's office, had the lead headline: DREAM GIRL NEW REP MARKETING VEEP.

The first sentence of the story said, "Susan-Marie Warmack, a newcomer from the Nixon White House who stunned the Women in Film meeting last week with her 'Movies are dreams made visible' mini-speech, has been made the new domestic vice-president of marketing at Republic following her last-minute save of *Trade-Off*."

In the third graf, the story continued: "Paul Belzberg, head of the motion picture division, noted that, 'This shows that Republic's long-standing commitment to bringing in quality people wherever we can find them works. It also vindicates Sid Bauman's policy of taking people from outside traditional entertainment industry circles to give us new insights."

In her office in Main Exec Deirdre read the article over and over again. She called Adele Lutz, who had also seen the article.

"I don't really think Paul understands how these end runs can really hurt his career," she said.

"Sometimes men are just so selfish that they don't understand anything," Adele Lutz agreed. She couldn't talk long because she was on her way to Robertson Drive to look at fabrics for new chairs for the Century City offices of National Linen. "You can't always be subtle. You've put up with an incredible amount. You've really been a martyr, and I think it's time you started asserting yourself."

"I just want Paul to be happy," Deirdre said. "I really have no life except what I can do for him."

"I know. But sometimes you have to try to think of yourself, too."

"I'll try," Deirdre said, "but I don't want to stand in his way."

She hung up, thumbed through the *Physician's Desk Reference* for a few minutes, and then called her father in New York. He was in a meeting with the principals of a waste disposal company in St. Louis who needed to raise money.

"I can only talk for a minute, princess," he said.

"I just wanted you and Mom to know I think of what great parents you are every minute."

"Thanks, but what did we do to deserve this call?" Needle asked.

"Oh, it's just that Paul's been giving me a pretty hard time and I wanted people who really cared about me to know I cared about them too. There's too much missed communication," Deirdre said.

"Well, I'll pass it on to your mom. She's up at Bertie's in Sharon, but I'll make sure she hears those kind words, I promise you."

"I'm not being maudlin," Deirdre said. "It's just that a lot of what's been going on lately gives me a far better perspective into what you and Mom gave me."

"Thanks, princess. I'll remember this call."

Deirdre thumbed through her *PDR* and made a list of who else she might call.

■　　■　　■　　■

"It would probably be good if you moved back to your house," Belzberg said. "I'm sure you already know that."

Deirdre stood next to the fireplace in the house on Chalon Drive. She ran her finger across the mantel and

197

looked at the dust. "I really think you ought to fire Elena if she can't even dust this room every day," she said.

"It hasn't been what you would call a love affair for a while now," Paul Belzberg said. He was sweating, even though the air-conditioning had the room temperature at sixty-eight degrees. He lit a Marlboro and inhaled a cloud of smoke. He coughed as he did, not from the nicotine but from a deeper inability to draw breath when he confronted Deirdre Needle.

"You really have to quit smoking," she said. "There is simply nothing good it can do for you. I used to smoke and I quit."

"I've been worrying about *Ladyfingers,*" Paul said. "But you're right. I should quit. I just don't have your discipline."

"No, you don't." Deirdre looked at a marquetry book on the mantel and then tossed it onto the couch. "It's because of that little whore from Washington, isn't it?"

"Don't call her that. She never did anything bad to you."

Deirdre sat down, crossed her legs, folded her arms in front of her, and ducked her head down toward her shoulder blades. "Oh, no," she said. "Not a thing. She only took the only man I've ever loved and stole him away right from under my nose and used every little slut trick in the book to undo all the good I've done for you all these years."

"That's not why this is happening," Belzberg said. "You know that." He coughed again.

"*I know that when I met you, you were desperate and I pulled you together, and when I met you, you couldn't write a good check, and when I met you you thought you were dead, and I pulled you together and brought out every good thing in you, and now you're throwing it away, throwing me away for a cheap fuck,*" Deirdre Needle screamed.

"You know it's not like that. You know it hasn't been right for a long time. You did a lot for me, but the connection just isn't there anymore. You know that." Again, Paul Belzberg could barely catch his breath.

"I know it's not there because that lying little bitch has ruined your life and my life. She doesn't care what people think about you in this town. She doesn't even know how to help you when you're in trouble. Who does she know? Who can she call? What can she do for you? In this whole business, except for Sid Bauman, whom she's probably fucking, too—"

But Deirdre didn't get that last sentence out because Paul lunged across the room, grabbed her by her shoulders, and said, "Shut up. That's enough. Just get out now. Just get out."

Then he let go, turned around, and said, "I'm sorry. But you're going too far. Let's part friends. We're still in business together. That was always the best connection between us, anyway."

"Oh, I'm already packed," Deirdre said. "I packed this afternoon. I'll go back to my apartment on Doheny Drive. I knew this was coming. I've known all about it all along. I hoped you would come to your senses, but you never did. I did a lot for you, Paul."

"I know it," he said. "I'll always be grateful."

"That little whore can never do what I did for you. Never. She knows she can get things out of you like that marketing job. Well, you're in over your head now. When things start piling up don't look for me," Deirdre warned. "Maybe your little mascot will know to work all night to clean things up at the studio. I doubt it. I suspect she does other things with her nights."

Paul Belzberg said nothing.

"I just want to know one thing. What does she know? Who does she know that I don't know? Just tell me that."

"She knows me," Paul Belzberg said. "And you don't."

18

REACH

■

High noon. Susan-Marie and Paul Belzberg on the private beach of dreams come true. Just the two of them walking on the sand, with an endless blue-green ocean flowing gently out to the horizon. The sun strikes their backs and makes happy shadows on crushed coral. Above them, a row of perfectly symmetrical palm trees offers a ladder to eternity. The waves roll and crash, and no one in her right mind would think to look for thunderheads at high noon of such a day.

■　　■　　■　　■

"I think I have a new way to do *Hawaii Kai*," Paul said. He sat with Susan on the deck of the Ojai Valley Inn, overlooking a vast lawn backing onto a hill filled with pines and oaks. He set down his Dewar's on the flagstone terrace. "This time, it's about the woman who finds the young man, but after he betrays her, she still trusts him. When he betrays her a second time she is about to be sucked in, but she goes for a swim to clear her mind. When she's swimming off Kahala Point, she starts to get carried out to sea by a riptide. She gets close to drowning, and all the young surfers standing nearby ignore her. So a guy her own age saves her. And then, when the young guy comes along, she tells him he's a loser. 'If you don't understand about what makes people feel, if you don't have respect for the human heart, if you can't feel except to take, you're not young. You're not even alive,' she says. And she and the older guy go away together back to the real world on the mainland."

"I like it," Susan-Marie said. She held out her hand and held Paul's hand. It was dark in the Ojai Valley. A distinct chill was following the blisteringly hot afternoon. "I like the way it has a happy ending," she said.

■ ■ ■ ■

At the end of the day one week after Susan-Marie moved into Paul Belzberg's house—at least moved in a few changes of clothes—Paul Belzberg and Susan-Marie worked late. They sat at the huge teak desk in Susan's office and spread out the cards that showed how *Hawaii Kai* would be laid out, scene by scene.

"I shouldn't be doing this," Belzberg said. "It's undignified for the head of the motion picture division to actually work on a movie with his hands."

"That's the only way it's going to come out right," Susan-Marie said. "It's your idea. How can anyone else possibly know what he's supposed to do?"

"There are a lot of other studio details I'm supposed to be working on. The contract with Coppola, for example. I'm supposed to be going over that with a team from legal."

"The way you told it to me in Ojai, the woman had a speech she gave to the surfer," Susan-Marie said.

"Right. Now I'd like to just cut it down to three sentences. 'You can't feel anything. You're not young. You're dead.' "

"Perfect. Absolutely perfect. Let the lawyers handle Coppola's contracts. That's why you have lawyers in the first place. That's not what you're here for."

Belzberg said, "I'll buzz Josh Wattles and tell him I'm out of the meeting."

"Now let's talk about the surfer. The bad guy. I have to wonder if that type has enough weight to carry off all the harm he does."

"That's just it. He's *against* type. He seems like such a punk, but he's really a bad, mean guy. That's why we feel so sorry for the woman."

"Then I think we should see that he's doing it out of an evil code of young people on the beach, who don't care at all about people's feelings."

"Exactly. It's the clash of two value systems," Paul Belzberg said. "Young and mean. Old and feeling."

"But then we have to show some young people who really do have good values. Otherwise, we're talking about completely turning off most of the viewers."

"Right. We want to show that the young woman's daughters have good values, and that there are other island kids with good values, and maybe they've been just as screwed over by the beach kids as the woman is. We want the good kids to be the proxy for the kids in the theater."

"All right," Susan-Marie said. "Now, maybe we ought to think about why the woman is in Hawaii in the first place. Maybe we should start it back in Ohio, where it's raining and it's cold, just to show that we're seeing a moment of paradise in her bleak life. . . ."

■　　■　　■　　■

One morning in November, right after the election, I watched Richard Nixon on the television news. He walked along the shore in San Clemente, wearing an electric-blue jacket, black trousers, and black wing-tip shoes, which occasionally got splashed by the waves. They had apparently not been fully advanced by the Committee to Re-Elect the President.

In the background Tom Brokaw explained that the president had just ordered all White House staffers to turn in their resignations, so that he could decide how he wanted the next four years to go with a clean slate. I felt a queasy feeling in my large intestine.

I watched Richard Nixon in the sunshine for a few minutes, then walked out into a cold rain. I got into my pitiful dark blue Subaru and headed west on Virginia Avenue on my way home. As I walked across the small, sodden grass strip to my back door, I could hear the phone ringing. I opened the door, shoved aside my howling weimaraner, and answered the telephone.

"This is the best place in the world," Susan-Marie said. "When can you come out here and see it?"

"I wish I could come tomorrow," I said. "Did you hear about what R.N. is doing to us loyal staff guys?"

"Benjy," Susan said, "leave all that behind. This is where you can actually get what you want."

"I don't even know what that means," I said. "I do know what 'settling for the best you can hope for without getting into trouble' means."

"You won't believe this," Susan-Marie said. "But you can actually get the things you want here. It doesn't come right away, and it's a fight to keep Deirdre away from my throat, but I think the worst is over."

"Get me out there right away," I said. "Can't you figure out a way?"

"How would you like to speak to a meeting of Women in Film?"

"When?" I asked, watching the sheets of rain seep through the ancient Georgetown masonry into my kitchen.

"How about tomorrow? That might be a good day."

"That would definitely be a good day," I said. "I'm off

to Dulles as soon as the dog-sitter arrives. Tomorrow would be a perfect day."

■   ■   ■   ■

At four-thirty that afternoon, Bryan Fitzpatrick had the flash figures on the release in New York, Boston, and Philadelphia of *Ladyfingers,* a black picture that had cost five million dollars for a negative pickup, a record figure for that time. Republic had put another three million against it in advertising pressure. The interest was almost a million. For a negative pickup of a black audience picture, Republic had an awesome investment. From what Bryan Fitzpatrick knew, and what he immediately passed on to Deirdre, Republic had an awesome loss. There were no lines on Lennox Avenue, no lines in Roxbury, no lines on Florida Avenue NW, no lines on Chestnut Street. The picture was a bomb. It was a mark of pure error and bad judgment against Belzberg.

Paul Belzberg got the news at six in the evening and took it well. It was a bad one, but perhaps something could be put together. Sid Bauman would be angry about it, because he did not trust the whole black exploitation phenomenon to start with. "Let's just say we'll ride with it," Belzberg said. "I should've put Susan in charge of the marketing instead of leaving it with Ann Jastrow, but that's water over the dam."

Susan and I sat with him at the first banquette inside the front door at Chasen's. He looked noticeably younger than when I had seen him in Washington. He wore a brown suit and a checked shirt, a college professor suddenly cast up in the world of agents and sharks. He also looked worried. To a novice like me, who was unaware of what a motion picture division chief should look like, he looked frightened.

Over and over again, while we talked about the election or the future of motion pictures in a video world, Paul brought the discussion back to *Ladyfingers.* Did we think it could be saved by remarketing it? Could it be recut as a comedy? Could it have a network sale? (Doubtful, since the heart of the story was about the slaughter of black prostitutes while they were committing oral sodomy.) Over and over again, Paul Belzberg, a man whom I would have thought stood at the pinnacle of worldly power and security, approached the *Ladyfingers* failure the way a college student talks about a question on the law boards. Maybe I *did* get it right. Maybe I didn't mark the box I thought.

Over the Hobo Steak and the Chili Chasen's, Paul Belzberg wanted to know how I thought Sid Bauman would react. How could I possibly know? How did Susan think that Sid Bauman would react? ("He won't like it, but he's a crapshooter. He knows you sometimes get boxcars." I was impressed at how quickly Susan had picked up the gambler's lingo.)

While we gasped at the flambé fumes and talked about success and failure, Deirdre Needle's perfect day unfolded.

At five o'clock, after hearing about Paul Belzberg's embarrassment with *Ladyfingers,* she consulted her *PDR* and her Merck manual again. Then she carefully counted out seven Dalmane. No, that was too many. She threw three into the toilet. Then she swallowed four. She also took two five-milligram yellow Valium. She took the remains of the Dalmane bottle, which had originally held fifty capsules, and flushed them down the toilet. She left the bottle—on its side—on her Carrera marble vanity in the bathroom. She did the same with a bottle of Valium that had originally held fifty of the pills.

Then she called Adele Lutz, who was due at five-fifteen, to make sure she would be on time. If she was going to be late, Deirdre would have to make herself throw up. But Adele was on time, had left "*sa casa*" right on time, so the housekeeper said.

Deirdre went to her bedroom. She made sure the letter to Paul was in plain view, with the words, "Good-bye. Without you, the entire point of my living is gone. I only lived to help you, and now you no longer need my help. I hope Susan-Marie loves you as much as I did. I do not hate you. In fact, I will always love you. . . ."

Deirdre also left out Paul's daily schedule, so Adele would know what to do. She even circled the part saying he would be dining at Chasen's.

Then Deirdre unlocked the front door and disarranged the living room, so Adele would know something terrible was in the air. Deirdre even left newsprint on the white silk couch.

Then Deirdre started to feel genuinely sleepy. She fell asleep in less than ten minutes. When Adele Lutz tried to rouse her she was groggy and unresponsive. Adele had her over at the Emergency Room at Cedars-Sinai in five minutes, propping her up on the front seat of her Coupe de Ville. "I'll kill that son of a bitch with my own hands," Adele Lutz said. "I swear I'll kill him."

Deirdre only moaned.

Do not underestimate Deirdre. She had picked two drugs for "overdose" that were completely water-soluble. That meant she could be given Antabus I.V. and would not need her stomach pumped. She could get into the room with the needles in her, with the heart-lung, blood-gas monitoring equipment attached to her within minutes, and still sleep pleasantly. Deirdre was an intelligent woman.

The hospital public relations director for nighttime operations recognized Deirdre's name immediately. Very special handling. If she did this right, she was a lock to get into the Republic P.R. department. She talked for a few minutes to Adele Lutz, who told her she must call Paul immediately at Chasen's. "Don't bother her parents," Adele Lutz said. "They're saints. They're old people. Her grandmother couldn't take it. They shouldn't have to be tortured because this *momser* behaved like a common criminal."

■   ■   ■   ■

Jerry Technopolis, the captain at Chasen's, approached our table at about nine o'clock, just as we were considering whether to order the flambéed cherries or the flambéed bananas for dessert. He bent over in his dinner jacket and asked Paul Belzberg if he might have a word with him.

Paul smiled at us and said, "It's probably in the *Reporter* that I've been canned and they need the table for the new production chief." He got up and walked to the small, oblong lobby, where he picked up the telephone.

When he returned to the table a few minutes later he looked shaken. He said, "Deirdre's in the hospital. She's tried to kill herself."

Susan-Marie looked down at the table and then held her face in her hands. "How horrible," she said. But her face was working. I could see that she was torn about saying anything.

For my part, I was tempted to say, "This I've got to see." But I said nothing. I was a guest, a stranger in the small town of Hollywood.

"Now, I think I'd better go over and see her. A woman from the hospital said there was a note and it talked about me."

"And me?" Susan-Marie asked.

"I don't know."

"Benjy and I'll take a cab home," she said. "Just go on and call me when you get back and let me know how it is."

We skipped the flambéed fruits. In the taxi I started to tell Susan a memory from David Paglin's psych class, where I sat across the classroom from Deirdre. The memory was about Dr. Paglin's lesson on how attempted suicide was always meant as a gesture of control rather than as a gesture of abandonment.

"It's possible," Susan-Marie said.

"Susan," I said, "I've known this woman through my cousin Laura for all my life. It's more than possible."

"Still," Susan-Marie said, "she was desperate. You have to be sorry for her for that."

"No, you don't. I'm not worried about her right now. I'm worried about you."

"Don't worry about me," Susan-Marie said. "I'm all set. I hope it won't be too awful for Paul. He's a big wheel, but he really isn't that tough."

■　　■　　■　　■

Belzberg walked down the tiled hallway at Cedars-Sinai. He took the elevator up to the fifth floor. He got off and walked where the public relations woman told him to go. He passed by all the lithographs that were not only for decoration but were also for sale, nine to four-thirty, at the gift shop in the lobby.

He stood outside Room 5842. The door was closed. He turned around to see a reproduction of a Chagall watercolor in deep blue of angels dancing with donkeys. Next to it was a Cezanne of a man preparing to ascend a gallows. The title was *L'ame pendu.* The Hanged Soul.

Perfect for a hospital, Belzberg thought, where the soul was always in torture from the weakness of the body and vice versa.

Mrs. Chernin, the public relations officer, appeared, wearing a light blue smock. She smiled at Paul as if she were welcoming him to a bar mitzvah. "She's sleeping now," Mrs. Chernin said, rubbing her hands together. Her blond hair was tied in a bun behind her head.

"What's her condition?"

"She's not in any danger right now," Mrs. Chernin said. "But we have a night nurse in there watching her, just in case."

"Can I go in?"

"Of course, Mr. Belzberg. By the way, the campaign you people did on *Respectable* was incredible. I'd surely be grateful for the chance to talk to you about that some time."

In the room Paul Belzberg saw first the outline of a tall, overweight nurse, apparently attaching a new I.V. needle to Deirdre's left wrist. Paul stood next to Deirdre and took the right hand that had in the past offered such welcome and unwelcome control on nights like this. Deirdre opened her eyes.

"Paul," she said. "Paul."

"Yes," he answered.

"Next time," she whispered, "do me a favor, okay?"

"Anything," Belzberg said.

"Don't bring me to the hospital. Just let me go."

"Don't say that," he said. "I'll never let you go."

"You already did." Deirdre's smile was pained.

"Well," Belzberg said.

"So I might as well be gone."

"No, don't ever say that."

"I understand what you mean," Deirdre said after a minute. "Just go to Manila. I'll take care of everything."

"Deirdre," he began, but then he did not continue, because he did not know what to say.

"I'll take care of everything," Deirdre repeated. "Everything."

19

FREEFALL

"Don't be too hard on Paul for getting over to Deirdre's so fast," Susan said.

"I'm telling you," I said to Susan, "Deirdre isn't like anyone you know. She doesn't have any rules."

We had gone back to Susan's apartment to get her little 280 convertible. There was a message on her Phone-Mate telling her that she might as well stay at her apartment. "I have to take a seven o'clock flight to Manila," Paul Belzberg said. "I love you." That was on a piece of recording tape.

Susan flinched when she heard Paul's message, but then she shrugged her shoulders. We drove out Sunset Boulevard, then up Pacific Coast Highway, then onto Malibu Canyon Road. It wound and stretched through mountains as if it were Route 80 by the Colorado River between Grand Junction and Glenwood Springs. But it was in the second largest city in America. Coyotes came out of the bushes and watched Susan's red Mercedes fly by. Occasionally a nighthawk shot out of his lair and dipped in front of Susan's headlights, then soared into the night.

"She must have some feelings," Susan-Marie said. "People don't try to kill themselves because they're not feeling anything."

"Deirdre has plenty of feelings," I said. "They're just all going in one direction—toward her, for her, not for anything else. Not ever. She has really intense feelings for taking from other people and giving to herself. A person like you can't even imagine that."

"Thank you," she said, "but I mostly take, too, just the same as everyone else."

"The hell you do," I said. "Susan, I worked with you for a year. You worked every day I worked. Every time we had a fight, you were there on my side. You did that for something that wasn't going to make you rich, that wasn't going to make you powerful, just for loyalty to something that was interesting. Deirdre would never do that. She's totally a bottom-line person. Totally. What's in it for Deirdre? Boom. That's it. That's the whole thing."

Susan turned off onto the Ventura Freeway and we hurtled into the ten-lane ribbon of light that ran north to Santa Barbara. It was almost midnight, but the freeway was choked with cars and huge, terrifying semis. Their drivers blasted Delco air horns as the trucks raced by. The trucks' onrush through the compressed air made Susan's convertible shake and swerve on the road. While we were still inside the city, the wildness of the coyotes and the hawks was replaced by the ferocity of the pitiless freeway.

"Look," Susan said. "I did that work at the White House to get ahead, too."

"You know what I mean. I'm telling you, Deirdre is focused. You're focused, too, but you just come at the whole thing from a different angle. Most people come to Hollywood to make money. Fine. Deirdre came out here to boss people around. I know it. I know Deirdre. I'm telling you. You came out here to get pictures made. You see the difference?"

Susan saw the difference. "Still," she said, "she helped Paul a lot. She really took charge and turned him around."

"Don't defend Deirdre," I said. "It's a waste of time. She doesn't need *your* help to cut *your* throat."

"I know," Susan said. "I'm really defending Paul. Ideally, he shouldn't be visiting her at the hospital. She did some terrible things. But figure it this way: He's head of the motion picture division. He's under pressure every day from fifty different people second-guessing him. The minute he takes the job, everybody in town says he's through. Every time he does something right everybody says somebody else is really responsible. On *Respectable,* Paul gets the awards, but all the gossips say it was some advertising agency somewhere in New York. On *Trade-Off* people say it's me. But then when they blow nine million on *Ladyfingers* everybody says, 'Oh, that's Paul's fault. He was a fuck-up all the time.'

"When you're hustling around Hollywood you're in a crowd. When you get to be head of the motion picture division, suddenly there's nobody with you. You're up front and all of a sudden everybody who was with you is behind you whispering. It's a bad place to be. And Paul's really never been that executive type. He has great ideas, but he's not really ready to take the kind of heat the head of production takes."

"What he gets there is nothing compared with what you're going to get from Deirdre," I said. "She doesn't like losing. You'd better watch out."

"I know. But she's in the hospital now. What can she do to me?"

A semi roared by and shook Susan-Marie's car, washing a wave of chill California night air and smoke over us. "I want to hear about your plans," Susan-Marie said. "For now, I'm in pretty secure shape. I want to hear how you can get yourself out here, too. You think you might work at the *Herald-Examiner?* It needs all the help it can get."

"Susan, I'm telling you, so do you."

"And I'm telling you she's in the hospital. I'm the one with Paul. I'm the one with the momentum, with Paul, with everything. What can she do?" Susan asked as we screamed past Thousand Oaks into the coastal night.

■　　■　　■　　■

Robbie stood at the door to Susan-Marie's office on the second floor of Main Exec. He wore his new dark blue uniform. He was now in the Republic Security Department. He still looked like a surfer, only this time in a policeman's uniform.

Susan's office door was locked. When Susan put her hand on the door Robbie grinned at her and said, "Hi, remember me? I drove you in from the airport."

"What's with my door?" Susan asked.

"You're locked out," Robbie said cheerfully, as if he were giving her directions. "Orders of Deirdre Needle. Locks have been changed. There're some more guys from the security department in there making sure you don't have any contributions."

"What kind of contributions?"

"Or contraband, or something," Robbie said. "Stuff you're not supposed to take with you when you leave."

"What the hell are you talking about?" Susan-Marie said. "Deirdre Needle can't give me orders. Anyway, she's in the hospital."

"Not this morning," Robbie said happily. "She wants to see you right away."

Susan grasped her doorknob and turned. It did not budge.

"I'm going up to Mr. Belzberg's office," Susan-Marie said.

"He's in the Philippines. That's way past Hawaii."

Susan turned her back and ran up the stairs to the third floor. Paul Belzberg's office door was closed and locked. She pulled on it and then ran back downstairs, dashing into Sid Bauman's office. His secretary, Miss Pilkerton, looked at her pleasantly.

"I hear you're leaving us," she said to Susan-Marie.

"You heard wrong. Do you have a line to Sid?"

"Sid's sailing today with President Marcos on his yacht. He can't be reached until tomorrow." Miss Pilkerton wore an *ao dai* and smiled as if she might offer a choice of champagne or orange juice at any moment.

Susan dashed downstairs again. She went to the first floor and into the Ladies' Room. Then she picked up the pay phone and called me at my hotel.

"Don't go see Deirdre," I said. "Leave the lot right now. Call a lawyer. Don't do this yourself. Get a really good lawyer and make sure he's with you every time you see anyone or talk to anyone. I'm coming right over."

"No." Her voice was deep, but it quavered around the edges. "No, I don't need to do that. I never used a lawyer before."

"You never had anything to lose before."

But Susan-Marie had hung up the phone. A moment later she called back and said, "Wait around there. Do you mind? I have to talk to Deirdre, and then maybe you and I'll see a lawyer."

"I know a killer," I said. "John Keker. He was in my class at Yale. He's a killer and a genius. That's what you need."

"No," Susan said. "I just need to reach Paul." She sighed and gave a very small laugh. "It don't come easy."

"I'm telling you, get a lawyer."

"I haven't done anything wrong," she said. "I just need to make one call."

Robbie was waiting for Susan outside the Ladies' Room. "Deirdre really wants to see you," he said. "Let's go and then we'll see what's what."

Deirdre's office was in the annex to Main Exec. It was the essence of industrial utility, actually predating high tech by a few years. The walls were gray. The carpet was a steely gray. On the wall were clocks with digital blue readouts. There were six steel-gray filing cabinets in her office, all ostentatiously marked PERSONNEL RECORDS—CONFIDENTIAL.

Deirdre herself, risen like a revanchist Lazarus, sat at her desk with patches on her wrists and the crooks of her elbows from where she had been fed intravenously. She still looked pale and shaken.

"I'm glad to see you're out of the hospital," Susan said. I am convinced that while you or I might have meant it sarcastically, it was simply not in Susan—those days—to be entirely facetious about it. She really was happy to see a fellow human being out of the hospital, even if that fellow human being was Deirdre Needle.

"You're fired," Deirdre said without preamble. "You're fired as of right this minute."

Robbie stood next to Susan, looking out the window and humming "California Girls" softly to himself.

"You can't fire me," Susan-Marie said. "You're not my boss. I'm in marketing, Deirdre. Paul's my boss."

"I can fire anyone if I find evidence of theft or misappropriation of company property or any act that might require criminal prosecution. That's part of administrative review." She glared at Susan-Marie. "You should have read your contract more carefully."

"I haven't taken a penny," Susan said, "and you know it."

"Really?" Deirdre smiled. "Take a peek at these."

She picked up a sheaf of papers from her desk. They were clearly legal, notarized documents. Deirdre picked one up and waved it at Susan-Marie. "This one describes your conversations with Schmooey Lipsher about continuing his program of payments from suppliers. In other words, kickbacks."

"I've never even met Schmooey Lipsher," Susan-Marie said. "Is this some kind of joke?"

"The next one describes your conversations with a stockbroker at Bache about your insider trading in the stock of Republic based on confidential data that only you could have known, that you did not even share with the other executives at Republic."

"I have never even had an account at a broker," Susan-Marie said. "You made all of this up."

"The third tells about how you paid for the airplane fare of your pal Benjy, that buddy of yours from the White House, with Republic travel money."

"I wrote on the travel order that I would guarantee reimbursement with my American Express," Susan-Marie said. "It's on there in black and white."

"The travel order is attached," Deirdre said. "It says Ben's working on *Ice II*, and you know goddamn well he isn't."

"That's a lie. Where the hell do those papers come from? Who wrote those things for you? Whose signature is that?"

"Your former secretary," Deirdre said. "Sheila Wallen. She felt it was her duty to Republic."

Susan felt the air rush out of her. "Sheila Wallen . . ." she said, and then she actually put up her hands to feel the wall, to see, to be certain that she was awake, that this was not a nightmare.

"Now, I'm going to make a much better offer to you than you deserve," Deirdre said. "If you just resign and leave right now, these papers will go into my safe and nobody but you and me and Robbie will ever know about them."

"Just a minute," Susan-Marie said. "I'm not resigning from anything. This is all trumped up, and I know it's got to violate every right I have."

"I have the affidavits right here. If you want to sue, go right ahead."

"Uh-uh," Susan said, shaking her head. "I want to talk to Paul. I don't need to go to court. I think maybe you were in the wrong kind of hospital."

Deirdre clamped her mouth shut, but her upper lip involuntarily curled upward. "We'll see who winds up in that kind of hospital. Go ahead. Call him. You can use my phone. But after you do, get the hell off this lot and don't ever come back, *and don't you ever even talk to Paul again. Never.*"

"You really must be crazy to think you can get away with this," Susan-Marie said. "You shouldn't be allowed out of the house."

"Just make your filthy little white trash call and then get off this lot before you get arrested," Deirdre hissed.

Susan-Marie saw a blinding white spot in front of her eyes. No time for that now. She pulled herself together, turned on her heel, and walked down to use the telephone in the Ladies' Room again. A huge fat woman in coveralls was using the pay phone. She ignored Susan's pleading eyes and turned her immense back to Susan.

Susan walked outside into the dazzling sun. She ran across the perfect green lawn, that touch of eastern gentility in the Hollywood madhouse, then ran across Barham Boulevard to the Taco Bell. There was a pay phone next to a table of bearded truckers eating burritos for breakfast. The truckers stared at Susan-Marie, who still looked cool and elegant in her blue silk dress and her high heels.

With trembling hands, Susan-Marie put her dime into the telephone, fumbled for her phone company credit card, and waited five minutes while the operator gamely struggled to put through a call from Burbank to Manila. While the phone rang at the Malacanan Peninsula Hotel, Susan looked at her watch. Nine-thirty in Los Angeles. That meant it would be seven-thirty in the evening in Manila. Paul was traveling with a party from Republic. Someone would know how to reach him, and then this nightmare . . . A surly Filipino operator said, "No reply. Call back, please."

In a flash of inspiration, Susan called the Republic office in New York. From a bored operator there, she got the number of Republic's exchange in Manila.

She called again, thanking God for her telephone company credit card. This time a distinctly American-accented woman answered the phone.

"Is Paul Belzberg in?" Susan-Marie asked in a rush.

"He's in, but he's just leaving for a meeting," the voice said. "Can you call back?"

"No. This is Susan-Marie Warmack from the Republic studios in Burbank. I have to talk to Paul Belzberg right now," she said. "It's an emergency."

"Okay, all right. No problem," the woman said. Susan heard the woman say, "Paul, there's a call you have to take," and then she heard the distinct sound of a hand being placed over the receiver, then muffled voices. For an agonizing thirty seconds Susan waited in the sunshine at the Taco Bell. A Mexican-American man in a torn T-shirt leered at her. Then the woman came back on the line.

"Hey, I'm sorry," she said. "I guess I was a little slow. He was just running out the door and he said he'd be traveling, but he'd try to get back to you day after tomorrow, and if it's anything really important, just send a cable to the Malacanan Peninsula Hotel. Do you have that address?"

Susan-Marie hung up the telephone. She walked back across Barham Boulevard to Republic. She did not go into the Main Executive building. Instead, she walked to her parking place. She took her Mercedes keys from her purse and tossed them on the seat of the car. Then she walked back across the grassy lawn toward Barham.

As she stood by the street, waiting for a taxi, she saw Ron Silverman walking toward her. He waved to her and smiled. "Is your car broken?" he asked.

"No, it's working fine," she said.

"You're crying," Ron Silverman said. "You look terrible. What's happened? Come on. Come to my office. Whatever it is, we can fix it."

"There's nothing to fix," she said. "I just want to go home."

"Well, where's home?" he asked. "I'll give you a ride if you tell me where it is."

218

20

MARSHLANDS

■

One week after her dismissal Susan-Marie and I drove west along Route 50 from Washington, through the rolling hills of Prince Georges and Charles Counties, down into the huge valley of the Severn River near Annapolis, and then into the flat plain on the western shore of the Chesapeake Bay.

It was late November. The ground was covered with tan grass. Leafless trees stood out by the highway. In the distance farmhouses watched the traffic of today from the sleep of yesterday.

We pulled up to the toll booth and paid our fifty cents. Then I put the Subaru into gear and headed onto the Chesapeake Bay Bridge. We climbed up a gradual defilement until we were gliding silently on steel trestles over an endless gray current that was the Chesapeake Bay. Below us, one oil tanker moved lazily north toward Baltimore.

To the south a flock of fishing boats with nets hung between their masts rode at anchor. Nearer to the Eastern Shore, small crabbers with sails moved slowly over their catch while men clambered abovedecks wrestling with huge wooden boxes.

The sky was completely gray. It was impossible to tell where the sun was above us. On the gray metal bridge, above the gray water of the Chesapeake Bay, below the gray sky of the Tidewater in November, we were wrapped in the gray cotton swathing of winter in eastern America.

We soared above the Bay for ten minutes, and then gradually descended onto the flat marshlands that make up the Eastern Shore of the Chesapeake Bay.

We turned south past Queenstown and entered the fringes of Caroline County, passing great fields of dead cornstalks, tan against the gray of the sky. The fields would run into the horizon for a mile, and then disappear into a stand of oak and maple trees, likewise dead-looking against the sky. Usually, just before the stand of timber, there would be a farmhouse. Typically, it was made of weathered frame, with a sharply sloping tin roof reflecting the bleakness of the morning, and a forking television antenna struggling to get some purchase on the outside world through the airwaves.

Occasionally we passed a weather-beaten, ancient billboard from another era. One showed a smiling black couple emerging from a 1955 Buick. The legend, in fading white letters, read, WHEN IN CAMBRIDGE, STAY AT THE DUNBAR HOTEL—FOR REFINED COLORED ADULTS.

There was almost no traffic on Route 50, and almost no signs of life anywhere by the side of the road. Once we passed a thresher in the right-hand lane, with a driver in a quilted jacket who waved as we passed by.

"Farm vehicles," I said. "Remember driver training with Mr. Moffatt back in high school?"

"Yes, I remember." Susan-Marie wore jeans and a white sweater with a blue wool coat over them. She sat cross-legged on the seat as if she were an Indian at a council of war, or else a woman mulling a great wrong.

"Remember all the time we had to spend learning about farm vehicles, and what happens if you ever run into a wagon pulled by a donkey?" I asked. "From that class, you would have thought we were going to grow up in the middle of Iowa in 1880."

Susan thought about that for a few seconds and then, for the third time that day, she began to cry. Tears fell down her cheeks, onto her blue coat, and then disappeared. She made no move to wipe them away or to pretend she was not crying.

"This whole Eastern Shore is really amazing," I said. "Did you ever study anything about it?"

"No," Susan-Marie said. "No, I didn't."

"Well, it was the most die-hard slave-holding part of Maryland. I learned that from a kid who used to be my best friend until his parents decided it wasn't dignified for him to have a Jew as his buddy."

"I see," Susan-Marie said solemnly, and then, through her tears, she laughed, and we both laughed together.

"Anyway," I went on, "when the Civil War ended there was the Emancipation Proclamation, freeing the slaves. But the Emancipation Proclamation specifically applied only to the states that were in rebellion, so it didn't apply to Maryland, which did not secede."

"I get it," Susan-Marie said, and then we laughed again.

"For about five years after the Civil War, even after the Twelfth Amendment, there was slavery here. And then, when Reconstruction came to the South and just tore it apart, there was no Reconstruction in this part of Maryland. So life here went on just as it had. This was the most southern part of America for a good long time."

"Ladies and their cavaliers."

"Exactly. There was no way to get here from the mainland except by ferry, and the ferry only went once or twice a day. From the north, you had to go by an incredibly roundabout way. So it was just asleep for a long, long time.

221

When I was a boy we used to have a house we rented for the summer in Rehoboth Beach. We'd take the ferry and go across the bay and stop at a diner in Denton, and then we'd go on our way. I still remember how we'd see the signs in the diner that said 'White trade only' and I had no idea what it meant."

"Very interesting," Susan said, and I think she meant it.

"But now all that segregation is long gone, and all you have here is a place that is somehow outside the mainstream, living quietly just on itself. People here take a long time to do anything, but they don't wake up screaming in the middle of the night."

"How do you know?" Susan asked.

"I know because the land here is too flat, and there are too many trees, and the Bay is just a mile away from anywhere, and in December you can smell the fires from every fireplace in the county when you drive into town to get dinner. Then, after dinner, you just read and then you sleep. That's how I know."

Susan and I drove down through Talbot County, past sprawling tobacco farms, past a silver bullet-shaped diner, into Easton. We had stayed one night in Los Angeles, then five nights in Georgetown, and now Susan and I were going to spend a week at the Tidewater Inn. We registered at the desk in a lobby with alternating black and white marble tiles, gleaming, polished wood paneling, and prints of mallards flying above the marshlands. The woman at the desk noted our request for two adjoining rooms ("We're Republicans," I explained) and gave them to us without a whimper. She told us about the breakfast and the included dinner in the nasal twang with the broad *á* that is the speech trademark of the Tidewater.

We had been staying in separate rooms for the last week. I have done, and still do, many low acts. But to pretend that Susan's devastation and betrayal and loss and need was love for me was too low.

In the afternoon we took a nap. At least I took a nap.

When I called for Susan she was sitting in a floral-covered wing chair in her room, looking out the sash windows at couples driving through scenic Easton and admiring its pre-Revolutionary-era shops. When she turned to me her deep blue eyes were rimmed with red.

"You always know the answers," she said to me later in the car. "You always know all the reasons. Why did this happen to me?"

"I don't know," I said. "There's no logic in Hollywood."

We were in the heart of the Tidewater, on a state blacktop road between St. Michaels and Oxford. On the right we saw endless forests of pine and oak. On the left there were great estates set in the midst of marshlands and the gentle waves of the Chesapeake. This was an area of fingers and necks and inlets, so that each estate was separated from the next by water and reeds and swamp.

We passed great brick entrance ways with wrought-iron gates. Fantastic names like "Sally's Delight" and "Content" were stenciled demurely into the brickwork.

We turned down a still smaller highway and soon came to a sandy spit leading into the Tred Avon River. Next to the point was a desolate, enormous fieldstone house set in a lawn of overgrown, dead grass. A wrought-iron gate hung askew at the entrance way. Above the gate, in elegant wrought-iron script was the estate's name: *Tamsey.*

I stared at the house with a wild hope, and then turned to Susan-Marie. She looked away to the west. Her face had a new vitality it had not had since Deirdre's coup.

"I had no idea life there would be like it was," Susan said.

"Yes, but now you know. 'You can't win if you're not at the table,' " I said. "You went to the table and you won a lot of passes. The final throw was a killer, but that's how most final throws are."

Susan-Marie did not say anything, but for the first time in a week the traces of a smile played around the edges of her mouth. I knew what they meant. She didn't even have to say it.

"You're kidding," I said. "You're not thinking of going back and trying again."

"Oh, no," she said. "Never. Not in Hollywood. Not there, where everything is such a sham. But somewhere. Paul was a son of a bitch. Deirdre was too much for me. But somewhere along the way, when things were going well, people were listening to me. People did what I said on *Trade-Off* and it worked. Those Women in Film liked what I had to say. I'll never go back to the phone company, and I'll never go back to L.A. But I'll promise you something, Benjy. I'll promise you something I just promised myself, right here at this place, this abandoned gorgeous *Tamsey*. They can drive me out of Hollywood. They can take the wind out of me. But they can't beat me.

"They don't even know it, but with their cunning and their tricks and their connections and their spies and their lies and their fancy houses and their fancy cars, they'll still never beat me. When I was ten years old, when I was twelve years old, I went through worse than this. Much worse, and I didn't have anyone to help me, anybody like you.

"I'll do something else, maybe politics, maybe public relations, maybe investment banking, and this time I won't feel so much. They took that away from me on the Republic lot. They taught me how dangerous it is to feel things, and I won't forget it. But I still have a lot inside me they'll never see, and I'll go away somewhere and have a great little life of my own, and they'll never beat me. Someday I'll be watching late-night TV in Connecticut or Florida or D.C. and I'll see a credit for Paul Belzberg and I'll say, 'Oh, is he still alive?' and then I'll know I beat them."

Susan's eyes glowed deep blue, deeply, beautifully blue in the gray of the afternoon.

"If they made you stop feeling things, they have beaten you," I said.

Susan's eyes, which had been so shiny and defiant, suddenly filled with tears again. "I'll never stop feeling for you," she said. "I'll never stop feeling for the people who care about me."

The rain beat on the car and the sleet made the car cold. I drove up the potholed driveway of *Tamsey* and then around to the back where it looked out over the Tred Avon River and the fish that were still out at dusk. The house had a magnificent row of French doors overlooking the lawn that sloped down to the water. I looked at the house and then at Susan.

"I love you, Susan," I said. "Stay here with me, and we'll make a whole new life where people value you and don't just try to fuck you over."

I said that and I looked at her, and just the minute flicker of her eyes away from me, westward, across the Bay, away from *Tamsey* told me more than I wanted to know.

"Our day will come," she said, and she hugged me, but did not kiss me.

While I hugged her, I tried in vain to smell the scent of Star Jasmine. But there was only the wet, deep smell of the Chesapeake Bay wind off the Tred Avon River and the smell of White Shoulders perfume in her hair.

I drove back to the Tidewater Inn. We changed for dinner, then ate Maryland turkey while around us the bankers and hardware-store owners and coupon clippers of Talbot County drank their National Bohemian Beer, ate their soft-shell crabs, their Chesapeake Bay clams, and their Virginia hams.

In the front of the room, by a row of domed French doors, a dance floor had been cleared. Behind it was a small band of ancient black men. One, so black he was almost invisible, played a guitar with his head crooked over the strings, hearing a rhythm no one else heard. Another played a saxophone, two played clarinets, another played drums, and a black woman sang. She was thin and high-toned. She wore a huge black dress that

225

must have been made for her when she was a younger, healthier woman. The band played "Moon River" and "String of Pearls" and "Try the Impossible."

Susan and I drank Courvoisier. We danced to "Tears on My Pillow," to "I'll Be Seeing You," to "Send in the Clowns," and to everything else that was played.

I held Susan in my arms. I felt that peculiar heat that warmed without burning through her striped silk dress. I could feel her pearls cool on my hand as I held the back of her neck. She felt small and intense in my arms. I felt as if by holding her I was also holding the only thing that would ever make me happy. I did not care that this was the rebound. I did not care that she was already thinking of what came next, and that "next" apparently was not me. If this sounds like the feelings of a dreamer, well, I never denied it.

I went to the bandleader and asked him to play "Our Day Will Come." I even handed him a crumpled five-dollar bill. He handed it back with a smile. "That's one of my favorites, too," he said.

The Modernaires played "Our Day Will Come" in such a long version that by the time I noticed, we were the only customers left in the dining room.

> Our day will come,
> And we'll have everything.
> No tears for us.
> Think love, and wear a smile
> Our dreams have magic
> Because we'll always stay
> In love this way,
> Our day will come . . .

We danced around in the room as if the song would never end. I thought that perhaps if I danced with Susan long enough, something in her would change. Just like the tiger changed into butter, maybe Susan-Marie would change and fall in love with me.

Then, just for us, the band played "Good Night, Sweetheart." Many people think of the Jesse Belvin song when I mention "Good Night, Sweetheart," but this one is different. The song has a much livelier, more changeable melody than most end-of-the-evening songs, so you can dip and pull your Susan back and then dip again. I did that with Susan for about five minutes until we were both laughing so hard that I didn't notice right away when Susan suddenly went limp as she faced the door. I did not notice anything for a few seconds until I wheeled Susan around to see a mournful, tired, but desperately eager Paul Belzberg tap me on the shoulder with one hand and hold out another to Susan-Marie.

"I'm sorry to cut in," he said, "but may I have this dance? Susan and I have a lot to talk about."

I looked at Susan's face and let him cut in. The three of us drove back across the Bay Bridge that night to Washington, D.C. An old friend of my parents, Judge David Bernard, stayed up until one A.M. to perform the marriage ceremony. I was the witness.

P·A·R·T

V

21

PLAYERS 2

■

A day in the life of Susan-Marie Belzberg one year after she returned from the Tidewater Inn to spend two weeks of honeymoon in Cap d'Antibes, then flew back by Concorde to New York and then to Los Angeles by the Republic Gulfstream II. That would have been about forty-nine weeks after she was named President for Worldwide and Domestic Marketing for Republic Pictures, and about six months after she was appointed to the four-person Office of the Directorate of Motion Pictures of Republic Pictures.

I do not say that this was a typical day for Susan-Marie Belzberg, but it was a day.

First, the studio limousine picked her up at the Belzberg house at 77 Malibu Beach Colony at seven in the morning. From the car, Susan began her day's telephone calls. A tough one with Sam Sohn in New York City about the rights to *Dreadnought,* the new British spy drama at the Helen Hayes: "I notice you haven't come back to me with a number yet," Susan-Marie said as her car sped along Malibu Canyon Road. "Are you getting shy?"

"It's just that the play is so new, Susan," Sohn said. "I'd like for a few other people to get to see it."

"You mean Bob Evans and Dick Zanuck. Fine. They have a lot more money than we do. If you're waiting for their bid, we probably couldn't have bought it anyway."

"I'll definitely be thinking of you," Sohn said.

"No," she said. "It's okay, Sam. I can't outbid those guys. Thanks anyway."

"Well, let me talk to the people in London who put up the money."

"I don't think so. Maybe we can do business on the next one."

There was a long sigh on the other end of the phone. "I'll make up a proposal and get it to you by lunch," Sohn said. "You're a tough lady."

"It's not my money," Susan-Marie said. "If it were just mine and Paul's, you know I'd pay anything."

By the time the limo was on the Ventura Freeway Susan was on the line to Jack Valenti at the Motion Picture Association. "You know I'd like to come to D.C. to get the award myself," Susan said, "but that's just when negotiations come up with IATSE."

"You have lawyers for that, Susan," Jack Valenti said.

"I have a lot of people for that. I also have a lot of pictures about to go into production. Let me ask you, Jack, if your shop were going to be closed down, maybe for a few months, would you let lawyers handle it? If it were your company, would you put it in some guy's hands when maybe he's got ten other things to think about?"

"Maybe not," Valenti answered in his usual deep tones.

"Well, look, try to get it rescheduled. If you can get it into the spring, I'll come, and maybe I'll bring a print of *Hawaii Kai,* and we can have a good time. But for now I have to take care of business. Paul's running ragged on *Cabin,* and I have to step up to the plate."

"I'll get it changed, Susan," Valenti said.

At the office, with doors to which only Susan-Marie had the keys, there were already calls from London. Susan took them crisply from Alexandra Hong, her secretary, whom she had recruited personally from a British finishing school in Kuala Lumpur. The only message from London she had to answer was a query about the Republic (U.K.) submission to the Exchequer on public subsidization of feature film production in the U.K. if made with certain required percentages of British participation. A country with top-drawer production facilities, the best actors on earth, and public money going in would make a big difference below the line on at least four negatives each year. She would make time for a trip to London herself on that one.

"Get me Jack Rubinstein in London on the phone," Susan-Marie said to her Chinese secretary. "Put the rest of these in my chron folder for today. Then call Costello and tell him I want a briefing on what we've done to get this subsidy thing through the House of Commons before he goes home tonight. Better yet, get him on the phone."

While Susan-Marie settled herself at her desk, she looked at the crystal decanter on its corner, right next to the photograph of her with Sid Bauman. In the decanter, as usual, were a dozen long-stemmed roses. They were there every morning before she arrived. "Think of them as a reminder every day that I'm sorry for the hell I put you through," Paul Belzberg said to her. That was exactly how Susan-Marie saw them.

In a few moments of studying a file on subsidies and a few more moments with a calculator, Susan-Marie was ready for her telephone call with Richard Costello, the general counsel of Republic. But Costello didn't call. Instead, he appeared at the door in white flannel tennis trousers and a white polo shirt.

"I was just finishing a set with Michael Douglas over on

the Columbia courts when I got your page," he said. "What can I do to help you out?"

Costello was a small, wiry man with eyes set deep in his face. Above his eyes were bushy, erratic eyebrows that reminded me of barbed wire. ("If you look at me too hard," those eyes said, "your eyeballs can get caught in this barbed wire.")

"Is this what you normally wear to work?" Susan-Marie asked cheerfully.

"Nope, this is what I normally wear to play tennis. I'll shower and change when I get back to my office. I heard you wanted me ASAP, so here I am."

"I like that." Susan's voice was genuinely enthusiastic. "I'd rather have somebody dressed like a shopping bag lady who shows up on time than somebody dressed like a male model who doesn't get here when he's supposed to."

"Then I'm your boy." Costello fell into one of Susan-Marie's yellow wing chairs.

"Have you thought about this Eady subsidy in England?" Susan-Marie asked. "What are we doing about it?"

"Nothing yet, because we don't know how it's going to turn out. When we get a complete law we'll get it analyzed. That's standard."

"Well, I just ran a few numbers on the thing." Susan-Marie brandished her calculator. "If we made four negatives there in one year, with what Heath's proposed, we're ahead about eleven million dollars over what it would cost to do the pictures here, and that's with the strong pound. With the pound going lower, we make almost three hundred thousand dollars for every cent the pound moves down."

"Wait a minute. You mean you just did that right now?" Costello asked.

"Come on," Susan said. "It was a completely simple regression and any eighth grader could do it."

"Not bloody likely. Hardly anyone I know could even hit the buttons right on that thing."

"The main thing is that it means a goddamn lot to us," Susan-Marie said. "I'll have an arithmetic lesson later. For now, let's get a show ready. Let's have me and James Mason and Richard Burton and maybe Glynis Johns go over there to make a presentation to the Treasury. I want some statistics on what we would be putting into the British economy in the way of jobs, taxes, that kind of thing."

"You're going to try to influence how Heath makes his decision? We've never done that before in a foreign country."

"It's eleven million in the first year alone. Discounted to present value over the next ten years it's close to seventy million," Susan-Marie said. "I think we'll try it this time."

"You're the boss," Costello said, wiping perspiration from his forehead.

"When we meet the Queen, try to wear a suit," Susan-Marie said.

Just before eleven o'clock in the morning Ron Silverman, the new deputy head of production for movies and television, appeared at the door, along with his assistant, the director for motion picture development, Jodie Sugar, the woman Susan had met on the back lot during the filming of *Stained Glass*.

"We have a little bit of a problem," Ron announced. "Eric Blume, who we thought we had locked down to at least go through development on *The Hider*, is giving us a lot of shit. He says he feels like he owes something to Columbia because they made his first movie when he was only twenty-two. So he's giving us problems about that."

"I feel like he might walk off the lot today and never come back," Jodie said. "I think somebody from there is ragging him about feeling guilty and all. Plus probably making threats about his picture."

"What was his picture?" Susan-Marie asked. "I didn't even know he'd made a picture."

Ron answered. "*The Receiver* was his first picture. It came out a year ago. The kid is twenty-four now and he doesn't know any better. It only got theatrical release for a few days, but somebody at Columbia's scared him."

Ten minutes later Susan-Marie walked down an alley on the Republic back lot and came upon a deserted small town, circa 1900, set. There was a village green, a band shell, trellis work everywhere, a white frame church, and a blacksmith shop. Standing in the band shell was a tousle-haired young man wearing a stevedore's cap over his head. He was scuffling his tennis-shoed feet on the boards, looking as if he might be called to the principal's office at any moment.

"Susan-Marie Belzberg," she said, taking Eric Blume's hand. "How are you?"

"Fine," the young man said, shuffling and looking ill at ease.

"I'm going to make this really simple, so that you don't have any hesitation about working on a Republic picture. Ron tells me you're the best young director in America, and I believe Ron Silverman."

The young man still shuffled and looked at the floor. He was accustomed to threats.

"There are people on this lot who thought *The Receiver* was a ground-breaking picture. I trust those people. I think Columbia gave you a bad deal. They didn't even spend a hundred thousand dollars on publicity and advertising. They had ten prints made. You get me?"

"I get you," Eric Blume said. "It was my first picture."

"I don't care," Susan-Marie said. "It was a goddamned good picture. So here's what I'm going to do. If you'll give us three pictures here, all things you get consultation on, we'll buy the negative of *The Receiver* from Columbia. We'll give you two fifty to recut it any way you like. Then we'll re-release it for you, and I personally guarantee we'll put it on three hundred screens in the first month. Do we have a deal?"

"Are you kidding?" Blume asked.

236

"Get him the papers. Make sure legal has them out to him this afternoon," Susan-Marie said. "That's got to happen if we're going to get this man to work." Then she shook his hand and walked back toward Main Exec.

Susan had lunch at her desk, as usual, with Paul eating at the coffee table. Each one had a Cobb salad sent over from the studio commissary. As Paul talked, Susan-Marie nodded enthusiastically.

"So this is how the problems lay out. We have the kids on a field trip from Washington, D.C., down to New Orleans. One of the boys is an innocent. But there's something about him that makes one of the teachers fall in love with him. She's from a small town in Mississippi, so in a sense, as the bus goes farther and farther into the South, they're going farther and farther into what makes her what she is."

"I understand that. I've always loved that story," she said.

"The payoff is that the teacher really loves him and really offers him something important. But he's so confused about what's important that he goes off to a whorehouse in New Orleans to satisfy a bet. When word gets out, everybody's giggling. The teacher doesn't get it. She thinks they're laughing at her and she's humiliated."

"It lays out like a dream."

"The kid is bewildered. He tells the teacher what's happened, and she realizes, in a second, that she is in love with a child. He's a child with a penis, but he's still a child, and the whole subject suddenly horrifies her."

"I understand. It's a metaphor about the minefields we have to go through to love. It's about how we always love the wrong man."

"Almost always."

"Until we find the right one," Susan-Marie said with a wide smile.

"The problem is that we've got Paul Newman as a teacher along for the trip, but he's also in love with the teacher. So that means we're already in for one point five for him. That was the director's idea. And then he says if we get him, we've also got to get Blythe Danner, and that's another half. And before we even get to that, we've got to wonder if anybody's buying the idea that Blythe Danner is going to choose a kid, maybe a Tony Channing, over Paul Newman. You think anybody's going to swallow that?"

"More to the point, does anyone want to see Paul Newman as a loser in any way?" she asked.

"On the other hand, what possible name can we put on the marquee? I mean who's going to go to a movie to see Tony Channing?"

"Is Newman pay or played yet?"

"I think so. Crovitz wanted that and I think we caved on it."

"Then can we switch pictures? Is there a right of substitution?"

"There might be that," Belzberg said. "We might put him into *The Chinese Day*. He would be a lot safer in that. He's a great actor."

"All right," Susan-Marie said. "Let's get Michael Crovitz on the phone and talk about it. I know you, Paul. You don't want Newman on the picture, and I'm not going to try to talk you into it. You're the artist. You know what kind of colors you want, and you know what kind of canvas you want."

"But we have to think about how we're going to promote this picture without a star."

"The story is the star," Susan-Marie said. "The kind of word of mouth that we're going to get laid down on this thing is the star. I'd rather have 'A Masterpiece' on the marquee, quoting a big paper, and half the kids at State talking about it at the Student Union than have anybody's name on it. Whose name did *Jaws* have on it?"

"Richard Dreyfuss."

"You think anyone outside three big cities even knows who he is?"

"You have a point," Belzberg said.

"In a way, I don't even want to have a Paul Newman in there competing with your idea," Susan-Marie said. "At the end, we should worry about the woman and the boy. We shouldn't worry about where Paul Newman is hanging out."

"And there's another thing. I hate like hell leaving it with the kid watching her drive away. That's just too vague. It's like ending a war movie with the fog coming in over the trenches."

Susan-Marie finished the last of her Cobb salad, sipped at an iced tea, and then stood up and stretched. "I've been thinking about that. I agree with you. I want to know that this kid has turned out all right. I want to know that the teacher hasn't become a shopping-bag lady."

"But the leaving is the third act," Belzberg said. "It flies like a lead balloon if he goes after her."

"Right. But it doesn't hurt if it has a narrator. Especially if the narrator is the boy, and he begins by saying, 'This is the story of the summer I learned about love.' Then if you go to the end and you see the boy meeting the woman for a drink at a restaurant in New York, and she still looks great—because, remember, she's only five years older than he is. And they only have to talk for a few minutes to let us see that now they're going to start again, and now they're going to make it work."

"Not only that," Paul Belzberg said, "but even if they're not going to start up again, if we see they've both come out of it all right, but they've still got feelings for each other, then that's an ending."

"She could say something to him in French, because she was a French teacher, and then he could say, 'I never understood French. I never understood anything. But I knew you loved me, and that's kept me warm when there wasn't any heat coming from anywhere else in my life . . .'"

"Something like that." Belzberg smiled. "I like it. A frame and a narrator. Let me see if we can get Goldman to do a polish."

Susan-Marie pressed her comm line for Alexandra Hong. "Get me Michael Crovitz."

■ ■ ■ ■

Alexandra Hong reached Michael Crovitz, thirty-year-old founder of Creative Factors Agency, on his car phone. Crovitz was driving his Ferrari to MGM, which was on the other side of the Santa Monica Mountains, so the connection was spotty.

Susan-Marie and Paul apologized, and then put the conversation "on the box."

"It's about Paul Newman," Susan-Marie said.

"He's gonna put *New Orleans* on the map," Michael Crovitz said cheerfully. "When do we get the papers from business affairs?"

"Maybe never," Susan Belzberg said. "We want to talk about that."

"Hey, he's pay or played on that picture. We're talking Paul Newman here. We're not talking somebody in off the street you just gave a test-option to. This is Paul Newman. The one the girls go to see. Remember?"

"There's a big story problem with using him," Paul Belzberg said.

"Rewrite it," Crovitz said. "I have an incredible writer. A new guy. From *Rolling Stone*. John Mankowski. Let him have a shot at it."

"I don't think so, Michael," Susan-Marie's voice was calm. "The problem is that it's Paul's idea, and you know, Paul has a pretty good idea of where it's supposed to go."

"You wanted him," Crovitz said.

"Yeah, but we hadn't thought about it enough," Paul said. "It's giving us problems."

"The problem is that he's just blowing the whole story line right out of the water," Susan-Marie said. "If we use him, it's one story. If we use somebody the audience doesn't love quite as much, we have a totally different story, and that's the one we want to make."

240

"So who're you thinking about for the part?" Crovitz asked.

"I don't know. Come in and we'll talk about it," Susan-Marie said. "We'll talk about where we might put Paul if we do take him off the project. Have you read *The Chinese Day?*"

"That's my client. That's Lance Harding," Michael Crovitz said.

"We can all talk about it. How about tomorrow at lunch?" Paul Belzberg said.

"No, I'm playing racquetball at lunch," Crovitz said. "Come over to our house Friday night. We're having Arlene Zeller. We'll see you a little before eight, and we can get everything straightened out."

"I think *The Chinese Day* is much more his kind of vehicle," Belzberg said.

"We may be talking about gross participation on this one," Crovitz said.

Susan-Marie said, "We can *talk* about anything."

"We'll work something out. It's a small town, and we're all in the business for keeps, so let's just know that we'll work something out. Paul's not gonna want to be in a picture where you don't need him, and *The Chinese Day* is a great script. We're all players here. We can work something out."

After lunch, Susan read a file on the deals that went into *New Orleans.* She got a personal briefing from Dick Costello on what "pay or play" might mean if push came to shove. "It doesn't mean a thing," was Costello's opinion. "It's just an expression of esteem. This studio has never had to pay off on a pay or play. Not once. No one ever wants to push the other guy to the wall. The town is too small for that."

At about three o'clock in the afternoon Susan left her office and walked out into the courtyard of the office quadrangle at Republic. She glanced at the workmen demolishing the cottage that had been Deirdre Needle's file room and the adjoining cottage that had been Bryan Fitzpatrick's western-style office cottage. He had simply been too close to Deirdre. He was now an "indie prod" and doing poorly. At Susan's suggestion, the buildings were going to be replaced by a small green area matching the green lawn in front of the Main Exec building. "It gives a feeling of restfulness that this building badly needs," she said to Sid Bauman, and he agreed. It's especially restful to know that the place is clean, rid of spies and secret agents.

Susan strolled through the back lot, past the sets that were being established for *Tornado,* yet another disaster movie. This set was an exact clone of the boyhood home of Dale Warmack, Prescott, Arkansas. Susan-Marie had spent four summers there as a small child before her father went to the Chosin Reservoir. She could still give minute advice to the production designer about the width of windowsills, the number of lights in a kitchen, how flat or raised the doors of the storm cellar should be.

She cleared her head of the file on *New Orleans.* In the sun, with the workmen swarming around the set, Susan had an almost overpowering urge to raise her wings out to her sides and see if she could fly. She remembered playing "airplane" in her playground in Silver Spring. Each child would raise her arms, run around making noise like a MiG fighter or a Sabre jet, and then pretend to land.

Only this time, on the back lot at Republic, Susan-Marie felt as if she would not land for a long time. She was gliding effortlessly through life as if life were an endless happy dream. Every call she made to a Sam Sohn or a Michael Crovitz, every deal she made with an Eric Blume or with the British Exchequer told her she was flying.

22

SUNDAY

■

Because Susan lived in a place where emotions go far beyond questions of gross participation and playing the dealstream game, there were other kinds of days in Susan's life than the days when she felt as if she were flying harmlessly down MiG Alley.

One Sunday about two months after Paul Newman was locked in for gross participation from an artificial break for *The Chinese Day,* Susan was awakened by a telephone call from Jodie Sugar. She picked up the phone next to her side of the bed. Then she noticed that Paul was already out at Jerry Perenchio's tennis court right across the alley at the Colony. In fact, she could hear him arguing with Perenchio about ins and outs above Jodie's side of the conversation.

"I need a doctor," Jodie Sugar said.

"Fever?" Susan-Marie asked.

"A lot worse than that," Jodie said. "My boyfriend was fired from Warner last week. He was a line producer on a project that got folded up. It was an MOW about a family from the fiffies through Vietnam told through the story of the family's pink Thunderbird."

"We've already got one in development about a 1962 Corvette," Susan-Marie said. "I'll try to use him if it gets a go from the network."

"That's not it, really," Jodie said. "The problem is that since he got canned he's been so worried about money that he's gotten me really worried."

"It's a real worry," Susan said. She could see a flock of pelicans soaring just above the edge of a wave. They sailed through the air inches from the wave as it curled from south to north, in a precise formation of predation. When the wave finally broke the pelicans were already lined up on the next one, like a machine for sailing over waves, automatic, graceful, effortless. "Are we paying you enough?"

"You pay me more than anyone else in town would pay me," Jodie said. "The worry isn't really that real. We have money in the bank and Rick always gets work. The problem is that he was so upset about it he talked to the rabbi at the temple in Hollywood. The rabbi told him that he was lucky to be working in Los Angeles and not a prisoner in a concentration camp."

Now the pelicans were farther out to sea, circling above something under the water.

"That was a week ago. The same night Rick talked to the rabbi he started to fall asleep and he had the terrible nightmare that if he fell asleep, he would find out that he had been dreaming that he was in Hollywood the whole time, and that in fact, he was really a prisoner in Auschwitz. He was afraid that when he fell asleep in West Hollywood he was going to wind up awake quarrying rock in Auschwitz."

"Good God," Susan said.

"So now he refuses to go to sleep, and it's been a week,

and he's so tired he's starting to think he's already in Auschwitz," Jodie Sugar said.

"I'll get you a shrink," Susan-Marie said. "A really good one who worked as a consultant for us on *Tornado*. And I'll get Rick something on the Republic lot right away."

"It's just that the business is so uncertain, and people here sort of forget what's real and what's not."

■   ■   ■   ■

Later that morning Susan drove into Santa Monica to the auditorium at Santa Monica College. The room was being used for an open audition for singers and dancers for one of Paul's musicals, a revival of *Hollywood Canteen* set during the Vietnam War. She had come directly from the health club on Pacific Coast Highway. When she walked into the modern, cinder block building she was still wearing her sweat clothes and her hair was pulled up behind her head in a bun.

In one corner of the room, Bonnie Zimerman, Republic's casting genius for the movie sat behind a folding table and interviewed five dancers at a time. "Jazz? Move well? How many years? Any ballet? Ever do ballroom with a choreographer?"

The dancers stood ramrod straight and tried to outdo each other in bright, cheerful optimism, even though there were over two hundred men and women brightly trying out for fifteen parts. "I love dance. It's my life. I never get tired. I would work for nothing as long as I could dance." The questions and answers went back and forth and then each dancer was given a straightforward six-step routine to do to the tune of "Feel-Like-I'm-Fixin'-to-Die Rag" by Country Joe and the Fish.

The dancers did their routines, and Bonnie made notes on a card. Then she thanked the dancers and told them they would hear from her.

In the bleachers on one side of the room Susan sat down next to a blond woman with straight hair in a chignon and a T-shirt that said NUCLEAR WAR? WHAT ABOUT MY CAREER?

The woman had large blue eyes and false eyelashes that were literally three-fourths of an inch long. She had the usual dancer's thick pink and blue eye shadow and the dancer's obligatory hundred-millimeter cigarette. "You're new," she said to Susan-Marie. "Are you new in town?"

"Fairly new," Susan said. "How about you?"

"I'm from Canada. My name is Sonja. Sonja LaPierre."

"I'm Susan-Marie Belzberg."

Sonja showed no sign of recognition. "Are you making any money dancing?"

"Not really," Susan said. "Not dancing."

"Anyone taking care of you?"

"Well, I mostly take care of myself."

"I know the name of that tune," Sonja said. "Eat tuna fish all week until you get one little check for two days' hard work, and then everybody thinks you're a bum if you don't have a BMW. It's incredibly tough here."

"Incredibly."

"Are you getting by?" Sonja asked. "You're really pretty. Especially your eyes. Someone should appreciate you."

"Thank you."

"There are a lot of men in this town who have money to burn who would kill for a chance to go out with a girl as pretty as you are." Sonja offered Susan-Marie a cigarette. Susan shook her head.

"I don't know," Susan said. "You think so?"

"Honey, go out to the parking lot. Look at the first row. There's an anthracite-gray 450 SL out there. The license plate says DANZR. That's my car. I didn't get it from going to these tryouts and getting a hundred dollars a day for extra work."

"I see."

"And you have a really classy way about you. Something about the way you talk. Honestly, some of the men just want to have someone pretty to sit across the table from at Ma Maison. They don't even want you to do anything with them afterward. And it's a hundred dollars an hour."

"A hundred dollars an hour." Susan quickly calculated if she were earning a hundred dollars an hour at Republic. She was. "But some of them do want you to do something with them," she said. "I assume that some of them want to actually do quite a lot with you."

Sonja took a deep drag of her cigarette. "That doesn't bother me. The guys I've been out with here who don't pay me, who just expect me to do it for nothing, are nowhere near as nice to me as the ones who pay. That's the truth. Figure it out."

"I can believe that," Susan-Marie said.

"Plus, even though they're paying me, I feel like I'm the one who's in charge, and I like that," Sonja said. "You know how it feels to be in charge of a man for once after you've been trying to get work in this town for five years? You know how it feels to be in control for once? I don't care if it's in bed with a guy I just met. I'm the one calling the shots for once, and that's what it's all about. I don't even care about the money or the car. You ought to try it some time."

"Maybe I will," Susan said, and then she left.

■　　■　　■　　■

When Susan got back to the house in Malibu she read a script about a man who tries to hide from modern life by becoming a hermit painter in Greece only to find that he becomes wildly successful after a tourist buys one of his paintings. Then he returns to New York and suddenly he becomes a failure when critics see that he is only a man with two legs just like them. The script was called *Goodbye to Mykonos* and it had been written by Bob Schallerberg, a longtime friend of Paul's. In fact, they had both waited tables at the Greenwich Village nightclub where Barbra Streisand had been discovered, The Bottom Line.

When she had finished reading the script she wrote on

the bottom, *Not for us. This is for a small crowd on the West Side of Manhattan and in Brentwood Park. Not for a mass-market audience.*

She went for a walk on the beach, waved to Ned Tanen, then went back into the house. Marco Castro was waiting for her in yellow duck trousers and Topsiders and a Princeton T-shirt. His face was unshaven and sweaty.

"I want to understand something," he said. "My girlfriend, Renee, works at William Morris. She's an agent for talent. She's a smart girl. Her father was an agent, too. For the last few months, every night when she got home from work she'd be so wired she couldn't sit down. Then, about two months ago, she was asleep every time I'd come home from work. So I finally got it out of her that she was taking 'loads' every day."

"What the hell are 'loads'?" Susan-Marie asked. "Some new kind of drug?"

"Loads are Doriden and Talwin." Castro paused for a moment to drink from a glass of iced tea that Elena brought to him. He looked out the window of the teahouse at a file of sandpipers moving precisely along the beach while two fat teenagers threw a Frisbee above their heads. The contrast between the corpulent, fleshy idleness of the boys and the slender, graceful purpose of the birds struck Susan as the underlining to Castro's story. "Doriden and Talwin together make you as high as heroin, at least that's what Renee told me."

"Great," Susan said. "She should quit the agency business."

"I told her that. She said she would be a total failure if she quit being an agent and she couldn't even consider doing anything else."

"Then she should leave town altogether. Get the whole mess out of her system."

Castro shook his head and stared at the terra-cotta floor of the teahouse. "A month ago I came home from work and she was lying on the floor of the kitchen, unconscious, barely breathing. The paramedics said she was lucky to be alive. She was in a coma for two days. The doctors at St. John's said she had so much Doriden in her she could have put all of William Morris to sleep for a week. When she came to she agreed to go into a drug treatment program at a hospital in Van Nuys."

"That sounds right."

"She was in there, incommunicado, for three weeks. Eight thousand dollars. Playing volleyball. The doctors would line them up every morning and tell them they were all shits for using. Then in the afternoon a 'family counselor' would get them in a circle and tell them they were all shits for using. When she got out she looked like a Moonie. I'm not complaining about the money, but what the hell could it have gone for?"

"It's like our distribution fee," Susan said. "It's just what they can get."

"So for three days she went to work and just smiled at everyone like she was a zombie, and then last night we went out to eat at the Palm. The waiter, Johnny, is walking by with a lobster, one of those great big ones with the claws waving all around, like it knows it's about to die and it's saying good-bye, and suddenly Renee looks at it and starts to scream that she's the lobster and they're going to cook her, and she just won't stop screaming."

"I'm sorry," Susan-Marie said. She felt a weight of sympathy so profound that she thought it might pull her down onto the floor, down through the foundations, into the mud under Malibu Beach. "This town is just too hard for a lot of people. It's not their fault."

"You want to know something?" Castro asked. "She's back at the psych ward at St. John's, and she's totally snowed under with chlorpromazines, but I know she'll come out of it. What worries me is that after this she won't feel anything. I'm not worried that she'll feel too much. I'm worried that she'll become the perfect Hollywood person. She won't allow herself to feel anything, not the phones getting slammed down on her, not the other agents bad-mouthing her behind her back, not having to fight for commissions, not having to lie as part of her daily business. She'll just become a machine for selling and for closing deals. She's too fine a woman for that to happen to. She loves piano music. She shouldn't be in this business."

"I agree," Susan said. "It's too tough for a woman who loves piano music."

"As long as I can feel sorry for her and not for myself, I'll be fine," Castro said.

"Does it ever make you think about leaving and trying something else?"

"Really and truly, how many people ever come here and then leave? You have to be almost dead before you leave. Hollywood isn't a business. It's a religion."

"Or an addiction."

"Or an addiction," Castro agreed. He paused for a moment and then said, "I'm glad you listened to me. Now, to change the subject, I think we can possibly get Jane Asher for *Bath House* and the price is well inside the budget."

Susan-Marie looked out at the beach. The sandpipers were gone, but now there were four overweight teenage boys throwing the Frisbee.

All of this happened on Sunday.

23

INVESTIGATION

Let me tell you how I felt when Susan-Marie left my life after we danced the last dance at the Tidewater Inn. To say that my days at the White House were empty would be an absurd understatement. To say that my daily transit through the Executive Office Building, into the White House mess, out to dinner at Bagatelle, out to Ward Circle to teach my part-time class at American University had lost its allure would be like saying that confinement to Attica had lost its allure.

Once, earlier in my life, the great economist, Milton Friedman, told me that I should not worry about losing one girl. "Statistically speaking," he said, "if there were only one right girl for every right boy, they would never find each other."

It was a good joke, but it didn't take away any of the pain. Susan had miraculously come back into my life trailing disappointment, failure, and sorrow. But to me, she was back, and that was all that mattered. I was certain that I could be enough to her to make up for all of the horror of her crushed fantasies. With sufficient time, I could make her forget the fairy tales and illusions of Hollywood. Instead, I was left with my own illusion, with a fantasy that might just as well have never been there. I wished, hoped, and prayed that I would wake up one morning and have forgotten that I ever knew Susan-Marie. The pain was so intense that I couldn't even cherish the memories of Susan-Marie. When I tried to hold them to me I found that I was holding a razor blade against my skin.

For almost two months I worked as well as I could on a new project about the political "inputs" on situation comedy. This involved studying the political messages of "All In the Family," "Maude," "Mary Tyler Moore," and "Bob Newhart." The contrast between the sweetened laugh tracks booming out of my television and the black, echoing silence in my heart almost made me laugh and did make me cry.

By night I walked my dog, Mary, in the streets of Georgetown, came home, wrote up my notes of the day's situation-comedy writing, and then went to sleep, with the help of chloral hydrate capsules.

One day, just after Valentine's Day, while I walked with Mary in Glover Park, snow began to fall. It was a Saturday afternoon and, suddenly, with the snow falling on the gabled, turreted houses of the neighborhood, an inspiration came into my head.

If I could only understand how this happened, I might stop hurting. If I could only study Susan-Marie, learn about her, scientifically detail and classify her surroundings throughout her life, then surely she would fall into the category of a boring chore—like investigating the sitcoms —and fall out of the category of "one who has pulled the bottom out of my life."

I had friends at *The Washington Post*. Tom Brogan was

one of them. Through him, I got an assignment from the "Style" section to do a long free-lance piece about Susan-Marie, the bureaucrat who had made good. With the carte blanche that *The Washington Post*'s name offered, I began to study Susan-Marie's life as if I were studying the origins and career of a Secretary of Commerce.

My schedule was my own at the White House. I was able to leave work and browse through school records in Rockville, military service records in Anacostia, even Warmack family records at a genealogical service in Kensington, Maryland.

Little by little, I began to accumulate a history of Susan-Marie Warmack Belzberg.

Then I began to widen my search to include the life of Paul Belzberg, from his ancestors in Lodz to his father in Albion, Alabama, to his films to Deirdre.

Of course, as any fool would predict, the endless exposure to Susan's life did not lessen my suffering at all. Every time I came upon an eighth-grade report card for Susan-Marie, I could see her there, and I fell in love with her again. Every time I read about her gym class accomplishments in tumbling or field hockey, I missed her the way a man in solitary misses daylight and voices.

Most especially, every time I read about Paul Belzberg, I thought—and this thought is a killer—"Why him and not me?"

As a way to ease the pain, to stanch the flow of life that was pouring out of the hole Susan had left in me, the research was a failure. But I started to understand something about Susan that perhaps she only glimpsed herself. In learning about Susan-Marie, I was constructing the biography of a woman who lives—and always lived—through dreams. Even now, scientists divide on what makes up a dream. But I was on the track of what made one woman a dreamer.

Once again, I have always been a dreamer myself, and that was part of the charm of the study. By seeing how Susan had become a dreamer, perhaps I would learn some key, some secret password of binding between us. Once uttered in her presence, perhaps it would keep us together forever.

In the late spring of 1973, something happened that allowed me to perform my experiments much closer to the subject.

One day in June I was called from the study of the West Point yearbook for 1944—Dale Warmack's graduation year—by a telephone call from Los Angeles. It was from Norman Lear. Somehow he had gotten the text of a speech I had given at the American Film Institute. The speech was about the implicit racism in "Sanford and Son." One line of the speech had struck him as particularly horrifying. The line was to the effect that " 'Sanford and Son' is an incomparably more racist vehicle than 'Amos'n'Andy' was at its lowest ebb."

Norman Lear did not call to shout at me. He called because, he said, he never got to hear any intelligent opinions from "conservatives." He disagreed with me about my ideas and frame of reference, but he needed to hear people like me. Would I care to come out and work for him in Los Angeles? He could use me in planning new shows.

I politely said I was busy working for the president of the United States and declined his offer.

At about one in the morning I awoke and looked out the window at the rain falling onto my Subaru. What the hell was wrong with me? What was I doing that was so great at the White House? Richard Nixon was himself on thin ice. What was my future in Washington? A deputy undersecretaryship of Housing and Urban Development? A condo on Cathedral Parkway and a cabin in West Virginia? Forty-five more humid summers and freezing, wet winters? An entire life of observing and never participating in what makes people laugh and cry and feel exultation?

As I saw it, I was being offered the chance to leave the sleet, dull skies, boxy buildings, and anesthetized faces of the bureaucracy behind, and live in the pink and yellow haze of creativity.

I left Washington three weeks later. That day the sky was a dazzling blue. The taxi took me out past the lush Virginia countryside. From the airplane, I saw the Tidal Basin and the glowing whiteness of the Washington Monument. When I arrived in Los Angeles the sky was overcast and a fine rain fell at the terminal gate, where Susan-Marie was waiting for me in a Republic limousine.

"Welcome to L.A.," she said, and she hugged me the way I hug my cousins.

The job with Norman Lear was easy. I had planned to write story ideas about why conservatives believed in prayer in school and liberals wanted higher corporate taxes. I had even thought of a whole sitcom based on a beautiful Southern girl like Norris Church married to a famous, two-fisted, boastful genius like Norman Mailer. But in the event, I was asked questions about whether it would be possible to smuggle a chimpanzee into the Oval Office or what the White House reaction would be to a gay marriage on the Ellipse.

Within a few weeks I was working only one hour each day, and usually not even that, at the tiny desk laid out for me at Metromedia Square.

On the other hand, I was well paid. I could spend my days watching movies being shot at Republic and not worry about the rent. I could linger for hours at the Palm and see the movers and shakers pound the table for more fried onions. I could and did walk up and down the beach at Malibu trying to understand why Western faces looked so much more angular, so much hungrier, than Eastern faces.

I had plenty of my own ideas, so I got an agent and began to have meetings. I pitched stories about economic disasters to agents who did not remember Kennedy. When I told them ideas like "a love story set against a catastrophe of Weimar level inflation in the United States" they looked at me with utter blankness. I pitched stories about

255

the second generation of Okies after the ones who had been in *Grapes of Wrath,* the ones who came to L.A. to work in real estate. Ron Silverman said I should call it *Perrier of Wrath* and that was as far as it got. I pitched a script about a reverse *Pygmalion* to two women executives at Warner. They looked at each other and asked me whether this was an animal story.

After a few months of these experiences I had new respect for Susan. She was able to see the forest. I saw the saplings: the rude agents, the foolish studio executives, the thoughtlessness of the producer/bureaucrat. Susan saw the pure cathedral of fantasy built by a multitude of blemished hands.

"I am a grown man," I would say to Susan-Marie. "The people in this business treat anyone under them as if he were a child. I'm not going to put up with it."

"Wrong idea. The only question worth asking is: 'Will this get something wonderful up on the screen?' If the answer is yes, then anything or almost anything is worth doing. I'm not talking about murder, but I am talking about slights and stupid rudeness."

"That's not true," I said, "because once I've seen a hundred agents who scream at their secretaries and fifty studio executives who bully people who need the money and seventy-five independent producers who use story meetings as punching bags, that starts to rub off on what comes out of Hollywood."

"No." Susan had the smile of the certain in her eyes. She would lean back in her chair in her office and smile at me with those perfect teeth. Then she would run a hand through her hair and I would start to hyperventilate. "No, because the fantasy stands alone, independent of where it came from."

"Let me ask you something." I remember the question because I remember Susan's hesitation before she answered. "Just tell me this. Does the steak stand alone from the slaughterhouse?"

"That was a low blow." Susan-Marie laughed. "This is

no slaughterhouse. We hurt people's feelings, but those people shouldn't be here in the first place. We don't kill people."

"People don't always have a sign on them saying they're dead."

"Well, we're all alive here. When you get your first really big break then you'll be singing hallelujah."

But I did not get a really big break from Hollywood. Instead, I learned something about why Paul Belzberg had cut in on Susan and me at the Tidewater Inn. I got an assignment from the *American Spectator* to write a feature on the designing dynamo of Republic Pictures, Sid Bauman. Susan set up the meeting on a day in early 1974 in Sid's house on Roxbury Drive. Sid had been at home for almost one week since he had left Cedars-Sinai's cardiology unit. He had gone there on New Year's Day 1974 after he passed out from angina on the seventeenth hole of the Bel-Air Country Club.

"The tests said I had a lot of constriction in the left main valve, and that's the key valve," Bauman explained. We were in his den, a paneled room with a marble fireplace and an enormous portrait of Amanda Bauman in a black sheath dress without any jewelry. Through three sets of French floor-to-ceiling windows, light poured into the room. Sid Bauman sat on a white couch, wearing a maroon silk robe and an ascot. He held a martini jauntily in one hand. "I'm supposed to go in for an arteriogram next week. That's when they stick a wire into your thigh and run it all the way into your heart, just to see how blocked up you are."

"Wonderful," I said.

"Let me ask you something. In your whole life, have you ever met anyone you consider competent to run a wire into your heart without killing you?"

"Never."

"Neither have I, so when they told me I couldn't have any alcohol before the arteriogram I just laughed. The problem isn't my drinking. It's some goddamned lab technician's drinking. That's what I'm worried about. You want a drink?"

"Yes, I do. I want a drink and I want to learn about where Susan-Marie is going here. I worry about her no matter how well she's doing."

"This is the payoff, right?" Bauman asked. "I almost forgot. You're in the line. You're in that line along with me. Standing out in the cold in line." He actually laughed, and then winced.

"What line's that?"

"The line of guys who're in love with Susan-Marie. That's why you're here. You want to know why you lost her to Paul Belzberg."

I shrugged. "Close enough. Very close indeed. But I also had to learn about martinis. That's a cross-generational gap in my education."

"Of course," Bauman said. "I remember now, you were looking at Susan-Marie when she was talking to Paul in the White House solarium."

"I was the one who was talking to Susan-Marie when she met Paul. I was the one who was dancing with Susan-Marie last winter when Paul came out of nowhere and took her away. What the hell happened?"

"Okay," Sid said. "You have to swear you won't tell any of this while I'm alive, or else I won't tell you. I'll die with it."

So this is what a combination of heart disease, martinis, and power do: they make you into a teenage girl at a pajama party. Still, there was something shining about the exchange of confidences with the largest stockholder of Republic.

"I swear," I said. "It will remain the secret of all those who love Susan-Marie." How many others, I wondered, were in that club? Was that man with the yellow trousers from The Barkentine in the club? Were there members of the Susan-Marie Fan Club everywhere? These were the bleary, whimsical thoughts of a martini afternoon in the home of a wealthy man. But I knew they would come back to cut me when I was sober.

"When I heard that Deirdre was in the hospital and had tried to kill herself I actually laughed," Sid Bauman said. "I know that whole family. They wouldn't even think of doing anything that didn't have ten percent off the top in it for them. That's their whole family."

"You thought it was a phony."

"I knew it was a phony. I knew Deirdre. She made extravagant gestures. That was her style. I was on the phone to the head of medicine at Cedars from Manila in an hour. He told me, in the usual medical crap that they throw in to protect them from malpractice, that she took a lot fewer pills to kill herself than most people in Beverly Hills take every night to get to sleep. By then Paul had already been to see her. I thought for sure that Paul would see right through it. But I didn't figure that Paul was feeling so guilty and so scared that he didn't see anything clearly at all."

"Have you ever been in a hospital, Sid?"

"Exactly. He saw the tubes and the wires and that's all he saw. But when he got to Manila I had no idea Deirdre had him so tied down. I thought he had just kissed Deirdre off and that was it."

Sid Bauman took a gulp of his martini and then got up to make himself another. "You know how I learned about what happened with Susan-Marie? Ron Silverman. An old comedy guy. I didn't even remember he was still on the lot. I think he might be in the club, by the way."

"I don't doubt it."

"Ron Silverman calls me from Republic. He tells my secretary it's an emergency, as serious as if the studio was burning down. When I came on the phone he told me the full story, including the part about Susan standing at the Taco Bell trying to call Paul, and Paul's not taking the call."

Sid Bauman told the story in his usual jaunty way, as if he might stop talking at any minute to take us all out to granddad's country place on the Sound for a weekend of polo. His movements were exaggerated inside his maroon silk bathrobe.

"I didn't plan to tell anyone this part, but here it is," he continued. "I want someone to know because some day Susan-Marie's going to wake up to Paul Belzberg and she's going to wonder if he fooled everybody else, too, and I want her to know that he fooled someone else for a long time, but that when you see the real Belzberg, it's a long way down, or whatever that metaphor is."

"If the occasion comes up, I'll tell her."

"When I heard about Susan in tears, Susan locked out of her office, I called all around Manila to find Paul. It turns out he's over on Tuarong Hill, giving a talk to the Philippine Film Students' Association. I got him back to the hotel. I took him out on the balcony and I put my arm around him and I looked at him, and he knew he was in trouble.

"So I said to him, 'Now I just got a call from Ron Silverman back in L.A., and I hope it's wrong. Because that call told me that Susan Warmack had just been locked out of her office by Deirdre, on your say-so. I hope that's a mistake and that Ron has been taking drugs and has lost his mind. Because if I thought he was right, I'd throw you off this balcony right now.'

"And Paul Belzberg says, 'I'll look into it right away.'

"So I said to him, 'Now let me get this straight. Your psycho ex-girlfriend, who's just put you through the wringer for nothing, illegally claims authority to fire the best person we have at the studio. This same lunatic completely humiliates Susan-Marie, who is the only person we've ever had at the studio who knows how to market a picture, who saved the studio from complete disaster on *Trade-Off*, who worked twenty-four hours a day for a month to take the marketing department into this century, who is the only human being in Hollywood who understands that advertising for a movie has to be connected to the movie, who is the only person we ever had in marketing who even came close to understanding how to make an undecided seventeen-year-old go to the movies, who never did any harm to anyone at the studio, who worshipped the ground you walked on. You let this maniac completely tear Susan's guts out, and then you wouldn't take her call. Is that about right?'

"And Belzberg starts to get really upset and says he didn't know what Deirdre was up to and how horrible it was to see her in the hospital and how he owes her so much, and I said to him, 'Paul, she owns your balls. She has made you into a robot. The only people who got hurt from Deirdre's stay at Cedars were you and Susan, mostly Susan.' Then I said, 'Look, Paul, I'm going to make this really simple for you. Susan loves you. I don't know why. I'm not going to let her leave Republic. I can go get her back. I'll give her your job if I have to, but I'll get her back here.'

"Then Paul starts to look really worried," Sid Bauman said, obviously enjoying this part.

" 'But if I have to go get her back, you're fired. Flat out. And no buying out your contract. You're through. Not only that, but I'll make your name dog shit in this town for a hundred years.

" 'On the other hand, if you go back to your room and think about this and try to act like you've got a brain and a couple of balls instead of acting like Deirdre's Stepinfetchit, if you go back to the States and find her and beg her to come back to Republic, this'll be between us, and I'll put Susan into a job at Republic where she can really start to run with production as well as with marketing. I'll put her into a place where she can take whatever she sees in you and make it better and where she doesn't put your nuts in a sling like Deirdre did.

" 'But let me tell you, boy, if you don't do this right, don't ever let me see you around Republic again. I'll make you wish you were shoveling shit in Biloxi.' "

"How did it work?" I asked.

"Pretty well." Bauman chuckled. "When he got back

he went right home, told Deirdre he knew what she'd done and that she'd better get the hell out while she could still walk. She started to scream. Then she took a fucking Tiffany decanter I'd given Paul for Christmas and tried to cut Paul's throat. When she couldn't catch him she smashed the thing against Paul's desk and then slashed two original Chagalls in his living room. She was still screaming three days later when her father had a private plane fly her to Chestnut Lodge. She was writing her name in shit on the walls for about a month. Now you know what she's doing?"

"No, I don't," I said.

"She's organizing the other patients. She's trying to get herself made into a kind of camp commander, like a counselor in training over the other patients."

"Jesus," I said.

"You have to say this for her: the kid doesn't give up." He shook his head. "You have to know a family like the Needles before you can see just how manipulative people can be."

I sipped my martini and savored the light-headedness that gin brings. To think that a whole generation wasted their time in back alleys scoring drugs when a simple bottle of gin, available at any Safeway, can do so much. The face of Amanda Bauman looked down at me and seemed to wink agreement.

"You can't mean to tell me that Paul ditched Deirdre and went back and begged Susan to marry him because his boss yelled at him," I finally said. "That's a bit hard to believe, even in Hollywood."

"Benjy," Sid Bauman said, "it wasn't because I was his boss. When a man gets to be as well known as Paul Belzberg is in Hollywood he really doesn't have a boss. Once the players in town know who you are, you'll always work somewhere, and you'll never have to worry about putting bread on the table. That's not what it's about at all."

"Then what?"

"Listen," he said, "I don't know then what. I'm not one

262

of you smart guys who went to Yale. I never learned that things were supposed to have explanations. I know that people do things and then when you ask them why, they make up reasons. The reasons they make up have absolutely nothing to do with why they really did anything.

"Life's not geometry. There are no proofs and no theorems that explain things. I threaten Paul and yell at him. Suddenly he does what I told him to do. Is it because of my yelling at him? I don't really know. Maybe, but he could just as easily have told me that it was none of my business. I thought that he was the kind of person I could push around, but I don't know that my pushing did it."

"Jesus, Sid," I said. "Give me a fucking break."

"I'm giving you a break. I'm telling you that you're wasting your time trying to figure everything out. Things happen. Nobody knows why. My mother, who worked baking bread and lived most of her life without riding in a car, told me that her mother, who never even knew there were cars, used to read the Talmud. Women weren't supposed to, but she did. She said that when she read the Talmud she learned one big thing, and that made forty years of it worthwhile."

"What was that?"

"Man makes plans and God laughs. So think about that."

Instead of thinking about that I walked over to Sid's bar and made myself another martini.

"Well done," Sid said. "That is the real answer."

"I think it is."

"You wonder why Susan isn't living with you in a colonial-style house in Chevy Chase?"

"Silver Spring."

"Wherever the hell it was," Sid said. "Ask nine out of ten doctors. They'll say she should be. You were pals. You talk her academic language. You're safe."

"Thanks," I said.

"Listen, by all odds, Susan and Paul shouldn't be anywhere near each other. Susan is a girl from an Army family and Paul is a hustler whose father owned a Jew store in Albion, Alabama. Susan should be teaching English literature at Oberlin. She's a dreamer. She's with a guy who used to be a dreamer, but it was a totally different dream from hers. That's pretty deep, huh? Almost Yale Law School deep?"

"Almost," I said.

"When Paul came out here after he was a waiter in New York he had great dreams. Great ones. And great ideas. He wanted to be an insider here. You think he wanted to make great art?"

"I don't know."

"He went around to the studios with two scripts. One was *Estonia*. The other one was Tom and Jerry in outer space. He didn't really care which one got sold. It so happens that *Estonia* got some attention from Dore Schary because Dore knew a big feeling when he saw one. But it was only after that came out and everybody said it was a masterpiece that Paul suddenly realized he was an artist. Then, when he made *Mother* and five others that didn't make a dime, he got to the point where he'd have been glad to make Tom and Jerry in outer space. You see what I mean? He wanted to keep making pictures so he'd be in the club. He wanted to keep hanging out with the guys at Nate 'n' Al's," Sid said. "That was his motivation. To be in the club."

"What's anybody's motivation here?"

"It's usually money," Sid said. "Alex Korda used to say that the only possible reason to be in Hollywood was for money. He was wrong. There are a lot of reasons.

"There are only about fifty people in this town who really control what gets made. That's a very fancy fraternity. It's about a lot more than money. A lot of people come out here to get into the fraternity. Very, very few do. You can't blame Paul for latching onto Deirdre when he was in trouble. She pulled him together enough so he could stay in the club. That's worth something. He was a wreck, gambling and not showing up on locations, and she got him buttoned down.

"So then Susan appears, and to Susan, Paul's not a guy who has to be dressed and given his lunch in a tin pail with a picture of Hopalong Cassidy on it. To Susan, Paul is that prince in *Estonia*. Paul's not blind, for Christ's sake. He sees his reflection in Susan's eyes. You know what that's like? To see yourself looking big in Susan's eyes?"

"I think once I saw it," I said. "Maybe not even then."

"That's bullshit," Sid said. "You must have seen it when you rescued Susan and gave her a place to stand at the White House. Don't be so fucking modest."

A sightseeing bus lumbered by outside. Through the double-pane mullioned windows we could hear the loud-speaker of the bus. As he pointed at Sid's house he said, "This is the magnificent home of Lucille Ball."

"All right," I said. "Maybe I saw that look once."

"So you know what that look is like. Paul falls for it like a ton of bricks, and then suddenly Dee's pulling on his nuts, and he doesn't know what the hell he's doing."

"So he kicks Susan in the teeth."

"Not once, but twice," Sid said. "Once when she came out and then when Deirdre had that fake suicide."

"So?"

"And Susan feels these things. She feels everything. That's written on her face. That's something you're born with. You can't be that sensitive and ever escape from it. You can cover it up, but you're covering up the real you.

"That day when she was first out here and got that shaft from Deirdre about the office, she was staggering. She pretended she was putting one over on me and that she was stringing me along into getting her a new office and that she was a helluva schemer. It wasn't like that at all. Susan was bleeding all over the lot."

"It's what makes her so right for the movies," I said.

"No." Sid shook his head. "No, I know what you mean. She knows what's on her mind. She knows what she feels.

That's what people used to say about Norman Lear. That he had the best record in TV because he was in touch with his instincts. That's different. People like Norman are in touch with their feelings, but there's some armor around those feelings. With Susan, everything's right out there in the open.

"Hollywood is filled with gangsters trying to look like artists. Susan is an artist, a real flower, like my mother used to say, and she's trying to look like a gangster."

"She doesn't want to look like a gangster. She wants to get pictures made."

"That's how you get pictures made, *boychik*. English lit professors don't get pictures made. *Shtarkers* get pictures made. Susan's trying to fit into that world, and you know it. It's not her, but she's trying to act like it is, and she's so smart that she can fool everyone for a long time, and maybe even herself."

"Okay," I said. "Okay, for a guy who doesn't see any explanations, you have a lot of ideas."

"Or I could be wrong," Sid said cheerfully. "That's also possible."

"Why is she with Paul?" I asked, although by then I was actually woozy, the way you get before the anesthetic puts you under.

"I don't know," Sid said. "I told you that. I spent my life trying to make things look pretty. Maybe after I yelled at him, Paul suddenly saw that Deirdre didn't look pretty at all anymore. She was the past, when he was weak. Susan was the future, when he was strong. I told you—maybe Susan saw him at that hotel in Maryland and suddenly he looked like Prince Alexei in *Estonia*. Maybe even the day Susan got thrown out made him look more like a savior, maybe after that she needed the fantasy more than ever. I don't know. I only know that you and I are out in the cold and I don't know the reason."

"And we're out there from now on," I said.

"Man makes plans," Sid said, "and God laughs. Don't

266

forget that. You want another one?" he asked, holding up a perfect Tiffany martini glass drained to the bottom.

"Definitely."

"A little heavier on the gin?"

"Much heavier on the gin," I said, and I don't remember the rest of the day.

24

CREDITS

About one month after Susan's bloody Sunday, Paul Belzberg came into her office and threw down *Good-bye to Mykonos* on her teak desk. He wore a red polo shirt and tan slacks, and had on his professor's horn-rimmed glasses. Susan wore her usual silk suit with her usual blue blouse.

"What's wrong with this story?" he asked Susan. "Bob Schallerberg is a very good friend. He's written a lot of pictures that made money."

"Which ones were those?" Susan asked.

"*Shoot the Tailor* and *It's Not My Fault*," Paul said. "Just for starters."

"I liked both of those pictures," Susan said. "I liked *Shoot the Tailor* a lot."

"I think *Goodbye to Mykonos* is even better," Paul said.

"How come this note like he was a student from AFI sending in his first script over the transom?"

"Because even though I liked those pictures, they aren't pictures we should be making right now. They might have been right for 1949, but they're not right for now."

"Are you kidding me?" Paul asked. "I just told you, two of his pictures made real money. Since when did you start to know more than the box office?"

"Do you really want to get into this?" Susan asked. It was a brilliantly sunny day in February, with light so bright it seemed to come through the walls, through the ceiling, through the floor. There was almost too much light on this particular day, just as there was too much light on the Sunday when Marco Castro had told her about his girlfriend, who had since died after taking one hundred Doriden in five minutes.

"Yes, I really want to get into this. The guy is not some loser to be dismissed by a woman who just came to town a year ago, even if she is my wife, and even if she is a fantastic braino," he said with almost a smile. He flopped into a yellow chair in Susan's office and turned up his hands as if to say *nu?*

"*Shoot the Tailor* was about a jewelry manufacturer in downtown Los Angeles who lives like a king and has to burn down his factory to keep himself afloat financially," Susan said. "It was maybe interesting to fifty people, all of them on the West Side of New York and on the West Side of Los Angeles. It had a negative of under five million because the star, Tony Schwartz, agreed to deferred compensation. They put another three million against it in prints and advertising. Interest was another one and a half."

"Jesus," Paul said.

"It took in eight million in rentals at a sixty-forty split against the distributor. It had a half a million network sale. You couldn't buy lunch with what it made in foreign. Okay? Tony Schwartz is in the dining room at the Hillcrest Club every day telling the garmentos that the picture made money. I'm telling you, it didn't."

"How the hell do you know so much?" Paul asked in genuine shock.

"I read and I'm not afraid of numbers, but I'm very afraid of making pictures that no one wants to see."

"You're a bottom-line gal. I would never have guessed that the girl who cried when Deirdre yelled at her would turn into such a computer."

"You wouldn't?" Susan asked with dead seriousness.

There was a moment's pause and then Paul said, "That was stupid of me. I know Deirdre did a lot more than yell at you, and you're not a computer."

"Anyway, *It's Not My Fault* was about a middle-aged Jewish folding-box manufacturer whose wife is a total loser and a bitch, and he gets seduced by a ravishingly beautiful sixteen-year-old girl who completely revives his self-esteem. I won't bore you with the numbers, but it lost money, too," Susan said.

"They were great pictures. Even if they lost money, they were great pictures."

Susan shook her head. "No, they weren't great pictures. I liked them, and you liked them, but they weren't for the real audience. They should have been little plays at an equity waiver theater somewhere. They had no point of connection with the college girl who's trying to learn something about life. They didn't mean a thing to the twenty-three-year-old salesman who's trying to escape somewhere after he's spent the day getting his brains kicked in on his bread route in Salinas. You see what I mean? Those pictures spoke to the fantasies of a tiny group of well-to-do middle-aged men. That's not what our audience is, and it's not what we're supposed to be talking about. Not only that, but they weren't particularly well done. If you look at them pretty carefully, you'll notice that the dialogue all sounds as if you can hear Bob Schallerberg typing it out at his swimming pool in Brentwood Park while he's waiting for Larry Gelbart to come over for a set. It's clever, but the writer is standing there chuckling between the screen and the audience."

"That's called good writing," Paul said. "Most people aren't used to it. We should help them, so they don't think 'Laverne and Shirley' is all that entertainment can be."

"I don't think so," Susan-Marie said. "The writing in those fake-smart movies is a group of old men sitting around playing pinochle telling their latest coup to each other. It's quips that go nowhere. 'Laverne and Shirley' do go somewhere. They're completely unpretentious, and they tell a little story about human nobility every week."

" 'Laverne and Shirley' is not about life," Paul said. "*Shoot The Tailor* is about life."

Susan got up from her desk and walked over to the yellow chair where Paul sat with a look of mock concern on his face. She took his hand and placed it against her cheek and then she kissed it. "You think so?" she said. "You've lived a lot of life. You think a garment manufacturer from Brentwood really has anything in common with those people in Albion, Alabama, where you wanted to be on the inside? More than that, do you think we're doing anything at all for those people when we show them the fantasies of well-to-do middle-aged men on the West Side of L.A.?"

"I don't care whether we do anything for those fucks," Paul said. "They're out lynching black people. What the hell should I care about them? I want to make movies that are what artists want to say. That's what counts. I assemble artists and I let them tell their stories. If I ran this business like Procter & Gamble, it wouldn't be the same business. It wouldn't be the business that made you want to come right out of the Silver Theatre and fly to Hollywood."

"Paul, come on," Susan said with a genuinely friendly caress of Paul's hand. "The business about lynching blacks was fifty years ago and it has nothing to do with anything. If they were lynching blacks it would be our duty to make movies that educated them and told them

271

that they would be bigger, better people if they didn't lynch blacks. But they don't, and that's just something that doesn't register.

"You know perfectly well that when you made *Estonia,* you had a perfectly good idea of exactly what those people at the record hops in Albion had on their minds. They were sick and tired after a day of working like dogs for two dollars and a quarter. They needed to feel as if life were something finer and bigger. They needed to go away on a trip, *a dream they could count on,* which is what a movie should be, and then they needed to have you deposit them back again at the Loew's Dixie, safe and sound. You knew that, and that's what you did. That's what *Mother* did, too, with the same whiff of how family life could be perfect, instead of being a constant round of fighting and squishing down people's feelings. That's what movies are supposed to do. That's what you knew when you wished you had the girl in your arms in the truck out by the lake."

"That was for a different era," Paul said. "That was before TV, when people would swallow any old lie about the world. Now they need to see something sharper, something with an edge. Something like *Shoot the Tailor,* which tells them about what's really going on in life."

"People already know what's going on in life," Susan said. "They're living life every day on the street while we're in our Mercedes convertibles playing tennis with the same friends we've had here for years."

"I know who that means."

"I don't mean you," Susan said hastily. "You still have the instinct. But most of the people making movies out here don't have any idea at all any longer what the rest of the country needs and wants to see. It's not true that people want to see things that throw life's failures back in their faces. People can turn on TV and see Watergate. People can stand in line at the grocery and see that their money won't buy as much. They can go out looking for a house and see that the American dream costs twice what they can afford. They can get a little escape from it by watching 'Happy Days.' But if they want to really get a glimpse into a whole new world where things are better, they have to go see an *Estonia*. They have to see Prince Alexei laying down his life for Princess Alexandra and having one last waltz before he goes off to fight against a sixty-ton tank on a white cavalry charger. That's what Hollywood is about, and not about Bob Schallerberg."

"Why do you think you know this when Bob and I don't, considering that we've been doing this since you were playing jacks?"

"That's why, Paul," Susan said with a pleading look in her eyes. "I'm new in town. I'm just off the boat. I've been out there in America. I've spent the lunch hour listening to information operators talk about their lives. I've been in line at the grocery hearing women talk about disappointment. I've taken night school classes at the University of Maryland and heard students tell each other how screwed up their world is. That's what I know. Most of what Hollywood makes comes from Hollywood. I'm telling you that what America wants is something that comes from east of Burbank, from somewhere out in America.

"That's why you have it all over most of the people in this town," she added. "You remember Albion so vividly that you can still bring that memory inside the lot. That's what people want to see."

"No," Paul said. He shook his head. "I love the compliments, but I'm not buying. The people here are artists. If there are other artists out there in America, they can come here and make their vision. I'm not going to run this studio like a detergent company, bringing in market research people to second-guess my writers. That's right for the plumbing supply business, not for the picture business. What plays in Peoria is a well-made movie, not what Audits and Surveys says will play. Look at *Midnight Cowboy*. That did pretty goddamned well, and it didn't have anything to do with people in Albion, Alabama."

"It did well because it took a situation of total misery and showed human nobility. Jon Voight and Ratso were noble to each other. They touched the kid who's just been totally shafted by the girl of his dreams at Bucknell. It touched the man who feels as if nobody appreciates his working like a dog to put bread on the table in Milwaukee. That wasn't like Bob Schallerberg's work. It worked because it had an artist named John Schlesinger lifting it out of the ordinary, taking it out of the slush and the germs and taking it up to the place where Don Quixote and Sancho Panza rode their horses. It was a real fantasy, even if it was set in SRO hotels."

"If you can do that with a gigolo and a bum, you can surely do it with a clothing manufacturer and an artist."

"You *could* do it," Susan agreed. "If you had real artists like John Schlesinger or someone even close to him, but we don't have too many of those people here. What we have here is the Hollywood buddy system, where people know each other's names and faces, and they give the jobs to the people they know. Hollywood isn't a community of artists. It's a network, the same as the network in foundation garments or P.I. law or selling real estate in Tyler, Texas. People work if they know the right people, not if they have talent. You know that."

"That's the system. I don't deny that there's a lot in that, but that's the nature of any business. You do business with people you know."

Susan became flushed and suddenly hugged Paul. She sat on the arm of his chair and pressed her face against his cheek. She pulled back and spoke to him out of a gusher of enthusiasm. "No, Paul. Nobody knew you when you got here and look what you did. Two Academy Awards before you were thirty."

"So, anybody with enough balls can still get his foot in the door here. You know that," Paul said. "Anybody with enough knowledge of what she wants. Anybody who's tough enough can still fight his way onto the lot. You did it."

"But it hurt, and people who have great ideas and great art in their heads aren't necessarily fighters," she said.

"What we can do here at Republic is something truly astonishing and new in Hollywood. We can actually make a home here for people who know fantasy, but aren't necessarily fighters or part of the Hollywood buddy system. Let the other studios deal with the writers who have ideas about middle-aged men in the *schmata* business. We'll do the stories that people who need movies need to go see. Let somebody else work with the people who he plays tennis with. We'll get the young guys and the librarians and the stewardesses who have stories that the sophomore at Indiana University and the mechanic at Chrysler want to hear."

"We'll have every nut in America knocking on the door," Paul said.

"Good. That's what Darryl Zanuck thought you were when you first got here. I *want* every nut in America knocking on Republic's door. I want to be positive that the next Paul Belzberg comes to our door and not anywhere else in town. If I hear that the next Paul Belzberg has gone to Universal, to my good friend Jules Stein, I'm going to be very pissed off."

She smiled at him and then hugged him and kissed his neck. He lifted her in his arms and twirled her around the office, knocking a copy of *Variety* onto the floor.

"My dreamer," he said. "My little dreamer."

"You're the dreamer," Susan-Marie said when they stopped kissing. "You're the one who made his dreams and made them my dreams when I was a little girl."

"Thanks," Paul said sarcastically. "Maybe you'll make mine when I'm in the Motion Picture Home in Calabasas."

"You'll never be there. When you have dreams, you're forever young. You've got it, Paul. You don't have to even think about people like Bob Schallerberg and Steve Somers. You've got everything. You can even read my dreams and tell me what they are. You read my dream about being in the pyramid and getting all wrapped up in cotton. How did you *do* that?"

"Lucky guess," Paul said, although the truth was that he did not know how he had done it. "Anyway," Paul said in Susan's office, "I'm just another schlepper out here, and I can tell you that it's a business. It's not dreams. It's work."

"No. It's work for some people. For the people who make movies great though, the people who made *Gone With the Wind* and *Quo Vadis* and *Jezebel* and *The Postman Always Rings Twice* and *House of Wax,* it's their dreams that make the town run."

"It's still work and you still have to depend on people who know the business."

"But you have to depend on them the way an architect has to depend on a bricklayer. You have to have the great idea, the picture in your brain first. After that, it all comes fairly easily for the bricklayer. But what I'm telling you is that we don't need to make the bricklayers into the architects. You're the architect of dreams. That's you. That's why I loved you even before I saw you, even before I ever knew you were a real person. You were the dream-architect of my youth, the dream-god who sent me a happy place to hide. That's what I love about you, and that's what you simply can't forget. You're bigger than people like Bob Schallerberg, bigger than the boys in the back room. That's why I love you. That's why you're my dream, even when you let Deirdre kick the life out of me, you were still my dream-weaver, and I'm not going to let you be anything less."

Susan-Marie talked like this for a long time, and all Paul could think was that something had gone terribly wrong. He was not an architect of dreams. He was only a man trying to earn a living, trying to get his ideas out. He was the son of the owner of the Jew store in Albion who had a vision, and that vision was that some day he would not be an outsider. He had found Hollywood, and by a miracle of luck and persistence and imagination, he had made *Estonia* and *Mother* and now he was not an outsider any longer. He was a member of the club in Hollywood, but nothing more than that. He did not have another *Estonia* inside himself to save his life. He had good ideas and he knew good writers. But he was no god.

■   ■   ■   ■

One day in early June of 1974 Susan looked up from her morning reading—a script called *Summer Rain*, about a sixteen-year-old girl becoming addicted to Methedrine—and saw Michael Crovitz standing at her door. The super-agent wore white tennis flannels, which were the height of chic that summer. Next to him stood Dick Costello, wearing a blue flannel suit, a cream-colored shirt, and a red Turnbull & Asser necktie with red ducks flying all over a field of blue.

"Can we come in?" Dick asked. "Just for a minute?"

"Of course," Susan said. "I don't have anything to do today."

Both men settled themselves wearily into Susan's enormous yellow armchairs. "I'll make it really quick," Crovitz said. "Paul Newman wants to know whether he's in or out on *The Chinese Day*. It's been close to a year and he's almost ready to start a new picture, and we still don't have a go."

"Jesus, I thought that was all taken care of," Susan said. "Is your client asking for gross participation again?"

"No way," Crovitz said. "The same deal he would have made on *Hawaii Kai*. Not a dime more."

"So?" Susan asked. She looked over at Costello. "What's the problem?"

"There's no deal problem," Costello said. "The problem is that I can't get the deal memo approved up above."

"What do you mean, up above?" Susan asked.

"I mean I can't even get in to talk to Paul Belzberg about it," Costello said.

"When I see him at the Palm and bring it up he just nods and pats me on the back of the head like I was a pet cocker spaniel or something," Crovitz added.

Susan took out a Viceroy cigarette and lit it with a

flourish of her Du Pont gold cigarette lighter. She glanced at the bottom of the lighter. A beautiful script read *To Susan from Paul—Forever Young.* She inhaled and then blew out a trail of bluish-gray smoke. "The deal is exactly the same as the deal on *Hawaii Kai?*"

"To the penny," Costello said.

"Including the back end, even including suspend and extend and weekly overages?"

"To the penny," Crovitz said.

Susan leaned forward in her chair. Then she stood and shook hands with Crovitz. "It's a done deal," she said.

"Are you sure?" Crovitz asked.

"What did I just say?" Susan asked.

"That's what I like about meeting with you. You're a player," Crovitz said.

"Have the papers sent over to him right away," she said. "Get one of the lawyers to stay here all night to get them drafted."

Susan walked Crovitz out to the parking circle. Along with the head of ICM and the head of William Morris, Crovitz was granted the right to park unannounced in the Winners' Circle, as that horseshoe was called. "Is Paul feeling all right?" Crovitz asked. "I mean, is something wrong? You know you can talk to me."

"He's all right," Susan said. "He was probably trying to bargain you down. That's all."

"It's a small town," Crovitz said. "I don't know how good it is to keep Paul Newman on the string."

"He's off the string right now. He's on the plantation. Let's start getting some work out of him."

Susan watched Crovitz drive away in his Jaguar. She turned to Costello. "Paul was just playing hardball with Crovitz. It's nothing."

"If you say so," he said. "But Crovitz would have been totally within his rights to have blown off the whole deal over this. You don't do this to Paul Newman."

"It's all taken care of now," she said. "Let's go on to the next crisis."

That night, in the teahouse at 77 Malibu Beach Colony, Susan handed Paul an iced tea before dinner and then stroked his cheek. "Paul," she said, "is there any particular reason why you didn't sign off on Paul Newman's deal in *The Chinese Day?*"

"You bet there is."

"May I know it?" She had changed from her usual suit into floppy silk trousers and a T-shirt with the Republic logo on it. She looked at Paul and smiled cheerfully. Paul looked back and squinted. He looked pained at having to answer the question and then said, "Because I don't like the idea of paying that kind of money to Michael Crovitz, especially when he isn't even handling the deal himself. That guy was carrying around the mail a few years ago and now he's asking for two million bucks and gross participation."

"He was carrying around the mail ten years ago. Now he's handling Newman. He's a genius now. There's a pretty big difference there. Anyway, there's no gross participation in that deal. And it'll be a million five."

Belzberg waved his hand airily. "I don't read every decimal point. Deirdre used to do that for me."

"Well, she's writing her name in shit on the walls now, Paul. So you have to do it yourself."

"Okay. But Crovitz didn't even handle the damned thing himself. He passed on the deal memo to some hotshot lawyer named Chris something. Am I supposed to deal on that level?"

"It wouldn't matter if he handed it over to his cleaning woman," Susan said. "The Paul Newman part was the important part."

Belzberg got up and looked out at the ocean. It was deep blue, with high surf coming in fast. Far off to the right the sun was almost down over Point Dume.

"You're right," he said after fully two minutes of silence. "You're right. Let's close it up."

"I did close it," Susan said.

"That makes me look great," Belzberg said.

"I did it to keep us from losing Paul Newman. I told them you were playing hardball negotiating with them, but I couldn't take the pressure."

"So it's closed."

"Right."

"So now you're making the decision to hire Paul Newman at one point five mil by yourself," Belzberg said. "That's a nice promotion."

"You know very well that we had already decided to hire him."

Paul looked out to the southeast, at the towers of Santa Monica overlooking the Santa Monica Bay. Without turning around he said, "Again, you're right. I don't really want to think about it."

"If you're too busy to think about it, we should set up some kind of mechanism to make these decisions," Susan said. "A committee or something."

"We don't need a committee," Paul said. "You do it. You do it so much better than anyone else that you might as well do it all the time."

Susan looked down at the tile floor. "I'm sorry," she said. "I guess I shouldn't have closed the deal without talking to you. I was just afraid of losing the deal altogether. I wasn't trying to take anything away from you." She smiled. "Believe me, the impression I left them with was that you were so tough they were getting a break not having to play with you."

Paul turned around and grinned at her. "But we know different, right?"

"Paul, come on. This is silly."

"You're right. I guess I shouldn't get upset just because Michael Crovitz, who was starting when I was producing major-budget pictures, sends a lawyer to negotiate with me. I guess I shouldn't feel as if anything wrong has happened when my own wife, who hasn't even been here two years, feels as if she knows the business better than I do and cuts me up right in front of my own head of business affairs and the hottest agent in town. Why should I worry about that?"

"It doesn't mean any of those things," Susan said. "We had to make a decision. Maybe I made it too fast, but nobody was trying to hurt you. When Paul Newman is negotiating with Alan Hirschfield, that same Chris something or other negotiates with him, too. And also if he's negotiating with Leo Jaffe. You ought to know there's nothing personal in this."

Paul walked over to the Lalique crystal decanter on the wicker sideboard and poured himself a tumbler of Dewar's. He drank about an inch of it in three large gulps, then smiled. He sat down next to Susan and kissed her on her long, white neck. "You're right," he said. "I'm getting old. I take all of this too personally."

"No," she said. "I was too fast."

"Forget it. That's why you're good. If you can't act fast, you don't belong in Hollywood."

She held his hand and squeezed it. "I'm sorry."

Paul waved her apology away and laughed. "I don't even want to think about contracts anyway. I have a way of doing *Good-bye to Mykonos* that will be just perfect. Before you start to argue with me, just listen."

"I'm listening," Susan said happily.

"When I was a kid back in Albion I was friends with this family. The boy had an older brother, Glenn Halley. That kid was the best jitterbug dancer you ever saw in your life. But fantastic. You ever see anyone do the jitterbug?"

"I've done it myself a thousand times."

"And he had the prettiest girl in the town as his girlfriend. One day, around 1942, he was out on some dirt road playing his guitar and suddenly he sees a black kid run by and right after him there's a mob of white men with shotguns. They're gonna kill that boy because he made some crack about one of their daughters."

"I'm with you."

"And the jitterbug boy stops them and says, 'Wait a

fucking minute. You'll do this over my dead body. That boy is my friend. We play music together.' So the crowd breaks up, but they don't like it. Glenn, the jitterbug boy, goes into the Marines and fights all over Europe. He gets wounded at Monte Cassino and then again at Okinawa when he's sent to the Pacific. Meanwhile, back in Alabama, the boys who hated him have killed that black kid and have raped the girlfriend. So when the jitterbug boy gets back, he pretty much has to fight the whole town. He has to be a sort of twentieth-century 'High Plains Drifter.' Finally he does justice and half the town is demolished."

"That really happened?" Susan asked.

"Not that violent," Paul said. "But something like it."

"It's an absolutely fantastic story. I love that story. Let's get started on that tomorrow."

"Well, wait a minute. That story is dated. World War II stories never make money. But let's take some of the elements of that story and put them in Mykonos."

"What do you mean?"

"I mean that we can take that element of the guy who's seen terrible evil in his hometown and he goes over to Europe and becomes really successful, and then he comes back to his hometown and gets revenge on all the people who were cruel to him when he was a kid. Maybe he does something with the Ku Klux Klan. Maybe we set it in the thirties when there was a big Klan in Alabama. The kid becomes wildly rich and then humiliates all the people who humiliated him, but then he learns there's no real triumph in revenge and he moves back to the town to lead a quiet life. I already talked to Bob Schallerberg about it over at the commissary at lunch today, while you were closing the deal with Crovitz."

"I guess I'll have to apologize for that for the rest of my life."

"No, I'll never mention it again," Paul said. "What do you think?"

Susan got out of her chair and walked back and forth in the teahouse for a minute, tapping her fingers on the wicker sideboard as she passed it. It was a moment, she thought, when she could take a deep breath after a conversation in which she was forced to inhale in teaspoons.

"I think your basic idea is incredible," she said. "I also think that the twist of having him realize that revenge is hollow is great. But what I really think is that you don't need to hook it up to *Good-bye to Mykonos* in any way. You have a fantastic classic of a story right there in front of you. Why clutter it up with Bob Schallerberg's garbage?"

"Bob Schallerberg had literally won an Academy Award for screenwriting before you were born. Literally. He won it in 1943 for *Twin Cities* and that was at least a year before you were born. You must really think you're pretty hot to knock him like that all the time."

"Let's not get into this again. You know that I don't care if a writer is fifty or fifteen. I care about what he's got in him. You know that. *Twin Cities* was a story about ordinary men and women in Minneapolis and in Leningrad during the war. It was a sentimental hit. He got blacklisted for it in 1949, which was a complete rip-off and I've always felt as if he didn't deserve it."

"Your pal, Nixon."

"It had nothing to do with Nixon, whom I barely know and who wouldn't recognize me if he fell over me. The reason I always felt that Schallerberg didn't deserve to be blacklisted was that he only did a re-write on *Twin Cities*, and the first draft was done by Tim Markison, who was killed in a plane crash selling War Bonds before the awards could be given out. Not only that, but Schallerberg did everything he possibly could to be a friendly witness before Martin Dies. He got tagged as an unfriendly witness because he told everyone at Junior's Delicatessen that he had refused to talk. The truth was that he had told everything he could ever make up, but one of his pals at Junior's worked for someone at Warner, and next thing you know, he was blacklisted for an act of bravery, if you can call it that, which he never even did."

"Jesus," Paul said. "I can't believe it. I have known that guy for thirty years. This doesn't sound like the same Bob Schallerberg. This sounds like someone else. How do you know all this?"

"I know it because I ask questions and I follow the movies. I've seen every one of his movies, including *Easy Ways Out*, which didn't even get theatrical release. He wrote it two years ago. Have you seen it?"

"No, I heard the director cut it totally wrong."

"No way. I've read the script and I've seen the movie. The script might as well be in Farsi."

Paul did not say anything while he sipped at the remains of his Scotch. He walked over to the sideboard and ate a handful of potato chips.

"You're a hell of a girl," Belzberg said. "Really amazing. If it's not brand shiny new with Susan-Marie stamped all over it, it's shit, right?"

Susan picked up Paul's hand as he walked by her and kissed the palm. "That's not what I mean at all," she said. "Your idea is wonderful. I can see it. Just hearing it is enough to let me see every scene."

"So, am I going to write it?" Paul asked. "It needs to have someone who really knows how to write work on it."

"That could easily be you and some new writer," Susan said. "It's your vision. Why not make yourself the writer? You can do it. You can do anything."

"If I did it, you might read it and tell me it's something Bob Schallerberg did."

"You know I won't."

"I'm not a writer. I think I'll just take the basic idea and have Bob Schallerberg develop it." He paused. "If that's all right with you."

"It's not all right with me," Susan answered in a rush. "It's not all right with me to see my husband take a fabulous idea and turn it over to a hack. Your idea could be a classic. It could be like *Inherit the Wind*, except with action. Pick it up and run with it."

"I am running with it. I'm letting a man I respect, a man who is *not* a hack, develop it. That's running with it."

"No. That isn't running with it. That's doing it so that if Sid asks what the hell happened you can say, 'Hey, Sid, it's not my fault. I gave it to a guy who won two Academy Awards. How could I have known he would screw it up?' That's covering your ass."

"You have a goddamn lot of nerve," Paul said, turning red and clenching his fists.

"It's not that. It's not nerve at all. It's that I believe in you. You're not a Bob Schallerberg. You're still an active volcano in this town. I won't let you sell yourself short."

"You really believe that?"

"I believe it totally. I believe in you. You're the man who made *Estonia*. You don't need to have hacks around you."

Paul Belzberg stood up, picked up Susan from her chair, and kissed her. "You really believe that?" he asked.

"You know I do, and you have to believe it, too."

"When I hear you say it I almost can believe it," he said.

That night, after dinner, Susan and Paul walked along the beach, past Lana Turner's house, past Ned Tanen's house, into the misty, cool evening.

"When I hear you talk about how great I can be, I feel small," Paul said. "I never thought of movies really as any more than a business. At the most, a way of telling the world what was on my mind."

"It doesn't matter if you conceptualized what you were doing. You were doing it and you were doing it right. You're still doing it right. You're giving that feeling to Americans that the frontier isn't closed after all. They can go and see a whole new way of life any time they care to take a short trip to the theater. The movies are America's last frontier. They are the most available link between the imagination and the concrete," Susan said.

"I really feel as if I'm just a janitor in some big museum in Paris when you talk like that."

285

"You're the prize exhibit. You're my prize exhibit," she added, hugging him more tightly.

Paul gently disengaged her arms and held her in front of him. He looked at her and said, in an excess of honesty and good faith, "I guess that's what I am, all right. Your exhibit."

"My Hollywood," Susan-Marie said. "My Prince Alexei."

25

AXES

Just to prove that no one knows anything about life, the interview with Sid Bauman got me a job. I wrote it up in a highly disguised way, making a lot of points that Sid had made about how Hollywood works on fear and envy. I sent it off to *Esquire*, just as a joke, and they ran it under the headline CONFESSIONS OF A MOGUL. It had a lot of blind items about people whom the really hip *Esquire* reader could identify as David Lean or Daryl Zanuck or Donna Wilkes. Sid had told me those items when I had awakened at midnight after passing out from the fifth martini. They were a sort of gift because he felt badly that he had told me so much about Hollywood. "I feel like a camp counselor telling a little kid ghost stories," he said, "and then the kid wakes up in the middle of the night screaming."

"Only these aren't ghosts," I said. "These are real."

Anyway, Sid told me the line of Hollywood gossip that he had probably been working out while he pretended to be tipsy, it ran in *Esquire*, and the next thing I knew, I had a call from Grassley Fauver, the publisher of *New View*.

Fauver had made a fortune with a magazine in Chicago called *New Wind*. It was a slick-sheet *cadeau* with articles about the best kielbasa on the South Side, where to get laid on a Sunday night, who makes the best pasta in Oak Park, and how to get rich quick while doing the crossword puzzle in *The Saturday Review*. *New Wind* was such a success that Fauver had been asked to start a prototype analogue in Los Angeles. The result was *New View*. Unfortunately, Fauver had staffed the magazine exclusively with magazine journalists from Minneapolis, Indianapolis, St. Louis, and Chicago. They had no idea of what Los Angeles was about except that they knew it was much warmer, drier, and farther west than New Trier High School. *New View* ran one article after another about how warm, dry, and far west Los Angeles was. Then they ran articles that discovered that there was surfing in California, that there were a lot of Mercedes in California, and that there were an amazing number of people who had gotten rich from the movie business in California, especially as compared with Minneapolis.

There were also articles about where to get the best kielbasa in Van Nuys, how to get laid on a Sunday night, who makes the best pasta in Redondo Beach, and how to get rich quick while working on your tan.

To be charitable about it, the magazine didn't fly off the newsstands at Gelson's in Studio City. Somehow, the discerning reader in Studio City was able to figure out that she was not being told anything about her city that she did not already know. Instead, she was given the treat of seeing it through the eyes of someone who had just gotten off American Airlines Flight #77 from O'Hare Airport to discover that there were *palm trees* on Sunset Boulevard! What the heck. The shopper at Gelson's great-grandparents had come from Illinois to learn the same thing fifty years before. She was not about to plunk down two-fifty to learn it again.

But in "Confessions of a Mogul," Grassley Fauver saw something new. "What we get with you, *boychik*," he said as we ate Mandarin Lamb at the Mandarin, "is gossip that people don't already know, with that, like, really sarcastic tone of yours. We're like telling people what's going on in tinseltown, only with wit."

I pitied the man who still called L.A. "tinseltown." I pitied the man who ate at the Mandarin. But I loved and worshipped the man who was going to give me my very own column every month in *New View*. The man who has a column has an axe. John Dunne once told me that, and I was in the mood to have an axe after I had been dumped on for six straight months by young men wearing Hawaiian shirts whom I would not have allowed to wash my car back East.

I was so excited to have my own column that I stayed up all night with "Grass" Fauver as we went from bar to bar along the Pacific Coast Highway, starting at The Jetty and making our way to the Point Dume Café by dawn. "Grass" was a cocky little sonofabitch, with his paisley tie, his suspenders, his midnight blue Brooks Brothers suit, and his dividend stubs sticking out of his vest pocket. He used them to pick his teeth, and I admired that.

"Go after the power players," he said. "Go after the people everybody else is afraid of. If you hate some guy at William Morris, tell us. If some guy pretends to be a philanthropist and makes his money off real estate scams, tell us. If you see something that's inside and really pisses you off, go to it. You're the Joe Pine of *New View*."

"I love it," I said.

At five in the morning, I made my way back to my apartment barely able to see over the wheel of my car, a new, black Porsche. Did I tell you I had bought a Porsche? Why not? After all, I was making six hundred dollars a week. As far as I could tell, I was rich. But when I got home I was not rich any longer. Just as a reflex before getting into the shower, I snapped on the Trinitron. There, in front of a crying knot of White House employees, stood the big enchilada himself. He was not quite as big as he had been that day in the solarium. He stood in his Saks Fifth Avenue suit, with his family arrayed behind him, looking as if they had been kept awake for forty days of siege, and he talked to the unconscious of America. For fifteen minutes a politician talked like a hurt human being. He talked about how no one in his administration had ever gotten rich from his job, how the White House was not the biggest house, but it was the best house because it had the best people. He swayed and tried to laugh and talked about how hard his staff had worked for him.

He wound into a little homily about how poor his family had been. His father had not been a shipping magnate or a wealthy bootlegger or a stock-market manipulator. No, his father had been a streetcar driver. His mother had been a nurse for babies other than her own. But she had been a saint.

He went into a long quote from Theodore Roosevelt about "when his heart's dearest died . . ." He fought back tears and the White House staff wept openly. That is the truth. That was the only truth I ever heard, before or since, on TV from the White House: that a boy child had been born. That he had tried, in the lemon groves of Yorba Linda, and in the dust of Whittier, to do better than his father. That he thought he had failed, perhaps because he had a mother who had been forced to nurse babies other than her son Richard. Most of all, that he was sorry.

In that speech Richard Nixon did something politicians are never supposed to do. He showed his wounds. He bled on camera. He told the schoolyard bullies that they had gotten him on his back in the mud at last. He hurt, and he showed it.

In my drunken, hung-over miasma, I watched the performance. I no longer felt rich, but I felt as if I had seen into the heart of a man who had been president, and I was dazzled by the labyrinthine fortress there. The moment was R.N.'s farewell address, to be sure. As far as I could tell, it was also his finest moment, the one he had been yearning to have all his life. It was the instant when he said to the world, "I am a human, a mortal just the same as all of you."

Or, as Sid might have said, perhaps I was wrong about the whole thing. One thing I was not wrong about, though. After that morning, I was ready to take up my axe.

One week later, when I was "interviewing" Sid, Susan strolled in. She looked like the president of Revlon, in a navy blue silk dress with blue shoes and long, thin fingers that would have made Princess Grace envious twenty years earlier.

Sid was lying on a couch in his pool house. He had passed his arteriogram with less than flying colors six months earlier. Now he was on a modified Pritikin program of exercise and diet. Sid followed the high-fiber, no salt, no sugar routine almost perfectly. He even swam for forty minutes at a time twice each day in his pool. The only variation from his regimen was that he still had two Bombay martinis every afternoon. As often as I could, which was plenty often, I joined him.

"I can't believe this," Susan said as she drank a Seven-Up. "Paul has put Bob Schallerberg on the *Jitterbug* project. What does he think he's doing? That was such a great idea, and Bob Schallerberg'll turn it into an episode of 'Starsky and Hutch.' He told me he was through talking about it when I brought it up to him."

"So, fuck it," Sid said. "It's not worth arguing about it. We'll do all right on the distribution side."

"But it's a great idea. I did charts for him about how it would go, and I got him a list of young writers, with some plot summaries, and I thought we were totally set up on that thing. I even got him some figures on World War II pictures and some survey dope on how kids are really, really interested in World War II. He just put Bob Schallerberg on it and that's it."

"You want a martini?" Sid asked.

"No, I can't," Susan said. "I was just on my way over to Century City to talk to Ken Ziffren about a few things and I stopped by to see the boss. You feeling all right?"

By way of answer, Sid pulled at the waistline of his trousers to show about seven inches of slack. "I'm hungry all the time," he said. "I'm starving all the time, but my serum HDL count is a lot lower, and maybe I'll live to see a few more movies."

"You'd better," Susan said. "I have to go. I'll call you tonight. Paul's going off to Rangoon, if you can believe that, to the Burmese theater owners' meetings."

She kissed Sid and me on the cheek, gave us each a soul handshake as she had seen it that week in the dailies for a prison movie called *Solitary,* and walked out.

We both caught each other looking after her too hungrily as she walked along the flagstone path out to her yellow Mercedes convertible. Then we went back out to Sid's pool house to watch the sun move across the sky and test different kinds of martinis.

"To Rangoon?" I said. "To the Burmese theater owners' association?"

"Go know," Sid said.

"I already know, because you explained it to me."

"So?"

"Over in Rangoon, Paul may still be able to find a little Burmese girl who looks up at him and says, 'Oh, you're the Paul Belzberg who made *Estonia,* and Paul knows pretty well that she's not going to suddenly pull out a sheaf of statistics generated by the research department of Burma University explaining why he never exactly understood movies in the first place."

"You got it," Sid agreed, jauntily shaking Bombay gin and vermouth in a Tiffany crystal decanter.

"It's an amazing thing, but just since I've been out here full time, I see Paul and Susan walking differently. It's like Susan seems to be walking a little straighter, a little taller, each time I see her. It's as if she's grown a few more vertebrae. But every time I see Paul he looks more hunched over. It's a little thing, but I think I see it."

"Her only sin," Sid said. "She's too fucking smart. She comes at Paul with all this stuff about the social context of the movies, and he could take it if she were just a philosopher. If she just could talk about AFI theory and didn't have any idea of where to find a decent script, he would feel all right. She would be a fumbling academic and he would still be in charge. But she's picked up the four best writing teams in Los Angeles in the last year, and she's signing them up so fast the development department at Fox is going berserk.

"And if she could do that, but couldn't negotiate, and didn't really have any idea of how to get her way in a meeting with Ron Mardigian and Stan Kamen, she would be all right also. Then Paul could say, well, she's really good in the abstract, on *story*, as if story wasn't what movies were all about anyway, but he was still a lot better than she was in sitting down and tummling her way through a meeting enough to get the signatures on the deal memos. But her problem is that she's better at that than Paul also. So where does that leave him?" I asked.

"Plus, she does the numbers so goddamned fast. That's the icing on the cake," Sid said. "If Paul were smart, he would just say, 'Wow, have I got a great partner,' and then he'd go on to push her as fast and as far as she could go. But he can't do that."

"Not at all surprising," I said. "If she was brought out here to be one of those fun house mirrors that makes Paul always look bigger than he is, and if she suddenly starts making Paul look smaller all the time, he can't very well change what he wants. He didn't want a partner. He wanted to be made bigger than he was. But he didn't know how fast Susan would grow. He didn't really know how far she was determined to go."

"I don't even think it was a plan," Sid said. "You say it like she secretly connived to get out here and make Paul look small. It wasn't like that at all."

He walked over to a small refrigerator and took from it a wedge of hoop cheese. With an ivory-handled knife, he smeared cheese on a Pritikin cracker. "I'm not even going to offer this to you," he said. "It tastes so awful that nobody should have to eat it unless he's in fear of imminent death."

"God forbid," I said. But, just to please Sid, I took pretzels out of a box on a ledge above the exercise bicycle.

"She didn't plan anything," Sid said as he sat down on a deep blue chaise and then lay down. "She didn't really even know herself how much she had in her. She knew she wanted to be here in Hollywood, but she didn't know at all how much better she would be than her competition out here. She didn't know that just because the guys out here are vice-presidents for production, that doesn't mean they know a thing. She didn't know that just because a man has been executive producer on six movies, he might still have no idea of what a movie should be.

"The most important thing is that she didn't know that the guy she idolized was going to be just another schlepper out here who happened to make a great movie but who couldn't really articulate what a movie should be as well as she could," Sid said. "She didn't understand how much better she would be than the competition."

"She didn't understand that Paul would be the competition," I said. "You're forgetting that."

"It couldn't be any other way," Sid said. He was restless. He stood up and walked out the French doors to the pool deck. I walked out and stood next to him.

"She wouldn't have felt that way about you," I said, putting my arm around him. "You own the studio."

"Yes, she would have soon enough," Sid said. "The difference is that I would have encouraged her to take over everything and I would have gone off to the United Nations. I always wanted to make things pretty. Once, Taft Schreiber told me that I could be a delegate to the UN. Not the ambassador, but a delegate to some conference or other. It would be in Paris. I would have liked that," he said. "Paris. My whole life, I've wanted to make things pretty. That's been my whole aim in life. I could have worked at some conference making sure kids in Mali didn't choke to death from whooping cough. That would have been pretty. When I lived in Brooklyn, when I was a boy, kids would still come down with polio. They'd be sick for a few weeks, and their families would be terrified, and then they'd either get better, or they'd never walk again. It would be pretty to make sure that never happened anywhere. Much prettier than a store window, even prettier than owning a studio."

"Well," I said.

"Susan could have stayed around the studio and run it. That would have been fine. But I knew she didn't love me. I was a businessman. Susan's not really interested in business. She's interested in putting *Jitterbug* on the screen so that people are in a trance for two hours. That's Susan's problem. She's not interested in business."

"She's doing just fine anyway."

"Yes, because she loves movies so much," Sid said. "She can do well even though she doesn't care about business. I don't mean that she doesn't pay attention to the bottom line or to getting contracts closed. She does that great. We've been able to get our contracts division caught up for the first time in five years since she's been here."

"Since Deirdre's gone."

"Yes, because Deirdre had to examine every page to see what she could use against somebody at William Morris or at Pollock, Bloom, but Susan just wants to get them out. Anyway, what I mean about Susan and business is that business, anyway, this business, is basically about being in the club of guys who play tennis together, who drink together, who fly off to Vegas to gamble and fuck hookers together, and Susan isn't really in that club. She's a player, and she makes deals and makes pictures, but she really cares more about the pictures than about being in the fraternity, the giant ZBT house that we call Hollywood, and that's going to be a problem. She's a dealmaker, but she's not a schmoozer."

"Sid, you're not a member of that club either," I said.

"I know, but to Susan, I'm a businessman, and that's nothing compared with being an artist, a man who made *Estonia* like Paul," Sid said. "So that's why she's with Paul, even though she should have been with me."

"That's funny," I said. "Because I thought she should have been with me. I wouldn't get mad if she were a bigger wheel in Hollywood than I was."

"That's because you're not even really in the game," Sid said. "No offense, but you're just standing on the sidelines watching. So you're not really in competition with Susan at all."

"Maybe that's better," I said.

"Maybe," Sid said. "But the point is that I have to go lie down, and you have to go swimming or something. And you asked me why Paul was in Rangoon, and the answer is that he's married to a woman whose only sin is that she's in touch with her own feelings and knows this picture business better than he does, and that wasn't what he bargained for, and so he goes on a lot of trips."

"What about Deirdre? Didn't she do the same thing to him?"

"Not at all," Sid said. He shook his head. "Deirdre is manipulative and tough, but she's not a creative type. She never could go head to head with Paul creatively and make him feel second-best. She could beat him up, but he always felt smarter, more of a moviemaker. She was an accountant, a handler, and he was the boss—until the last gambit at Cedars-Sinai. But with Susan, he sees this sweet, non-bitch who knows the craft as well as he does and who cuts through all of his prejudices to see what a movie is. In some ways, Deirdre was easier for him."

We walked out to the front lawn, immaculately green just like the lawn at Republic. Sid shook hands with me. His wrists seemed thin inside the sleeves of his bathrobe.

"So?" I asked. "What's next?"

"Oh, Susan can handle it all," Sid said. "She's just begun here. She'll make Paul feel like he's part of it, like he's doing the most important things for a while, like he's still big. For a while, and then everybody'll know who's pushing and who's riding. Believe me, Susan's just begun. She's the first woman who could have it all, who knew how to get a picture done right, and even more than that, could do something new, better, outside the club."

"Then what?"

"Then I don't know what," Sid said. "I told you, there aren't answers for everything. This is life. Haven't you figured that out yet? Life is different from an examination in school. And Hollywood is so fucking hard because it's everything in life crammed into four square miles, and there are never any long-term answers for anything. If you want answers go back to New Haven."

"You know what I mean, Sid."

"When the doctors at St. John's first told us that Amanda had the wrong kind of receptors and that she'd need radiation, we made all kinds of plans. We would go to the Mayo Clinic. We'd go to Sloane-Kettering. We'd go to someplace in Zurich. We had a plan for everything. It didn't mean a thing. In the middle of the night. I'd just be there holding her hand with her not even awake, and that was what it came down to. If there was ever an answer, that was it—I held her hand while she was dying. That's the only answer I ever knew.

"So, I don't know what to answer. You want me to answer that you'll wind up with Susan? I don't know. Maybe you will."

"It would be nice," I said. "I would never be envious."

"It won't be me," Sid said. "I know that."

"How do you know?"

"I know because by that time I'll be holding Amanda's hand again," Sid said, and I left.

26

AMENDS

∎

In the spring of 1975 something happened at Republic. Word had gotten around that Susan-Marie and Paul were willing to take a chance. They would not go to the same thirty screenwriters that everyone else went to over and over again. They would look outside Nate 'n' Al's for talent. Mountains of new scripts began to pour over the transom. Word had gotten out mostly because Susan had spoken at film classes in Bloomington, Indiana, and Durham, North Carolina, and Clovis, New Mexico, where the students once believed they had no chance at all of having work considered in Hollywood. She had spoken at the 92nd Street YMHA and at the Bible School in Spartanburg, South Carolina. She had told anyone who would listen that Republic was not a closed shop.

More to the point, she had allowed the development department—part of Marco Castro's bailiwick—to act" ally lay out money for optioning six scripts from places like Lincoln, Nebraska, and Ellenville, New York, from three film students, two editors at New York publishing houses who wrote scripts part-time, and one widow in Boca Raton, Florida. One of the scripts by a new editor in New York was about the world of young editors in New York—always underpaid, always having to look as if they came from inherited means, always trying to combine a snappy appearance, scholarly demeanor, and the eye of a hawk with the personality skills of a politician necessary to advance in the house and to get the salesmen to love their books. Susan had loved that script so much—largely because it recalled to her the love of fantasy that had moved her through circumstances to the executive suite at Republic overlooking the green, grassy lawn—that she had rapidly put it into production with two young actors —Tim Hutton as the young editor and someone named Debra Winger as his lover, also an editor, only this time for a paperback house.

Word that money is changing hands had moved a flood of brown envelopes with scrawls that read PRINTED MATTER to come from the post offices all over America to the mail room at Republic. The usual staff of readers and development V-Ps was simply overwhelmed. "I need help," Marco Castro said to Susan. "The development office is paralyzed. I know you like to run a lean ship, but this is ridiculous."

"Hire new people," Susan said. "Figure it out. We pay a few executives forty or fifty thousand a year. If they work for five years and find one good script, they've paid for themselves ten times over. I want a lean staff, but I want good scripts."

Marco hired three new executives. Two of them were former agents, from APA and Kohner-Levy. One of the new executives was from the MBA program at Stanford. His name was Chris Wohlstetter. He was twenty-seven years old. His father was a major player in venture capital in Palo Alto.

I met the new executives one afternoon while I was visiting Susan in her office. They had a sharp, edgy look about them, as if they were perpetually on the lookout for food. That look of anxiety and menace was blended with a look of cockiness and condescension that made them perfect examples of their type—the young Hollywood player.

After Chris Wohlstetter had been at the studio for a few months he was approached by a young man who had been teaching at Fairleigh Dickinson University in New Jersey in a minor staff position in creative writing. The details were never easy to come by, but the gist was that the former teacher at Fairleigh Dickinson submitted a script about suicide to Chris Wohlstetter. Wohlstetter took a call from the man and told him the script was great. When the writer came in for a meeting Wohlstetter was out. He kept the man waiting for ninety minutes. Then he came back to his office and told the writer that he had not read his script and that he must have been thinking of another script.

The writer phoned Wohlstetter every morning for two weeks. Wohlstetter only took one call, when his secretary was out and he thought that Mark Canton was on the line.

"Listen, I just haven't had time," Wohlstetter told him. "I have meetings with important deal-makers in this business every day."

"Could you just read a few pages of it, maybe?"

"Maybe," Wohlstetter said. "I'm busy though, so don't bug me all the time. I'll get to it eventually."

On the fifteenth day after his meeting with Wohlstetter the writer wrote down his experience with Republic studios in a short story. He mailed the short story to a magazine where the editor was a friend of mine. Then the writer took a taxi to the Continental Hyatt House right on Sunset Strip. He took an elevator to the tenth-floor rooftop restaurant. He walked right through a luncheon of the West Hollywood Chamber of Commerce. He went to the rail, shouted back to the crowd, "I'm sorry for disturbing you," and jumped.

The editor of the magazine gave me the writer's story. It had real names. I brought it to Susan-Marie. She called together all the creative executives in the dining room at Republic. There were six of them. Two of the men, Wohlstetter and Goodman (who was the son of an owner of theaters in Oregon), started an argument about who had the more expensive Italian shoes.

Susan-Marie asked me to come with her in case the story ever got out the wrong way.

She started the meeting by reading the six-page short story aloud. When she got to the end, where the writer had written, "Why I deserved this when I only came here to write and tell a story and have never done anything to Republic but go to their movies, I will never know. I know that people like me have no chance in this world. I never knew that before."

She paused for a full minute and then Chris Wohlstetter said, "Look, I was really busy. I had no idea the guy would act so crazy."

Still, Susan did not speak.

"We're the power in this business," Mike Goodman said. "If he can't take a tough business, he should never have come to this town."

Susan-Marie looked at the young executives, none of whom showed the slightest sign of sorrow. One of them was openly reading *The Hollywood Reporter.*

"First of all," Susan-Marie said, "that man is being buried tomorrow in Short Hills, New Jersey. I'm going to make this really simple. Republic will pay for anyone who wants to go to that funeral. Anyone who's too busy to go is on three months' leave without pay as of this afternoon. You understand?"

Wohlstetter, the MBA graduate of Stanford, said, "Susan, we're all sorry, but we have work to do. This isn't a charity. It's a business."

"Chris," Susan-Marie said, "you're fired. Be off the lot

in fifteen minutes. Now, who wants to go to the funeral?"

While the executives were still stammering, Susan-Marie said, "That man was only asking for a minimum of courtesy, to be treated like a man. We have readers just twiddling their thumbs watching 'Days of Our Lives.' You could have gotten his script read and talked to him for five minutes even to tell him it wasn't right. Once you made an appointment with him you shouldn't ever have kept him waiting for an hour and a half. If we treat creative people like dirt, what does that make us? If we lord it over little people who love movies, what kind of people are we? If we take people who love our movies and make them feel as if their lives are worthless, we shouldn't be in this business at all. If you got into this business to beat people up, you're in the wrong goddamn business. You want to fight? We'll get some stuntmen up here and you can fight with them.

"Chris," she said, "do you want to go to the funeral now? I'll change my mind if you do. I'm not going to treat you the way you treated that writer."

"Of course I'll go," Wohlstetter said.

"This business isn't about who's the biggest thug," Susan-Marie said. "It's about making fantasies. You show you're tough here by making a picture you believe in, that makes money, not by beating up defenseless writers. If you take a tough position to defend a creative point of view, I'm with you all the way. When you use your jobs to hurt people for no reason except that they're weaker than you, if I hear about it, you're out of the business altogether. I'm telling you, I'm not going to have this business run as if it were a slaughterhouse," she said with a nod at me that went unseen by the other people in the room. "We are in the fantasy business. That's not the kind of business where you torture people just for the heck of it. We want to make money, but we make stories for people to escape to. We have to have the right frame of mind to do that. If we have a contemptuous attitude about the ordinary moviegoer, we're never going to make the kind of movies that man or woman wants to see."

"We're hip," Chris Wohlstetter said.

"Good," Susan answered. "It's a business where people's ideas pay our salaries. Let's take care of them. Besides, going to the funeral will give you a whole new idea about America. We'll go on the Republic G-2, and we can read a few scripts while we're on our way. Get some work done. Learn a few things. Okay? Meeting's over."

■   ■   ■   ■

Paul Belzberg saw the story in the *International Herald-Tribune* while he was in the first-class cabin of a Swissair 747 returning from a meeting of Bernese Theater Owners in Lausanne. He saw the photograph of Susan and the young development executives at the graveside, with the caption A NEW DAY IN HOLLYWOOD. The story began: "Short Hills, New Jersey. In a light drizzle, Daniel Napolitano, 29, was buried at Our Lady of the Angels cemetery while officials of Republic Studios paid their respects. In a startling departure from normal motion picture practice, Susan-Marie Belzberg, executive vice-president for production of Republic and the wife of noted Hollywood producer Paul Belzberg, the president of Republic, told reporters that while Republic had no reason to know if the behavior of its executives had contributed to Mr. Napolitano's death—officially ascribed to a fall while depressed over his rejection in Hollywood—she wanted all of America to know that Republic studios values the creative mind and grieves when even one is lost. . . ."

Belzberg became flushed, stopped his conversation with Karin, a twenty-four-year-old former art student from Newport Beach who had just come from a visit with the Shah in Teheran, and asked the stewardess for a double Scotch.

By the time he had arrived home in the Malibu Colony he was no less furious, but was substantially less articulate.

He lay under a blanket in his bedroom for an hour, then sat in the sauna for fifteen minutes, then ran along the beach as far as Louise Lasser's house, and then came back, showered, changed into his jeans, and got ready for Susan to return from the studio.

"Let me get this straight," he said when she walked in the door, carrying her Bottega Veneta briefcase, crammed with scripts and budgets. "You have been in this job for two years. You have been in the motion picture business all told for less than three years. You have seen one picture through to completion. You own no stock in the company..."

"I own a hundred shares," Susan said. "What's the matter? I've missed you."

"The fucking matter is that you have terrorized our executives, made the studio a laughingstock, and dragged our good name through the mud of a little cemetery in New Jersey all because some nut case happened to kill himself after he had a meeting with Chris Wohlstetter, whose father happens to be a good friend of mine and of Sid's. What the hell is wrong with you?"

Susan put her briefcase on the glass-topped table with the gray cross-hatching that she had ordered from Knoll because it reminded her of precision and vision, two qualities she valued. She walked over to the gray couch in the living room and sat down. Elena came into the room automatically. Susan asked for an iced tea and then said, "Paul, let me explain it to you. I am trying to make a studio where ideas are welcome. I am trying to get us out of the mold. Chris Wohlstetter humiliated that man from New Jersey just because he didn't know him. I'm trying to do something dramatic so that it'll stop."

"So you got us in the newspapers as if we were criminals?" Paul asked. "You made us look like bastards as a way of expiating our guilt?"

He had already started toward the sideboard and the Scotch decanter when Susan got up and grabbed his arm. "Just a minute," she said. "I might have acted too fast.

Maybe I did. But you have to know that *New West* had a long letter that man had sent, making us look like Eichmann. It was going to look terrible if that article appeared, right below a picture of the kid standing in front of Republic, which his mother apparently also had. I saw that I could get some sense into the executives' heads and tell America something about what makes us different. I consulted with Sid before I did it. I would have asked you, but every time I called you in Lausanne you sounded as if you were running out the door."

"So, Sid knew about this. I guess Sid knows everything you do before I do. I don't care. He's wrong. You're wrong. You should've taken out the editor of *New West*, given him some little piddly script deal, done something to keep it out of his magazine. You have all the charm. You can do it."

Paul pulled his arm out of Susan's grasp and walked into the teahouse for the decanter of Scotch. "Instead of doing the right thing, you did the grandstand play so your picture would be in the newspapers, so all of a sudden you look like the one who's calling the shots at Republic, while Paul, that old schlepper, is in Switzerland getting shots of monkey glands."

"Please, Paul. Don't do this to me." Susan-Marie took both of Paul's hands in hers. She held them up to her face and pressed the right hand against her lips. "Please don't act like this. You know it was a gamble, but we've already gotten an official resolution from the WGA thanking us, telling us it was right."

Paul gently took his hands away from her face. He lifted his heavy tumbler of Scotch to his lips and swallowed. "I've already gotten three telephone calls from people I've known in this business for twenty-five years asking me if I'm still running the studio or if I've turned it over to you. You know how that feels?"

Susan walked back into the living room and toyed with her iced tea. She ran a finger along the edge of a book about astronomy that she had picked up in Hunter's in

Beverly Hills the day before. "It could feel terrible if you didn't know that they were trying to jack you out of your mind and they were jealous that Republic was getting some good publicity. More important, that we were getting some good scripts."

"Elroy Robinson and Edgar Pittman. Two of the calls. Guys I worked with on *Estonia*. Guys who used to take me out to lunch when I first got here, when I was too broke to afford a decent meal at a restaurant. There were calls from them at the office about how this business at the funeral makes everybody in the business look bad. About who the hell is running the ship and making us into a whipping boy for every neurotic failure in Topeka."

"They wouldn't have called if they didn't think we had beat them to something. You and I both know that. We're already getting scripts from people with real new ideas, not just people in the club. More than that, we're getting across to the writers and the directors and everybody who loves movies that Republic is the studio they can deal with. That we'll not only make deals with them, but we're the same as them."

Susan paused for a minute. "Please. Just think about it. If it was that bad a thing to do, we wouldn't have gotten that letter from the Writers' Guild."

Paul thought for a minute and then he said, "Maybe. It might have some merit as a way to get in writers. But writers can be bought for a nickel anyway. What really makes me crazy is that you humiliated Chris Wohlstetter. He's our boy. He's part of our company."

"No. He's not part of the company. Our company doesn't treat people like shit because we don't know their faces and we haven't been to their daughter's bat mitzvah. That's not Republic, and it's not me and it's not Sid. Most of all, it's not you. You wouldn't do that. I know you wouldn't."

"I might," Paul said and then paused. "But Susan, please. Maybe this wasn't such a bad idea. Maybe it makes sense. But look. This is important."

306

"What is it?" Susan-Marie asked rapidly. Paul's voice suddenly had changed from bullying to almost pleading, and Susan-Marie was taken by surprise at the change in tone.

"You're a very smart girl. Very smart woman. Full of good ideas. You can argue like Abe Fortas. Great. But I didn't marry Abe Fortas. I didn't marry David O. Selznick. I didn't marry someone who was supposed to argue with me and make old friends call and ask what's going on."

"I'm trying to help," Susan said softly. "I'm trying to help everybody."

"You can help by just doing your job, reading scripts, keeping track of where the production budgets go, and just keeping yourself quiet for the next few years. You've got a great job. You can see everything happening. You can learn the business from what gaffers do to what the best boy does to all the back-end parts of the deal, and then see if in a few years you still want to go charging off to funerals in Short Hills. You can just lay low for a while, and that would make it a lot easier for everyone." Paul's voice was even, measured. "Just take a rest, move along a little more slowly, work yourself into the club. Get what I mean?"

Susan-Marie took Paul's hands once again and held them against her cheeks. She looked into his face with those magnificent deep blue eyes and then kissed his hands again. "We're together. I'm not working against you. We're a team. If something good comes of what I've done or thought of, it's good for you, too. I never thought of it any other way."

"Then just lay low," Paul said with a new edge of anger in his voice. "Don't go around like you're the female Louis B. Mayer. Just lay low and let somebody else have the bright ideas for a few years."

"Paul," she said calmly, "you married a woman who has ideas. You married a woman who loves movies. You didn't marry a little mouse from the Congregational Church. I am who I am. I love you, and you're the most

important person on earth to me. But I am who I am. I'm
not going to do an abortion against myself and kill who
I am so that your pals won't call you up and make jokes.
I have my ideas, and I'll fight for them. And I'll do it now.
In three years I might be just another member of the club
and I might not have a single new idea. I love you, Paul,
but I want to do something with movies, just like you."

After a long pause Paul said, "I understand. But you
have to understand that it costs something."

"I understand that I love you," she said. "I understand
that you love me, too, and we can work it out. Even if you
don't think so, I know we can. I'm planning on it."

27

SUSPICION

■

My book, *Mirrored Sunglasses*, came out. It was a survey of the social attitudes of Hollywood TV writers and producers. In the glorious East, reviewers thought I had discovered something important: that the small clique who make prime-time TV are an ideological monolith, with identical views on crime, small towns, businessmen, minorities, and religion. The book appeared in the windows of bookstores and I appeared on TV talk shows. It was swell.

More luck came when Norman Lear extended my contract to consult on yet another show. That meant I had a tiny little bit of notice and enough money to live on. When in Hollywood, one always wants more, so I continued trying to sell my ideas and my screenplays. That was how I saw the jungle.

I wish I could catalog someday the infinite varieties of

rejection that came my way as a peddler of stories in the seven studios and three networks.

One day I went to sell a story about a minister's wife who had fallen away from faith and had started an affair with a real estate developer. The woman executive at the network told me that they were not going to do any real estate stories. One day I went to see a producer who asked me if I had any stories about how the fear of nuclear war had turned all those ghetto kids into juvenile delinquents.

I learned that Hollywood had a different lingo from the rest of the nation. For example, if a studio executive says, "I love it. It's fantastic. I can't wait to make that picture," that really means, "Get out of my office. I hate you and your filthy story." I learned that when an agent says, "Don't worry. I'll get on the case immediately," that means you will never hear from him about it again. If a Hollywood lawyer says, "The deal is closed," that means that after another year of negotiation, you might possibly get a little bit of money, but don't expect the lawyer to help you collect. If a woman whom you meet at the bar of The Palm while you wait for a table says, "I'm a producer on the lot at Universal," that means she is a secretary to a property manager. If you go out with a woman and she tells you that she loves writers and she loves to read, that will almost certainly be followed with, "I even read the 'Calendar' section of the L.A. *Times* every Sunday, at least the parts about the business." If you go out to a party and you meet a well-dressed, intelligent, well-read man whom you remember from the East and he tells you that he is about to start production on a picture, you can be certain that he is lying. On the other hand, if you meet a ratty-looking kid with herpes blisters on his lips who tells you that he has twenty development deals and has just made a picture that made forty million in rentals, and if he tells you this while he is snorting cocaine off a Porsche key, he is almost certainly telling the truth and will probably soon be up for an Academy Award.

I had no schedule, no regular day-to-day life in Los Angeles, so I found myself wandering the streets of Beverly Hills in the mornings, along with the housewives and mistresses. I began to examine their faces carefully. I stood on the corner of little Santa Monica and Rodeo and watched the women drive by in silky black Corniche convertibles. Their heads were bound in Hermes scarves. Their wrists were completely planted with gold. Beside them on the seats were ranks of Louis Vuitton accessories arrayed by size.

To me, a simpleton from the East, they would seem to have life completely by the throat. But on their faces were etched lines of toughness, rage, anger, and fear that would have made a member of al Fatah look like a Norman Rockwell mother by comparison.

Sometimes I lingered for a yogurt at The Cultured Cow on little Santa Monica by Camden. After school was out at Beverly Hills High School the boys and girls appeared there, driving silver 450 SLs and red Ferraris. The girls had the same gold-plated wrists and the same mounds of Louis Vuitton purses as their mothers. The boys had looks of almost complete contempt. All of them looked as if they would not be surprised if they got to the doctor and the old quack told them they had inoperable sarcomas in their necks.

Other days I drove down to little Tokyo and ate tempura at a Japanese stand called Nigiri-Sushi. The customers were apparently a mixture of gardeners and washerwomen and East L.A. Chicanos. Their faces looked calm and untouched by grief, even if they had actual scars from gang fights.

I made friends with a man who often was at my bank when I was. He had made fifteen million dollars in a scam in videotape. He was five years older than I was, but looked as if he had been dipped in sulfuric acid while his toenails were being pulled out. He and his wife, a medical doctor who owned a chain of emergency-care clinics near

National City, owned a home in the flats of Bel-Air that would have made Mussolini envious. They could not sit still. They sat in a living room with an authentic Flemish renaissance tapestry and smoked dope with shaking, twitching hands and talked about diseases that could not be cured.

I had lunch with agents who could not remember the last time they had been in love. "It's the business. It's just not possible to be really hustling and to have time for other people," they would say, as if it were perfectly obvious which option any sane man would choose.

On Saturdays I often drove out to the Malibu Colony to visit Susan-Marie and Paul. They had calls to make and scripts to read. I, the perpetual tourist, would walk along the beach and look at the millionaires. The more spectacular their manse, the more angry, terrified, and vulpine were the looks on their faces, like Damascus street assassins in gold and tailored leather, perpetually on guard against a return to dusty souks and goat's cheese.

On the other hand, the blacks and the Mexicans who were waiting on them in little white bolero jackets and dresses with white aprons looked perfectly calm and unafraid and uninterested in a fight.

From all of this restless observation, I derived my axioms of Los Angeles—by which I mean "Hollywood"—and its inhabitants.

In Los Angeles, and only in Los Angeles:

· the women are more frightening than the men
· the children are more frightening than the adults
· the elderly are more frightening than the young
· the rich are more frightening than the poor

To me, these were inversions of normal experience, and I wondered at the incredibly powerful gravity of a city and a way of life that had pulled people literally inside out.

Still, I could easily see the attraction of Hollywood

despite its liars, its thieves, its heartbreak, and its fundamental confusion about human life.

For six months a redheaded waiter served me and my various dates seaweed, dumplings, and spicy beef at Mr. Chow. Then one day he sold a script to Columbia. He got forty thousand for a first draft and a set of revisions, and then he was officially a writer. A manicurist who lived down the hall from me on Horn Street went to Paramount every day to manicure the nails of an executive in the TV department. She told him a story of a nun who became a detective. In three weeks the deal was made at NBC. The show was called "The Sister and the Tramp." It only ran for forty-six episodes, but it paid Veralynn Procter fifteen thousand per episode and then she became an executive producer on "Aladdin's Laddies" and now she lives in a house in Pasadena that was built by one of the founders of Bethlehem Steel.

One of the messengers who used to come over to take my articles down to the *Herald-Examiner* happened to strike Lionel Charing right for a part in *Take My Wife, Please.* Charing, the head of casting at Universal Pictures, thought the messenger had the right look for a *febissineh* stockbroker who turns into a rock music drummer. The messenger got scale for six weeks, which was about fifteen hundred a week. When the dailies appeared in screening room S behind the commissary at Universal, Franck Bleckner saw the messenger. He put him in the second lead in *Interiors by Diane,* the story of an interior decorator who becomes a surgeon, and the messenger's price was a hundred thousand for six weeks' work.

The poolman for my apartment building used to bring around his girlfriend. She was a red-neck with tiny features and dirty blond hair. The pool man also serviced the pool of Leonard Spellberg in West Hollywood. He saw her stretching out to rake the bottom of the pool one day while she was wearing tight white shorts. In a year, she was a regular on "The Emperor's New Clothes," a long-running series about the play and intrigues of the rich in Boca

Raton. One year after that she owned the apartment building where I lived.

Seemingly, Hollywood was the Philosophers' Stone of human morphology. It could make small people big and poor people rich. More important, Hollywood could do all of this as if by magic, overnight, while the subject of the experiment in metamorphosis was sleeping, so to speak. You simply came to town, put down your number by being thin and available, and you took your chance.

The fact was that Hollywood did not make the waiter strong and happy. It did not make the poolman's girlfriend serene and contented. It did not make the manicurist comfortable. Hollywood took those people and gave them a lifelong anxiety attack: Will my contract be renewed? Will I be able to afford the ten-thousand-dollar-a-month payments on my house? Will I wake up to find that my show has been canceled? Will I be young enough for the part? What if sitcoms fall out of fashion? Will I have the right story ideas so that a studio executive thirty years younger than I am will give me the deal? I am up in the stratosphere, but will I be able to stay here? Will someone younger and thinner and hipper and *luckier* come along to take my place on Parnassus and Vine?

After all, if the manicurist and the waiter and the poolman's girlfriend were sent heavenward by divine interference and not by any kind of real world effort and discipline, if they had simply made it because of a stroke of luck, they had to know that it could all be taken away by another stroke—of *bad* luck.

I saw a raft of men and women come to town about the same time I did. The ones who were touched by greatness were invariably more tormented by fear, by the terror of the unreturned call, the fury of the cool turndown, the lash of the missing mortgage payment than the ones who were still waiting tables or raking leaves in fifteen pools each day.

I thought those thoughts, which may have just been the ramblings of a loser, and I thought of my darling Susan, who had walked home along Sligo Creek Parkway with me not fifteen years before. I remembered her long legs and her graceful, confident carriage, and her deep blue eyes lighting up the autumn afternoons in Maryland. I remembered her black hair against the reddish-yellow maple leaves falling onto Dale Drive. I remembered her smile and the smell of her girlish perfume against the aroma of burning leaves.

Those were the days when I realized that Susan-Marie's worst fate would be to succeed in Hollywood and to join the club.

The day she became one of *them*, even if it were the day she had her tenth top-grossing movie, could just as easily be the day she slipped seamlessly out of the old, gloriously alive Susan-Marie and became a robot of self-promotion.

It was a terrible thing, but I often longed for yet another shock to awaken Susan-Marie to just exactly where she was.

Once I ate lunch with my agent at Joe Allen's in West Hollywood. At the next table two neatly dressed men with little mustaches and short hair ate spinach salad and talked about a meeting they had just come from with Susan-Marie.

"She has this thing she does," one said. "It's like really effective. She looks at you when you're pitching to her."

"I know," the other one said. "It's a fantastic trick. Really amazing. It actually makes you believe she's paying attention."

"It's a really good device," the first one said. "It almost makes me want to believe she's interested."

"Maybe she is," the other one said. "She's buying stuff from a lot of new writers."

"Oh, *right*," the first one said. "Give me a break. A studio executive who really cares about anything anyone else says? No way."

"Yeah," the other one agreed after a moment's thought. "It's a good device."

That was exactly what I was afraid of. But once again, as Sid told me, there were no easy explanations in Hollywood. Maybe I was only feeling the rationalized pangs of the loser and the hack for missing the woman I loved. Anything is possible.

28

ETHER

■

A man named Lloyd Turtletaub called me one afternoon while I was writing my column. He was a producer of the evening news for Channel Two, the CBS affiliate in Los Angeles.

"I've been reading your columns for a while now," he said over the telephone in a voice so sharp that it could have scraped barnacles off the hull of an Indian Ocean trawler. "I like them. I'd like to have you come in and read for us."

"Read what?"

"Read to see if we could get you on the nightly news doing a little humor commentary about the lighter side of Hollywood life."

"When can I come over?"

I made up a few little commentaries about beer commercials and movies about little girls with makeup, and I read them in front of a camera manned by two large lesbians. My reading was mediocre, but, as Lionel said, that could be turned to advantage. I would be the station's resident braino, an Oscar Levant type minus the Demerol and sick jokes. They would use my stiff manner in front of the camera to my own advantage, sort of like Julia Child doing commentary.

They started me out between the sports analyst and the Surf-to-Sand Gourmet. It was not a huge hit, but it was big enough for them to put me on twice a week, once at 6:35 P.M. and once at 11:21 P.M. I told little stories of teenagers at the car wash and alternated them with stories about the impending doom of Western Civilization. The other staff, the get-happy boys and girls with their three-hundred-dollar haircuts, thought of me as a sort of newsroom oddity, the Cassandra who might possibly know something. When I passed Connie Chung in the hall she always winked at me: her way of avoiding the braino's evil eye.

When a man living in a miserable apartment above Sunset Strip has a TV commentary spot, even if his voice is too slow and too deracinated, an audible analogue of Joan Didion's heroines, he is a small celebrity. Suddenly girls at parties talked to me. Little thin ones with great legs and silicon breasts leaned against me at houses on Shoreham Drive and asked me if I could mention them in my column. The request was the approximate equivalent of asking Bill Buckley if he could mention them in his column, but I listened far into the night. I often made something out of the stories of the starlets.

"A few weeks ago, a dweeb in a Mercedes ran into my Toyota," said a ravishing brunette with blue eyes at a party on Kings' Road. She wore tight denim cutoffs, tight enough to make me dizzy. "The guy didn't hurt me, but my father scammed him out of about eight thousand."

"Great," I said.

"So my father and I split the eight grand. He took it and bought two ounces of really fantastic coke. He brought home all the strippers from the Kit-Kat Klub and they were high for almost a week. Then he had a thousand left over and he bought a used Porsche."

"With a thousand dollars?"

"Well, that was just the down payment. It was a really old one."

"A good investment."

"That's what he said, too," Stacey agreed. "He also won twenty-four hundred at Hollywood Park, and you know what he did with that?"

"I can't guess," I said.

Stacey thrust her two perfect breasts in my direction and laughed. "He bought me these," she said. "The best. From Cedars-Sinai."

"Another great investment," I said.

She leaned even closer to me and whispered, "You won't believe it. They don't even move. They're like rocks."

When I put the anecdote in my column it was picked up by Liz Smith and I got on Tom Snyder, talking about the glory that is Los Angeles. Amazingly, the starlet, the lovely Stacey, sent me flowers.

Stacey and I ran into Susan-Marie and Paul at Mr. Chow. Stacey was and is a hot-looking chick, as my friends at KNX used to say. When she wore a tight black suit of pin-striped silk she looked like a million grams. (She had a look that was a perfect combination: bursting with life and bursting with death.) Susan-Marie kissed me and Paul shook my hand and winked. "Enjoying Hollywood, Ben?" he asked me in one of the only friendly conversations I ever had with him.

"Are you the ones who are always in the newspapers?" Stacey asked.

"Not really," Susan-Marie said. "We're the ones who're always in meetings. I'm happy to see you having a good time," Susan-Marie said with genuine good feeling. She passed by on the way to Michael Crovitz's table, and occasionally looked over at us and smiled. Just before the sesame prawns arrived she sent over a bottle of Pommery '68. I don't know much about wine, but I knew it was worth about what I earned from *New View* in a year.

I also knew that for me to be with Stacey Darvon when Susan-Marie sat two tables away with Paul Belzberg was like being told that I had one more day to live, and that day had to be spent on the subway to Coney Island. The fact was that Stacey or Janet or Vicki or Andrea or any of the girls I met as a celebrity were simply nothings compared with Susan-Marie. She was flesh and they were plastic, or more precisely, silicone. She had life, and they had self-obsession. There was a big difference.

So I worked on my consulting gig for Norman Lear, which ended a few months after I started at KNX, my column for *New View,* and my endlessly unsuccessful efforts to sell ideas and scripts in Hollywood. In a tiny way I became a well-known figure in Hollywood. Valets got my car right away. The car wash threw in a wax job for the price of a wash. I spoke at meetings of the Glendale Republican Women (Federated). After a lifetime of dwelling in the crowd I started to come into a small corner of the limelight.

Frankly, it was better than obscurity, but the limelight was not my jackpot. My jackpot went home every night with Paul Belzberg, who feared and distrusted her. I passed the smoggy days and the balmy nights above Tower Records with a succession of pale losers on the fruit machine. Not one of them was a criminal—although they often stole money or Seconal—but all of them were simply games of solitaire.

29

SPACE

◼

Go know, as Sid's mother used to say. All of my hopes and fears, all of the scheming and plotting of the parts of Hollywood who competed with Susan-Marie, all of the built-in flight plans of a lifetime came to their crossroads because of an abnormal McGoo.

It happened when Susan was trying to make a better connection with the viewing public through what was supposed to be a sophisticated form of audience-reaction testing. This must have been around Christmas of 1975.

"This is how it works," Marco Castro said to Susan-Marie. They were in the glass-fronted control booth of Preview House on Sunset Boulevard at Stanley. In front of them was an auditorium filled with middle-aged viewers. "We get about sixty people in here. We give them tickets when they're at Universal on the tour or on Hollywood Boulevard watching the winos or at Disneyland. We pay them each five bucks and we wire them up to these dials. The dials are wired up to this electronic graph, sort of a continuous bar chart in liquid quartz to show how they're reacting to whatever we show them. We say a concept, like 'lady con man robs richest man in Texas.' Then we see how they react. If they like it, they twist their dials right. If they don't like it, they twist their dials left. And we can tell if they're a normal crowd because we have a five-minute 'Mr. McGoo' cartoon we show first. If they respond the way the average of the last hundred other groups have responded, we know we're all set to test our movie ideas. Are you ready?"

"I'm ready," Susan-Marie said, shaking her head in amazement. "This is unbelievable," she whispered to me.

"It must work," I said to her. "Look at this huge building."

"Exactly." Susan shook her head again. "Can you believe they called this sophisticated concept testing?"

The lights in the auditorium dimmed. The audience of men in plaid Bermuda shorts and women in muumuus with their hair in rollers began to giggle. Onto the screen came the familiar Mr. McGoo, who promptly bumped into his own titles. Then he turned around and miraculously did not bump into an onrushing truck. The audience did not laugh. The continuously moving bars on the bar chart stayed stationary.

An authorized Preview House technician let out a long sigh. "Hold it," he said. "We've got an abnormal McGoo. This whole thing's a wash. We might as well go out and get lunch and wait for the next group. We can't do anything with an abnormal McGoo."

■　　■　　■　　■

The abnormal McGoo was what led Susan-Marie to fly to Aptos, California, in March of 1976. "I can't believe they were really basing go decisions on how sixty losers responded to Mr. McGoo," she said as we flew up to the San Jose airport in the Republic Gulfstream. Sid Bauman had invited me along for the ride. Besides, there might well be a story in it for the second book I was writing about Hollywood, *Walking Wounded—How Hollywood Works.* The book contracts had given me some small status with Sid, whose grandfather had been a rabbi. Sid rewarded me for it by considering me his confidante, his California Boswell. That was why I sat in a leather seat in the Gulfstream and schmoozed with Susan and Sid Bauman on the way to talk to high-school kids in Aptos, California. Paul was in Rio, at a meeting of Brazilian theater owners.

"We have no idea if those people at Preview House were representative. We have no idea of how their feelings about Mr. McGoo related to any other feelings they might have about anything," Susan said. "High-school kids are the audience who see a movie five times if they like it. I want to talk to them myself, without some fool showing a Mr. McGoo cartoon."

"Aptos is perfect," Sid Bauman said. "A suburb of San Jose, sort of affluent, all different kinds of kids. It's a little bit of America."

"Procter and Gamble uses it to test pimple medicine ads," I said. "It must be right."

Susan-Marie had made certain that we arrived at the high school in a Chrysler sedan. "I don't want to show up there in a Cadillac limousine. I want something that shows that we're adults, but doesn't intimidate anyone. We want the kids to talk. We don't want them to bow down."

The high school itself was set about a mile from the ocean near a hospital and a Burger King. It had about eight low buildings, a large athletic field carved out of a hill next to the freeway, and a huge entranceway, like the entrance to a corral, that read APTOS HIGH HELLRAISERS.

The principal, Mrs. Croner, was a middle-aged woman with a wide, friendly, lopsided smile. She incessantly ran her fingers through her hair as she introduced us to the twenty students who had been selected as being just average enough to help.

We sat in the cafeteria. Sunlight streamed through

clerestory windows high above the yellow Formica tables. On one wall was a long strip of posterboard on which was a basketball team cartoon, with the phrase HANG 'EM HIGH, HELLRAISERS. On another wall was a selection of materials from the CAREER GUIDANCE OFFICE. Off in another corner from where we sat, a pretty girl with dark blue eyes sat alone at a table. She read *The Paris Review*. When Susan saw her she stopped to ask her to join the group of "discussants." The girl looked up and, in a distinctly Southern drawl, said, "What're we going to discuss?"

"What you like at the movies and what you don't like."

"No, thanks."

"Why not?"

"I don't go to the movies too much. They're too serious. Too sad. When I saw *One Flew Over the Cuckoo's Nest* I promised myself I wouldn't go to the movies any more."

"What about *Dog Day Afternoon?*"

"Too sad. Too much killing. Not for me. I lost my father in Vietnam. I've seen enough about killing."

"And this isn't sad?" Susan-Marie asked, pointing at *The Paris Review*. "Nothing upsetting here?"

"In here it's all far away. It takes me really far away. At the movies I feel as if somebody's holding my head underwater. Are you that woman I read about all the time? That woman from Hollywood who's married to Paul Belzberg?"

"Yes, I'm Susan Belzberg."

"I'd love to be where you are," the girl said. "I'd love to be where I could make up things that would take people's minds away from the freeway. I guess there's some reason why you can't do that kind of movie any longer, huh?"

"Maybe not," Susan-Marie said. "Come and see me some time in Hollywood. I'll pay." Susan-Marie handed the girl her card and then walked over to the "focus group."

We had not gone five minutes into the afternoon's discussion when we started to realize that the "abnormal McGoo" was going to change Republic's life.

"I love movies where you can see some unbelievable something going on and still believe it's really happening," said a girl with blond hair and a white-and-red cheerleader's sweater.

"I can't stand it when there's a real heavy message, like about how we should all hate our families," added a boy with broken glasses, mended with a Band-Aid.

A tall thin boy with a prominent Adam's apple said, "There's no movie now that's even close to as much fun as the comic books we used to read."

Several other students nodded as they sipped at their Diet-Rite Cola.

"What comics do you particularly like?" Susan-Marie asked. "What comics would you like to live in, if you could move from Aptos to that world?"

With one voice, fully twenty of the students shouted *"Laser Tracks."*

Susan-Marie smiled girlishly, as if she were a traveler in a foreign country. "What is *Laser Tracks?*"

The children fell over each other to answer. "It's about a boy who lives at home with his mom and dad. But every night a space ship comes for him to take him way far up into outer space, where he's a wizard and has magical powers because he came from earth," said one girl who had previously been silent.

"It's like in outer space, people aren't anywhere near as strong as they are here, so he's got incredible strength, and he can fly, and he can read other people's thoughts," said the boy with the Adam's apple.

"And he's incredibly good-looking on all those outer planets," said a boy with red hair. "So all the girls in outer space just love him. And they have magical powers so they can make themselves look like anything they want. He can tell them he wants them to look like a girl he has a mad crush on back in Ohio, and right away she looks just like that," the boy added.

"It's fantastic," a boy in running clothes said. "He fights duels and always almost gets killed, and then the spaceship takes him back to his bedroom, and gives him this special thing to say, and he goes to sleep, and he's never tired, and no one knows where he's been, except that he has this magical vest that he's allowed to keep. . . ."

From across the room, the girl reading *The Paris Review* suddenly appeared at the edge of the group. "You really feel like you've been away when you read one of those comics," she said, still clutching her magazine.

"It's not exactly science fiction," the boy with the Band-Aid on his glasses said. "Because the world he goes to really looks just like this world except that the sky is always a kind of vivid pink."

"But he can just do anything he wants there. He's just a kid, sort of like us," the *Paris Review* girl said, "only he's the one in charge. And everything that happens is real clear. You can tell right away who's good and who's bad. The good guys look good, and they sort of glow. The bad guys have a gray look about them and they're always scowling."

"Nobody's double-talking him," said the girl in the cheerleading sweater. "It's like on this planet, everything is right out in the open, and he can just do right for whoever's in trouble, and he can knock down whole tanks and battle cruisers with his fists."

"When you see him you really feel as if he's taking you far away from everything that's bothering you on earth. You feel like you've been on a vacation after you read one of those comic books. It's like he's in another world, just like this world, only everything you want to have happen happens." The girl who had been reading *The Paris Review* was positively flushed with excitement. "The guy who makes that comic book up, he's like made up a whole better place for us to live. When I go to sleep at night I sometimes pray that I'll be like that boy in *Laser Tracks,* only when I go to that other planet that looks just like earth, my father will be there."

The girl spoke totally unself-consciously. All around her, the other students were as immersed in *Laser Tracks*. I looked over at Susan-Marie. When she lifted her face from her yellow notepad she had tears in her eyes.

■　　■　　■　　■

"It's not exactly science fiction," Susan-Marie said. "It's more of a fantasy using science-fiction devices to put across the idea of escape."

Susan-Marie, Paul, Sid, and I were sitting at the first booth in the front room at La Scala. Susan had a plate of angel's-hair pasta in front of her, as we all did. She toyed with it while Paul glared at her.

"It's science fiction. I'm telling you right off the bat, if you call something *Laser Tracks,* it's science fiction. It's that simple. And if it's about a boy going to another planet, it's science fiction."

"No, it's only got a science-fiction name," Susan said. "It's in many ways like *Gone With the Wind,* but set in a vaguely science-fiction context."

"Science fiction never works," Paul said. "It's been dead since Buck Rogers. The only time it works is if it has some drug subtext going for it, like *2001.* Otherwise, it's a giant yawn."

Sid lifted a Bombay martini to his lips and sipped at it. "It's really something much bigger than *2001.* It's an escape story for children, not for college kids."

"Doesn't matter," Paul said. "Science fiction is not what people want to see."

"Why do you have to fight me on everything?" Susan asked, looking straight at Paul. Her voice had an edge.

"I'm not fighting you," Paul said. "I'm trying to do what's best for Republic. Isn't that what you always tell me when you cut me off at the knees?"

"*Laser Tracks* is the movie for right now, and if you could have seen those kids' faces, you would know it," Susan-Marie said. "It's the movie for the kids who grew up during Vietnam and Watergate. It's the movie for the kids who saw that everything was turning black and gray, and nobody could exactly explain what had happened. It's the movie for the kids who grew up seeing napalm falling on children, being dropped by smiling guys who looked just like their uncles. It's for the kids who grew up seeing Sam Ervin talking on TV, and they didn't exactly know what he was talking about, but they knew that their parents got real upset when they watched it."

"You were always great with the sociology," Paul said. "I guess that's why you've made so many great pictures."

"I'm new in the business. That's why I can see what's going on outside this town, when you can't see anything beyond Junior's Delicatessen. I can see what kids want to see. You see what your pals from the Hillcrest Country Club want to make. That's the difference. That *Laser Tracks* has to be made."

"It has to be made by somebody who wants to take a bath. The special effects alone are going to be four million," Paul said. "Who's gonna want to pay that much?"

"Somebody smart," Susan said.

"It needs stars," Paul said. "Who's gonna play the kid? You have any ideas? Who's going to play the evil Stentor? Richard Burton? You know what that'll cost?"

"It doesn't need any stars. It has a great story. The story is the star." Susan's voice was agitated, barely under control.

"I wish you could have seen the looks on those kids' faces," I said to Paul. "You would have been impressed."

"Another major moviemaker," Paul said with a derisive smile. "Everyone has an idea except the guy who's actually made the movies."

There was a moment of silence at the table while the waiter brought a new round of drinks. Sid Bauman sipped at his, and I suddenly realized something about him. He held the drink to give the impression of conviviality, but he never got drunk. It was a prop, like his window dressings when he was eighteen. It was a way to regard the world from behind the crystal of the martini glass. As if he had read my mind, Sid winked at me and said, "I've made a couple of movies. I think it's a great idea. The adults just go once or twice. If the kids love it, they go over and over again. That's where the real money comes in. They make their mom and dad come, and suddenly you have a family tradition—you go see *Laser Tracks* over and over again until you've seen it six times."

"Sid, science fiction is dead," Paul said. "You're just doing this to torment me."

"Nobody is doing anything to torment you," Sid said in an even tone. "We run a business. We need to make pictures that will bring in kids more than once. We should all be on our knees thanking Susan-Marie for finding this *Laser Tracks* thing. It's a goddamned disgrace that none of us found it any sooner."

"Oh, yes, let's all get on our knees to Susan-Marie, the new goddess from the East. Let's especially thank her for letting us know what a bunch of idiots we were before she came along, especially that old fool, Paul Belzberg. Imagine that anyone thought he knew anything about making movies. Thank God we found a woman from the telephone company who *really* knows movies." Paul glared from one of us to the other as if we had cornered him in a jungle clearing. In a sense, we had.

"Paul, nobody's trying to make you look small," Susan-Marie said. "We want to make the breakthrough to a new kind of movies, and I don't care one goddamned bit if my name is even on the screen or if I have any interviews or anything. How would that be? If it works, you can have all the credit."

"Oh, gee, thanks," Paul shot back. "Charity from my wife, who was answering four-one-one two years ago. Gosh, thanks."

"Shut up, Paul," Sid said. "You really should go home. You want me to have the car take you home?"

"No, I don't want any car to take me home. Why don't all of you go home and I'll stay here? Sid, why don't you go back to making windows, and Susan, you go back to the phone company, and Benjy, you go back to writing your little articles. I was here before any of you, and I'll be here when you're all gone."

"Jesus, Paul." Susan's voice was suddenly tired, strained, almost embittered. Almost resigned. "Why do you have to fight against everything new that anybody brings up? It's not aimed at you, Paul. Why do you have to try to squash me every chance you get? I'm not fighting against you."

"Yes, you are," Paul said in a hiss. "You don't fool me. You want me to look like a has-been, like an idiot who's punch drunk. A producer with cauliflower ears. Why don't you just keep your big ideas to yourself and let somebody else who knows the business make some decisions?"

"It's made," Sid said coolly, blowing smoke from his pipe across the room. "We're going to have two different writing teams working on it right away. Meerson and Krikestein and Madsen and Hanberg. All of them brand-new. Found by Susan. From Indiana University and from Hofstra on Long Island. If all's well, we'll be in production in June."

Paul let his head drop for a minute and then he raised it and looked almost plaintive. "What about *Jitterbug?*"

"We'll go with Bob Schallerberg's script," Sid said. "I agree with you that Bogdanovich should direct."

"So they're going toe-to-toe," Paul said.

"That's the way it should be. That way, no matter what, a good chunk of the box office some weekend a year from now will be all Belzberg product." Susan-Marie smiled in a conciliatory, cheerful way and reached out for Paul's hand.

But Paul did not take her hand the way a man takes his wife's hand. Instead, he shook it as if he were making a wager. "You take all the credit for *Laser Tracks,*" he said. "No matter how much it flops, you get all the credit. Also if it's a hit. I'll take what comes from *Jitterbug.* Then we'll see who knows about making pictures. That whole fiasco is your affair, and if I'm wrong, I'll eat it."

"Why do you have to fight me all the time?" Susan-Marie asked, taking her hand away. "I'm not your enemy. I'm trying to do something right here. Why do you have to fight me about it? Wouldn't you be glad if I were right? I am your wife, after all. Wouldn't it make you happy if I did something right?"

Paul looked down at the table. He was a fighter licking his wounds, trying to get his strength back for another round.

"I'm your wife. I work for you. We both work at the same studio. Aren't you happy I have something for us that's new and original and different? If it works, it could turn this town upside down. Even if it doesn't, it's new. Isn't that worth something? Don't you want me to have good ideas? Don't you want me to show what I can do?" Susan-Marie's voice had lost its edge. Now it was almost begging.

Paul said nothing for a few minutes while we all studiously ate our appetizer. Then he said, "I want you to try to learn a little from me. Then, in a while, we'll see what you can do."

"I'm not playing ingenue for you. I'm not playing dumb for you," Susan said. "You want someone dumb, go find one of those little stewardesses from Swissair. I'm in the picture business, not in the being dumb business. This is an idea that'll work. You want to try to make a better picture with *Jitterbug?* Go do it. You think I wouldn't cry with happiness if you won the fucking Academy Award? You know goddamn well I would.

"But you, Paul, what if I'm right about *Laser Tracks?* Are you going to love me for it or hate me for it? Which one?"

Paul did not answer right away. Susan suddenly stood up and threw down her napkin. In a voice loud enough for Aaron Spelling to hear across the room, she said, "I'm your wife, goddammit. I'm your wife!"

Then she ran out the door onto Santa Monica Boulevard. I was on the end, so I ran after her. I caught her on the sidewalk in front of Doubleday Books. I touched her and she spun into my arms. She put her face against my shoulder. I could feel her shaking with confusion against my chest. "Why?" she said between gasps. "Why does it have to be like this?"

I was too moved at the touch of her to answer with any smart words. "I don't know," I said. "Jealousy. Fear. He knows you're right. We can see that."

"Oh, God," she said in a rush. "I'm not going to play dumb for him. That never works. Never. I've done that. I've kept it all inside. That's all I ever did when I was a little girl. I'll never do that again. I'm never going to put a cork in my head again, never going to play like I'm just another silly girl, with a man showing off while I can do it twice as fast, twice as well."

"You're right," I said. "You never have to play second best. Not ever. Not to anyone. Never again."

I thought my meaning was clear, and I could feel Susan's extraordinary heat and the memory of years ago. But Susan-Marie abruptly pulled herself out of my arms. She looked at me with her sapphire vapor eyes and held both of my hands.

"What would I do without you?" she asked. The words cut into me like a tattooist's needle. I knew what they meant: best friend, period. "Paul won't be like this when he sees how good *Laser Tracks* will be. We'll show him. Together. Won't we?"

"Yes," I said. "We'll show him."

"When he sees he'll know I was right and he'll be glad."

"I hope so," I said.

"I know it." Susan-Marie's eyes were suddenly clear and confident again. "We'll see it. He'll be the first one to admit he was wrong. I know him. I know he will. Don't you think so? He's really a much bigger person than he looks like when he's around you and Sid. You two make him nervous."

"Maybe," I mumbled to myself, but I said nothing.

"I know so. I just can't have been so wrong, I can't."

By then Paul and Sid were out on the sidewalk moving toward us. "I'm sorry," Paul said. "I'm sorry, Ben. I'm just tired, and maybe I had too much to drink. I'm sorry. Let's go home, Susan."

They walked back to the valet station together, and I watched them go. When they left Sid looked at me with pained regret on his face. "My mother used to have a saying," he said. " 'It's a pity the bride is so beautiful.' "

"Let's go have martinis," I said. "Even though I know now you never get drunk."

"It's company," Sid said as the limousine pulled up. "That's enough, isn't it?"

"More than enough," I said, and we drove off.

30

RIGHTS

■

On the hottest day of 1976, September 6, Susan-Marie drove out Route 5, the Golden State Freeway, to Newhall, onto Route 126, where Bron Gless was filming second unit work on *Rodeo*. The site was a dried-out riverbed. Normally it was used for ATC racing and off-road motorcycle stunts. Today it was the background for a scene of a group of cowboys rounding up a pack of terrified mustangs.

Susan and I got out of her red 280 SL and walked through the dust to where a cameraman recorded the mustangs' capture and branding. The mustangs were first stampeded into a small pass, then tripped with fine wires spread across the gully floor. After they were tripped they were more malleable and could be lassoed and branded.

The horses were thin, noble animals, with the look of terror in their eyes on a bleached-out, blindingly dry day. They whinnied and stamped their feet, sometimes rearing high into the air and screaming animal screams of fear. When they tripped we could see their anguish.

Susan-Marie watched in horror for two minutes and then shouted at the director. Bron Gless was covered head to toe in leather chaps, denims, spurs, and vest. Only his bald head and his wire-rimmed glasses told us that he was the director and producer.

"What the hell are you doing?" Susan-Marie demanded. "Trip wires are illegal. You know that."

"They save two days' shooting and ten thousand dollars in training fees," Gless said, as if that ended the discussion.

"The horses don't care how much it saves," Susan-Marie said. "Neither do I."

"It's second-unit work. I just happened to be here today."

"Like hell," Susan-Marie said. "I heard you thought up the whole idea. And another thing, are you actually branding those horses? It sure looks like it."

"Of course we are," said the director in a thick Queens accent. "I don't make movies that aren't real."

"Does that mean you actually shoot people when the script calls for it?" Susan-Marie trembled with anger.

"Susan." Gless's voice was so condescending that it seemed to pick up a ball of dust on the valley floor and turn it to mud. "This is a man's business. Sometimes animals get hurt. What do you think happens when you eat a hamburger?"

Susan-Marie grimaced. "You torture these horses just to save a buck. It's illegal and it's stopped from right now."

By now the shooting had stopped and a cameraman shouted up to us, "Set up for the next one?"

"Go ahead," Gless shouted back. Almost instantaneously, several men dressed as cowboys began shoving branding irons into a fire.

"Wait a minute," Susan-Marie said. "Does this mean you're getting ready to brand those horses?"

"Look," Gless said angrily, "this is the way Westerns are always done. I've done eight of them. It's a man's way of making a picture. It's my picture, and I work directly under Paul Belzberg, and when it's done I know you'll do a great job making up ads for it. Now get off the set."

"You're fired," Susan-Marie said. "Get off the set, close down shooting, and tell those people they have a few days off until we get a new director."

Gless looked stunned down to his brand-new snakeskin boots.

"You can't fire me for breaking a few little guidelines from a few little old ladies at the ASPCA. I've made eight Westerns. This one'll cost you a fortune to finish with another director."

"This is a Republic picture. I'm in charge. You're fired. Now get the hell off our property or you won't work in this town again until I leave it, and that'll be a long time."

Gless looked furious, then tried to laugh, then sauntered away toward his Rolls-Royce convertible, now gathering dust under a tent nearby. "This is a small town," he said. "You can't get away with this kind of thing."

"I just did," Susan-Marie said.

■　　■　　■　　■

On Thanksgiving Day, 1976, Susan-Marie and Paul Belzberg had Sid and me over for turkey dinner. By this time Sid and I were virtually inseparable. An old man read to by a young boy in a dry season is the way the saying goes, I believe, and it was only wrong about my age.

As we finished with the stuffing and the cranberry sauce, Sid said, "I think maybe we should start thinking about the merchandising for *Laser Tracks*. I can see some mileage there. Maybe in clothing, maybe in toys. The caves could be a whole inspiration for a line of toys. Maybe we should get someone over to talk to Milton Bradley, Hasbro, Mattel."

Paul stiffened. "Sid, when was the last picture that made money off merchandising? Everybody always thinks he's in for a pot of money and there never is any. Really, can you tell me the last picture that made any money in merchandising?"

"I can't tell you the last one," Sid said cheerfully. "I can tell you the next one."

There was no more conversation until we went into the teahouse for dessert, a perfect raspberry sherbet that Elena had made herself. Then Paul made himself a large Scotch, while Sid and I drank martinis. Susan-Marie drank only tonic water with bitters.

"How do you like the *Jitterbug* dailies?" Paul asked everyone.

"No picture is ever as good as its dailies or as bad as its rough cut," I said, and for once everyone laughed. Everyone except Paul.

"What is that supposed to mean?" he demanded. "Am I supposed to be the butt of jokes from everybody, including journalists who don't know which end of a camera to use?"

"Maybe I'd better leave," I said. "I only intended a goddamned joke, Paul. We're not reading anybody's will."

"And what's that supposed to mean? That I'm dead, or what?"

"It's supposed to be a joke, Paul, that's all," Susan-Marie said. "A joke."

"Nobody's even noticed in the general hoopla about *Laser Tracks,* but I'm getting some fantastic dailies out of Schallerberg and Bogdanovich," Paul said to all of us. "Quality stuff. Not the kind of stuff for eight-year-olds. The kind of stuff that thinking people appreciate. The kind of stuff that lasts after *Laser Tracks* is just another thing on Saturday mornings for kids."

"You know we all love the dailies from *Jitterbug.* And you know very well that there's no way on earth *Laser Tracks* is going to be just another kids' show." Sid's voice was calm, but I noticed that he was stroking his chest idly as he spoke.

"I could understand it if it were just coming from

Susan," Paul said. "I mean, by now everybody knows how she thinks about Jews making movies, with all her cracks about Nate 'n' Al's and Junior's Delicatessen—"

But Paul did not get a chance to finish. Susan-Marie was on her feet and in one fluid, furious movement had thrown her tonic and bitters in Paul's face. While he scrabbled at his eyes with his shocked fingers, Susan-Marie screamed at him, almost unrecognizable in her anger. "You dare say that to me? You sick, sick man. My father was with the first patrol to reach Dachau with the Third Army. He still had shrapnel in his hip from fighting just outside the gates to get inside. Even when I was a little girl he couldn't stop crying whenever he talked about it. His best friend in the whole world was Sam Fairstein. You think he was a Moslem? My best friend for my whole life has been Benjy. What do you think he is?"

"I'm leaving," Paul said. "I don't have to take this."

But Susan-Marie would not let him leave. With surprising strength, she grasped the lapel of his blazer and spun him back into his seat. "You try to wrap any criticism of you and your pals in some grimy cloak of anti-Semitism. I'm fucking sick of it. No one in this room thinks *Jitterbug* is anything but great. But if you don't have everyone on earth bowing down to tell you it's another *On the Waterfront*, you're suddenly the victim of anti-Semitism, the innocent victim of Nazis. Don't you dare try that shit on me. My father walked with half a pound of Krupp steel in his leg fighting Nazis. You're not doing anything but throwing mud at your own wife."

Paul hung his head for a moment and then said, "I'd better change. I'm late for a meeting at the DGA. I'm supposed to introduce a screening of *Estonia*. An antique. Someone found a print."

After he left Susan-Marie sat in her chair for a while. The timer threw on the sodium vapor lights that illuminated the surf, breaking just outside the wall of the pool.

"I was too hard on him," Susan-Marie said. "I don't

know. For a few days there we were getting along great. I don't know what made me do that."

"He was acting like a crazy man," Sid said, puffing on his pipe. "You don't need to make excuses for him."

"No, but I was too angry," Susan-Marie said. "Especially now. For a lot of reasons. You shouldn't do that to your husband. Not for any reason. He's just always picking, always needling. As if I didn't know *Jitterbug* was a far more important picture than *Laser Tracks.*"

"No," Sid said. "*Laser Tracks* is electric. It's a throwback to when people understood that movies were meant to take you away, not put you in the shit. It's a breakthrough. *Jitterbug* is a fine picture, but it's been done in other ways. It's *Bad Day at Black Rock* in Alabama."

"I don't know," Susan-Marie said. "I just know that for my husband to always be attacking me, always acting as if I were the enemy, it's really making me wonder what the hell I'm doing here. And this latest business about my being anti-Semitic. It's incredible. It's really incredible."

"You can handle it," I said. "You always do. Always."

"I'd better this time," Susan-Marie said.

Sid got up to call the driver, and Susan went to her desk drawer in the teahouse. "I think this is putting me on edge. This and a few other things."

She handed me a postcard of a large shopping center. On the card was Susan-Marie's name and address in an impeccable, schoolgirl script of robin's-egg blue.

Dearest Susan-Marie White Trash, it read. *You're entirely to blame for my being here. This has been the worst time of my life. I don't belong here. You do. I'm getting out soon, and then we'll see who's boss. If you're as smart as you think you are, you'll leave town and leave Paul before I get there and break you in two.*

The card was signed *Much love, Dee.*

31

DEBITS

∎

Jitterbug was finished in January of 1977. It was shown to a small group of buyers for the major chains—Sack, Diller, Picker, Cinema General, K-B, Syufy—after a dinner at the St. Regis Maisonette. The buyers were enthusiastic. In the next few days deals were struck to open the picture at the prestige houses in New York, Chicago, San Francisco, Los Angeles, and Boston. Because the theater owners could expect good business for at least the first two weeks, they offered Republic a fifty–fifty split on gross box office. Republic countered with seventy-five–twenty-five. The deal was closed at fifty-five–forty-five.

The movie opened on Valentine's Day of 1977. It drew respectful audiences, especially from the cinema-buff generation who remembered *Estonia* and *Mother*. The reviewers were complimentary. Pauline Kael called it a "triumph of mature moviemaking . . ." Roger Ebert said it showed the "powers of hindsight and memory of a true pillar of the movie industry."

Jitterbug went into wide release three weeks later, in March of 1977. The Republic statisticians figured that based on what it did in the bellwether theaters in its first weeks, it would do about $4,500 per screen in about nine hundred situations. That would have made it a definite hit.

The only problem was that it opened—at Paul Belzberg's insistence—in a wide break the same weekend that *Laser Tracks* opened nationally in wide release. "I'm doing this as an education for you," he told Susan-Marie. "It's Sid's money, so what the heck. I want to show you that the theatergoing audience just won't buy science fiction anymore. If we open wide with a lot of theaters, we may get enough word of mouth to get a good network sale, which is all we can really hope for."

"You're wrong," Susan-Marie answered. "When we had the studio screening they stood and cheered. When was the last time a studio audience stood and cheered?"

"They cheered because everybody at the studio loves you," Paul said. "Ever since you fired Bron Gless you're a goddess. Mind you," he added, "I have to agree you made a good movie there with *Laser Tracks*. I enjoyed it myself. But it's a cartoon, not a movie. It's fun, but not commercial, not on a wide scale. It's for little kids. That's all."

On the weekend of March 2, 1977, when *Laser Tracks* opened wide, it did average business on Friday. By Saturday at noon every matinee all over America was sold out. By Saturday night there were lines around the block at every theater where it played. By Sunday night there were riots in Westwood and Astoria because the theaters were sold out for every show.

By Monday the clamor from the theaters to extend the

play of *Laser Tracks* was so intense that Republic re-negotiated its deals with all of the major chains. The new split was eighty-five for Republic and fifteen for the theaters.

In the first week of release *Laser Tracks* set a new record of $11,321 per screen. In the second week the number of screens went up to thirteen hundred and the per screen gross was an even $12,500.

In the third week of release the covers of both *Time* and *Newsweek* showed Susan-Marie Belzberg. One split the cover with Susan-Marie and Eniwetok, the adorable stuffed teddy bear from the hero's Ohio bedroom who became a ferocious sidekick in outer space. The other cover showed Susan-Marie atop the planet "chessboard" as it spun through "another eon, far away from wherever you live."

The headline of the *Time* cover was A NEW WOMAN FOR A NEW ERA IN HOLLYWOOD. The headline of *Newsweek* took off from the space-hero's frequent comment to Eniwetok in *Laser Tracks*. THE NEW QUEEN OF HOLLYWOOD—CAN ANYTHING STOP HER NOW?

On the fourth weekend *Laser Tracks* was rapidly closing in on the total all-time American box office for *The Sound of Music,* with gross receipts of over $64,000,000 dollars.

On the sixth weekend, when Susan-Marie arrived at her office, Pal Lassiette, the director of *Laser Tracks,* Mel Tolkin, the child star of the movie, Stacy Trane, a former librarian from Elkhart, Indiana, who had written the final draft of the script, a photographer from *The New York Times Magazine,* Sid Bauman, and I joined together in the blue room of the Republic commissary. When Susan-Marie walked in with Paul Belzberg for lunch the waiters pulled back a screen and a Frank Sinatra imitator stood revealed with a small band.

While the entire staff of the Burbank Studios pressed around and looked through the windows, Susan-Marie heard "Frank Sinatra" sing "My Way" to her, closing with a stanza Sid Bauman had written himself.

> *And through it all,*
> *I took the falls,*
> *I took the thorns with all the roses,*
> *Came up with only . . . new world record grosses,*
> *And did it my way.*

Susan-Marie whispered to me, "I don't know whether to laugh or cry or hide my head."

"Be proud," I said. "You've showed the whole world what movies are."

Paul Belzberg overheard me. He looked at me as if he were going to commit murder. While Susan accepted a bouquet of roses, Paul Belzberg whispered to me, in a furious rush, "There are flukes in this business. Remember hula hoops?"

"No, I don't," I said, "but I remember *Gone With the Wind.*"

"We'll see," he said. "There are a lot of surprises in this business."

• • • •

Susan-Marie was given an award on May 25, 1977 by the Writers' Guild of America, West. She sat on a dais along with Jack Valente, Paul Newman, Paul Belzberg, Charlton Heston, Michael Chasman, and Lila Garrett. On the dais also was Ron Silverman, a new member of the Office of the President of Republic, and Stacy Trane, the librarian-scenarist of *Laser Tracks.*

After eating appetizers of mushrooms stuffed with cracked crab and a main course of squab on asparagus, after a chocolate mousse in the shape of Eniwetok, the spokesman for the Writers' Guild, Isaac Leon Churchill, creator of the ten-year-running sitcom "Take It As It Comes," read from a prepared text.

"This woman, Susan-Marie Belzberg, had the courage

to fight for what she believed in. She had to test new waters, knock a few heads together, and do that most difficult of all things, actually put her career and reputation on the line for a movie she believed in. I think that every man and woman in this room knows there is nothing more difficult than that. To risk your future and your name on something new, well, that's courage."

There was enthusiastic applause.

Susan-Marie took the little gold baton and shook hands with Leon Churchill. "Thank you, and thanks especially to my wonderful husband, Paul, who stood by me every step of the way, who knew this picture would work and went far beyond the bounds of duty of husband to wife to make sure it did work."

I listened and watched Paul. He stared at his untouched dessert. I remembered how he had done whatever he could to put *Laser Tracks* into inner-city theaters where it couldn't possibly compete against the suburban extravaganzas showing *Jitterbug*.

"You know, this town owes a lot to people like Paul, who have ushered in one change after another. It owes a lot to men like Sid Bauman, who put their money behind what are the most insubstantial quantities on earth—mere ideas. And it owes thanks to newcomers like Pal Lassiette and Stacy Trane, who took a chance on Hollywood with their hopes and dreams.

"I am flattered indeed by what Leon said about me. But it's more than I deserve. In every sense, I simply had no choice but to make this movie. As soon as I saw the looks on young people's faces when they talked about the clear, unqualified world of *Laser Tracks*, I knew I had to make this picture. If it was a failure, I would still have had to make it. Frankly, I would have looked stupid, but I would not have starved, and I would have had a roof over my head. We have another breadwinner in my family."

(Polite applause. A small smile from Paul Belzberg.)

"But it just is not fair to say that pushing to get a movie made is an act of high courage. In the last ten horrible years in this country, fifty thousand young Americans gave their lives for something that never should have been. Some of them threw themselves on grenades to save their friends' lives. Others endured torture in small chicken coops until they died of starvation. Others fought with bayonets so that their buddies could escape. That's high courage, not arguing in Hollywood.

"In my own family, twenty-five years ago, a man fought for six straight days and nights in below-zero blizzard conditions in Korea so that his battalion could get out. When they were finally surrounded and there was only one truck left to get them out he gave his place in it to a wounded Korean boy he had never seen before. That man's body was never found. *That* was courage. That was something to admire, something to move men's souls."

The men and women in the room looked flushed, amazed, as if they had been slapped on the face.

"There was a funeral for that man. Ten people were there on a hillside in Arlington, Virginia. It lasted fifteen minutes and then the chaplain had to go on to the next funeral. There was an award later in the mail for his wife and his daughter. That was the reward of real courage. That, and remembrance. For real courage, there are rarely lunches at the Beverly Hills Hotel, mushrooms stuffed with crab, little gold batons. This country has a great many men like my father in it. I intend to make movies in the future that celebrate their courage.

"What we do here in Hollywood takes persistence and imagination and hope. It's hard work. But the real heroes are out there, in the place east of here they call America, and it is their courage that has always moved and inspired me. I will leave here grateful for this award, and determined, again, to be worthy of the men and women who have shown what real courage is. We are all their heirs and we must work to be deserving."

Susan-Marie sat down. There was about fifteen seconds of silence. Then the audience did something I have never seen the Writers' Guild do before or since: they broke into a five-minute standing ovation, complete with whistles and foot-stomping. Susan-Marie looked down at her plate. Paul Belzberg leaned over and kissed her. When he took his face away I saw that his fists were clenched so tightly that his knuckles glowed.

■　　■　　■　　■

On June 1, 1977, Sid Bauman reached a decision. He called Susan-Marie down to his office at eleven in the morning. Susan-Marie walked past his two secretaries. On that day they were dressed in full parachute regalia, with baggy trousers and real parachutes strapped to their backs. They looked completely nonchalant about it. Susan breezed into Sid's office without knocking and sat down on a beige leather chair. She smoothed her yellow skirt and smiled at Sid. "I hear the merchandising's all finished at the lawyers'," she said.

"Sixty million over five years for the rights." Bauman beamed. "Split among Coleco, Mattel, and Hasbro for toys, and among Russtogs and J.C. Penney for children's clothes. Sears gets lunchboxes and tool kits and that kind of *chazerai.*"

"Pretty good," Susan-Marie agreed. "I would have paid more attention, but I've been working with Pal Lassiette and Stacy Trane every day on *Zero G.*"

"We did all right anyway. As near as I can figure, we got as much as every other picture put together has ever gotten for merchandising. I can't complain."

Susan-Marie nodded and said nothing.

"It's especially nice for a picture that was at most going to be an 'ABC After-School Special.' That's what I wanted to talk to you about," Sid said cheerfully. "That's topic A."

"Topic A?" Susan asked with a smile. "Have you been talking to John Ehrlichman?"

"Every day." Sid laughed. "Listen, is Paul still in Thailand?"

"At the Southeast Asian Theatre Owners' meeting,"

Susan acknowledged. "Reassuring them that the flow of American films won't be affected by the end of the war in Vietnam."

"They must be relieved," Sid said.

"Overjoyed."

"Listen, I have an idea about restructuring this company. I've talked about it with Estelle van Amburg and Rick Hunneycutt. I can tell you that they agree."

"What might that be?" Susan-Marie asked.

"I think you should be head of the motion picture division, with corporate responsibility for TV as well. You know you're right for it."

Susan-Marie got up from her chair and walked over to Sid's wall. She looked at a photograph of Bauman with President Sukarno and Dewi, taken in happier days for the Indonesian leader. "I think someone already has that job."

"You know Paul's not right for it," Sid said. "You've carried him for the last two years. You know that in your heart. He's a great idea man and he made some good pictures twenty years ago. But he's nothing on administration. That little creep, Deirdre, carried him for a few years, and you've been carrying him lately."

"I'm surprised at you, Sid. That's just not fair. *Jitterbug* was a great picture."

"It was a good picture. But it played for two weeks and it's a genre that shouldn't even be made anymore. Besides, I hear you had a lot to do with keeping the original story line when Paul and Schallerberg wanted to fuck it up. Be fair to yourself. This job is right for you."

"No," Susan said. "For all anybody knows, I just had a fluke with *Laser Tracks*. I might never make another picture that makes money again."

"That's Paul's brainwashing, and you know it. You have vision. You had it from the first day you were on the lot when you gave me that fairy tale about just walking onto the lot and not knowing where your office was. You had it when you gave us advice at that first meeting about marketing. You had it when you made us open up to new writers. You've got it, and Paul doesn't. It's wrong for you to spend another day not being in real control, not having to argue with Paul about every little thing."

"I can't do it," Susan repeated. "Paul's trying very hard to adjust to how well *Laser Tracks* did. If I took this job, it would kill him."

"He's a big boy. This is Hollywood. He's not looking for charity."

"I know. But I'm not going to kick him in the teeth. I'm not an agent. I'm his wife. If somebody else does it, that's one thing. But I wasn't brought up to wreck my own marriage with ambition."

"Jesus Christ, Susan. Think of the shit Paul put you through about *Laser Tracks*. The meanest guy at William Morris wouldn't have done that. Think of yourself for once."

"I'm going to tell you again. I want our marriage to work. That's more important to me than any job, and it's more important than the earnings per share of Republic."

"But it has to be a mutual thing. You really think Paul is trying as hard as you are?"

"I know he isn't," Susan-Marie said. "But I think now he's trying a lot harder, and I'm not going to do anything that makes him give up. If he'll just go a little way to seeing that I have something to contribute to movies, to seeing that I can be somebody here, I'll meet him all the rest of the way."

"You're making a mistake," Sid said. "Take it from someone who really loves you."

"Sid . . ."

"No, I mean it. Take this job and let Paul sort it out for himself. We'll make him chairman of the Finance Committee, give him a rich indie-prod deal on the lot, and he'll realize what's inevitable."

"I can't, Sid. I pushed really hard for *Laser Tracks*. It was a blow to Paul. Now we're going to try to pull it together. He means something to me, Sid. He's my husband. He's not my co-producer. He's my husband."

"I never could talk you into anything," Sid said. "But you're wrong here. Do for yourself and you'll be doing both of you a favor in the long run."

"No," Susan-Marie said. "Besides, I was going to ask you for a meeting this week anyway to tell you I'm going to need a year off soon. Maybe more."

"What the hell for?" Sid asked irritably. "We're almost in production on *Eniwetok* and we're finishing script on *Zero G*. Not only that, but we're negotiating with Newhall Land for a theme park for Republic . . ."

"Paul and I are going to have a baby." Susan-Marie smiled. "It's corny as hell, but there it is. I want the baby to have a mother and a father. So now you understand everything."

Bauman's eyes flashed, then clouded over. "Studio executives don't have babies when they're on the hottest streak in the business. Children are for people who aren't making it," he said slowly.

"No. Children are the whole reason for everything," Susan-Marie said. "They're the point, not deals or grosses."

There was a moment of heavy silence in the room. Then Sid got out of his chair and walked to Susan-Marie. He opened his arms and folded Susan into them. "Congratulations. God, that's a lucky baby to have you as its mother," he said.

Susan-Marie blushed and Sid held her, rocking her in his old arms. "That's a lucky baby," he repeated. "Jesus, that's a lucky baby." Then he put his hand over his eyes.

32

CREDITS

◼

Of course, I called Parisian Florists and sent a summer arrangement of flowers—jonquils and hollyhocks and daisies and birds of paradise—to Susan and Paul in their dream house in Malibu. I drove out there and spent an afternoon with her, remembering the past—at that point all that we had was the past—and telling her how happy I was for her.

But the truth was that for Susan-Marie to mix her light with Paul's darkness was the last straw for a good long while. Hollywood had never held the charms for me that it held for Susan-Marie. It had never even begun to reward me the way it had paid Susan. In a sense, I was a perpetual stranger there, always amazed and shocked to see Jane Fonda at Ma Maison, but even more shocked to see myself there. Each time I passed by the windows of Hunter's in Beverly Hills and saw myself reflected, I was surprised and bewildered. With the imminent arrival of Susan-Marie's baby, I had had enough.

In October the Personal Dignity Foundation offered me a job writing a book for them on the history of libertarianism. The foundation was funded by a group of Texas land millionaires and Korean steel manufacturers who were fixated on the idea that the individual's worth transcended that of the state and was prior to it. These worthy people had read Rousseau and von Mises, Jefferson and Hayek. They believed that if they could have a book about the dignity and preeminence of the individual, they could print literally one billion of them in paperback. That would stop Godless, atheistic Bolshevism dead in its tracks. See this here book, Comrade Brezhnev? Take this and suck on it!

It was a lush deal. For a year of writing I got about what a beginning scriptwriter gets for a first draft and a set of revisions. On the other hand, a condition of the deal was that I had to work in an office of the PDF in Washington, at 1000 Connecticut Avenue, NW. That was the good part of the deal.

I also could do my column for *New View* and occasional TV spots about the lighter side of Washington for KNX. I could keep my status as a very, very minor celebrity in Los Angeles, but remove myself from proximity to the pain.

Susan-Marie wanted to give me a going-away party. But even that signified more of a connection with her and with Hollywood than I felt at the time. Sid Bauman made me a better offer. "Keep your apartment here, *boychik,*" he said. "I'll have Republic pay for it. Once a month write me a letter about anything you hear about laws or regulations about the movie business. I'll have you come back here whenever you want. First class."

We were in his pool house when he spoke, watching the blue waters of the pool ripple in the three P.M. breeze that always blows through Hollywood. As usual, we were drinking Bombay martinis. As usual, I was unsteady and my vision was blurred, while he was as steady as a rock.

"I accept," I said. "You are a pal."

As for my year in Washington, D.C., you can get a good idea from a brief listing of a few of the women I went out with there:

- The legislative assistant to a New England senator who had found God in a tavern in Framingham, Massachusetts, after a five-year stint as the live-in girl-friend of ten Hell's Angels in Revere, and, after finding God, had found that she could go to Radcliffe and become a leading member of Americans for Democratic Action.

- The doctor at George Washington University Hospital who had decided to give up medicine in favor of becoming a specialist in medical real estate. "In the hospitals, people are dying," she said to me. "In real estate, nothing ever dies."

- The statistician for the World Bank who introduced me to her mother after our third date. The mother had been born in County Clare, Ireland. When my friend left the dining room the mother leaned over to speak to me. With a strong Irish accent she asked me if I knew what Hitler had done wrong. "A great many terrible things," I answered. Mom shook her head and said, "Nay. He didna finish the job."

- The legislative analyst for the Heritage Foundation who, when I asked her about the homeless men sleeping by the grates in Lafayette Square, said to me, "Every society has its expendable men. It would save everyone a lot of trouble if we sent them off to Alaska to die and be eaten by the wolves. Wolves," she said with true admiration, "are efficient animals."

The art student at American University who wore little blue suede shoes and who was studying the works of the nineteenth-century masters. When I asked her which was her favorite she said, "Vincent van Gogh, because he was the only one of the great masters who signed only his first name on his canvases. That showed genius."

Most of the time I walked Mary, my dog, who had been so neglected in Los Angeles, and thought about individual dignity. In the leafy hills of Battery-Kemble Park, along the jogging paths of the C & O Canal, by the softball diamonds of Rock Creek Park, I walked with Mary and thought about Locke.

One day, in the early fall of 1978, after I had been in Washington for eleven months, I walked past the picnic table in Sligo Creek Park where I had met Susan-Marie Warmack for the first time twenty years before. I looked at that spot and I looked up at the boundless blue sky and I knew something I had not known: that I would always love Susan-Marie, that time was neutral and would not heal that wound, that I missed being around her even if she belonged to a man I hated. I could practically feel the heat of life from the spot where we had first talked, and I longed for the warmth of her company again. Washington had been a change, and I certainly bore no ill will toward the Korean steel men and the Texas land men who had brought me back there. But I needed to return to Los Angeles. I could do without the pitch meetings and the turndowns and the sharks. But I needed the *action* of closeness to Susan-Marie. She was so much more alive than the statistician from the World Bank or the art student from AU or the doctor at GW Hospital that their very presence made me miss Susan more. This is an embarrassing thing to say, but love does not disable women only. I had become addicted to Susan-

Marie so that just having a few percent of her meant more to me than having all of the statistician or the legislative aide.

Of course, Susan-Marie was a mother by then. In March of 1978 as *Time* reported in its "Milestones" column: "Born: To Susan-Marie *Laser Tracks* Belzberg and Paul *Estonia* Belzberg, a girl, seven pounds, one ounce, Ava Elizabeth Warmack Belzberg, in St. John's Hospital, Santa Monica. First for both parents." She had called to tell me the news from her hospital bed. I was at home with the former girl from the Hell's Angels. Frankly, I felt dirty being with another woman when I talked to Susan, but then again, I never denied that I was a fool.

I thought about the baby Ava, and the maple trees under which Susan-Marie and I had walked long before, and I looked at my darling Mary with her blue weimaraner eyes, and I said, "Mary, how would you like to go back to Hollywood?" Mary jumped up on me and cried, and I have to believe that meant "yes."

■　　■　　■　　■

Susan-Marie had changed. I asked Sid's driver to take me directly from LAX to the house at 77 Malibu Beach Colony. Ava Elizabeth was magnificent. She looked at me from the infinity of babyhood with deep blue eyes that laughed and saw with what I was sure were perfect Susan-Marie insights. When I held her she seemed to me to feel unusually warm against my chest, almost like a girl I had danced with at the Senior Prom. She pressed her baby palms against my chest and I felt dizzy. But Susan-Marie had changed.

We ate lunch in the teahouse, with the windows open to the ocean. "I want Ava to get used to the sound of the waves," Susan-Marie said. "It's a strong sound, and if you listen to them right, it's a reassuring sound. I want her to hear strong noises and not be afraid of any of them."

354

"It's hard to believe she could ever be afraid," I said. "What would she be afraid of?"

Susan-Marie only looked at me as if I were a lovable but dim creature who had suddenly been washed up on the shore.

"I'll tell you what a little girl can be afraid of," Susan-Marie said. Then, for the first time, although there had been hints before, she told me about the little bedroom with the knotty-pine furniture and the posters of Tab Hunter and Elvis Presley and the sound of footsteps on the stairs and about feeling numb and escaping into another world out in space, far, far away, or maybe into one little cell hidden somewhere in her body.

Susan told me about that pain for about half an hour, maybe longer. I didn't look at my watch, which was set for the wrong time anyway. While she talked, Elena dozed in a deck chair. Susan took Ava out of her crib and held her, rocking her gently back and forth in the teahouse, her soothing motions in shocking contrast to the words she was saying. After she had finished, I said, "It's terrible. It's just terrible, but it's a long time in the past. You've beaten it, gone way beyond it. That's the only thing that counts. You've defeated your own past, and that's what counts for right now. There is no way that the fear from the house on Dale Drive could ever come inside a house like this," I said, gesturing again at the Belzberg dream house.

"No big scary man can ever come and use me because he can't deal with real life," Susan-Marie said. "No big scary stepfather can ever act like I'm a love doll with no feelings of my own. That's true."

"That's something," I said.

"But I can live with a man who hates me. I live in that fabulous house with a famous man, and Barbara Walters has asked us three times if she can come interview us, and it doesn't mean a goddamned thing. I'm not scared of being raped anymore. But I'm scared all the time that he's going to start yelling at me because I said something smart or because I told him the truth or because I didn't act small enough or because I wasn't enough of a plastic praise doll for him."

"My sweet Susan," I said. "Why don't you just get the hell out?"

"Paul was in Seoul at the Korean Theatre Owners' Association Convention when Ava was born. When I called him he said he was going to go to Hawaii for a few days' rest before he got home. I could hear a woman speaking Korean in the background in his hotel room. When he got home he hugged the baby for five minutes, then he said he had to go see Chris Wohlstetter's father about an investment in some apartments in San Jose. When I looked sad he slammed the door and walked out."

"I'm sorry," I said. "Why put up with it?"

"You have to understand that I'm not scared of being beaten up or being raped. But I'm scared all the time that just for being me, Paul hates me and is going to hurt me some way or other. If you think it didn't hurt when I heard him walk out after he had just seen our baby, you're wrong. If you think it didn't hurt to know he hated me because I had not only made *Laser Tracks* but had also made a baby, something he couldn't do, you're wrong."

"Then leave," I said.

"I can't," Susan-Marie said. "I grew up without a real father. I don't want it to happen to Ava."

"Paul must be scared to death," I said.

"I know he is." Susan-Marie's voice was low and soft. "My stepfather was probably scared to death as well. But what about me? I don't deserve this," Susan-Marie said. "But I'm not going to waste my time feeling sorry for myself. I'd rather feel sorry for Paul than feel sorry for myself. I wish I were you," she said. "You're never scared of anything."

356

"I only seem that way because I'm scared of everything."

Susan-Marie took my hand and squeezed it. "Let's not talk about this any longer. Let's talk about the movies. After all, that's what movies are for. To make us forget what's real."

33

ZERO

■

In July of 1978 I drove out to Malibu on a Saturday morning and went with Susan and Paul to the gym at Pepperdine College. We rode on bicycle machines in a glass-walled room overlooking the Pacific. In her white leotard and tights, Susan-Marie pumped away at her bicycle, looking like a schoolgirl. Paul Belzberg rode even faster in his gray sweat pants and his scarf from Hermès, of fine checks against a yellow background. We were the only people in the room. It was a big day for me. The night before my TV gig had been bought by Viacom to be shown on TV stations all over America. Now my "wry and penetrating" insights would be in small towns all over America, between ads for Plymouth dealers and hog price forecasts.

We rode furiously for fifteen minutes, and I had the distinct feeling that although no words were spoken,

Susan and Paul were trying to somehow pedal away their differences, as if the most fundamental personality conflicts could be worked off like burning off a cheeseburger.

After fifteen minutes, we all got off the bikes and looked out the gym windows and panted. "This is good," Susan-Marie said as she wiped her brow. "I can see some people out there on the campus. Usually the only people I see all day are Elena and my babysitters, Julie and Vicki."

"Her Valley Girls," Paul Belzberg said indifferently.

"I love them, I really do. They both go to USC and live over in Agoura. They're in this sorority, Alpha Chi, and on the one hand, they're completely naive and trusting. On the other hand, they're scheming and clever. On the one hand, they have great ambitions and plans, and on the other hand, they're like babes in toyland. They don't know where Washington is, or where New York is, or where Russia is. But they have incredible ideas about how to snag a rich husband."

"Perfect California girls," I said. "They know what counts."

"They have it down to a science," Susan-Marie continued. She was now on the floor doing leg-raisers while she talked. "They check on guys' license plates through this detective they know, and they get Dun and Bradstreets on the boys, and then they take the classes where the rich ones hang out."

"Very mercenary," Paul sniffed.

"Not really, because the plan is only in their minds. Basically, they'll love anyone who loves them. When push comes to shove, they're always with guys who don't have a dime."

"Hmmm," I said.

"Don't tell me," Paul said.

"Of course," Susan-Marie said. "A college gang comedy. A cross between 'The Three Stooges' and 'How to Marry a Millionaire.' But very broad. Physical humor, physical gags. Black and white people. Heroes and villains. The girls are in a sorority that's been the doormat of the row for as long as anyone can remember—"

Susan-Marie was cut off by a long groan from her husband. After a moment's pause, she went on. "Only despite the way everybody's dumping on them, they still have a lot of spirit. When guys are mean to them, they steal the guys' cars and paint graffiti on them. They break into the fraternities and steal stereos and toss them off the roof, and they call that 'rooftesting' and whenever they see something they like, they say, 'Let's rooftest it.'"

This time Paul said, "Really, Susan."

But Susan-Marie continued. "And the dean is always threatening to sue them or throw them out of school or call the police, but the girls just aren't afraid of anything. That's their beauty."

"What's their beauty? It sounds as if they're a bunch of young thugs," Paul said. "It sounds like it's the lowest kind of pandering to the youth market."

"It's not pandering to give moviegoers something that'll make them happy and give them a place to escape to when the real world is kicking their brains in," Susan-Marie said. "It's not great art, but it's new and and it might make people forget what's bothering them and feel happy for a few hours and give them something to laugh about in the future."

"And that's what movies have come to," Paul said, "under the kindly hand of Susan-Marie Belzberg. An hour's laughs for sixteen-year-olds."

"No. Something that ordinary people can relate to," Susan-Marie answered. "Something that's full of life and excitement and challenge. Something that's real, instead of the *geshreying* of twenty middle-aged men because they have more money than they know what to do with. It comes from life, not from complaining all the time," Susan-Marie added. "It's like *Estonia*. That's what's so great about it."

"Really," Paul said. "Really? A movie about a group of ignorant USC girls is like *Estonia*? A movie about throwing stereos off rooftops is like *Estonia?* I must be losing my mind. I actually thought I heard you say that."

"It's like *Estonia* because it celebrates life," Susan-Marie said. "It's not elegant and it's not courtly and maybe not even romantic. But it says how wonderful it is to be alive, and that's why it's like *Estonia.* You know what I mean, Paul."

"I have no idea what you mean," he said, "except that you obviously never understood the first thing about me or about *Estonia,* and I have to leave to talk to some of us old people about script work."

With that, he picked up his Porsche keys from a bench and walked out. Susan ran over to him and grabbed his arm. "Paul, you know I love *Estonia* more than anyone ever has on earth. You know what I meant."

Paul looked at her as if she were a piece of dirt that had somehow attached itself to his sleeve. He firmly took her hand, that warm, white, fine hand off his arm and said, "Have dinner with Benjy. I don't know when I'll be home. I may sleep in town at the Beverly Hills Hotel if it's too late to drive home. You might want to screen *Estonia* so you'll have some idea of what you're talking about next time."

Susan-Marie walked back to her bicycle and started pedaling it again. Looking out the window at the ocean, she set her chin and said, "Anyway, the thing that's the beauty of these girls is that everyone in the audience knows that the world is filled with crocodiles and alligators, and the sorority girls sort of know it, too, but they go out there and fight for what they want as if there was nothing that could ever hurt them. As if they were going to win every battle and live forever. That's what's so wonderful about them."

"I'll go see it," I said.

Susan stopped pedaling and took my hand. "It's already in script. I'll make it. I'd make it even if Paul liked it," she said with a laugh. "It'll make so much money that then

I can get Sid to let me make *Chosin,* which is about people who are really brave, who really deserve to have a movie made about them."

"That, I really love."

"And Paul will hate it, too," Susan-Marie said. "Let's go home and eat."

34

PAYMENTS

In August 1978 I was rehearsing a television show for KCET, the Los Angeles public affairs station. The idea was that I would interview celebrity Angelenos about what the city was all about. With a camera crew, I stood in front of Gazzaris, a teenage nightspot in West Hollywood, on Sunset Strip. With a stand-in supposed to be Gore Vidal, I was practicing questions that would get his usual witty answers. My director, a twenty-four-year-old woman from the University of Wisconsin Film School, stood behind the camera playing with her ponytail. Every few minutes she would say, "No. Say it as if you were giving a fire truck instructions to get to a fire."

While I was trying to put more life into it, and while a fat shopping-bag lady nodded approval of the director's suggestions, a bus passed by. It was almost completely empty, as buses in Los Angeles usually are in daylight. There was only one passenger on the bus, sitting in the rear seat.

It was Deirdre Needle. She wore a plain white blouse and a red, checkered bandanna over her head. She looked at me carefully and then waved to me. In her eyes was a stare that told me that she had been in touch with the Almighty and wanted to pass on to me what He had said.

■   ■   ■   ■

Alpha Chi opened in nine hundred theaters during the last weekend of March 1979. Frankly, Sid Bauman had insisted on making it as soon as Susan-Marie had told him about the idea of a gang comedy set in a Southern California sorority house. Morgan Fairchild played the house mother, but otherwise it was a low-budget picture. Marco Castro handled the marketing and Ron Silverman was the studio executive. A newcomer, Diana Baer, directed. The picture was brought in for six million. Republic put another four million against it in advertising. The campaign was a masterpiece. It ran almost exclusively on late Saturday nights for three weeks before release. It showed a row of Alpha Chi Omega sorority sisters lying on their stomachs in bathing suits. In front of each one was a computer keyboard and a videoscreen. The background was a beach and palm trees. Above the girls ran the line, "Just when you thought it was safe to go into the Perrier water . . ."

Roger Ebert said it marked a "new day of vitality in film comedy . . ." Peter Rainer said it was "a final declaration of independence from the tired middle-aged crisis syndrome of American comedy . . ."

There were lines around the block at almost every theater on opening night. By the second weekend the picture had added two hundred and twenty screens and the gross per screen was above $13,000. By April 1, 1979, *Alpha Chi* was the highest-grossing picture of the year. The runner-up was a re-release of *Laser Tracks*.

Susan-Marie didn't get on the cover of *Time* again. She was at home with Ava Elizabeth. "I don't care," she said merrily while she and Sid Bauman were blocking out ideas for a sequel to *Alpha Chi*.

Paul was upstairs in his bedroom—right next to Susan-Marie's bedroom—reading a script.

"I don't care," Susan-Marie repeated. "The point is to get the best possible picture and get people to see it and to love it."

"Everyone in town knows it was your idea," Sid Bauman said. "So there's no problem there anyway."

"My idea. Not my project."

"Kids are going every night of the weekend in some cities, and coming dressed like girls in Alpha Chi," I said. "It's a cult thing almost."

"Fiddle-dee-dee," Susan-Marie said.

On the floor in front of us Ava Elizabeth played with a doll of Eniwetok and a doll of Killer Joe, the main character in *Alpha Chi*. She looked as if she were in the warm center of the universe, and I guess she was.

There was a polite knock on the door of the teahouse and Paul Belzberg made an ungraceful, mocking bow. "I hope I'm not disturbing America's sweetheart," he said. "But I need to come in here for a Scotch."

"It looks as if you've had plenty of Scotch already," Sid said. "But, if you want more . . ."

"You don't tell me how much to drink," Paul shot back. "Who the hell do you think you are?"

"Take it easy," Sid said. "Nobody's ordering you around."

"It's not enough that you've all made me look like the town pansy," Paul said. "Not enough that you've made me look like my job is to carry around Susan-Marie's garbage. But you have to push me out of my house, too."

"We'll leave," I said. "C'mon, Sid. We can go into Westwood and see what's playing."

"Try to get control of yourself," Sid said in an affable way to Paul, clapping him on the shoulder as he walked past.

Paul flung Sid's arm off his shoulder. "Don't condescend to me, you fat nothing. It's not enough that you were banging my wife before I could even get back to town. You have to make me look like a moron, too."

"Are you crazy?" Sid asked. "You'd better check yourself out at a hospital very carefully, and don't waste a minute. We're leaving, Susan. Good-bye, Ava." Sid waved cordially to the baby, who waved back.

"Who's baby is that, anyway?" Paul asked. "I don't know who's baby she is. For all I know, you've both been *shtupping* her every time I turn around. It wouldn't surprise me. She rose awfully quick, awfully fast in this town."

Sid swung on Paul like an enraged gorilla. The blow hit him just as I was also leaping for him. Paul ducked out of the way, slipped, and fell against a heavily cushioned yellow chair. He was out cold before he hit the pillow, far more from Dewar's than from Bauman.

But just as we all panted with fury, Sid grabbed my arm. His hand was cold to the touch, even through my shirt. "Call an ambulance," he said. "I have the most terrible pain . . ."

He sat down heavily on an embroidered couch while I picked up the phone and called the Malibu paramedics. Sid looked at me and said, "Thanks."

"Just sit quietly," I said. "Don't talk."

"Just like the days in the Young Communist League beating up the Social Democrats, even the Trotskyites, that was great. Those were big days," he said, panting heavily. "Amanda would sit up late at night and listen when I told her those stories. It was wonderful. Like a baby listening to a lullaby. Pretty stories."

"Don't talk," Susan-Marie said. She held his head against her chest and pressed her cheek against the top of his head. "Don't talk."

366

It is a measure of something essentially fine in Sid Bauman that Susan and I both jammed ourselves into the front seat of the ambulance to ride with him to the coronary intensive care unit. The male paramedic, who looked as if he had come straight from the Yeshiva of Flatbush, pausing only long enough to learn how to hang ten—long, drooping nose, pale, *shtetl* complexion, prominent, bobbing Adam's apple, laconic, Malibu manner—put a needle and digitalin into Sid's arm before we started up.

Sid started to breathe more regularly and he took his hand away from his chest. He also began to sigh deeply and to shift his head back and forth from the Malibu hillsides to the ocean, as if he were looking at air, water, and earth for the last time, and wanted to make sure he remembered them right.

Traffic cleared out of our way and we were in the outskirts of Santa Monica in less than ten minutes. "I'm telling you," Sid Bauman whispered to us from his place in the ambulance, "make your move now. Paul's not worth protecting. I think I'm dying, so I can say anything," he added with a self-deprecating laugh.

"Just rest. We can talk about this later," Susan-Marie said.

"He had talent. I don't deny it. He still does. He found *Estonia*. It was from some Russian emigrant who died broke. Paul fought to get it made, but it wasn't his story. He's been running scared for a long time now. You've protected him enough," Sid said in a low wheeze. "Let him go. He'll do all right on his own."

"I know," Susan-Marie sighed. "Just rest now."

"This is your time in the sun. Take it and be happy. You've always had it in you to have the whole shooting match."

"I will, Sid," Susan-Marie said. She held Sid's hand as they wheeled him up to the ICU, and then kissed his cheek when they put him into the elevator for the operating room.

We sat in the ICU waiting room until well after midnight. Then a woman doctor said that Sid was alive, that he was in the ICU, and that we could talk to him. We found him next to a man without legs and a woman with burns over her entire body, writhing silently in agony.

Sid was attached to an infinitude of wires. One went to a computer that measured blood gases. Another went to a continuously reading cardiograph, still another to a continuously reading pulse rate, and another to a continuous, digitally expressed temperature. There was also a band across Sid's forehead measuring brain activity.

I had never seen anyone look like Sid Bauman looked that night in the intensive care unit. His skin color was light green. His hand was waxy to the touch, and cool. His breathing was so slight that we could barely detect it. He had no tracheotube, and he was slowly coming back to consciousness. The doctor was a Filipino who looked extremely proficient with knives. "I would say he is doing well considering that we did three bypasses including the left main, and that was a replacement bypass. He had bypass surgery back in 1970, before it was fashionable."

The idea of Sid leading in fashion, even in the fashion of bypasses, was perfect, even in that ghastly place. By a process I cannot begin to explain, it must have seemed perfect to Sid as well, because he opened his eyes, looked at us, and said, "Eat an apple a day."

Then he closed his eyes again. Susan-Marie and I sat with him for an hour and then he opened his eyes again and said, "It's silly to make plans. Foolish, even. I became a Communist and that didn't work, and I became an artist and that worked a little better. Then I bought Republic, and that worked because I found you." He squeezed Susan's hand. "I wish I could have painted you. I used to be a painter when I was younger. I never saw anyone with eyes like yours. They were the tip-off."

At about four in the morning he looked out the door of the ICU and saw the faintest pink light of Southwest morning. "I've only learned one thing in my life," he said, "and I just learned it today. You want to know what it is?"

"Yes, I do," Susan-Marie said.

"There are only two kinds of people, the live and the dead. Remember that. That's the only thing that matters in the whole world. Only two kinds of people."

■　　■　　■　　■

When Susan arrived home (I stayed at the hospital) Paul was still asleep in the chair in the teahouse. Susan-Marie grabbed his shirt and shook it until he awoke and looked around himself groggily.

"Wake up," Susan-Marie said. "Time for you to get out."

"What?" Paul asked.

"Get out," Susan-Marie said flatly. "You're through here. Last night was the last straw."

Paul shook himself awake and said, "It's about time. I'm sick of looking like a schmuck in front of all of this town. I'm sick of taking all your shit."

"Just get out," Susan-Marie said. "I'm too tired to argue about it."

Paul looked at Susan-Marie. He picked himself up and asked, "Just tell me. Is Ava my baby?"

Susan-Marie slapped him so hard he fell back into his chair. "You dare to ask me that? I never looked at another man after we made love. Never. Not when you were fucking the stewardesses, not when you fought me and tried to kill my projects and tried to make me into a nobody and tried to make me scared you would leave me if I tried to be who I am. I never looked at another man."

Paul glared at her. "How did you get so hard? What made you so angry?"

"You can ask that? After you brought me out here and ditched me twice? After you pulled that stunt with Deirdre when you were in the Philippines and kicked my guts out? After you tried to squeeze me down and squeeze me down until I was nothing? You can still ask that? After you connived with Deirdre and then fought me every day

369

on every idea I had? You tried to make me a zombie. You wanted to bury me and then make me work for you like a slave."

"So tough," Paul said. "So hard. What makes you women so hard?"

"You kick us around and fuck us over and try to break our spirits in every possible way, and use one of us against the other, and blame everything on us, and you still expect us to be soft? Are you crazy? Start packing and get the hell out."

"You always put your career ahead of mine. You had an in with Sid so that my pictures played in the slums while you got the best houses. All my scripts were shit to you and Sid. You never cared about anything but getting rich and famous."

"That's a lie. A ridiculous lie. A ridiculous, disgusting lie. I loved you. That was first. I wanted to make movies. I wanted to help you make a studio where dreams were safe. Where dreamers were safe. You tried to keep your own wife out in the cold. I always wanted to work with you as your partner. You wanted to have me as your servant, to treat me like a stenographer or a little researcher or a professional flatterer. Then you started insulting me and fucking around with your little stewardesses, but I still stuck up for you with Sid."

"That's because you were fucking him."

Susan-Marie slapped Paul again and hissed, "We were finding good scripts, Paul."

"That's even worse," Paul said in a sudden surge of self-awareness. "You never loved me."

"Just get out," Susan-Marie said. "Go to one of your stewardesses and get out."

"You won't get Republic. You might just as well go over to Universal right now. You'll never get Republic. Never. Not against me and Deirdre."

"We'll see," Susan-Marie said.

As Paul started to go out the door, Susan asked him if he had any message for Sid.

"What fucking message would I have?" Paul asked.

"That you're sorry and hope he gets well soon."

"That's a laugh," Paul said. "He used me and screwed me over, and now it's time to get even, not to send him roses."

Susan-Marie looked at him for a long minute. Then she fished in her pocketbook and threw him the keys to her 450 SL. "Here. Take my car. Yours is out of gas. It won't get you as far away as I want you to be."

Paul threw the keys on the floor, walked out, and the marriage was over.

■　　■　　■　　■

After Paul left, Susan-Marie went to the teahouse. She watched the waves pound against the sand for ten minutes without speaking. Then she walked upstairs and into the pale pink nursery and picked up Ava Elizabeth. Elena came in and stood silently by the door. Susan sat down in a wicker rocking chair and began to sing to the baby, "I've got a little book with pages three . . . And every page spells liberty . . . All my trials, Lord, soon be over . . ."

Ava opened her eyes. They were a deep, peaceful, far-seeing blue, completely unlike the disoriented, glowing, hate-filled eyes Susan-Marie had just seen. Thank God, thank God.

"Woman come here last night while you at hospital," Elena said. Susan's blood froze. "Look like this." Elena made a squeezed face of anger and rage. "Eyes blue, but very light, very light. Come to see you and Mister. She want to see Ava, but I not let her in room. She leave. Very angry."

"Thank you, Elena," Susan-Marie said. "I won't forget this."

"Mister asleep. She not talk to him neither. Leave name with me. Call herself like this," Elena said, and then she let out the elongated sound of the letter D.

■　　■　　■　　■

This time around Susan-Marie was playing for keeps.

She called me at noon. We did not sleep again for almost twenty-four hours. "If you help me with this," she said, "if you help me make sure Republic is nailed down tight for me, if you work with me and use every connection you ever made anywhere, especially your connections at the White House, I'll give you any deal you want at Republic."

"You don't have to give me anything. I want to help you. That's all. I want to see you get what you deserve, which is Republic. That's the only deal I want."

35

DESSERT

I got to her house by noon. We went right down the list of directors of Republic. We started with Rick Hunneycutt, the great-grandson of the founder, Meyer Kotlowicz. The "Hunneycutt" was an actress from Missouri who took Meyer away from Hilda Kotlowicz in 1915. Rick was in his cabin in Snowmass. "Look," he said, "I only want to know one thing. If you take over, will you buy me out and let me just put the money in bonds? I'm sick of worrying about it."

The next call was to Alphonzo Bell from the Bank of America. He was in Newport Beach, learning roller skating from his granddaughter. He was no problem at all. "I think that if Sid is going to be out for a long time," he said, coughing discreetly, "you don't need to look any further. Paul never was very good at this kind of thing."

I made the next call. It was to Dick Costello, the general

counsel. "I'm acting as Susan's lawyer on this," I said. "It would be awkward for Susan to call you herself when she works with you every day. But I think you know the score far better than anyone else at the studio. You see the kinds of deals Susan's made, and you know how Sid feels about her work."

There was a long silence on the other end of the line. "I've known Paul for a long time," Dick said.

"That means he's already called you today."

"I won't say yes and I won't say no. It's hard for me to do this when I've worked with Paul so long. I've never had much trouble with him."

"What kind of trouble do you think Republic would have if Susan were at Warner?"

There was another long pause. Then Costello said, "If the vote is kept completely secret, I won't vote against you. That's as far as I can go."

Susan herself made the call to Estelle van Amburg, the comic genius of the golden days of TV. She had made her show, "It's Momma," into the Union Jack of television. There was no large city in America where a rerun of "It's Momma" did not play at least once per day. It was playing somewhere in America at any time of the day or night. When Estelle answered, I got on the line, too.

Estelle had sold her company, Momma's Boys, to Republic for three percent of the stock and she had been an extremely active member of the board ever since. She actually went over the supporting documents from Price, Waterhouse for the annual statements after they had been audited and certified.

"I can see it," Estelle van Amburg said. "It can make the stock move. I'm only sorry I can't buy it this afternoon from Jeffries and Company. I know the stock's gonna move on Monday." She paused. "I read your articles. How come you never wrote about 'It's Momma'?"

"I'm writing an entire book about 'It's Momma,'" I said. "That takes time."

We could not reach Frank Hills, a former treasurer who

now lived modestly on Fisher Island, Florida, and who could tell where every corporate body was buried. He was in New York. His reservation had been made at the Carlyle, but he had not showed up there. The maid at his house innocently said, "Why don't you try Mr. Melvin Needle. They've been talking a lot lately. They may be together."

I called back Estelle van Amburg. "Honey," she said, "I don't worry about what Melvin Needle says. He can make the stock move half a point. Susan can make me rich."

"Isn't that your house that takes up a whole block on Roxbury Drive?"

She laughed. "I want two blocks."

I called back Bell and asked about calls from Deirdre and Paul. "They called the minute you hung up. I didn't take the call."

Rick Hunneycutt had had no calls since ours. "But I'm going hang-gliding anyway," he said, "so he can't reach me anymore today."

"If Sid is incapacitated, which he most certainly is, we've made the first big step right now," Susan-Marie said.

"I think we'd better have that lawyer Ken Mitropoulos there in the building just in case. He's the best in this kind of thing. He's the one who handled a lot of Carl Icahn's work," I said.

"No," Susan-Marie said. "I want to be there alone. It's my fight. You can have him on the line, but not on the lot. I want to know I did it myself."

■　　■　　■　　■

When Belzberg arrived at his office on Monday morning he had Deirdre Needle with him. He walked across the always perfect lawn to the Republic building, opened the door for Deirdre, and bounded up the stairs. When he got to his door it was locked. There were two Republic Security Department guards at the door. There was a padlock on the outside of the door, and a large paper seal across the front of the door. SEALED BY ORDER OF THE BOARD OF DIRECTORS OF REPUBLIC PICTURES CORPORATION read the seal.

Deirdre wore a denim skirt and a peasant shirt of cotton paisley. Paul wore a tweed jacket of tan wool and blue jeans. They had apparently believed they were going to a picnic.

"Is this some kind of joke? I'm the president of this company," Paul said.

"No, sir," Robbie, the guard, said. "Miz Belzberg is the new president of Republic. You're to be escorted off the lot. Your lawyer can take your effects out of your office."

Paul shoved Robbie out of the way and clawed at the seal on his door. "You little son of a bitch, get out of here."

Robbie and the other guard, a work-release candidate from Atascadero State Prison, had Belzberg on the floor in less than a second, with his arms pinned behind his back. In his usual calm manner, Robbie said, "Better be careful, Mr. Belzberg. At your age, you can break bones really easily."

Deirdre tore at Robbie's face with her nails, making a line of blood across his forehead. Robbie reeled backward in shock and then, in one instant, threw Deirdre against the wall of the office. "You're going to jail for that," he said.

"You little punk," she said, "you work for us."

"I used to work for you," Robbie said. "Now I work for Miz Belzberg. I'm gonna put you off the lot, and if you come back, you're going to the Burbank jail."

"I'll get you for this," Deirdre said. "You can count on that. I'll get you for this."

When Belzberg was back on his feet he said, "Can I call Mrs. Belzberg?"

"Yes," Robbie said. "There's a pay phone you can use right across the street at the Taco Bell."

■　　■　　■　　■

376

Susan and I watched Paul and Deirdre being led to their cars. We watched them drive away. When Robbie came back to Susan's office she said, "From now on, I want an armed guard at my house around the clock for the next month at least."

"Okay."

"And, Robbie," Susan-Marie said, "you did good work."

"Just doing my job," he said, and he seemed to believe it.

When Susan and I were alone she went into her bathroom. Because she turned up the shower loud I could not hear what she was doing in there. When she came out she looked white and thin. "It don't come easy."

"It never does. But you have most of it now."

"No way," Susan-Marie said. "All I have now is a fight."

P·A·R·T

VI

36

CAMPAIGNERS

■

I took the office next to Susan's in the Main Executive Building at Republic. It was her original office, the one that had belonged to Schmooey Lipsher an eternity before. I spent almost all of that first day on the telephone to Joe Flom in New York and to Bruce Montgomery at Arnold & Porter in Washington, D.C. If we were going to have a fight, we might as well have the best lawyers on earth.

By three in the afternoon we got the first word of the Belzberg/Needle counterattack: Melvin Needle had filed papers asking a federal district court in the Southern District of New York to dissolve the present Board of Directors of Republic and declare that Paul Belzberg was chairman pending Sid Bauman's recovery or a new election. Among the charges that a paralegal at Skadden, Arps read to us were: ". . . waste of corporate assets, looting of corporate assets, undue influence including emotional influence upon Sid Bauman, physical assault upon an officer and director, condoning of drug use on the Republic lot in Burbank, California, gross negligence in the performance of duties in connection with motion picture production, and theft . . ."

"Anything else?"

"Yes, yes, indeed," the paralegal said. "Paul Belzberg has also filed for divorce. He's asking for half of Susan-Marie's bonuses on *Alpha Chi* and *Laser Tracks.* He says they were his ideas all along and Susan-Marie stole them from him."

■　　■　　■　　■

At about six in the evening we had two visitors. The first was Ron Silverman. He had been at a preview in San Jose and had flown home to find out what had happened. He sat in a large yellow chair in Susan's office and listened, alternately laughing and hissing. "So now it's a fight," Susan-Marie said. "To see who's going to run Republic. And I wouldn't blame anyone who wanted to stay out of it. It's my fight. And maybe Benjy's. It's not for anyone else to lose his job over."

"It's definitely my fight too," I said. "But my job isn't at stake. If Paul wins, he'll take reprisals. It would be smart to lay low."

Ron Silverman stood up and walked to Susan-Marie's desk. As nearly as a sitcom writer can do, he pulled himself to attention and snapped off a salute. "There's not an executive at this studio that I know of, except maybe for a few of the younger little weasels, who won't quit if you want us to. If you want our resignations as a weapon, you can have them too. This studio used to be a decent place to work, and then Deirdre made me feel like I was dirt for showing up. And now you make us feel as if we're somebody. You make us feel as if we're not just trying to make a few bucks. With your pictures, we feel like our job is to make people happy. I've actually started jogging and getting up early so I can get more done. I feel like a *mensch.*"

"You're a good friend," Susan-Marie said simply. "You've always been a good friend."

"Because I believe in you, pal," he answered.

With that, he gave another crisp salute and then turned on his heel and walked out of the room, Tyrone Power having volunteered for the suicide mission to bomb the Japanese rail line into Burma.

Before Susan-Marie and I could digest Ron Silverman's delivery there was a discreet buzz and Wing Hoi Ping, one of Susan-Marie's receptionists, told us we had another visitor.

"Mr. Melvin Needle is here, please," she said. "If you have a moment, he would like to see you."

"We have a moment," Susan-Marie said.

Melvin Needle walked into Susan-Marie's office with a short, thin man carrying a litigation case. I had not seen Needle in years. As far as I knew, Susan-Marie had never met him. He was a large man—above six feet, at least two hundred and twenty pounds—in a huge black suit, with black hair slicked back from his forehead. He had the air of a thug sent on a gangland mission of extortion. You may have seen wealthy investment bankers who were suave in movies, Claude Rains or Edward Albert types. Not Needle. You do not come out of the parking lot, Jewish funeral home, and hauling businesses to Wall Street by being a shrinking violet. He had not come out of Harvard Business School or St. Mark's. He had come up from the streets, and he looked it. The look was, as Sid used to say, *prust*. Low.

"This is my lawyer, Marty Siegel," Needle said. He did not offer to shake hands. He just sat down in the yellow chair Ron Silverman had just been in.

"This is my lawyer," Susan-Marie answered, gesturing toward me. She did not blink or smile. Neither did Melvin Needle.

"So you're the little girl who's caused me so much trouble," Needle went on, as if he were inspecting a cricket, deciding whether to step on it or to spray it with malathion.

"I'm the woman who's running Republic."

"I think you should be talking to our lawyers in New York if you have a proposal," I told Needle.

He looked at me with surprisingly incurious eyes and then said, "I thought maybe I could save a little time. I was up in San Francisco at the Bohemian Groves, and I thought I could possibly work this out with just the two of us now."

He nodded at Marty Siegel, who started to take folders out of his litigation case. "For Christ's sake, just tell them what we want," Needle hissed at his attorney. "This isn't a goddamned slide show."

The lawyer pulled himself together. "We think you're on pretty thin ice. We think we have you on a number of counts of corporate waste, abuse of the bylaws, improper influence on Sid Bauman, and physical assault on Miss Needle and Mr. Belzberg."

"You had your goons rough up my daughter," Needle said. "That's not nice."

"We didn't rough up anyone," I said. "You know that. Deirdre tried to kill one of our guards."

"You little punk," Needle said. "You stay out of this."

"Get out of here," I told him. "Just take your fat face and your skinny lawyer and get out of here. You want to talk? Talk to our lawyers."

"Wait a minute." Needle smiled. "I was gonna give you a break. I was gonna use my connections to make sure you walked away from this deal with about eight million in Republic stock. Just because I don't like to see people fight. I was gonna do that before I have my friends at the *Daily News* start writing about a few little facts about Susan-Marie and Sid, and about Susan-Marie back in college with a few of her teachers. I thought I might even do Benjy here a favor and see if my pals at CBS might put him on the network."

"Talk to our lawyers," I said. I got up and grabbed the lawyer's briefcase, opened the door to the receptionist's office, and tossed it out onto the floor. "You want to run stories? Okay. How about Deirdre at Chestnut Lodge, writing her name in shit on the walls, sending threatening letters to Susan-Marie, coming over to Susan's house to see her daughter while no one's home. You want to start throwing around dirt, go ahead."

"Why, you nothing punk," Needle said. "You couldn't even buy a first-class ticket to New York. . . ."

"I can't," I answered. "But I can make sure you and your wife and your whole family can never walk into the Harmonie Club again, never go swimming at the Century Country Club again, won't ever go into Gristede's without somebody laughing. You get it? Now get the fuck out of here."

I stood next to him and hoped, just *hoped*, that he would swing on me. I was no fighter, but I was in the right mood. Needle apparently sensed something. He got out of his chair slowly and looked at me. "Okay. But fights like this are won by two things. Money and connections. You don't have either. I've got both. You could have walked away from this as rich kids. Now you're just nothing. Money wins these fights. You'll see. And Sid can't help you. This is way out of his little window dresser's league. You poor schmucks."

"Oh, we'll win," I answered in a rush. "There are still some things you can't buy. Republic's not for sale to you. Neither am I, and neither is Susan. Go pick on Guatemala."

As Melvin Needle left the room, he turned to us and laughed for the first time in the conversation. "At least we understand each other," he said.

■   ■   ■   ■

Susan sent a studio car to my house to pick up Mary, the dog. We drove home to Malibu at midnight with the dog sitting in the front seat looking at the waves lapping along

385

the Pacific Coast Highway. A new moon sent a cool blue shaft along the water, up the rocks, and over the sand.

"We can tie this up in court forever," I said. "I've been on the line to Marvin Chirelstein, and there's really not much doubt about where the law is. It's with us, and even if it weren't with us, we can tie it up forever. There's no way that Paul can get a TRO stopping his getting kicked out."

"I'm glad you went to law school."

"For the very first time so am I."

"That was a piece of work back at the office. How do you know I didn't want to take the eight million?" she asked with a twinkle in her eye.

"I know because I've never heard you even talk about money ever in your life," I said.

Susan-Marie nodded and took my hand. "How come you know me so well?"

"I've been studying you for a long time," I said. "Listen, I have to thank Hollywood. I could never have been that angry or that rude if I hadn't spent time here."

"Oh, I think you could have."

We laughed and Susan-Marie looked out at the waves while I suggested that we fire Dick Costello, get all of Chris Wohlstetter's files out of his office, and probably write a few memos to the files about Chris Wholstetter and Bron Gless. "I think I'd fire Costello first thing tomorrow," I said.

Susan-Marie smiled. "I fired him last night. The problem is, and I wouldn't tell this to anyone, but Melvin Needle is right. How the hell are we going to win this? I mean, he is *Mr.* Capital, *Mr.* Wall Street, *Mr.* Connections. We're out here on the edge of nowhere trying to fight against Wall Street. I don't think it can even be done. I mean, I know movies, but I don't know this kind of fight, with lawyers and proxies." In a much smaller voice she said, "I'm scared, Benjy. I think we're going to lose."

I thought for two full minutes. "No, we won't lose. Because you didn't have a father who was a hero and didn't go through all that hell with your stepfather to lose."

"It's a lot more than that. It's Merrill Lynch and Paine Webber and First Boston, not Susan-Marie Warmack."

"I don't think so. People don't win wars for money. Money is just shit. People win wars because they have to. And that's why you'll win."

"You believe in me that much? How come you believe in me when no one else does? How come you did back there in Washington when I was buried at the phone company?"

The ocean slipped by against the rocky shores of the Santa Monica Bay. "Because you went to the Senior Prom with me when I didn't have a date."

We laughed again and Susan-Marie leaned her head against my shoulder. "And you kissed me out on the balcony. And gave me a drink of vodka. Then you didn't go to that party at Betty Jones's house even though you could have because I had to be home early."

"Ever since then," I said, "I knew you would someday be head of a movie studio."

"You always make me laugh and cry at the same time," Susan-Marie said. "I wonder what that means."

We arrived at the house in the Colony. I went to sleep in the guest bedroom after I took Mary for a walk along the sand of the Colony. As I passed Robbie in front of the floodlights, he said, "Man, this is buff duty."

■　　■　　■　　■

When I was a child I always dreamed I would be a captain of industry. People would stand in awe of my power. That was only a dream and it never happened.

When I was in high school I used to fantasize that I would wake up one morning and I would suddenly be popular and handsome and have a red 1960 Corvette, and everyone at Montgomery Blair would like me. That was only a fantasy, and it would never happen.

At the Shoreham Hotel, on a balcony next to the room

where we had our Senior Prom, I formed a new dream. One day I would know a woman who had deep blue eyes, jet-black hair, full red lips. She would smell of White Shoulders. She would understand all there was of fantasy and of the real world of chrome and paper. She would see through the lies of other men after a long journey through hills of pink Cadillacs and graceful flamingoes. One night she would come to me and she would say, "I've been such a fool about you, Benjy. That's my worst mistake. Not seeing you for all these years because my ambition got in the way." Then she would lie beside me and press her lips against my neck, and I would pull her toward me until we could not get any closer. When our lovemaking was over I would say, "This is what life is all about." She would fall asleep with her head on my chest and her hair spread across my neck.

In the distance I would hear the ocean crashing against Malibu Beach, and I would feel her breast. It would be abnormally warm to the touch, as if it were five degrees above 98.6. She would stir in her sleep, kiss me again, and say, "This is it, Benjy, from now on. Just the two of us."

I would hear those words, feel that touch, and think that for the first time I knew why I was alive. From then on every act, every thought would be for the woman I loved. My life would not run from envy and frustration any longer. Instead, I would draw limitless energy from the pool of love for the woman with the jet-black hair, the deep blue eyes, and the full red lips, from protecting her and keeping her close. A life that had been led around curves and down alleys would sail along a limitless blue ocean under warm, dry tradewinds and a cloudless azure sky. I would feel whole, and in that feeling I would sleep holding the smooth, warm hands of my Susan-Marie.

This was real, and it happened.

■　　■　　■　　■

In the morning we drove to St. John's Hospital. Sid Bauman was sitting up in bed, although he still had all his wires attached. "I'm a puppet," he said cheerfully. "There's a puppeteer somewhere in this hospital, and he pulls these strings and I live or die."

A nurse came in to change his nitro patch. Then she drew blood. While Sid studied the puncture, he huffed and puffed even without his pipe. Then he looked at us with his artist's gray-blue eyes and said, "So you two are finally an item, huh?"

I swear we had not exchanged a word or a touch or a look, and yet Sid knew.

"It's good, Susan," he said. "He's always been *meshug* for you."

We did not say anything. Susan started to laugh and Sid said, "Let's go. *Tuchus aften tisch*. What's happening now at Republic?"

"I think we're all set, especially if you can get yourself out of here soon."

"I think you'd better not plan on that for a while," Sid Bauman said carefully. "We've got to take every day as it comes."

"You look so much better," I said. "I don't get it."

"I feel better too. But I remember, when my mother died, she was a lot better, at least she looked a lot better before she died. She looked like a schoolgirl the day before she died."

Susan-Marie touched his arm. "This is a new age. Much better medicine."

"Yes, but it's my same old body." Bauman sighed. "Now, tell me everything."

We told him about Belzberg, about Deirdre, about the lawsuits, about Flom, about Montgomery, about Chirelstein, about witnesses and depositions and blocks of stock.

"Listen," he said, "I had my lawyer, Irving Fishman, in here this morning. My stock is already given to you for CEO. The value goes to Amanda's children, but you get the votes. If I'm gone, though, and can't testify differently, Needle may be able to tie it up by charging undue influence. It's happened before. You have to have enough votes to beat them even without mine. That means forty-one percent, and here's where they are."

Sid Bauman then went through an exhaustive list of risk arbitrageurs who held small amounts on any takeover chance, pension funds, bank trust departments, mutual funds, wealthy people, former employees, Estelle van Amburg, Al Bell, Rick Hunneycutt, and Peter Flanigan. "Flanigan's the key—well, almost the key. He's got the cleanest reputation on Wall Street. Get him, and you've got right and goodness on your side. He's very quirky, but the thing you have to remember is that you pulled Republic into the number-one spot. Paul Belzberg was just letting it drift. Hire somebody from Wall Street, this Dan Paluch guy from Lazard who follows pictures for them. Get him working with you every day.

"You have to hit Belzberg hard. Say that he's a fuck-up. He's a slob. Hint that he's a thief. It's not a gentleman's game."

"I know that," Susan-Marie said.

"The one to watch out for is Deirdre. Even more than her father. She's totally unpredictable, and she could do anything. I mean absolutely anything."

"We'll watch her," I said.

"I'd make a trip to New York and Washington immediately. Don't wait for anyone to tell you Melvin Needle's already called. You get there first and get them zipped up. Once those Wall Street guys make a decision they don't like to change it. Get to them first. Benjy, you should go down to Washington and make sure there's not going to be any problem from that end. You've got the connections. That's good here. It looks like you're just talking for the good of Hollywood. Now listen," Sid said, "I'm getting tired." Indeed, his face was starting to look pale and sweaty.

"We'll go," Susan-Marie said. She started to lean forward to kiss Sid good-bye. When she did he winked at me. Then he laughed, which was the last time I ever heard him do that.

"This whole town," he said, waving his hand toward the window. "This whole town is for people who know what they want.

"It belongs to you because you know movies. You deserve to have Republic. When it's almost sewed up go to Walter Burns at Citibank last. If he knows you're going to win anyway, or if he suspects it, he'll throw in with you, and then you know you're over the top."

The last thing Sid said, just as we were walking out the door, was, "One thing Amanda used to say was that as long as we had enough money to eat, none of this was real, none of this Hollywood stuff. What was real was this kind of thing." He pointed at us, describing a sort of invisible web between me and Susan.

"And this kind of thing," I said, describing with my hand a web including Sid as well.

Sid looked almost uncomfortably moved. "All right. Just go and have a good time and call me from New York. Go tonight. Take the Gulfstream. Call me from the Helmsley Palace. In the morning put me on with Peter Flanigan if you think it'll help."

We worked for most of the five hours between Burbank Airport and JFK on lists of possible problems, answers to possible interrogatories, allies in the financial press, documents that would prove Susan's authorship of *Laser Tracks* and *Alpha Chi*, witnesses to her creativity since she started in marketing at Republic.

When we were above Chicago the sun went down and the sky turned a deep, dark blue. We were above a cloud bank that covered everything east of the Mississippi. The light of the stars made almost palpable hills and valleys among the clouds. Susan had fallen asleep in a chair, her yellow pads on her lap. The pilot had put the cabin lights on dim. In the light Susan looked like a child again, almost as she had looked on the first day I met her in the park when I was reading *The Count of Monte Cristo* and she was all arms and legs. Her face was relaxed for the first time in months. There were no lines in it at all in that starlight sky.

When we arrived at JFK a Republic driver handed me an envelope. Inside was a telex from Ron Silverman. "Sid Bauman died this afternoon at 6:37 P.M. Call for further details." But no further detail about Sid really mattered after that.

37

VICTORIES

The fight went much as Sid had described it. There is no special need to go into it now, because it has been carefully summarized in *Fortune* and *Forbes*. The rumor is that Western Publishing will bring out a Corporations case-book that will make many of the proxy fight principles of Susan-Marie Belzberg into the accepted norm for that kind of struggle. When it comes out you can garner the details about when equitable relief is appropriate and when application to the Securities and Exchange Commission can make a difference.

Susan was an artist everywhere she went. Her fight for Republic was no exception. She made up her own rules of whom she should conciliate, whom she should bully, with whom she should plead. She fought the battle in court-rooms in Lower Manhattan, in hearing rooms at the Federal Communications Commission, at breakfasts with the financial editor of the *Los Angeles Herald-Examiner*, at lunches of boiled fish at the Manhattan Club with the editors of *The Wall Street Journal*.

Of course, it all came down to the Citibank decision reached the day of the fire, the day Susan was shot, but when she started she didn't know this, and so she fought everywhere she could.

From those weeks that Susan and I traveled around the country to keep her at the top of Republic, only a few memories are etched permanently into my mind.

There is Susan at the luncheon of the New York Security Analysts at the Yale Club. She sat in front of them on a dais, beautiful and confident in a white and blue silk dress. In front of her were a legion of young men with neatly combed hair, all going from left to right across their heads, all eyes watching her through wire-rimmed glasses, all heads bobbing over their chowder in a workmanlike fashion.

Susan sat next to me, and on the other side sat Roy Rachmil, acting head of the analysts. Susan talked to him for over an hour about the possibility of instituting defeasance for the Republic retirement liabilities and thereby increasing Republic earnings. When Mr. Rachmil turned to his companion on the other side, Marina Frost, a corporate treasurer, Susan turned to me. In a perfectly pleasant way she said under her breath, "When this is over let's go back to the hotel and ball our brains out."

∎　∎　∎　∎

Susan-Marie answering interrogatories in a room at Kaplan, Livingston & Drysdale. A Mr. Lescaze was asking Susan questions obviously put to her by Paul and Deirdre.

> Q: *Did you at any time have sexual relations with Sid Bauman?*
> A: I will not answer that or any other personal and insulting questions. I am engaged in a process to take Republic past that kind of small, petty, venge-

ful thinking that adds nothing to the welfare of the stockholders.

Q: *If you do not answer the question, the judge will compel an answer in open court.*

A: He will do no such thing, and if you attempt to browbeat me any further with your specious, two-bit back-alley tactics, I will not answer any further questions at all.

Mr. Lescaze motioned to the stenographer to stop taking notes, said to our lawyer, Ken Mitropoulis, that we were off the record, and then said, "Wow. You are a helluva tough witness. "I'd like to get down some money on your side." The stenographer winked.

"Talk to Nick the Greek," Susan-Marie said. "Let's get on with this. I have a lot of other work to do."

■　　■　　■　　■

In the hallway of the SEC building on Fifth Avenue in Washington, D.C., we traveled by convoy of lawyers and accountants to see Kathryn McGraff, head of enforcement. On our way down the hall we passed Paul Belzberg. He was dressed like a college professor with a wool, checked jacket and brown slacks. With him were his lawyer and two accountants, all in dark blue pinstripes. Deirdre was with them, dressed in a white silk dress, as if she were going to lunch at the Woods with my cousin Laura.

When Deirdre passed she actually bared her teeth, the snarl of a wolf when it is half crazed with hunger and cold and senses danger.

"You little redneck piece of trash," Deirdre said. "I'll get you . . ." And she began to reach for Susan-Marie. No one was close enough to them to stop them. Susan-Marie stuck out her hand and grasped Deirdre's free wrist and squeezed it.

"If you touch me, you'll go back to the insane asylum." She said it evenly and with perfect confidence.

"Maybe," Deirdre said, "but it won't do you any good, because you'll be dead."

Paul arrived and pulled Deirdre away. "How are you, Susan?" he asked, still holding back Deirdre, trying to look calm.

Susan-Marie looked at him from his shoes to his head. "It's amazing," she said. "I thought you were taller."

■　　■　　■　　■

A meeting with Raymond Giusti, head of research for Keyworth Associates, an investment firm in New Canaan, Connecticut, in an office building overlooking a small forest. Mr. Giusti first wanted us to know his bona fides. He wiped a huge hand across his white shirt and then drank from a stained coffee cup.

"I didn't study at a business school," he said. "I worked loading cement at a plant in Canarsie. That way I got to see how human beings worked under pressure, if you get what I mean. In a few years I had my own truck. Then I had ten trucks. Then I had a garbage disposal business. Then I sold that. You get the picture?"

"We get it," I said.

"I work by the seat of my pants. I don't go for the computers and slide-rule types. I have a feeling about businesses. My nose, my ass, call it whatever you want, it's always right.

"I've been in business with Melvin Needle for a long time now. He used to bankroll that cement company. Then he worked with the garbage disposal company. He's a stand-up guy."

"He may be," Susan-Marie said. "But I've been adding to Republic's income faster than any other manager they've ever had there. Gross receipts from the film division have tripled in two years."

Giusti waved his large fingers in the air in a gesture of dismissal. He drank another loud drink of his coffee, then wiped his mouth with his hand. "Could have been a fluke," he said. "I go with management that can stay in there and take the punches. Whiz kids come and go."

"Maybe so, but when they're at Republic they make a lot of money for the stockholders," I said.

"The picture business is a tough game. It's not just brainstorming. It's a man's game. If you see a horse getting a little roughed up, you can't start crying about it. Time is money."

"I'm not going to apologize for that," Susan-Marie said. "If you make your investment decisions on that kind of basis, it may be hard to persuade you anyway."

"We started out in what you might call the dirtier ends of business," Giusti continued. "Garbage disposal, linen supplies, parking lots. Movie theaters, for that matter. The places where the fancypants don't even want to go. Gradually we've moved out into a few other businesses where we see potential—fast food, franchised auto repair. That kind of thing. Nothing complicated like computers or defense equipment. We learned that you go a lot farther if you stay away from the high-fliers and just do business with people you know, people who may not be geniuses, but you know where they live."

"You know the stock has moved five points just because people think I'll probably get control. Doesn't that mean anything to the people who gave you their money to invest?"

"Mrs. Belzberg, in my business we've got a saying," Giusti began.

"Don't tell me," Susan-Marie said, holding up her palms. "You make more money with your ass than with your head. Right?"

*　　*　　*　　*

We flew in the Gulfstream to El Paso for a meeting with the financial director of the Texas State Teachers' Pension Fund. They had 300,000 shares of Republic.

While we waited on the runway for a gate, Susan-Marie looked intently out at the desert landscape. "This is where

I lived when my father died. Fort Bliss. We lived in a barracks that had been separated with paperboard into two-bedroom apartments for young married officers."

"It must have been pretty dismal."

"Every summer my parents would drive me to Idabel, Oklahoma, to spend the summer with my grandparents, Big Mama and Big Daddy. I remember the last time I saw my father we were somewhere in Texas and it was so hot sweat was pouring off all of us. My mother was in a terrible mood because my father had just been given orders to go to Korea, and she was going to be scared to death again.

"But my father said, 'Oh, I think MacArthur's got everything nailed down all right. It won't be so hard. It'll mostly just be boring.' I remember he said those things and he held a map in front of my face in the car so the sun wouldn't beat down on me too hard. He told me he'd send me a kimono from Tokyo as soon as he got there. I remember I fell asleep dreaming about that kimono with my father shielding my face from the sun. That was the last time I ever saw him. I don't even know for sure where his body is."

"It must make it hard for you to go on with this shit when you think about it."

"No." Susan wiped tears from her eyes. "No, it makes it easy for me to go on. My father didn't die like that for me to be kicked around by a psychotic bitch like Deirdre and a losered-out, jealous cheater like Paul. I didn't live my life and my father didn't die for me to run away from a fight."

We met Mr. Lacey Dalton at the terminal in El Paso. I swear to you that Susan might as well have worn blue pinstripes in her brain. She was that precise and that buttoned-down. She even had a slight Texas accent at the meeting. We got the votes.

"You're doing the right thing," Susan-Marie said. "I'm gonna pay you more money for your dividends, and Paul isn't, and it's that simple."

398

"Yes, ma'am, I believe it is," Mr. Dalton said, doffing his Stetson.

On the airplane I said to Susan, "That was some story about your father."

"Forget it," she said. "I was just nervous about meeting Dalton. I never think about it anymore."

■　　■　　■　　■

Ron Silverman came to Susan in her office at Republic with a new writer. Steven Greene was a pale, nervous man with a beard. He had an idea that had captivated both Ron and Jodie Sugar, the head of development in the Susan-Marie regime.

"The idea is that a group of kids are in a small town in Alabama, and there's a terrible flood. The kids seek shelter in an old, abandoned church out in the middle of a field. The storm gets terribly bad, and just when a flooded river is about to swamp them, it turns out the church is a spaceship and it can take them out into outer space, where there's a whole new, better way of life, and where the kids learn to forget all the things that had caused them problems on earth. It's only at the very end that you realize that the kids are all in heaven, and they've been so good they get returned to earth to live out the rest of their lives as earth people."

"God, it sounds wonderful to me," I said. By then I was constantly at Susan's side.

Susan gave me a meaningful look and said, "I'll have to think about it. The problem is that to do it right, it'll take very special effects, and ever since *Laser Tracks* the price of special effects has gone through the roof."

"It's a great story," Ron Silverman said. "It goes to a whole new place in kids' stories."

"I know it does. But I can't see that getting made for less than fifteen million just in the negative. When you get up to the point of fifteen million and above the chances for making a profit go down by a factor of five from what a ten-million-dollar picture gets. You have more advertising pressure, more overhead, more interest from day one, and you can think it's a great concept, but the numbers are against you."

"Susan," Jodie Sugar said, "it's what kids think about all the time. It's their world."

"It may be their world. Could very well be. But I'm in a fight to show I can run this studio and pay a dividend." Susan-Marie tapped her H-P desktop computer keyboard with a fingernail. "This is my world right now."

■　■　■　■

In mid-April Susan-Marie and I flew to the airport in Westchester County to have lunch with Skip Topping. Skip was head of the trust department at the Morgan Bank. He had just come back from Kuwait and he did not want to miss seeing us. So, on a Saturday, we had a Republic car and driver take us along the New York State Thruway and then along winding country roads to Topping's house in Lakeville, Connecticut. It was a rambling colonial structure with huge French doors overlooking a pond and a swimming pool next to a lawn tennis court. Skip met us wearing green-and-yellow-plaid trousers, Topsiders, and a white shirt with the emblem of a duck over the breast. He handed each of us a gin, without our asking for them, and then led us out to a white metal table in a glassed-in solarium.

The house had that particularly sharp-lined New England elegance that only the country houses of the New York and Boston rich ever have. I have wondered now for many years why no architect in California can ever get it right, with its contrasting mullions, windowsills, and masterpieces, why California architects routinely produce houses without any intelligence in them at all, the residential equivalent of those Kean paintings of children with big eyes.

"I like the way you've made the stock move," Topping said. "I have to admire that. It's made some money for us already. In fact, a lot of money."

"The company can do a lot more. I think we can eliminate an awful lot of the downside by turning the production end over to limited partnerships more and more, and turning the company more into a development and distribution entity, at least dollar-wise."

"It makes perfect sense. The dentists in Oak Park can use the write-offs far more than you can. And after all, you have control over the whole process anyway," Topping agreed. "It works if you can show the limited partners that they're not just going to see their money shoveled out the window like manure, going for payoffs to your pals. That's the way some of these things have been in the past."

"My record in making pictures that people want to see speaks for itself," Susan-Marie said.

"Indeed it does," Topping agreed. He was a pleasant-faced man with regular features, sandy-blond hair, and a pair of carefully selected horn-rimmed glasses on his nose.

"Can we count on you?" Susan-Marie asked.

"Well, that's something we have to talk about," Topping said. "The fact is that you're already sort of a legend around Wall Street for your work at Republic. But it's a mixed legend. Chris Wohlstetter, Sr., is not happy about the way you treated his son. Paul's been able to make a lot of mileage out of something you once told him about how you don't care if your pictures make money as long as they work for some little farmer in Minnesota. Word's around that you're smart, filled with good ideas, but you're a dreamer."

"Skip, the fact is that I've given Republic the two biggest pictures we ever had."

"That's true. But sometimes in business you make more money by just taking the quiet, ordinary path, even if it is less glamorous. We're handling money for widows and orphans. We have to make sure that we take it very carefully. You can keep making expensive pictures and then you can one day come up with three in a row that are busts, and the studio's dead. Sometimes you make more money just sitting tight than you do with great ideas."

"Does this mean you're voting against us?" I asked.

"It means that a committee is still thinking about it," Topping said pleasantly. "The committee's decisions are always confidential."

■　■　■　■

The next day Susan-Marie and I rode in a limousine from the San Francisco International Airport to the headquarters of the Bank of America on Montgomery Street. The numbers were not coming out the right way, and, as far as Susan, Daniel Paluch, and I could determine, a trend was starting to work against us. The trend even had a name: "We can't put a dreamer in charge of a New York Stock Exchange Company" was the name of the trend.

Susan-Marie sat next to me, adding up numbers on a hand-held calculator. She wrote down notes on a sheet of lined paper, not even taking her eyes from the calculator. Outside, the cloudy magnificence of San Francisco slid into view.

"We're going to lose this one if we don't pull ourselves together," Susan-Marie said. "The court's not going to let Sid's children vote for us, and the trust departments are going against us."

"We still have a lot of people to see," I said.

"I know, but we're hearing the same song over and over again. It's sort of like the song I used to hear from Paul. It's about being in the club and being out of the club. Sometimes I think that's what everything in the whole world comes down to—who's in the club and who's not."

"The man at the Bank of America has the second largest block of votes after Citicorp," I said. "He has a fantastic reputation."

"They all do," Susan-Marie said. "That's because reputation comes from being in the club."

An hour later, in the executive dining room at the B of A Tower, Stanley Armatrading looked sadly from one of us to the other. He was an elderly man, apparently so valuable to their trust department that his retirement had been waived. He wore a pin-striped suit that was far too big for him, wire-rimmed glasses, and a hearing aid. His face was genial, even appealing, with its wrinkles and its pale blue eyes. What he had to say was not funny at all.

"Personally, I like you a lot. I took my grandchildren to see *Laser Tracks* four times. I went to see *Alpha Chi* by myself and laughed out loud in a movie for the first time in twenty years. But I'm a trustee. You're a young genius. I'm required by law to go with what's cautious, what's safe. Sometimes that means taking a slower, surer route."

"All of the evidence shows that I can take Republic to higher earnings than the last management even dreamed of," Susan-Marie said, trying to look calm in her black silk dress with its white collar.

"Maybe so," Armatrading agreed. "But dreamers have problems. That's the history of the business. They fly high, they put their faith in visions, and then they crash, and we're left holding the bag."

"I have three pictures in development, sequels to *Laser Tracks* and *Alpha Chi*. You know I can do them best, and you know I can get them distribution that'll make money for the stockholders." Susan-Marie was becoming flushed.

"I know that," Armatrading said. "But I also know that you're a dreamer, that you turned the studio upside down with a lot of talk about new ideas and new writers and being kind to animals. That scares people. I don't want a widow to come to me in three years and tell me her son can't go to college because I trusted a thirty-five-year-old dreamer to run a New York Stock Exchange company. Don't get me wrong. You might be a fine head of production. Perhaps at Universal. Maybe under a seasoned management."

Susan-Marie flushed and began to speak. Before she could, a doddering messenger in a gray cotton jacket entered the room and told Armatrading he had a call. The elderly man left the room with a toothsome smile.

"Goddammit," Susan-Marie said. "I'm not going to lose this game." She grasped my arm tightly. "I didn't come this far to lose. 'Honesty may not be the best policy, but it's worth trying some of the time.' You ever hear that?"

"Yes," I said. "At the White House."

"Right. Now we'll try something else."

Armatrading came back into the room and sat down gracefully. "Naturally," he said, "we have nothing but respect for your creative imagination . . ."

"Just a minute," Susan-Marie said forcefully, like an Oklahoma minister about to begin a total body immersion. "Things have gotten totally turned around here. I'm not the dreamer in this piece of work. Paul was the one who was running the studio as a playpen for directors. I'm the one who told him to put auditors on every location second unit. I'm the one who told him we'd fire the first director who put his wife on as costume designer. Paul wanted to run the thing as if we had a license to print money. I'm the one who told him we had to run Republic like a business. He was the one who was always talking about his goddamned fantasies and his pie-in-the-sky ideas for fairy tales. I'm the one who told him to use market research and learn from Procter & Gamble."

"Well," Armatrading said. "This is more of what I want to hear."

"Sid Bauman was a businessman. He wanted me to take over for him. That's because he knew I wouldn't put up with all of this crap about dreams and fantasies and that nonsense. That's fine for writers and for little children. But I want to have market research tell me there's no way we can lose—at least in their opinion—before I spend a dime. I'm not running a charity for unemployed writers. This is a business, Stan. The bottom line is what counts. That, and making sure we're not out on a limb."

"That's the way it has to be," Armatrading agreed enthusiastically. "Business is business."

"Paul used to come to me with his crazy ideas about *Jitterbug* and a remake of *Estonia*. I'd say to him, 'Paul, these are great ideas for a book or for a short story. But this is a business, and it doesn't matter how great your ideas are if they can't bring something to the bottom line.'"

"I think I can go back to the Trust Committee with a very favorable report," Armatrading said with a broad smile. "And I can talk to some other officers of banks."

"I used to tell Paul, 'Ideas are all very well. But out here we make more money with our ass than with our head,'" Susan-Marie continued, "and he just could never learn it."

"It's crude, but it's true." Armatrading nodded.

"I have a plan for the studio for the next five years that will play off the success we've had with *Laser Tracks* and with *Alpha Chi,* but without taking any of the risks we took with those. That was enough gambling. We'll try to make five to ten movies a year, mostly with people we know."

"That makes perfect sense," Armatrading said. "You can't go wrong dealing with people you've known for years."

"Instead of looking at five or six twenty-million-dollar pictures that might just have no bottom, we'll do small pictures that have an audience we already know, with writers and directors who've been around the track a few times. That way we won't be eating a negative nut of a few hundred million a year that could take us nowhere."

"Susan, I like very much what I'm hearing. Now, I know you had a problem with Skip Topping back East. I'd like to just put you on the phone with him right now. I can't believe he heard the same woman I just heard."

"I'd love to do that, Stan," Susan-Marie said. "I might have given the wrong impression back there. I get tired out just like other people. I'm just a numbers person basically, not a genius like Paul."

■　　■　　■　　■

As we drove back down Highway 101 to the airport in the limousine, I looked out at the Bay and the city of Oakland rising on the other side of its polluted waters. "The problem with Oakland," Gertrude Stein had said, "was that when you get there, there's no there there." I started to tell the epigram to Susan-Marie, since I thought it might save a lot of time telling her what I thought about the meeting, but she was on the car phone getting farther away from "there" moment by moment. She had reached Raymond Giusti as he was walking out the door. Word travels fast, and he had already heard about the sudden warmth toward Susan in trust departments at money center banks.

"I was tired, Raymond," Susan-Marie said. "I made a mistake."

Mercifully, I couldn't hear Giusti's part of the conversation.

"I think that when I have control, which is pretty much inevitable, I would like to see Republic signed on a wall-to-wall contract for haulage with your companies. We had been using our own teamsters, but the administrative savings in having you do it would be enormous, and a lot of that could be put into safe investments. We've taken all the risks we're going to take for a while. The studio needs a chance to calm down, to play it safe for a while, to just remember where we came from and who our friends are . . ."

I listened to the conversation and all I could think of was that perhaps there might be even greater administrative savings if we moved the headquarters of Republic to a safe, sane, no-nonsense place like Oakland.

■   ■   ■   ■

But I was wrong in my self-righteousness. A few minutes later, when the Gulfstream was above Santa Cruz I looked over and saw the ribbons of light going out to the amusement park, out to the yacht harbor, running up in sodium vapor green to the redwood forests of the university. "I hope you understand that the only person you were making fun of back there was yourself," I said. "It wasn't Paul who got the shaft. It was you. You weren't selling out Paul and Deirdre. You sold out yourself."

Susan-Marie looked at me in the dim light of the cabin and took my hand with her warm hand. "Lighten up, pal," she said.

"That hurt me," I said. "To see you belittling yourself, turning yourself inside out. If you believe it, it's bad. If you don't believe it, it's also bad."

"No, it's not at all bad." Susan-Marie smiled. "What I suddenly realized back there in that big tall building at the Bank of America was that business is a bunch of dogs meeting each other and sniffing each other's behinds. That's all that business is—just a bunch of dogs sniffing each other.

"I suddenly knew that if I started making the right sounds and grunting the right grunts about 'safety' and 'conservative' and dumping on dreamers, then I would smell like one of them. That was all I had to do, and I would get them to vote for me. It might be too late, but that's the way the game is played."

"So you just *made up* that stuff you told him?"

"Of course," Susan said emphatically. "I made the right sounds. That's all that counts. And don't start in on me about lying."

"I won't," I said. "Everybody lies all the time."

"Exactly," Susan-Marie said. "Paul and Deirdre are complete liars, even under oath. So if I lost, liars would get control of the studio. And if I lie, I might just be able to get control. So either way a liar's going to have Republic. But at least this liar makes movies people can get lost in, and that's the difference."

We were over Salinas, and I could see the lights of the town and then the lights of the straight highways leading into the San Joaquin Valley.

"This is the big one," Susan-Marie said. "I was in that office with that son of a bitch from the Bank of America, that smug bastard with his pin-striped suit, and I thought, if my father's looking down at me, he's saying, 'Go do something. Don't just let it slip away because you hurt.'

Sometimes I have to play hurt, Benjy. But I'm through losing."

■　　■　　■　　■

The next day Susan-Marie, Daniel Paluch, and I all worked with telephones from six in the morning until two in the afternoon. The scenes and the stars are made in Los Angeles, but the money still comes out of New York City, and we had to live by their time zone.

At two-thirty Susan-Marie and I walked out of her office at Republic. We walked across the green lawn and then across Barham Boulevard to the Taco Bell. Susan-Marie ordered a burrito and I ordered an enchirito, and then we sat down at a steel table next to the pay phone. Next to us two men from a private garbage-hauling truck ate tacos.

"Someday I'll have a picture painted of that telephone," Susan-Marie said. "The lowest ebb of my life. Making a call to a man who was terrified of me, asking him to save my life from a pay phone at a Taco Bell in Burbank. It should be a monument."

"It's a monument to you," I said. "The bottom notch on the graph."

"The way I figure it, of the eighty percent of the stock that can vote we have about thirty percent, with another fifteen or sixteen leaning our way."

"And Needle has maybe got slightly less," I said.

"I feel sure that the portion that Merrill Lynch has, about two percent of the total that can vote, is going for Needle."

"The only one who's really big enough to vote any damn way he pleases is Burns," I said. "We can count on him to do what he thinks has the money in it. Whichever way he goes, that way wins."

"I'm not sure," Susan-Marie said. "That's the big question. If he's going to be a member of the club and play it safe, he'll go with Paul and Melvin Needle. He can always play 'cover my ass' that way."

"Well, bankers aren't big poker players. But at this point you're the smart, cautious thing. You've got it covered now in about fifty different directions."

"That's what I thought before I made the call to Manila from that telephone," Susan-Marie said with a tight smile.

"This time you do," I said. "This time you've got it wired."

"Anyway, it'll be just like last time in one way."

"What's that?"

"It'll all come down to one telephone call."

■　　■　　■　　■

On a Friday one day before the Malibu fire Susan-Marie sent her Korean secretary, Lo Ching Samsung, to Bullock's-Wilshire for blouses and stockings. She was far too busy to take on that kind of chore herself. I was at the UCLA Graduate Business School talking with an expert on proxy battles. Robbie was at the house on Warner Boulevard in Toluca Lake where Susan was keeping Ava Elizabeth and her nurse, Miss Birkestrom, just to know where they were while she was at the studio. She did not like for them to be so far away from Burbank on the long days she spent there. When they were in Toluca Lake, in the bungalow next to Bob Hope, she could spend lunches there with her daughter, love her, and still be near enough to meet the visiting head of the Welsh Coal Miners' Pension Fund.

Susan was back at her office making notes for her conversation with Walter Burns when Paul Belzberg walked in. He wore an Irish tweed jacket with leather elbow patches and a tattersall shirt. He took four steps across the Oriental rug and sat on a red wool and chrome chair.

Susan looked up at him. "Get out." She did not rise from her desk.

Belzberg ignored her order. "I want to talk compromise with you."

"No compromises."

"I think this one'll make sense."

Susan-Marie sighed and leaned back in her chair. She twirled her dark blue Du Pont pen in her fingers and nodded. "Go ahead."

"Okay. You take Republic and I'll take Ava."

Susan-Marie's breath exploded out of her lungs. "Are you insane? Are you crazy?"

"No, maybe you'd be better at running Republic than I would be. Maybe I should just retire and stay home with Ava. Maybe that's best for everybody." Paul leaned against the chrome arm of the chair and smiled.

"I don't know how you got in here," Susan-Marie said. "But if you don't get out this instant, you're going to be making your calls from the Burbank jail. You miserable schemer. You never cared a goddamn about Ava when we were living together. Now you're using her as a pawn for money. You're dirt."

"Look," Paul said, starting to retreat from the chair, "I've read articles. Sometimes a man makes a fine parent by himself."

"Maybe so," Susan-Marie said, biting off each word. "But you're no man. You'll have Republic when I'm dead, and you'll never have Ava. Now, get out. I have a lot of work to do. Melvin Needle and his flunkies are trying to take Republic away from me and give it to a sleaze who uses his own daughter as a bargaining chip. Get out."

Paul Belzberg looked at her deep blue eyes, driven by a dynamo of decision, and then walked out. That was the day before the Malibu fire.

38

JUSTICE

■

I sat by Susan-Marie's bedside at UCLA for two days straight. I still believe that if I had been able to get some sleep in those first days the whole business with the knife would never have ended the way it did. The doctors operated on her for three hours after she arrived at UCLA. They removed a thirty-eight caliber slug from her abdomen, where it had lodged next to her pancreas, grazing it, and then removed another from her shoulder, where it had smashed her collarbone and ruptured the triaxial artery going into her arm. They sutured her large intestine and made repairs to her pelvic bone, which had apparently been splintered by the erratic movement of the bullet inside her abdomen.

Susan needed nine units of Type O plasma. She required the services of three surgeons and a team of internal medicine specialists from the UCLA Medical School. She was fed an intravenous solution of sucrose, water, potassium chloride, and other nutrients known better to Squibb than to me.

While I waited for Susan to go through the initial surgery, I looked out the window of UCLA Medical Center toward Malibu. The fire burned on. It gave a red-brown color to all of the northwestern sky, and even when darkness fell the sky in that direction was still illuminated by flames and capped by smoke.

To the south, in the shopping area of Westwood, lights came on. Cars passed by in dazzling profusion, carrying them and their occupants through plenty of nothing on the strength of the mighty river of getting and spending. The air in Westwood was smoky from the fire in Malibu, but there was no diminution of teenagers slogging along the streets looking for the shoes or the movie or the boy or the girl that would give them something to get up for in the morning.

There were no rules for women like Susan-Marie or her lover, so I stayed in her room on an orange vinyl chair with wood-veneer arms through the morning. Susan was not brought back from surgery until almost five A.M., and the doctors were too tired to do any more than tell me that her condition was "guarded."

Susan was attached to the usual plethora of wires, which in turn ran to computers and then to green and red liquid-quartz digital readouts of her life story: half dead and half alive at the age of thirty-five. Across the screens in her room ran the latest up-to-the-minute bulletins of her struggle for life like moving electric light signs across Times Square in World War II.

Too many hospital rooms, I thought. Something about the Hollywood life drove people to be charging racehorses of creativity and power one day and patients in intensive care the next day. In some way I could not figure out, Hollywood drained so much life, required so much of the human spirit to fuel its fantasy apparatus, that its top players were sent reeling backward to hospitals far too often. The glamour and Technicolor had been squeezed from the blood of real-live men and women, and then the men and women were in hospitals. Not always, but far too often.

Two sheriff's detectives from the Malibu office came in to interview me about the dead gunman. The detectives wore Hawaiian shirts, shorts, and sandals. They had perfectly manicured mustaches, like characters in "Magnum, P.I." They had "run a make" on the dead man's fingerprints. He was named Elroy Trammel. He had been in and out of mental hospitals for most of his life and had been arrested twice for carrying a gun near Senator Cranston.

"Has he ever been a patient in a hospital called Chestnut Lodge?" I asked.

The detectives read down a list of references and qualifications for attempted murder and one of them, with watery green eyes, nodded. "Chestnut Lodge, Rockville, Maryland, June 1977 to October 1978. What does that mean?"

"It might mean something or it might mean nothing. I'm just too tired to think straight."

The detectives left. On day number two a parade of hospital public relations people came in and out. There was a major story about Susan-Marie in *The Wall Street Journal*. It was in the works. Did I care to talk to the reporters about it? There was a lawyer from a Los Angeles firm representing Citicorp. He handed me a letter telling me that Burns's support of Susan-Marie was firm "no matter what the condition of her health . . ." Another public relations woman appeared, telling me that a camera crew from KABC-TV had been camped outside the hospital for thirty-six hours. Did I care to make a statement? At almost midnight still another publicist for the hospital (small wonder they charge a thousand dollars an hour for intensive care) asked me if I would spend a minute with a reporter for *People*. "They're talking about both of you on the cover," he said, as if mere *talk* of such an event would remove any possibility of refusal. On the morning

413

of Susan's second full day in the hospital yet another publicist came to tell me that the Dow-Jones wire carried the story of Melvin Needle admitting defeat in the struggle for Republic and selling his shares to a Canadian mutual fund. He also wanted to tell me that he had heard that Paul Belzberg had flown to Cozumel for an unspecified purpose with a nineteen-year-old Dutch starlet named Mieke Vermeer. "That was in Hank Grant's column," he said with a wink, "in the *Reporter*."

On the night of the second full day I walked around the lobby in clothes that still smelled of smoke. I bought a paperback book of English and American poetry. In Susan's room at two in the morning I read a poem that struck me so hard that I read it aloud to Susan. Of course, she was unconscious.

I no longer remember the exact words of the poem, except that it was about the inspiration of seeing the ruins of Tintern Abbey in the last days of the eighteenth century. The poet said that the serenity of nature had moved him to feelings such as offer unremembered pleasure, feelings that have "no slight or trivial influence on that best portion of a good man's life, his little, nameless, unremembered acts of kindness and of love . . ." I guess I do remember them after all. I thought about them, about Susan-Marie and the writer who committed suicide, about Susan rescuing the horses in Newhall Canyon, about Susan-Marie crying when Jodie Sugar told her about life in the concentration camp, about Susan going with me to the Senior Prom.

A nurse with pale blue eye shadow stopped outside the room while I read to Susan. "Who's that by?" she asked. "Or did you just make it up yourself?"

"William Wordsworth," I said.

"First draft or re-write?" she asked and then left.

On the third day a nurse told me that there was a call at the nurses' station from a man who said he was Susan-Marie's stepfather. He was calling from a hospital in Lin-

414

coln, Nebraska. I walked out to the desk and picked up the phone.

"The thing is," the man said in an embarrassed voice, "she was always a good girl. She always knew how to treat people better than they deserved."

"You should know."

"So when I read about her being shot and all, and how she practically owned that whole movie studio, I thought, well if she knew I was in a hospital in Lincoln, just a miserable old county hospital, she wouldn't let me stay there a minute. She'd send a check right away to get me to a decent place. I hardly drink at all anymore. Maybe you can even write a check for her until she comes around. . . ."

I hung up and went back to watch Susan-Marie. Her beauty was so perfect, at least to me, that she looked magnificent even half dead. Her face rose and fell with her breathing. I took her cool hand and rubbed it, and she mumbled something, which I think was, "Thank you, Benjy," but I could be wrong.

If she dies, I thought, I am going to blow up Republic Studios and as much of Hollywood as I can before I'm caught. If she dies, I might just as well have my revenge, and then be done with living. There really would be no meaningful life after Susan-Marie.

Then I napped for a few minutes, and when I woke up I felt differently. None of this was Hollywood's fault. Susan-Marie took Hollywood as it came. There was no special council of war to "get" Susan-Marie when she came out. Hollywood is a small town. We don't like strangers here. Someone had said that fifty years before, and he was right.

Susan-Marie did not lie in the UCLA Intensive Care Unit because she had been the victim of a Hollywood conspiracy. She was a dreamer in a world of businessmen. She had loved a man who was possessed by a jealous, sick woman. She was famous. There was nothing personal in it.

The personal part would be that if she died, I would be a zombie for the rest of my life. The arc that began with the morning in Sligo Creek Park and took off with the Montgomery Blair Senior Prom would have gone askew, taking me alone into the coldest parts of outer space, far from any balcony that smelled of Star Jasmine.

I went home on the third day. I had been calling Miss Birkestrom and Elena every few hours at the cottage in Toluca Lake. Ava Elizabeth was fine, but she cried at night for her mother. Robbie played with the baby in the backyard. "Should I go home now?" he asked. "Looks like the fight's over no matter what happens with Miz Belzberg."

"No way," I said. "Stay there. There are still a lot of strange people out there."

I thanked the neighbors for taking care of Mary. Then I slept for twelve hours, got up, took a shower, and took Mary to the park. In the park a camera crew from KNXT took my picture and asked me about Susan's condition. "It's in God's hands," I said, looking straight at Connie Chung, and the funny thing was, I was right.

When I got back to the hospital Susan was starting to come around. She was talking in her sleep until about one A.M., talking about Eniwetok and *Laser Tracks* and the Chosin Reservoir. At one she opened her eyes, looked around her, and said, "Are we there yet? Are we halfway there yet?" Then she closed her eyes again until three A.M., when she opened them and said, "I guess we won."

I took Susan home two weeks later in an ambulance. She wanted to be at the house in Toluca Lake with Ava while she recovered. Robbie came from the cottage—"for just an hour, in broad daylight"—to ride with us. In the ambulance Susan-Marie looked at the cars, the parched hills, the light blue hazy sky, the billboards, the children with orange hair, as if she were a newly hatched chick looking at the world for the first time.

"When I'm better," she said, "when I'm really all better I want to get started on that movie Ron liked about the kids in the church that turns out to be a spaceship and takes them to outer space."

"Why not?" I asked. "You can do anything now."

"I want you to be head of story," Susan-Marie went on. "You can do it. You can work out a contract that lets you do it and do your books, too. Why not?"

"I don't know. Hollywood doesn't have the same magic for me that it does for you. Anyway, that's not the kind of association I had in mind."

"We can have any kind of association you want," Susan said. "In Hollywood anything is possible."

"That's exactly the problem."

We stopped in front of the house at 4223 Warner Boulevard in Toluca Lake. There were no camera crews, no reporters, no one at all on the street. "The publicity department did great work on this one," Robbie said. "No one here to disturb your homecoming."

I pushed Susan up the walk in her wheelchair. As I turned the key in the lock, Susan said, in a kind of playful prayer, "Ava, Ava, Ava, Ava . . ."

Deirdre was in the living room. She had a long, sharp kitchen knife clutched in her hand. Behind her, Elena lay in a heap, blood oozing from her stomach through her flimsy cotton dress. In front of Deirdre was a pink high chair. Ava Elizabeth sat in it. She wore a look of overwhelmed, bewildered terror in her dark blue eyes. She was gagged with a yellow silk scarf.

Deirdre had the knife pointed at Ava's neck. Deirdre's eyes were a ghastly, unreconciled aqua, spinning crazily about the room like saucers of madness. She wore leather slacks and a white silk blouse. Her hair was done up in a bandanna.

"Now," she said, "I'm going to show you who's boss. Finally. You're finally going to know who's running the show here in Hollywood."

"We already know, Deirdre," I said.

"You shut the hell up," Deirdre shouted. "I'm talking to

that bitch, that Susan-Marie bitch next to you. She's got to see who's in charge."

I could hear Robbie outside saying good-bye to the ambulance drivers.

"I want that bitch to come closer now, so I can show her what she's done to people. That Elroy fucked up. I have to do everything myself."

"We're coming," I said. I pushed Susan closer to the pink high chair, across the Oriental rug of ivory and red squares. Ava tried to cry. Because she was gagged, she started to choke, and Susan reached for her.

Deirdre shoved the wheelchair back. "No," she said. "I told you I was in charge. You think you can come out here and turn this whole town upside down and do everything you want? You think that, you white trash piece of shit? Now you'll see what you've done."

Ava choked again, gagging under the scarf, and began to turn blue. A tiny drop of dark red blood appeared on the point of the knife. Susan-Marie shrieked a cry that had been building up in her for her whole life. The scream was so wildly loud, so piercingly unexpected that Deirdre involuntarily recoiled for an instant and that was all it took.

I took one step forward and grabbed Deirdre's wrist. I twisted it back toward her as hard as I could, but she was strong. Deirdre took one furious, snarling step toward me. She tripped over the leg of the high chair and slid as she tried to get her footing on the rug. Robbie burst through the door with his revolver in his hand. The high chair went down onto the floor. Susan lunged out to catch Ava. Deirdre wrenched once more in my grasp as she fell. I twisted again and her wrist buckled toward her. The knife suddenly unexpectedly pointed straight toward her heart. As Deirdre fell, it went in like a carving knife into a raw rib roast. Deirdre's eyes opened wide at the complete surprise of who was finally in charge.

39

COMMENCEMENT

After the inquest we went to Easton, Maryland, for almost six months. We rented a decrepit estate on the Chesapeake called Sally's Delight. It had whole frame wings that had been unoccupied since the Civil War. We sometimes took Ava and walked into the abandoned parts of the house as if we were exploring caves. Once we found a yellowed newspaper, the *Baltimore Sun* of November 12, 1860, announcing that Abraham Lincoln would be the sixteenth President of the United States. The *Baltimore Sun* predicted that there would be no war.

Each day we walked along the marshes with Mary happily running and barking at the ducks. The house came with a gardener. We had him lay in beds of hollyhocks and roses and star jasmine. After about three months we bought the house and made plans to stay there. Susan-Marie would teach at Washington College in Chestertown. I would write about what had happened in Hollywood. We would open a little bookstore in Easton. Those were our plans.

At night we sat on the porch and watched the moon rise over the Bay. Flocks of geese flew by and honked at us. Susan-Marie read "Mother Goose" to Ava. We talked about how impossible Hollywood was, how a dreamer like Susan-Marie never belonged there. We talked to Ron Silverman, the interim president of Republic, every few days, heard his crises, and felt happy that we were not there to worry about writers' strikes and directors who would not deliver on time and production executives who had approved Winnebagoes for Sylvester Stallone and his entire family.

Sometimes we would drive down back roads and watch the families getting ready for church on a Sunday morning. We put Simon and Garfunkel into the cassette deck and listened to the sounds of silence. We sometimes stopped at the edge of fields and watched the corn wave in front of the stands of oak. Then we pulled into hamburger stands made out of old Airstream trailers and had lunch.

While we ate our food, we talked about what a wonderful, quiet life we would have on the Eastern Shore, far away from the shrieking and clawing of those who want to make certain their names are heard, their faces seen, their dreams known to the world.

We got an official letter from the LAPD telling us that Elroy Trammel had been adjudged to be a "publicity-seeking maniac" and that the case was closed.

We got a telephone call from Cedars-Sinai telling us that Elena was out of the hospital, well and eager to start working again.

One afternoon in September the wind came across the Bay without the moist heat of summer. There was a distinct coolness in the air. The summer boaters were not out on the water in their yellow slickers and their Topsiders.

In town at the Tidewater Inn the dining room was closed to allow for remodeling for the fall season.

We went home and watched television while we ate reheated pizza. At about eleven Channel Eleven from Baltimore put on the worst print of *Estonia* I have ever seen. Susan-Marie watched it for two hours without moving from her chair. When Prince Alexei gets into his small boat and waves to the shore for the last time as the elegant world of *Estonia* crashes into the tumult of the twentieth century, Susan-Marie took my hand and cried against my chest. I could feel her tears against my skin. They were the warmest tears I had ever felt.

I looked at her blue eyes and said, "I guess it's time to go home to Hollywood."

"I think so," Susan-Marie said.

We still have Sally's Delight, just in case. The bookstore and the class at Washington College never happened. But Republic started production on the story of the children in the church that gets struck by lightning and the kids go to heaven, and I think it will make audiences cry for about one century.

We did not rebuild in Malibu. Too many bad memories is the long and short of it. After a few months of searching we found an old Spanish house on a knoll off Outpost Drive. It overlooks virtually all of Los Angeles, from east L.A. to the towers of downtown, across Hollywood and the green lawns of Beverly Hills, into the geometry of Century City, and then out over Santa Monica to the ocean. At night the view is spectacular, with lights cascading over one another, almost like the view of the galaxies from a clear mountaintop in Snowmass.

Susan-Marie is at the studio all day and often until late at night. She is always tired, but always engaged. In Easton she was a mothballed dynamo. Back in her element—she made it her element—she is pumping electricity and light into the air of the nation, which is her destiny, I hope.

She has twelve pictures in production right now—including *Heartbreak Ridge*, a story of the Korean War that maybe no one but veterans will see, but that she had to make. The headquarters of Republic are in the Bauman Building, a perfect reconstruction of a Spanish mission, which was always Sid's favorite design, back where Building H once stood. There are lawns and grassy places everywhere on the lot now. "Dreams grow better in parks than in parking lots," Susan-Marie told the directors, but they did not even listen.

Paul's name occasionally flickers past us in the trades or in the credits of an old movie. We do not talk about him.

At times, in the middle of the night, I wake up and walk down the hall to Ava's room to watch her sleep. Susan-Marie and I make no plans for her. She is in the land of dreams, anyway, not the land of plans. She holds her stuffed Eniwetok doll and smiles and laughs in her sleep.

I walk down to the pool and over to the edge of the knoll and look out at the lights, and I try to understand what happened, even though Sid warned me against it. Each human being, it seems to me, has a richly worked edifice of experience, exultation, despair, fear, and courage inside his soul. The exciting, tragic, revealing moments of a lifetime are woven into a structure that is what sustains all of us with its strength, its promise, its very interiorness. The great, unbearable tragedy of death is that when we die those chapels inside each of us also dies—unless we can somehow put them outside of us as well. That is the meaning of art, of great scientific enterprises, of magnificent business accomplishments—to place some of the ethereal insides outside in concrete or newsprint or canvas or celluloid.

Susan-Marie Warmack had not a chapel but a cathedral inside her. From the losses and terrors and escapes of her youth, she had woven a Chartres of the imagination, a cavern of incalculable grandeur inside the small vessel of her person.

She had to come to Hollywood to root that cathedral somewhere in terra firma. Unfortunately, Hollywood is the least firm terra on earth. Still, it is the bridge, the spaceport, where dreams touch down to earth and are made into fact, so it is the only place she could have come.

The tragedies for Susan-Marie were that once dreams touch down to earth they run into all of the problems of earth. The fantasies that had been so vital to her as movies on a screen or make-believe in her head suddenly were mixed with the gritty reality of running a business, fighting the jealousy of a Deirdre Needle, fending off the rage and envy of a Paul Belzberg, and pledging a fraternity of men who believed that you made more money with your ass than with your head.

Susan-Marie loved the movies and wanted to be a part of them to escape the pain of her life as a child. But manufacturing dreams on celluloid in Los Angeles was far different from dreaming them in a room with a knotty-pine bed. The dream business is part dream, part business, and all human feeling.

Susan-Marie is a genius, a real one like Vincent van Gogh or Renoir. Geniuses have trouble when they touch ground.

A brilliant woman named DeAnne who invented the Made-for-TV movie once told me that she thought that Susan-Marie's only sin was that she loved the wrong man. An article in *American Film* said that her only sin was that "she had feelings in a business where you are not supposed to have any feeling besides ambition. . . ." The London *Sunday Times* once wrote a feature about her that said her only sin was in thinking that Hollywood really had anything to do with the rest of America.

In a way, every one of them was right. All of them said that Susan-Marie's only sin was that she was a dreamer, and they are all right. Susan-Marie's only sin was that she believed with all her heart—and still believes—that the line between what is a dream and what is real is insubstantial, malleable, inevitably yielding to the superior power of the dream. To Susan-Marie, the dream—not only hers, but the dreams of children of whatever age in whatever place—was always prior to any real world obstacles. That was her strength, and her only sin.

Now, she can work on erasing that line for the rest of her life. She works at a studio that will always be "safe for dreamers" as long as she runs the show. She can pour America's dreams out to the nation and give them the delicious narcotic of imagination and escape as long as she is strong, and she will be strong as long as she believes in the power of the dreams, as long as dreaming is her only sin.

Perhaps this is not even a sin. At two in the morning I look out at the city, brightly lit with the products of man's imagination and this earth, where there was nothing here but dirt and cactus one hundred years ago, the span of a few afternoons. How else could this have happened but through the mixed labors and dreams of a race who believe that the dream is as real as the fact, only it comes first. Who else but dreamers shape anything that lasts anywhere? No, Susan-Marie's faith in imagination was not a sin at all. It was a legacy.

I think these thoughts, with Mary standing beside me, staring out into the night. Often I imagine that I am telling them to Sid in his pool house, with him laughing at me jauntily from behind the screen of the martini glass, wishing me well with all the heart of a man who only wanted to make things beautiful.

"I'm not making any plans, Sid," I say to the darkness, lift my glass in his direction, and then I go back into the house to sleep next to the woman I love.

Sex...
Glamour...
Money...

PRETENSIONS by Sally Rinard

Set in the glittery world of high fashion and high society, where money is a weapon and sex the means of exchange, this dazzling tale combines the erotic, exotic, and the cutthroat world of business.

"A glitzy contemporary novel that's a delight to read." —*Publishers Weekly*

___90301-4 $4.50 U.S.   ___90302-1 $5.50 Can.

LISA LOGAN by Marie Joseph

Ambition and pride take Lisa Logan from poverty to the heights of success in haute couture. Money, power, fame, she finally has it all—except the man she wanted most.

___90218-2 $3.95 U.S.

DECISIONS by Freda Bright

Dasha Croy rockets to the top in a brilliant law career, but will her marriage be the price? Can love and security compete with the seduction of power?

___90169-0 $3.95 U.S.   ___90171-2 $4.50 Can.

GREAT READING FROM
St. Martin's Press

THE FALL RIVER LINE by Daoma Winston
The raging saga of four generations who made fortunes, love and history with a fierce pride and passion.
_____ 90184-4 $4.95 U.S.   _____ 90402-9 $6.25 Can.

MAIDEN VOYAGE by Graham Masterton
Sail away on a sea of champagne, money and outrageous passion with the heiress to a fabulous ship, a charming millionaire, a decadent countess, and an unscrupulous dealmaker.
_____ 90225-5 $3.95 U.S.

SOUTHERN WOMEN by Lois Battle
Vividly drawn saga of three women you'll never forget, by the author of _War Brides_.
_____ 90328-6 $3.95 U.S.

THE DECATUR ROAD by Joe Coomer
A touching, triumphant novel of life lived close to the Southern earth—the story of Jennie and Mitchell Parks, their triumphs and sorrows.
_____ 90160-7 $4.50 U.S.   _____ 90161-5 $5.75 Can.